SHELL GAME

"Shell Game," by Douglas Clark. ISBN 978-1-60264-431-1 (softcover); 978-1-60264-432-8 (hardcover).

Published 2009 by Virtualbookworm.com Publishing Inc., P.O. Box 9949, College Station, TX 77842, US.

Manufactured in the United States of America.

To Josie for her sustaining encouragement and considerable editing contributions.

SHELL GAME

A NOVEL

DOUGLAS CLARK

Where happiness had dwelt,
Were devastation, woe and death.
And these words were written of the fall:
While watchman slept
Rats undermined the wall.

Albert Annett, *Rats and the Wall,* **1920**

CHAPTER 1

KADUNA, NIGERIA

M ark Reynolds arrived in Lagos, Nigeria within 48 hours of hearing about the disaster. He was on assignment from his newspaper, the New York Daily Press, researching a story about African corruption when reports of a major chemical accident became public. He was early onto the scene since he was already in the nearby Republic of Congo at the time. Nigeria was a short plane trip north to the city of Lagos.

With an introduction from a Congolese colleague he quickly forged a friendship with a local Nigerian journalist. Reports were sketchy. Rumors identified a chemical plant located near the northern city of Kaduna. The Nigerian Government had no official comment. However, the airport in Kaduna was reported closed. The official reason was an unexplained security alert.

Reynolds and his new Nigerian colleague decided to hire a vehicle and driver to take them the 300 miles north from Lagos to Kaduna. It proved an uncomfortable drive. The old Land Rover was a rough ride, long overdue for a suspension overhaul. With no air conditioner, the 100 degree heat and 90 percent humidity added to the unpleasantness.

After a few hours, they stopped at a small town along the way for beer and sandwiches. The place advertised itself as a bar but it consisted of only a few derelict tables protected by a sheet metal roof. The beer was lukewarm. There were plenty of flies.

"What do you think we are going to find when we get there, Abejide?" Reynolds asked his Nigerian associate Abejide Ojukwu.

Ojukwu was a small man in his forties. His still crisply starched white shirt suggested he was immune to the oppressive heat.

"Hard to say. Inquiries made to the operating company are not answered. The Military has sealed the area. My inquiries to various contacts in Kaduna have not proved enlightening," Abejide Ojukwu said in perfect British accented English. "There are rumors that there have been casualties at a village not far from the pesticide factory."

Reynolds had just received a brief research report by e-mail from his New York newspaper. The factory was owned by a company named Nigerian Agriproducts Limited. It was a wholly owned subsidiary of a London firm, Pan Africa Holdings Limited. Pan Africa Holdings was traded on the London Stock Exchange. Sixty percent of its common stock was owned by various Cayman Islands registered corporations. The research stopped there since Cayman Islands laws do not require public financial reporting, or any corporate organization information. The Government further protected the secrecy of its client companies against all inquiries.

The ownership particulars were for the moment secondary to the events of the disaster. The principle product at the plant was a carbaryl classification pesticide called Tricarb. According to various scientific articles it was economical to produce and highly profitable. Carbaryl is a general use pesticide used throughout the world. Tricarb is a particular type of carbaryl formulation. Unfortunately, Tricarb carries enough toxicological effects, such that is was not licensed for use in the United States or Europe. Of more interest was the speculation that methyl isocyanate was used in the manufacturing process at this plant.

Methyl isocyanate is a highly toxic gas that attacks the respiratory system. It is best known as the source of thousands of fatalities in Bhopal, India in 1984. A Union Carbide pesticide manufacturing plant leaked tons of the gas in the worse industrial accident in history. Had another such accident occurred twenty-five years later in Nigeria?

They arrived in Kaduna eleven hours after leaving Lagos. Ojukwu directed the driver to a small bar and hotel. Reynolds collapsed into a chair in the bar. His shirt and shorts were soaked with perspiration. Ojukwu excused himself to use a payphone to attempt to contact a local Kaduna journalist. The driver sat down with Reynolds. His dirty shirt was dryer than Reynolds', but he still welcomed the cold beer.

"You are American, Mr. Reynolds? A newspaper reporter like Mr. Ojukwu?" the driver asked. He had a British influenced accent to his English, not as polished as Ojukwu but still better than the common pidgin English. Where Ojukwu was well groomed with handsome features, the driver clearly had lived a different life. His cheeks had a three-day growth of gray beard. His teeth were a cigarette yellowed nasty display with several missing, accented by one gold one.

"That's right. Do you know why we came all the way here?"

The driver's face turned grim. "I have heard things. Don't need newspapers for news to travel."

"What have you heard?"

"They say something bad has happened in Mobatu."

"Well that's what Mr. Ojukwu and I have heard."

Reynolds ordered another round of beers. Ojukwu returned and sat down. He asked the driver to go check out the best restaurant nearby.

After the driver left, Ojukwu said, "We will take rooms here for the night. It's not luxurious but we will not be noticed. My local newspaper contact here thinks the Military closed the airport to impede access by foreign journalists. He was denied any information from the local military headquarters. They have also blocked access to the plant. But we will see for ourselves tomorrow."

"Before trying to go to the plant site, what about trying to get an interview with someone from the Company? Reynolds asked. "Maybe they have offices other than at the plant, especially if they're trying to isolate things there."

Nigerian Agriproducts Limited did have offices in downtown Kaduna. Ojukwu's local contact provided the name of the managing director. The local Kaduna journalist also warned Ojukwu that he had tried unsuccessfully to talk to anyone representing the Company. More than that, the journalist was warned off pursuing any further inquiries by the Military.

Reynolds suggested they first approach Nigerian Agriproducts management. Maybe his being an American journalist with a major newspaper might at least gain some sort of interview. After that they would approach the Military command.

Ojukwu agreed with the plan, but felt compelled to educate Reynolds in the realities of Nigeria. "Mark, do not forget that this is a Third World country. It is not like a Western democracy. The Government controls all things with the threat of the Military. It is my country; a country with a rich culture and a warm people. But it is a country with entrenched political corruption, enforced through the Military. Being an American is leverage only so far."

The next morning, their driver delivered Reynolds and Ojukwu to the Nigerian Agriproducts offices located at a modest, nondescript business address. Two police officers however guarded the entrance.

With Reynolds in the background, Ojukwu attempted to negotiate entry to the offices, but the police officers rejected his arguments.

"These police have been ordered to refuse entry to anyone. Their pretext is that this is a security situation," Ojukwu told Reynolds.

"Do they speak English?" Reynolds asked Ojukwu. He answered that they did.

Reynolds approached the police officers. "Officers, I believe my colleague told you we are journalists. We need to talk with someone from Nigerian Agriproducts management. I believe he also told you I am an American journalist. What that means is that I will publish a story throughout the world that will not be good for Nigerian Agriproducts. I will say that the local police prevented the Company from providing correct information. If you don't want that to happen, I suggest you place that decision on someone in that office." Reynolds pointed to the office, and then gave one of the officers a business card.

The two officers conferred in Swahili. After a heated exchange, one officer entered the building. The remaining officer glared at Reynolds. Reynolds glared back with as much feigned arrogance as he could muster.

It was ten minutes before the police officer returned. "Mr. Mbala has agreed to meet with you briefly. Follow me, please."

Reynolds and Ojukwu were ushered into a palatial office, in sharp contrast to the building exterior.

Managing Director Oliver Mbala's large office was appointed with exquisite furnishings, but in a tasteless display of wealth. A Waterford crystal bar set on an antique colonial-era Africa sideboard. African art hung along side an original impressionist oil. A heavy Henry XIV style desk sat on a Persian carpet.

Mbala was dressed in a light gray Armani suit, gold-colored knit shirt, and Rolex watch. With much exaggerated politeness and shaking of hands, Reynolds and Ojukwu were offered seats. Reynolds thanked Mbala for seeing them.

"Can I offer you gentlemen tea? Perhaps a good Scotch?" Reynolds and Ojukwu declined.

"There are many rumors about a major accident at your plant, Mr. Mbala. We understand the Military has secured the area against any entry. Can you tell us what has happened?" Reynolds asked.

"I am not at liberty to discuss details, Mr. Reynolds. You see it has not yet been established that the problem was the result of an accident," Mbala said.

"I 'm not sure what you mean, Sir."

"I believe I can tell you gentlemen of the press this much. There is reason to believe this may be an act of terrorism. That is why the Military is involved. You see, Agriproducts is very important to the Nigerian economy. Its products boost agricultural yields throughout Africa. Being an American, Mr. Reynolds, I am sure you can appreciate the sensitivity of the situation."

Ojukwu asked, "Can you tell us what happened? There have been reports of casualties. Specifically, has there been a release of toxic gas the same as in Bhopal, India?"

Mbala was obviously displeased with Ojukwu's question. "Mr. Ojukwu that would be speculation at this time. I would further caution against printing any such speculation here in Nigeria. You may find yourself in conflict with certain laws. You, Mr. Reynolds, are bound by no such laws; however I would appeal to your journalistic integrity against wild speculation. I would expect that the Government will issue information soon. I too am bound not to discuss details of the investigation."

"Can you comment on another report we have? According to a number of witnesses from a village southeast of your plant, there has been a constant polluting of a stream that runs through that village. They trace those pollutants to your factory.

Witnesses say that many people have recently been suffering from a range of medical problems. Domestic animals are also experiencing problems."

"Mr. Ojukwu," Mbala paused. "I granted this interview believing you and Mr. Reynolds were responsible journalists. I will answer your question, but then must terminate our discussion since it appears to be going down avenues of irresponsible rumor. I have no time to respond to such nonsense. As to your question, Agriproducts does not release harmful chemicals into the water. Furthermore, there has been no such formal accusation from anyone."

"Mr. Mbala…." Reynolds started to say, but was interrupted by Mbala.

"Pardon me, Mr. Reynolds, but I really must terminate this interview. It is unfortunate that you journalists continually seek to demonize business."

Mbala rose from his chair and opened the door. "Good day gentlemen," he said without shaking hands.

Returning to their car, Reynolds asked the driver to take them as close to the plant as the Military would permit.

It was a forty-minute drive on a paved road. At the roadblock they were turned away with no information. The driver then took them on another route that would access the village near to the plant from another direction. Again, they were prevented from going further by the Military.

Several two and a half ton military vehicles passed them going toward the village while they argued with the young officer commanding the roadblock. In the rear of one of the trucks, there were men in full contamination suits. Reynolds started to take a photograph with his digital.

"No!" The officer yelled holding his hand in front of Reynolds camera. "No pictures. Let me see your papers."

Several soldiers brought their assault rifles to a ready position when the officer yelled. They surrounded Reynolds and Ojukwu.

After inspecting their documents, the officer said, "Turn back. Do not return. This is a restricted military area. If you return you will be arrested."

After retreating a couple of miles back up the road, Reynolds ordered the driver to pull over in order to study the map.

"Abejide, it appears that the village is maybe three kilometers to the east of here. Can we walk there?"

Ojukwu considered what Reynolds was suggesting before answering. "That is possible, but you must consider that if we are found out we could be arrested, perhaps even shot."

"I understand, Abejide, but I think this is something big. Worth the risk. The Military is not going to expect someone trekking into the area from the bush. We get close, take some photos and get back within a couple of hours."

Ojukwu nodded in agreement then instructed the driver to return in five hours. The driver became agitated, shaking his head negatively. Reynolds produced a hundred dollar U.S. bill to appease his concerns. Another one hundred dollars was promised upon his return in five hours.

Reynolds and Ojukwu started off into the high grass as the driver drove off. They were dressed in cotton slacks and white shirts with only two bottles of water. Even though the terrain was fairly easy walking, his shirt was soon soaked in sweat. This was an impossible climate for anyone foreign to equatorial Africa.

Within an hour they came over a slight hill that looked down over the village of Mobatu. It was a typical impoverished Nigerian village. Mud-brick structures with corrugated metal roofs. A few beat-up trucks shared the area with rusted automobile carcasses and assorted debris.

This scene however was unique. It could have been a film set for a science fiction movie. White-clan men in contamination suits were moving about the village. Several could be seen carrying bodies to a central area. There were as many as one hundred bodies laid out in rows. At some distance, there were Nigerian military vehicles and several eighteen-wheel tractor-trailers. The trailers had Agriproducts logos. Standing next to the trucks were several soldiers looking none to happy. They were not wearing decontamination gear which gave Reynolds some comfort.

Reynolds captured the scene in digital photographs but wanted closer shots. Over Ojukwu's objections they moved to a concealed place within a hundred meters of a crew bringing out bodies from some sort of public building. Reynolds subjugated his concerns over his proximity to whatever caused these widespread deaths. If it was a toxic gas release he assumed it was now contained and the residual effects dissipated. But the fact that the rescue personnel were in emergency gear still gave him and Ojukwu concern for their own safety.

They were perhaps at the scene for only thirty minutes before starting back to meet their driver. Reynolds had captured photographs of the bodies, the contamination hazard suits, the trucks, and the presence of the Nigerian army. With their adrenalin high, Reynolds and Ojukwu returned to the road in half the time. Their driver was not due back for at least a half an hour. They concealed themselves in a dense thicket of scrub trees twenty meters from the road. It would be turning dark in another hour.

"What do you think happened, Abejide?" Reynolds asked.

"I think it is the same disaster that happened in Bhopal, India." Abejide said. "I researched this Agriproducts plant and their manufacturing processes. Most assuredly they generated the same intermediate product that caused the Bhopal disaster. It is known as methyl isocyannate. It is denser than air, so if there is a discharge, it will not dissipate into the atmosphere. It will collect near the ground and pool in low areas. Mobatu is at the end of a valley sloping downward from the plant. If there was a release and the wind was from the west, it would have pushed the gas down into the village."

"Well, if that's what happened, they won't be able to hide this," Reynolds responded.

"And why not, Mark? This is not India. I believe that India has at least a semblance of a free press. But this is Nigeria. If a toxic release happened, neither the Company nor the Government will ever acknowledge it."

"But we have the pictures. The foreign press will make this a big story," Reynolds said.

"For a couple of days perhaps. The Nigerian government will publicly disavow any such incident. Agriproducts will have no comment. The Government will suppress any mention in the newspapers. Behind the scenes diplomatically they might acknowledge the incident, but they will claim it was a terrorist act."

Reynolds and Ojukwu waited in the brush for their driver to return. He was now two hours past due from the agreed upon time. It had turned dark with a half-moon casting some light. Automobile lights then became visible in the distance. The vehicle stopped. The driver got out and called out for them in a low voice.

"Let us go quickly, I was stopped by soldiers. I told them I was to pick up a priest in a village to the East. It was with much persuasion that I convinced them to let me proceed. This is not worth the money you are paying, Mr. Reynolds."

Reynolds would have thought it was a ploy to extract a larger fee, but the driver was clearly shaken. They drove a different route back to Kaduna. It was close to midnight when they arrived at their hotel.

Reynolds gave the driver an extra hundred dollars.

"Thank you, Mr. Reynolds. It is without offense that I say that I hope not to see you again. Good luck," the driver said.

The next day, Reynolds and Ojukwu gained a meeting with the local military commander for the area. The Colonel was a large, barrel-chested man, well over six feet tall, with close-cropped hair. He was dressed in a starched kaki uniform with a polished black leather sidearm holster.

"Mr. Mbala of Agriproducts indicated the Government was investigating this incident as a possible terrorist attack. Can you provide any information on what happened at the plant, Sir?" Ojukwu asked.

"Gentlemen, this is a matter of national security. I cannot comment on any aspects of our investigation. For that matter, Mr. Mbala should not be making such comments. I expect that we will have some information to provide to the Press soon," the Colonel said.

"Colonel, was this a release of the toxic gas known as MIC like in Bhopal, India twenty years ago?" Reynolds asked.

The Colonel said sharply, "There has been no release of toxic gases. I am afraid I cannot comment further. There is no story here, gentlemen. I strongly suggest you return to Lagos, Mr. Ojukwu, and you Mr. Reynolds to the United States. The Kaduna Airport will open tomorrow. I trust you will take that opportunity." He stood and like Mbala made no attempt at shaking hands.

Back at the hotel bar, Reynolds and Ojukwu ordered beers.

"The Colonel was not very subtle."

"That my friend was an order to leave Kaduna. If not for you being a foreign journalist, I might have been arrested."

"If the photos I took are published will you be in trouble?"

Ojukwu rubbed his temples. "Probably. But what is a journalist to do? At any rate we can discuss what to do next once we are back in Lagos."

They spent the afternoon drinking and exchanging war stories. Reynolds had taken a genuine liking to his new found colleague.

As the Colonel said, Kaduna Airport was open the next morning. Reynolds and Ojukwu found seats on the 45 minute flight to Lagos. Ojukwu told Reynolds that Agriproducts parent company, Pan Africa Holdings, had a wide range of companies operating in Nigeria. There was Pan Africa Petroleum, probably the largest oil company in the country. Pan Africa Minerals was a major player in coal and tin. There were other operations in various agricultural products. The construction company, East Africa Construction was the largest government contractor. Relatives of the President held management positions at East Africa Construction.

"All told, Pan Africa is the largest economic entity in the country. In fact, with its political ties, you could say it controls a large part of the Nigerian economy. And considering that Nigeria is a politically corrupt county, Pan Africa might then be said to control Nigeria."

"That's interesting," Reynolds said. "I only knew that Pan Africa Holdings was the parent company of Agriproducts. It will be interesting to do more research and see who runs Pan Africa."

Reynolds and Ojukwu exited the aircraft and entered the Lagos Airport terminal. Six police officers stopped them. Ignoring their questions, the police moved Reynolds towards an office while Ojukwu was taken outside.

"Mark, you must tell the story," Ojukwu yelled, and was then struck in the mid-section by a police officer with the butt of his assault rifle.

"What the fuck is going on?" Reynolds yelled. He was then pushed into a bare room with only a table and two chairs. A rusted ceiling fan did little to abate the stagnant heat.

It was an hour before an officer entered the room along with two larger policemen.

"What the hell am I being detained for? And what's happened to my friend?"

"Enough, Mr. Reynolds. You are in serious trouble. So is Mr. Ojukwu. You entered a restricted military area. An area I might add that was under investigation for national security reasons."

"I demand that the U.S. Consulate be notified."

The officer ignored Reynolds. He grabbed Reynolds duffle bag and emptied the contents on the table. It was a modest assortment of a couple of changes of clothes, a dictionary, and a toiletry bag. Everything was examined meticulously. His notebook computer was turned on. The officer expertly looked through the computer folders and various files. The digital camera contained only innocuous photos of Kaduna and the trip up from Lagos.

"Very well, Mr. Reynolds, where are the photographs?"

"What photographs?"

"The photographs you took in the restricted area," the officer said. "Your driver said he deposited you and Mr. Ojukwu on a road some miles from the village of Mobatu. You have a camera. Are you saying you took no pictures?"

Reynolds hoped the driver was not in serious difficulties. He assumed Ojukwu was, just as was he. "The driver did drop us off. Ojukwu and I never found Mobatu. We got lost for some time before returning to the road."

"Several hours according to your driver."

"Well he's wrong. Maybe two hours at most," Reynolds said.

The officer stared at Reynolds, perhaps trying to intimidate, perhaps trying to decide what to do next. "Take your clothes off, Mr. Reynolds."

Reynolds complied. "Your underwear and socks also," the officer said.

The officer went through the clothing thoroughly, then went through everything again from the bag. Standing there naked,

Reynolds felt more intimidated. He was less certain if he was going to be able to bluff his way through this.

After some moments, the officer turned to one of the soldiers and said something in a local dialect. The soldier roughly picked up all the items and stuffed them back into the bag.

"Get dressed," the officer said. "It would not be my choice. However I am ordered to see that you are on the next flight out of Lagos. In twenty minutes there is a flight leaving for Nairobi. You are being deported. Do not return to Nigeria again, Mr. Reynolds."

Once the flight was airborne Reynolds ordered several scotches. He was badly shaken, partly by his near arrest, but more over concern for Ojukwu's fate. The assault on Ojukwu at the airport implied at least harsh treatment by the security forces.

Reynolds pulled his bag down from the overhead storage bin and took out the dictionary. With the aid of a comb inserted into the spine of the hardcover book, he pushed out the small flat digital memory storage card from the camera. Viewing the photos would have to wait since his camera and notebook computer were confiscated at the airport. But he had quickly looked at the results as he took the photos. It was one hell of a story. One that might cost the life of his friend, Abejide Ojukwu.

CHAPTER 2

MANHATTAN, NEW YORK

F orty-eight hours after being thrown out of Nigeria, Mark Reynolds was back in his Manhattan apartment. He had slept only a few hours on the last leg of a twenty-four hour journey from Lagos, Nigeria, to Nairobi, Kenya, to Rome, Italy, then onto JFK in New York City. He tried to call his live-in girlfriend once he arrived but she never picked up on her cell phone.

It was nine o'clock in the evening when Denise Fisher returned home. After the hugs and kisses, Denise said, "Christ, Mark, you look like shit."

She held him at arms length and examined him.

"Well, I've had a slightly difficult adventure," he said. Her critical tone stuck a defensive nerve. He was also a little put out that she was so late when she knew his arrival time. "Just witnessed a major environmental catastrophe, then I was interrogated, then I was deported out of Nigeria. Other than that, how are you, Mark? Just fine I answer."

Denise held up her hands, "I'm sorry, Mark, I didn't mean to greet you like that. But you didn't tell me much when you called from Rome."

Reynolds could feel the conflict that started long before this recent assignment to Africa. Denise turned the conversation to some practical matters at home before asking him about what happened in Africa.

Reynolds chronicled his recent events. Even when describing his brush with Nigerian Security and the unknown fate of Abejide Ojukwu, Denise seemed preoccupied elsewhere. Reynolds hoped that they could have a romantic reunion; a good bottle of wine, a make-do dinner of something simple like an omelet, hopefully followed by love-making. Denise's demeanor suggested that was not to be. They settled on having dinner at a favorite Italian restaurant close-by.

He tried to engage her in talking about how things were going for her professionally, but she seemed disinclined to say much.

It was a good dinner, but a shitty homecoming. Later, Denise pleaded exhaustion. No romance. No sex.

Denise was gone when he awoke in the morning. He vaguely remembered her giving him a kiss on the forehead but fatigue carried him back into sleep until mid-morning.

It was twenty minutes by taxi to the offices of the New York Daily Press. He called his editor and suggested they meet for lunch.

The Dubliner was an Irish pub on Greenwich Avenue in the West Village, serving hearty Irish fare. Reynolds and his editor, John Fredericks, lunched there frequently when Reynolds was in town.

Reynolds was seated in a booth when Fredericks entered. He was pushing sixty, short, loosing his hair, and moderately out of shape. He smiled broadly and extended his hand to Reynolds. "Goddamn it, Mark, it's good to see you. Hell of story we've got," he said after clasping Reynolds' hand in both of his, then sitting down.

"Those photos you dropped off last night are dynamite. Rachel has been busy researching this methyl isocyannate and the Bhopal disaster. I want you to finish writing tomorrow's lead story on this. Looks like we're the only ones that have anything of substance. We'll go with one of your photos on page one, the rest on three and four. Headline will read *Nigerian Chemical Accident Like Bhopal.*"

A waitress took their lunch orders.

Fredericks continued, "The wire services only have sketchy stuff. The Nigerians have sealed this up pretty tight. Reporters can't get close to the facility. The Government puts out a bunch of horseshit. Their security forces intimidate anyone who might have information. What we have classifies as a genuine scoop, my friend." They both hoisted pints of beer in a mock toast.

"Have we been able to get a line on what happened to Abejide Ojukwu?" Reynolds asked.

Fredericks shook his head no. "I talked to Ojukwu's editor by telephone. Seemed a strange conversation. The guy said he knew nothing about Ojukwu's whereabouts. Didn't seem to want to talk or even speculate. Short time later I got an e-mail from him. He explained he was concerned about the phones being bugged. Went on to say in the e-mail that he had feelers out all over. Unfortunately, he speculates that Ojukwu might have been killed by Nigerian Security Forces. Might be why he can't get any information."

"Or he might be killed if we print this story," Reynolds suggested to Fredericks.

Fredericks considered the question for a moment. "You're not suggesting we hold off publishing the story are you?"

Reynolds took another drink of his beer. "No. We'll publish. Don't have any real choices do we? Just wish I could know that I wasn't sending this guy to his death. You'd like Abejide. Good reporter. Works under impossible conditions there. It's as much his story as mine. Wonder if I should give him credit for the story, or might that be worse for him?"

Fredericks didn't have an answer.

They ate their lunch without further reference to the story, or Abejide Ojukwu.

Rachel Stern gave Reynolds a hug and a kiss on the cheek when he walked into her tiny cluttered office. Rachel was the senior staff researcher for the Daily Press. It's what you did with an advanced degree in library science, if you didn't want to be in the library business. Her work fleshed out stories by providing necessary background information. Sometimes it unearthed new lines of inquiry.

"You've got to tell me about this latest adventure, Mark," she said.

"Maybe tomorrow. I've got to write tomorrow's front-page story this afternoon. I've got the bones of it down, but I need your background stuff," he said.

"All right. Lunch tomorrow then? We can read your front page over a glass of wine," Rachel said.

"Ok, you're on. Now let's get to it."

Rachel had done her usual thorough job. Her material was organized in a hierarchy starting with a summary then progressing to an outline that acted as a table of contents for specific elements of the subject. The bottom of the pyramid was a source appendix. Quotations were carefully attributed. She laid three report folders in front of Reynolds.

"What's all this, Rachel? I've got a story to complete this afternoon. I can't go through all this material."

"Hang on, Mr. Star Reporter. I'll go over enough of the material right now for this first story. John expects this will play front page for at least a couple of days. You can use the in-depth stuff for your subsequent pieces. Open the folder titled *Methyl Isocyanate & Carbaryl Pesticide Manufacturing*."

"That sounds interesting," he said sarcastically, but opened to the first page of Stern's report.

"It is actually; interesting and scary. I'm certainly no chemist, but I think I now have a pretty good handle on pesticide manufacturing and particularly this nasty stuff. I took the liberty to contact a couple of professors in the field. They helped frame the explanations in layman language. Besides this report, I did a workup on the Bhopal, India disaster in 1984. The third report is about the Company, Nigerian Agriproducts Limited. That material is interesting from several angles apart from this accident itself."

"All right. Educate me sufficiently on pesticides and this gas so I can write something that makes technical sense," Reynolds said as he paged through Stern's report where she had highlighted key points.

"I want to go into some detail about Bhopal. Frame this story as a tragic repeat. We'll use archive photos of Bhopal along side the Nigerian photos. The Company stuff about who actually operates this plant we'll use in the following days."

Stern went over her research materials with Reynolds for over an hour before he went off to write the story. On his return flights from Africa, he had already written a personal account of how the Nigerian photos were obtained. It slammed the Nigerian Government hard with a direct allegation of covering up a major industrial disaster. He planned to use that as the day-two story.

It was now only necessary to expand the piece with the explanation of how these materials were manufactured, and the dangers involved. Resurrecting the horrific tragedy of Bhopal would thrust this event into a worldwide issue. How could a repeat of that accident occur decades later? Why had technology not been implemented to avoid such an accident? Who is covering up? He would relish investigating who Pan Africa Holdings really was for subsequent follow-up pieces.

Reynolds worked on the story for the next few hours. He consulted frequently with Stern and had her edit draft portions for accuracy. Simultaneously, the story layout was being shaped. John Fredericks was personally supervising selection of the photos. The story would dominate page one, with the Nigerian and archival Bhopal photographs on several interior pages. Reynolds was to write the story in 3000 words.

He was an hour away from deadline to get the newspaper to press that night when he walked into John Frederick's office. Fredericks had finished reading Reynolds' copy.

"Hell of a piece, Mark. We're out in front of everybody on this. Great job. Some pretty strong editorializing at the end though." Fredericks was referring to Reynolds' treatment of corporate responsibility and inferences of collusion with corrupt governments.

"The conclusions are obvious, John. Are you going to let it stand as I wrote it?"

Fredericks removed his glasses and rubbed his eyes. "Yeah, I'm leaving as you wrote it. What about crediting Ojukwu's contributions? Any second thoughts?"

Reynolds reflected for a couple of moments before answering. "Sure I have second thoughts. But I think if I was in his shoes, I'd want it out there that I was responsible for telling this story." Reynolds' eyes teared slightly. "Besides, my instincts tell me the bastards have already killed him just like his boss thinks they did. This is a real shithole beat for a journalist, John. He's owed a joint byline."

Fredericks nodded his agreement. "As for tomorrow, who are you going to call for comment?"

"Nigerian Ambassador of course. Some Under-Secretary at State for African Affairs. A United Nations guy that Rachel found who was very close to the Bhopal accident. The parent company, Pan Africa Holdings in London of course. But we suspect that Pan Africa is just that, a holding company with little operational involvement in Nigerian Agriproducts. Since Pan Africa Holdings is itself owned by several Cayman Islands corporations, it's a matter of untangling who the real parent company is at the top of the ladder," Reynolds said.

"What do you mean? Is this some big multinational like Union Carbide or some Third World player that was not up to the technology?"

Reynolds answered, "Well it's definitely not that clear, John. Rachel's still working on it. The corporate associations are complicated to say the least. I know something of business structure and the ownership trail is obscured. I'm hopeful she'll be able to identify who's at the top of the food chain when we go to print. That will be who controls these offshore incorporated companies."

"Tax havens you mean?"

"They can be, but they're also useful in hiding things like ownership. Or like Enron who used them to disguise business transactions as something else. Offshore subsidiary corporations like this Southern Group don't run anything. They exist only for tax reasons or to hide something."

"Sounds like that's the next piece in this story," Fredericks said.

"Such insights are why you get paid the big bucks, John," Reynolds said with a smile. "I'll start working that investigation as soon as I get the next couple of days pieces completed. I would guess that depending on the level of the shitstorm tomorrow's story brings down, that the next day will also be page one."

"Greedy byline hog aren't you?" Fredericks said jokingly.

"The best an editor like you could hope for," Reynolds responded.

The New York Daily Press hit the street the next day with their lead story using Reynolds photographs. The wire services had put out only scant details about the event for several days, but the story never gained any traction. The Daily Press's story was something different. The headline read, *Nigerian Chemical*

Accident Like Bhopal, India. The byline read, *Story by Mark Reynolds and Abejide Ojukwu.*

New York Daily Press - Kaduna, Nigeria:

For several days the Nigerian government has failed to explain reports that there has been a major industrial accident at a pesticide manufacturing plant in central Nigeria. The plant in question is operated by Nigerian Agriproducts Limited. Both the Company and Nigerian government officials have been reluctant to even confirm what has happened.

The photographs published in this newspaper were taken clandestinely by Mark Reynolds and Nigerian journalist Abejide Ojukwu. The Nigerian government has attempted to suppress this information by expelling Mark Reynolds of the New York Daily Press from Nigeria, and detaining Nigerian journalist Abejide Ojukwu. Mr. Ojukwu whereabouts or status are unknown at this time. The Nigerian Government has ignored all inquiries.

The full range of photographs shows over two hundred victims of what is believed to be a release of the highly toxic gas methyl isocyanate, or MIC. Methyl isocyanate is an intermediate product in the production of a certain class of pesticides. It is also found in the manufacture of certain plastics and polyurethane foam. It came to world attention in 1984 with the accidental release into the atmosphere of forty tons of the gas in Bhopal, India by a Union Carbide subsidiary. That release killed nearly 3,000 people within a few days of exposure. Another 10,000 people were permanently disabled. Additional tens of thousands of people have claimed injuries.

Methyl isocyanate is denser than air, therefore it will not dissipate upward into the atmosphere, but instead will collect in low areas. In high doses of exposure, it causes death principally by pulmonary edema, or an abnormal accumulation of fluid in the lungs. Secondary effects include pneumonia and bronchitis. Death is agonizingly painful.

Photographs reveal the presence of personnel suited in contamination protective gear. Nigerian Army personnel are clearly present at the site of the causalities in the small village of Mobatu.

Repeated attempts to get more complete information from the Nigerian government have proved un-successful. Nigerian Foreign Minister Madu Achebe has announced only that there has been a terrorist attack in that region and authorities are still investigating. Minister Achebe has cited national security concerns for the secrecy, but suggested that the incident may have been the work of Islamic fundamentalist insurgents also responsible for recent attacks on oil field operations. U.S. State Department spokesperson Marilyn Wilson has indicated that they are in close communication with the Nigerian government, but cannot clarify the situation at this time.

The story expanded on the incident by quotations from many experts and a resurrecting of the details of the Bhopal, India disaster. Reynolds concluded the piece with a focus on Nigerian Agriproducts:

Nigerian Agriproducts Limited, the operator of the pesticide manufacturing plant has not provided any information, even to confirm that some sort of accident has occurred. This newspaper has learned that the pesticides being manufactured at this plant would not be licensed for use in the United States or the European Union. Nigerian Agriproducts is a wholly owned subsidiary of Pan Africa Holdings of London. Pan Africa has refused all inquiries, issuing only a statement that events in Nigeria were under investigation and they could not comment further until details were clarified. This newspaper has found that Nigerian Agriproducts is ultimately controlled through a hierarchy of offshore companies by the large international firm, Martinelli Global, headquartered in New York. Martinelli Global has also declined to make any comment.

SHELL GAME | 25

CHAPTER 3

Corporate headquarters for Martinelli Global were located on the top ten floors of the Martinelli building at the end of Broad Street in the Financial District of Manhattan. The office of Chairman and Chief Executive Officer, Steven Martinelli, occupied a thousand square feet on one corner. Full length windows on the outer two walls gave a panoramic view over the East River. To the northeast was the Brooklyn Bridge, to the southwest the Statue of Liberty.

Assembled around comfortable chairs were two other senior executives of Martinelli Global.

"I read a minor article about reports of this accident in Nigeria a couple of days ago. Now this front page headline story in the Daily Press," Steven Martinelli said. "Martinelli Global is implicated. How is that, Conrad? I thought we were insulated."

Conrad Redek was the Chief Operating Officer. He was also the architect of Martinelli Global's complex international organization of foreign subsidiaries and offshore tax-haven shell companies.

"Well, we are actually. At least Martinelli Global is," Redek answered. "Nigerian Agriproducts is wholly owned by Pan Africa Holdings in the U.K. Pan Africa is traded on the London Stock Exchange. Around sixty percent of Pan Africa Holdings stock is owned by a number of our Cayman Islands corporations. Another Martinelli Global owned Cayman corporation, New World Finance, is the principle secured creditor to not only Pan Africa, but the other offshore entities involved with Pan Africa."

"So with that layering, how did Martinelli Global's connection become known?" Martinelli asked Redek.

"One of the offshore entities, Southern Group Limited, is listed in our annual report. Some enterprising researcher dug into financial reports of Pan Africa Holdings, then dug a little deeper. Structurally, there is still substantial distance between Martinelli Global and Agriproducts."

"Paul, where do we stand?" Martinelli asked Corporate Counsel, Paul Belden.

In sharp contrast to Martinelli's trim build, his full gray hair, Belden was paunchy and balding. His suit had none of the elegance of Martinelli, or even the stylish, more fit, Conrad Redek. Nonetheless, his intelligence was every bit the match to the others.

"Pan Africa Holdings is going to be dumped on with a load of international shit. They are in the same position as the Union Carbide partly-owned subsidiary was after the Bhopal accident," Belden said. He moved to sit forward in his chair, intent into the subject.

"Nobody remembers that this pesticide plant in Bhopal was owned and operated by an Indian company, with about 51% of the stock owned by Union Carbide. Of course, the world claimed it was a Union Carbide disaster. The CEO was even arrested when he went to India."

"I'm not planning on going to Nigeria, thank you, Paul," Martinelli said. All three men smiled. "What are you suggesting we do?"

Belden resumed. "Like I said, Pan Africa Holdings stock will take a big hit. Insofar as the disaster, liability insurance will pay for a good deal of whatever settlement is eventually negotiated. As for Martinelli Global, we stick to our position, legal as well as public I might add, that Martinelli Global's association was only as a distant investment. Martinelli Global had no involvement in direct or even indirect management of the pesticide plant."

"What is the situation in Nigeria, Conrad?" Martinelli asked.

"Fairly well contained. The Nigerian government is sticking to the story that the event was a terrorist attack. I've talked personally with the Foreign Minister who is close to President Enzinwa. They're also giving out no details. Journalists have been kept out of the area. Looks like only that Daily Press reporter got anything. The plant is now stable. Casualties will run about 200 to 300 dead, maybe another 1000 injured."

"You're saying this was not a terrorist attack by insurgents? What did happen then?" Martinelli asked.

"It was some sort of industrial accident. Could have been equipment failure or human error. They haven't got to the bottom of it yet. Doesn't ultimately matter," Redek said.

"It's imperative that the Nigerian's keep this contained, Conrad. Does the local management of this plant understand? What's the situation there?"

"The Nigerian's will stick to the terrorist story. There'll be a quid pro quo with the President of course, but it's manageable," Redek answered. "One of our best people from London is in Nigeria. Knows Africa. Knows how things operate there. Everything gets channeled through him. He's already met with President Enzinwa personally. He's reporting to me directly every day."

"Very well. Get out a press release. State our position succinctly; very indirect investment by Martinelli Global, not involved with this local company's operations, regret the loss of life, another example of terror being used as a weapon, et cetera.

No direct comments from anyone to the Press. Personally, I must respond to calls from a White House staffer and several members of Congress. They want assurances this won't turn into a scandal."

The three executives discussed details for another twenty minutes. As Redek and Belden were leaving Martinelli's office, Belden stopped and said, "Here's an interesting number, Steven; Union Carbide paid out $350 million dollars in a settlement for the Bhopal accident. Assume that was for 3000 dead and another 10,000 injured. Kaduna, Nigeria casualties appear only to be ten percent of that number. So any settlement is going to be pocket change. After all, this isn't like it happened somewhere in America."

The second day's story was now front page in most international newspapers. Reynold's account of his escape from Nigeria gave a second punch to the story with its conspiracy overtones. Having the lead on the story, the Daily Press now focused on attempted interviews with Nigerian officials. The Nigerians were feeling the pressure, but no useful information came out although several angry responses did make good copy.

Reynolds' personal inquiries into the fate of the Nigerian journalist, Abejide Ojukwu returned disturbing news. Speaking from a cell phone, Ojukwu's editor spoke briefly with Reynolds. He explained that it would not be safe to have this discussion over a regular land-line. Ojukwu had not been seen since the incident at the airport. A senior police official had personally warned the editor off any further inquiries. The editor suspected the worse.

He explained that most of the able bodied men of the devastated village worked at the pesticide plant. The village itself was within the security zone established by the Army. No witnesses or survivors had yet come forward. If they did, no newspaper would be allowed to report it in Nigeria.

"But this is Africa, Mr. Reynolds. It is not possible to keep such a terrible event secret," the editor said. He told about heavy equipment and medical units moving into the cordoned off area. Rumors told of mass graves, and hundreds of injured people.

"Many people died a terrible death in the village of Mobatu. Your photographs are the only evidence of that disaster. Agriproducts and the Nigerian government will never reveal the truth. The people here know the truth though, but I wonder if the world really cares."

Since Reynolds could not return to Nigeria, for the next several days he relied on a freelance British reporter for local information. Ojukwu's editor had facilitated the contact. There was little in the way of official information. The Nigerian government still had a security lid on everything. Reporters were discouraged from even asking questions. The Brit was resourceful and was at least able to provide enough copy to give the continuing story local color.

However, it was Rachel Stern's research that had developed some interesting insights into the scope of Pan Africa's operations in Nigeria. Feeding this intel back to the Brit was providing him with targeted lines of inquiry.

The British reporter had canvassed a range of companies operating in Nigeria under financial control of Pan Africa Holdings of London. Some were wholly owned subsidiaries, in others Pan Africa had substantial interests. They covered a range of industries from agricultural products, to mining, to construction, to transportation, and most importantly, petroleum.

A major construction company, East Africa Construction was the largest firm of its type operating in Nigeria. They enjoyed well over fifty percent of all major government construction contracts. Several major stockholders were relatives of senior officials.

Pan Africa Petroleum was the second largest producer in Nigeria to Shell Oil. The managing director was the President's uncle. The pipelines were constructed by East Africa Construction.

Reynolds called the British reporter. "Some interesting information you've dug up. My compliments."

"Thanks. Been reporting from Africa for eight years, but never looked into corporations like I have here. I tell you, this is a study in how corruption really works. Apart from the operations I described, there are smaller supplying companies that have incestuous business relationships," the reporter said.

"I'll give you an example. There's this company called Kaduna Communications. I'm in the lobby of East Africa Construction waiting to see the Managing Director. He's a right piece of work, but that's another story. Anyway, this bloke comes in. Talks to the receptionist in the local dialect. She calls the Managing Director then shows the guy into the office. Five minutes later he comes out, now carrying an attaché case."

The reporter continued his story. "I overheard the name of this bloke's company when the receptionist introduced him. So I track down Kaduna Communications. They have this dump of an office in a low class retail district. I go in and there's this fat girl behind a metal desk in an area the size of a closet. There's a small office to the side with the door open. Inside is a guy talking on the phone. Same bloke who went into East Africa Construction."

"I tell the guy I'm a reporter. He's nervous as hell. I ask him about his company's association with East Africa Construction. This dumbshit tells me they provide computer services to East Africa. I start to ask him how he does that with only two employees, and he gets agitated. Says they outsource the work. Then he tells me to get the hell out."

The British reporter recounted several other investigations of companies associated with the array of Pan Africa's companies in Nigeria. It would make good copy to expand on a story of corruption, but it was still just background to the present disaster.

"If we publish your stuff, will you be ok there in Nigeria?" Reynolds asked.

"Doubt that. But it doesn't matter. I'm leaving this shithole tomorrow, so fuck'm over good, Yank."

The Nigerian Disaster as it was now known continued as a major international story for days. Casualties were officially reported at 410 dead, over 1500 injured. The Nigerian government officially announced that the pesticide plant had been the target of a terrorist attack by an unnamed anti-government insurgency group. Information was still limited. The area around the plant still sealed off. There was no request for outside assistance. The Government reported that Nigerian medical and military resources were adequate to the relief effort, and that ample financial resources had been provided by Agriproducts and its parent company, Pan Africa Holdings.

Reynolds wrote a major article on the collection of companies controlled by Pan Africa Holdings, and their impact on the economic structure of Nigeria. Rachel Stern's research and the ground level work by the British reporter gave the story its fusion of Third World government corruption and the big business angle. It built perfectly on his original project to report on African corruption and Western corporations.

The piece suggested to Reynolds further investigations into large multinational firms doing business in Third World countries. How were they part of the cycle of corruption? Did Martinelli Global actually control the Nigerian economy? Research showed Martinelli Global did business in some interesting places throughout the world. Martinelli Global would be the perfect focus of his continued investigation.

CHAPTER 4

MOSCOW, RUSSIAN FEDERATION

A middle-aged man and woman walked arm in arm down the sidewalk. It was a cold, overcast April day with a chilling wind, colder yet as they walked through long shadows cast by the buildings as the sun was about to set. The sidewalk was piled with shoveled snow, now a sooty gray color. Spring had not yet arrived. The neighborhood would be considered middle class, but the drab apartment buildings were still 1950's Soviet-era ugly.

As the couple approached the entrance door to an apartment building, a black Mercedes pulled abruptly to the curb in front of them. Two men in leather coats got out quickly.

The man and women tensed. Two other men were approaching on foot from behind them. No one else was on the street. The man attempted to push the woman toward the apartment building entrance. Bewildered, the woman hesitated. It was too late anyway. The four men now surrounded them.

"Upstairs," one of the men ordered. "The key!"

The man handed over the apartment key to the extended hand of one of the leather coats. All six people ascended the stairs to the third floor and entered the couple's apartment.

"You were warned to stop your articles about Caspian Enterprises," said the one apparently in charge. He was perhaps thirty. The other three were younger, but with more muscular builds. "Your editor was warned. What is wrong with you? Are you stupid or do you not give a shit about the consequences?"

"Sergi, what's this about?" the woman asked. She clutched her husband's arm tightly.

"Let her go. Your quarrel's with me," Sergi said. It was a meek response, his voice cracked with fear.

The same man said, "Afraid we can't do that. You see, if we beat *you* I think you are stupid enough to continue to write your stories. Now I think if we beat your wife, perhaps you will come to a new understanding. So I think that is what must be done."

Two of the men grabbed Sergi from behind, one on each arm. One man grabbed the woman. The leader stood in front of the woman. Her eyes widened in terror. She knew she was about to be hurt.

"No!"

The leader smashed her in the jaw with a gloved fist. The woman slumped with the blow, but was held fast by the man restraining her arms. Another blow broke her nose and sent blood flowing down her front. The man hit her twice more, restraining the blows enough for her to remain conscious.

Screaming pleas for them to stop, Sergi Astapkovich slumped at the sight of his wife being beaten. The leader drew a knife and held it to Sergi's throat. "Viktor. Get to it," he said.

The one called Viktor released the husband and approached the woman. He ripped open her coat. She was wearing a sweater, a long skirt, and tall calf-length boots. Barely conscious, she struggled vainly under the restraint of the man holding her arms from behind.

Victor extracted a spring-loaded knife. Although barely conscious, the woman gasped at the sight of the five-inch blade. He proceeded methodically to cut away the sweater, then the skirt. Victor looked the terrified woman straight in the eye as he separated her bra with his forefinger and slit the fabric.

The woman gasped as her attacker grabbed her breast roughly. He cut away her slip, then her underwear. Covered the woman's mouth with his large hand to silence her screams, he proceeded with the rape.

"There shall be no further articles in your newspaper, Sergi Astapkovich. If you pursue inquiries, both you and your wife shall disappear. Do you understand?" The leader held his knife to the side of the man's neck. The man's wracking sobs caused the point of the assailant's knife to draw a drop of blood.

Sergi Astapkovich slumped to the floor. The four men left the apartment. Crawling to his moaning wife, he vomited as he looked at her battered face.

The editor of a prominent Moscow newspaper was sitting down to dinner with his wife when the telephone rang.

The caller said, "We warned you and your reporter Sergi Astapkovich about pursuing his current story. Perhaps we were not clear. Tonight we warned him again. I believe he now understands. I am sure his wife does. I hope you also understand." The caller disconnected.

At an up-scale Moscow strip club, two men sat drinking French champagne. The older of the two looked the part of a prosperous businessman; late fifties, thinning gray hair, slender build. He was dressed in a western-cut gray suit with a cashmere overcoat laid over the back of a chair. He wore a silk necktie with a white shirt. The younger man had full and unfashionably long black hair. In contrast to the other man's business style of dress, he wore a black turtleneck knit shirt and casual slacks. A Rolex watch, designer Italian shoes, and an expensive kid-leather coat suggested equally expensive tastes.

Although just early evening, the club was reasonably full. Most of the patrons appeared to be businessmen. Most were dressed in suits. Some English and French could be heard suggesting many were foreign. The only women were the waitresses and the performers. On the stage at the moment was a dark haired beauty with the requisite long legs and large breasts. She was totally nude.

"And how about her, General?"

The older man in the suit could not take his eyes off her. "She's extraordinary. Do you know her?"

"Of course. Her name is Leysa. She's Ukrainian. Like to meet her?"

The older man turned to face the younger man, "Of course I would like to meet her. I'd like to do much more than just meet her, Feliks."

"Perhaps I can arrange that as well, General," Feliks Garnitsky said.

The older man smiled and nodded. Garnitsky motioned to a waitress. She smiled broadly and bent to hear Garnitsky over the music, as well as to reveal her own breasts. Garnitsky whispered something in her ear and gave her enough of a tip that she kissed his cheek.

Fifteen minutes later, Leysa strolled to their table. She touched Garnitky's cheek with her palm and kissed him full on the lips. She was dressed in a tight knit dress, heels, and no nylons.

"Leysa, I'd like to introduce my very good friend, General Ryndenko." He did not bother to mention what branch of the military. Leysa did not ask.

"Oh my, a general. You look like a military man, General. I bet you are even more handsome in uniform," Leysa said. She laid her hand over his.

Garnitsky sighed at Leysa's overplaying it. But what could he expect from a whore, even one as beautiful and expensive as Leysa.

"Leysa. Perhaps you and one of your friends would like to join the General and me upstairs for a party. We can have dinner sent in. Champagne and French wine. Caviar of course."

"Oh that sounds wonderful. And I am so hungry," she said while looking intently into the General's eyes.

A well-built man in the ubiquitous black leather coat approached their table. Garnitsky gave him a slight nod. He stood to one side as Garnitsky said to the General and Leysa, "Leysa, please escort the General upstairs and I will be along in a few minutes."

After they left, the man sat down and said to Garnitsky, "It's taken care of, Boss. The reporter Astapkovich will not be writing any more stories about Caspian."

The next morning the same man at the strip club who brought him the information about the reporter the night before woke Garnitsky. It was ten o'clock. Garnitsky lived in a large luxury apartment that occupied the entire top floor of one of the best addresses in Moscow. There was sufficient room for his maid and bodyguards. It had been a long night of sex and drinking. He was badly hung-over. The bodyguard poured him a glass of water and lit a cigarette for him.

"And you woke me for a fucking good reason I suppose?" Garnitsky said.

"Mr. Krasin called. Said it was important. He wants you to call him as soon as you can."

"Shit. I need some breakfast first. Get me some sausages and fried potatoes." Ganitsky put his feet on the floor and pulled on a robe. "You see, Pyotr, the best thing for a hangover is to put some grease in your stomach. Then a touch of vodka in some fruit juice. And lots of fucking coffee." Garnitsky said. "See to it will you, Pyotr?"

An hour later, he called Nikolai Krasin from a phone that was secure from any electronic eavesdropping. It was the latest technology installed with the assistance of people he knew at the Russian Federal Security Service, or FSB. The FSB was the successor agency of the former KGB. Garnitsky himself was ex-KGB prior to its dissolution along with the demise of the Soviet Union in the early nineties.

Garnitsky left the intelligence service to pursue other personal opportunities, but retained strong alliances with senior FSB officials. Like the old KGB, the FSB conducted intelligence operations both within Russia and abroad. In reality, Garnitsky still had access to the highest levels of Russian intelligence, for which he paid handsomely.

Nikolai Krasin was one of the most powerful men in Russia, but he did not flaunt that power with Garnitsky. He ignored his associate's dissipative excesses because of his value. Garnitsky was himself powerful with his access to intelligence and his criminal associations. Primed with Krasin's money, the association yielded mutual powerful advantage to both.

"I have arranged for a top level meeting to propose our concept for the purchase of controlling interest of Transneft," Krasin said. "Attending will be the Industry and Energy Minister, Tkachenko, the Justice Minister, Rumiantsev, the managing director of Transneft, Dyakonov. None of their staff. Someone from Eastern Capital Funding will discuss the financing details. Our Far-North Oil & Gas managing director will be there along with a British oil industry consultant named Edward Burke to help sell the deal. At least the public face of the deal. The deal gets sold if these officials see enough personal gain."

Garnitsky understood the basic plan for Krasin's bid to invest in the Russian state-owned oil pipeline company, Transneft. The deal was worth billions in U.S. dollars or Euros. More than that, the financing and construction work would be through companies controlled by Krasin, and ultimately controlled with his partner the multi-national, Martinelli Global

Incorporated through various off-shore, tax-sheltered corporations.

"After the Yukos re-nationalization, our competitors in the private sector are being cautious about expanding investment. It's a unique opportunity for us. Our pitch to the Government is a major investment commitment to double existing Transneft capacity within three years. With oil prices at historic levels and continuing to rise, that will play well for the Government," Krasin said.

"I have the major players agreeing in principle. What we need is to understand the personal appetites of these individuals. I want to ensure that we make a proposal that will be personally difficult to refuse. In brief, I need your intelligence insights. How quickly can you assemble the requisite information, Feliks?"

As cultured as Krasin seemed, Garnitsky knew he had a heart of stone, perhaps no heart at all. Krasin thought himself an aristocrat, a White Russian in post-revolutionary times. In reality he had some aristocratic blood, his grandfather somehow having survived the civil war in the twenties. His uncle was Deputy Minister of Finance with powerful government and international banking contacts. Garnitsky knew this since he had researched Krasin extensively.

Garnitsky told him he would have the information within a few days. Krasin said the meeting was scheduled within three weeks.

"I'll need your special assistance in pulling this off, Feliks. By the way, has the problem with that newspaper been resolved?" Krasin asked.

CHAPTER 5

N ikolai Krasin owned a large estate, a forty-minute drive outside the Moscow suburbs. The dacha was built in 1885 as the summer home of a wealthy aristocrat. After the revolution in 1917 and the civil war that followed, the last of the landed aristocracy was swept away by the Bolsheviks. The building fell into neglect until the fifties when it was given a utilitarian restoration for use by the KGB as a training center. Krasin acquired the property in 1992. Spending a considerable amount of money, mostly not his own, he returned the property back to its tsarist-era splendor. Exquisite new woodwork, frescoed ceilings, millions of dollars in artwork, and period antique furniture made one feel as if they were in a Romanov palace at the end of the nineteenth century.

Krasin ostensibly operated the estate as a non-profit charitable corporation, devoted to preserving historical properties. This was the only property in that portfolio. The various companies under his management all *contributed* to the restoration, the artwork, and even the upkeep. For this meeting to sell the pipeline deal, the non-profit organization billed Far-North Oil & Gas for the entire cost as *maintenance*. Krasin personally pocketed the seventy-five thousand dollars by charging consulting fees to the non-profit organization.

Garnitsky did his research well - easy enough through his FSB connections. One of his senior lieutenants made all the arrangements and would manage the staff during the weekend. Garnitsky would not attend. Krasin played the lead in this play. Garnitsky was the stage manager.

Limousines began arriving on Friday in the early evening. The plan was to have a lavish dinner and a night of pleasures. Saturday would be a day of leisurely negotiation. The weather was expected to be warm. The garden and grounds would offer the opportunity for individual private discussions. Dinner would be followed by a continuation of the previous night's entertainment.

Krasin greeted each of the guests and his own people as they arrived. At his side was a tall handsome man, dressed in an Armani suit, and an equally tall woman with a magnificent figure, advertised in a tight dress.

Industry and Energy Minister, Vassily Tkachenko could not take his eyes off the woman. "Vassily, this is Yuri, and this is Leysa. They are in charge of all the staff here. If there is anything you should require during your stay, please just ask them," Krasin said.

Tkachenko made an exaggerated gesture to kiss Leysa's hand, which was the only break in his stare at her deeply revealed cleavage. Leysa had been selected primarily around Tkachenko. She would captivate him with his known appetite for women.

"Minister Tkachenko, may I escort you outside for drinks before dinner?' she said.

Outside, a string quartet was playing Vivaldi. Waiters moved about with champagne and chilled vodka.

The Justice Minister and the managing director of Transneft were already drinking champagne. They were engaged with the executives from Eastern Capital Funding and Far-North Oil & Gas.

A short, paunchy, bald man was at the buffet table heaping caviar onto toast and talking to another beautiful young woman. Unlike the others dressed in dark suits, he wore a tweed jacket and brown slacks. He was speaking English to the woman.

"Edward, I see you have made a friend," Krasin said in Russian.

Edward Burke answered in flawless Russian, "Nikolai Mikhailovich, this beautiful young woman is most remarkable. She is working on a graduate degree in international economics. She has an extraordinary grasp of energy economics."

"If you might excuse us for just a few minutes, Miss?" Krasin said to the woman who smiled and retreated gracefully.

Burke followed her with his eyes.

"I am relying on you to convince Tkachenko of the international benefits of this sale. If he is won over, the others will agree," Krasin said.

"I have constructed what I believe to be a persuasive case. Not too technical so Tkachenko will be able to grasp the salient points. Of course, there is a fair amount of fitting the facts to the desired perspective," Burke said.

"Well, be at your most persuasive. You personally stand to gain a small fortune," Krasin replied. "Enjoy the evening, Edward."

Eventually, Krasin suggested they move to the dining room. He introduced the chef from a five-star Moscow hotel who in turn explained the dishes to be served. Krasin concluded with a list of selected old Bordeaux and Burgundy wines, specifically paired with each dish by the chef.

With a subtle choreography, the men were all paired with beautiful woman. Only Krasin had no escort. Tkachenko and Rumiantsev were both in their sixties. Encouraged by the liquor, both were trying to impress the pretty young females seated next to them. The Director of the state-owned pipeline company

Transneft was becoming slightly drunk as dinner proceeded and his wine glass was continually refilled.

Transneft Managing Director Dyakonov was not as polished as the more senior two government ministers. He was a large man with a swarthy complexion with the hands and thick fingers of a construction worker. Next to him was a woman, much younger than the other females, with less makeup and a less provocative dress. She looked almost like a teenager. As dinner progressed to dessert, he had his hands on her thigh under the table.

The next morning, Garnitsky's man Yuri Dratshev gave Krasin his report of events of the previous night.

"Tkachenko had a fulfilling night with our Leysa," Dratshev said with a broad smile. "It's all on video. Makes for some great watching if you . . ."

"Skip the voyeuristic details. Go on," Krasin said sternly.

"Yes Sir. Minister Rumiantsev suffers from erectile dysfunction. However, the two young women were successful in overcoming that problem."

"And Dyakonov?"

"Mr. Dyakonov has a liking for young girls. You may have noticed that the woman we paired him with looked to be in her teens. Small breasts, dressed ..."

"Yuri, get to it," Krasin interrupted him.

"He was certainly enticed with her. But it got ugly. He continued drinking vodka even though he was already fairly drunk. Wanted her to drink with him. She tried to keep on drinking but got sick. Dyakonov became violent. Beat her up. Pissed on her and then started kicking her. Got bad enough that one of my people had to go into the room and get her out."

"This is all on video tape?" Krasin asked.

"Yes Sir."

There was a breakfast buffet set out in the dining room. The women were not in attendance. The guests and Krasin's people wandered into the dining room over the course of an hour.

Justice Minister Rumiantsev and Krasin were the first at breakfast. Krasin suggested they take their coffees and walk in the garden.

"I trust this is proving an enjoyable weekend, Pavel," Krasin said to Rumiantsev.

"Most enjoyable, Nikolai. The amenities at your dacha are most exquisite."

"That is excellent, Pavel. You are a special friend. You must profit handsomely by lending your support. I would think perhaps two million U.S. dollars. Swiss numbered account of course."

"You are certainly not subtle, Nikolai. This will be difficult to spin as a good policy move," Rumiantsev said.

"Ah, my dear friend, the sell will be easy. There will be other considerations attended to that will preclude any repercussions," Krasin said.

"The President will perhaps question this purchase."

Krasin stopped walking and looked the Justice Minister in the eye with a knowing expression. "Pavel, the President's office is on-board. All is taken care of."

The two men continued their stroll. "I hope that we can consolidate a united position, Pavel. And I do hope you enjoy the remainder of the weekend. Now I must be the good host and see to the other guests."

Krasin turned to leave, then said to Minister Rumiantsev, "Pavel, from your position this is just a legal issue. This deal will be of great benefit for everyone, including the Government. But the economic success is our problem. Any risk on your part is deniable based on your involvement from a legal position only."

Krasin returned to the dining room. The key figure in the negotiation, Industry and Energy Minister, Tkachenko was seated at the dining table. Before him was a huge plate that he had heaped with the buffet offerings.

"Nikolai, I am famished. Join me in this feast that you have provided," Tkachenko said.

"Vassily, I have already breakfasted, but I will take coffee with you."

Krasin sat down next to the Industry and Energy Minister. "I hope you are enjoying the weekend so far, Vassily."

Vassily Tkachenko leaned close to Krasin so that no one could overhear. "Nikolai, this woman that I . . . that I was with last evening. Her name is Leysa. I tell you, I never experienced such an extraordinary woman. She can make you forget everything."

"That's wonderful, Vassily. Then you have much to look forward to the rest of this weekend. Do I assume that you are supporting the deal?"

Tkachenko whispered, "I would like to discuss the particulars further. While the remuneration you offer is substantial, I have the most to lose if this sale to you is viewed unfavorably."

Krasin and Tkachenko excused themselves and went into the library and closed the door. It was a spectacular room in a round turret of the house. Glass extended two stories with a view onto the garden. Leather bound books lined walnut paneled shelves on the three walls. Krasin offered Tkachenko a cigar.

"I believe Edward Burke will be able to dispel any concerns you may have on the technical and economics aspects of why this is good for Russia."

"That may be so, but as Minister of Industry and Energy I will be held responsible."

"What is it you are looking for, Vassily?" Krasin asked.

Tkachenko took several moments before answering while he cut the tip and lit the cigar. "I was thinking of a sum double what you had proposed."

Krasin made no facial response to indicate his reaction. "And that is truly a vast sum. I am buying your support, Vassily, not the entire Ministry. Besides support for the purchase, what can you offer?"

"Long term government oil and gas contracts. At very profitable prices of course," Tkachenko answered.

Krasin finished his cigarette. "Very well, Vassily. You shall have your king's ransom. For which, I expect you to work on convincing anyone important to the venture. That includes Dyakonov," Krasin said.

"I will do what I can, Nikolai, but Dyakonov will be difficult. After all, he sees himself losing power. He will not be the top boss after you take over. Will he?"

"Christ no, Vassily. That fat pig has mismanaged Transneft for years," Krasin said. "He'll have a figurehead position, make the same amount of money, but run anything? Certainly not."

Oleg Dyakonov did not present himself for breakfast. He only joined the others at ten-thirty for the start of discussions. Dyakonov may have been fat and possessed of degenerate sexual appetites, but he was also shrewd and understood the energy business. He had architected many successful schemes that allowed him to secure powerful allies in the government. He had amassed a modest fortune, but at fifty-five, he was not yet ready to retire. Dyakonov probably could not stop this deal since it carried too much power at a level over his head, but he could secure a better deal for himself.

The first session of discussions lasted two hours. All three of the government officials knew each other were being paid handsomely for supporting the sale of the state-owned Transneft. They also knew others, all the way to the President, were being paid-off as well. But they also knew that they carried the most visible responsibility for the sale of Transneft because of their positions.

Dyakonov proved defensive on many of the issues. He knowledgeably argued technical points with the British consultant Burke. Ministers Tkachenko and Rumiantsev stayed apart from the debate, but were visibly irritated at Dyakonov's resistance. It was a strained two hours. Krasin was clearly displeased with the course of the discussion. He suggested they adjourn for a lunch break.

Krasin took the opportunity to divert Dyakonov to the garden for a private conversation.

"So, Oleg, you seem to have reservations about this deal," Krasin said once they were outside.

"Reservations? This is a brazen move to enrich your company, Krasin. You offer me some money to rubber stamp your coup and then step aside. Why should I do that?" Dyakonov said.

"Some money? I believe it was a very sizeable amount. And you are not being pushed out. You will have a senior position at the parent company of Far-North Oil & Gas. A generous salary and all the benefits of the most senior executives," Krasin said.

"Krasin, your fucking offer is chicken shit. I don't think you understand the economics here. If I raise objections about this deal in the right places, it simply will not happen."

Krasin betrayed no emotion when he asked, "Then what will it take for you to be onboard with the deal, Oleg?"

Dyakonov had anticipated this moment. His response was rehearsed. "Five million Euros, plus a salary of half a million per year. A five year contract. My guess is that is probably equivalent to your offers to Tkachenko and Rumiantsev."

Krasin responded, "You have an inflated value of your contribution to this project, Oleg. Perhaps I should consider just ignoring your opposition."

"I don't think you will do that, Krasin. You want this deal to move forward without any major obstacles. And rest assured I can create formidable obstacles. I'm not without substantial influence in the Government."

Krasin considered Dyakonov's threat for several moments before responding. "Very well, Oleg, you will get your five million. For that I expect not only your support, but your wholehearted lobbying for the project. Agreed?"

"Agreed," Dyakonov said.

"Shall we now have lunch?" Krasin said.

The afternoon session was productive with Dyakonov not obstructing the process. The general elements of the deal were finalized. Ministerial staff and the accountants for Far-North Oil & Gas and Eastern Capital Funding would conclude details. The purchase price was finalized at 7.1 billion Euros.

With the deal essentially concluded, all of the participants enjoyed another night of food, drink, and sexual debauchery. Feeling substantially richer, the government officials celebrated by consuming excessive portions of all three.

Several days after the conference at Krasin's villa, Moscow newspapers carried the headline that the managing director of the state-owned oil pipeline company Transneft was found dead in a third rate hotel. Initial reports suggested suicide. There were some suggestive references to illicit sex being involved.

Two days later, the tabloid publication, the London Daily Mirror went further. It splashed the story not only on the cover, but four inside pages exhibited explicit photographs showing Oleg Dyakonov having sex with two clearly underage girls. Even though the Daily Mirror blacked-out genitalia and the girls' faces, it still pushed the envelope on British public decency laws. The tabloid did not acknowledge the source of the photographs. The Moscow newspapers subsequently speculated that Dyakonov committed suicide because he was trapped in a blackmail scheme that was bleeding him financially.

Feliks Garnitsky was seated in Nikolai Krasin's elegant corner office. It was on the fifth floor of an eighteenth century palace, not far from the ancient city center. Like the dacha outside the city, Krasin's office was a study in elegance. Antique French furniture in dark woods dominated. Krasin sat behind a massive eighteenth-century black-walnut desk. The walls were done in gold tones with elaborate white moldings. The walls were hung with oil paintings. Many were of Venice. Several were originals by Canaletto and Sargent.

Garnitsky started to extract a cigarette from his pocket when Krasin said, "Feliks, I prefer you do not smoke in here. It's bad for the paintings."

The two men were seated in comfortable armchairs in an area to the side of the office. Garnitsky scowled but nodded his understanding.

"It appears that the death of Dyakonov is working out well. The photos are the focus of attention, not Dyakonov. We made sure the Russian press got the same materials as the foreign tabloids. All of his allies are distancing themselves by making no comments.

"Yuri did well. The two twelve year old girls were a real find. Dyakonov was such a degenerate, that Yuri lured him to that hotel with a promise of more of the same with them. The police have no evidence to conclude murder," Garnitsky said.

"Spare me the details, Feliks, but I agree that Yuri did an outstanding job," Krasin said. "Now we need further support for the sale by leaking information about Dyakonov's corruption at Transneft. That will add to the argument for privatization."

CHAPTER 6

MANHATTAN, NEW YORK

S everal weeks later, Conrad Redek told Steven Martinelli that Krasin had concluded the Transneft deal with the Russian Government.

"Good afternoon, Nikolai," Steven Martinelli said. He was calling Krasin from New York, eight hours earlier than Moscow time. "I am just now having my coffee. Perhaps you are enjoying champagne? Well deserved."

"Steven, so good of you to call. No, I am not celebrating. Too much work to do," Krasin said with a laugh.

"I can appreciate that. Obviously negotiations worked out to your satisfaction. Any difficulties?"

"Of course, but they were overcome. My more immediate attentions are to pursue opportunities in the Caspian Sea that I touched on some time ago."

"Yes, I recall our discussion. The Caspian Sea is considered maybe the last frontier of oil and gas exploration according to the experts. Everyone seems to want something there," Martinelli commented.

"Exactly, Steven. Every country in the region, plus the European Union, even the United States. The United States has been a hindrance to Russian efforts. The U.S. wants to strengthen ties to the smaller regional countries to counter Russian influence. Apart from the other chief producing countries of Kazakhstan and Turkmenistan, there are pipeline alternatives to Russia that could be routed through Georgia or Azerbaijan to Turkey.

"Plus the American's want to curry favor with the Muslims of the region. Now with the acquisition of Transneft, Far-North is positioned to participate in a major way. Transneft carries almost all of Russian produced oil. Being Russian state-owned, it was not considered in the equation for new non-Russian reserves projected out of the Caspian Sea. Privatized, Transneft is now in a much better position."

"What are you considering, Nikolai?" Martinelli asked.

"Expanding Caspian Enterprises through acquisitions in the region." Krasin answered. "With the Transneft acquisition, there will be opportunities to throw a lot of new business to Caspian. We'll form subsidiary companies underneath Caspian in the principle countries. This will allow us to promote nationalistic interests to our advantage. We expect to secure inducements from the Russian government to route any new Caspian Sea petroleum production through Russia."

"Do you have any political influence in these countries?"

"Just in Georgia. We have Tbilisi Industries there," Krasin said. "We will have to develop our positions in the Muslim countries, though. The British petroleum consultant, Edward Burke, is proving helpful there. He's currently employed by Azerbaijan as part of their bilateral negotiations with Turkmenistan on oilfields in the middle of the Caspian Sea. He has already provided some important intelligence. We pay better than the Azerbaijanis."

"Very well, Nikolai. That all sounds very promising. Let's talk further as you make progress. Don't let any funding limitations retard the opportunity. Perhaps you could come to New York next month and update us and the Board with more specifics."

Krasin signed inaudibly. "That would be good, Steven," he said cordially.

It was not that he had anything to hide from his partners across the Atlantic. Martinelli Global was every bit as ruthless. They were equally risk-taking opportunists. But their concerns inevitably turned to the detail of any audit trails. It was a function of their Western legal systems contrasted with the freewheeling environment of Russia and the other former Soviet republics. They spent more effort on covering their tracks than on getting things accomplished. But Martinelli and the financial resources of the Martinelli Global empire had made Krasin enormously wealthy. So a trip to New York was better than them coming to Moscow and involving themselves more intimately in Krasin's operations.

Krasin had the best of two very different worlds. The association with Martinelli Global gave him access to vast capital resources. Partnered with a Western multi-national corporation provided added leverage. Coupled with Krasin's government connections, these resources provided unlimited opportunities in the Russian business landscape as it continued to develop since the fall of the Soviet Union.

Krasin spent a part of his early years getting a graduate degree in economics at the Sorbonne in Paris. He understood the complexities of Western business. Competition in sophisticated capital democracies with intricate government oversight was a different playing field than in Russia.

Twenty-first century Russia was a comparative infant in market economy. It was like the late nineteenth century in the West where the Morgans, Carnegies, and Rockefellers created vast business empires with little government constraint. Even these robber barons operated in environments less dependent upon official corruption than modern Russia. As the Soviet Union collapsed, chaos reigned as state owned assets were liquidated, and official corruption became the currency in an unregulated economic environment.

Krasin became a shark among sharks. At a point, his ambitions required not only new sources of capital, but international leverage to grow. Linking with Martinelli Global provided those elements. Steven Martinelli also proved to be a kindred spirit in the pursuit of empire. Both had profited handsomely with the association, but neither was really able to fully understand the business environment of the other.

"How is the situation in Nigeria progressing?" Krasin asked.

"I believe it's under control. It's still major news but abating. Martinelli Global has not been linked to blame in any compelling way," Martinelli said. "There has been some attempt in the U.S. press to implicate Martinelli Global but it has not gained any real footing. Our London subsidiary, Pan Africa Holdings has taken a beating. Pan Africa stock prices plummeted on the London Exchange after the story broke. They've now stabilized and have recovered somewhat."

"That is all very good news, Steven. So, I will plan on coming to New York next month to discuss ideas on the Caspian venture."

CHAPTER 7

MANHATTAN, NEW YORK

B y the third week, the story of the Nigerian pesticide plant disaster had moved to the inside of the newspaper. Mark Reynolds was no longer writing the pieces. A staff reporter was essentially just massaging wire service copy. The story had quickly lost traction after the initial international shock. The Nigerian government continued to effectively limit information. Some countries were even acknowledging Nigeria's continual labeling of the incident as a terrorist attack. Even in the United States some groups citied the incident to make the case for increased security at chemical plants.

Reynolds got up late on this Saturday morning. Denise was already sitting at the kitchen island having coffee and reading the newspaper. He bent to kiss her. She offered her cheek and continued reading. The atmosphere was a little strained. The previous night had not gone well. Both had drunk too much. A colleague of Denise's and his wife had been over for dinner. Reynolds thought the guy was arrogant, his wife an airhead. Differing political and social views had lead to some heated disagreements.

"Seems the Nigerian incident has played out. I should have thought it would have been a bigger story with all that shit you went through," Denise said. Her tone was mocking.

"It would've been if the Nigerian government hadn't sealed off any information. That and calling it a terrorist attack."

"And why do you think this wasn't the work of terrorists like they claim? The place is a hotbed of all sort of violence, yet you seem to be on this campaign to prove it was another big bad corporation thing."

Reynolds knew she was goading him. One of the arguments from the previous night involved his position on the social impact of large multi-national corporations.

"Not likely. Just like my last piece pointed out. This was not the style of the Islamic insurgents. They've engaged in attacks on oil production, kidnappings, and targeted assassinations. There's been no claim of responsibility. To the contrary, they've even disavowed any complicity."

"So you believe a bunch of terrorists?"

"In this case, yes," he said, a little too sharply. "Besides, so do a lot of experts. Sources at the CIA and State I've interviewed. This was a militarily secure area. No rebel activity. Even these gangs that make a business out of stealing oil and gasoline from pipelines don't operate in the area."

"So you conclude the Government of Nigeria is in league with this pesticide company to cover-up the incident? And of course, this company is part of a big multi-national so the conspiracy is on a grander scale."

Reynolds took a breath trying to back away from this escalating into a larger argument. "Listen, Nigeria is a cesspool of corruption. You can't do anything there without paying off somebody. At every level right up to the President. Especially the President. They've given no credible information that the deaths of these people resulted from some terrorist attack. No matter what the real story is, Agriproducts paid out money to keep the Government on its side."

"So now that this story is dying away, what are you going to do? Go after the corrupt Nigerians?"

"Fuck the Nigerians. I'm going to do a series on multi-national companies doing business in places like Nigeria. How they use offshore tax havens to mask what's really going on. They plunder resources and ignore environmental damage. The corruption they fund stifles democratic institutions. This is the sort of shit that went on in the U.S. in the late nineteenth century. Only this is more sophisticated. This Agriproducts, where the accident happened, is just a complicated extension of the multi-national, Martinelli Global."

"Spoken like a true communist. I'll tell you this, Mark; your political opinions make me sick. You're a pain in the ass to our friends, and I . . ."

"Friends? You mean that arrogant jerk-off colleague of yours, Larry, and his simple-minded wife, are now *friends*?"

Denise got off the stool and walked out of the kitchen. "You're truly an asshole, Mark."

Reynolds refrained from calling her a bitch, and chose to make a smart-ass remark that was just as inflammatory. "So a blow-job is probably out of the question?"

Denise slammed the bedroom door.

The remainder of the weekend was spent avoiding each other. When necessary, they forced a minimal politeness. Monday was a relief to be away from each other.

"How was your weekend?" John Fredericks asked when Reynolds entered his office.

"Had better, but I'll survive," Reynolds answered and sat down. "Can we talk about my idea for my next series?"

Fredericks suspected that Reynolds and his girlfriend were having some difficulties but was not going to pry. He liked Reynolds and felt it was mutual, but Reynolds kept his emotional distance.

"Sure. What are you proposing?"

"I want to complete the series about African corruption. Even before this Nigerian accident, it was clear that Western corporations are part of the corruption problem. There's a whole variety of reasons why the West gets in bed with these dictators and generals, but they all lead to profits. They're not the reason behind third-world corruption, but they're a contributing component as they flow into these areas of opportunity like water seeking a level. The story goes beyond Africa."

"Ok, so what's the story?" Fredericks asked.

"The story is Martinelli Global Incorporated. As Rachel and I researched these guys, we came to the realization that this isn't just your ordinary international corporation. These fuckers are in a class by themselves."

"You want to do a profile on a corporation?" Fredericks asked with undisguised sarcasm."

"No, no, John. It's not a piece about Martinelli Global. Martinelli Global's just the poster child for literally all kinds of big corporate issues. They're perfect. I can get into these wider issues, but make it more specific by using Martinelli Global as the example."

"Wonderful. So what makes Martinelli Global such a bad guy?" Fredericks said.

"Not sure they're any worse than a lot of others. That's the whole point. Corporations of this size are more amoral than bad. They act more like governments. The pursuit of profits trumps everything else. There's more inertia than malice to their actions. But Martinelli Global seems to be something else. They use all the tools in the box. Their origins go back a hundred years, but they're strategically on the cutting edge."

"Mark, this sounds like a yawner. Why Martinelli Global and not Walmart or Microsoft? How about General Electric, they go back a hundred years? Or why not do postmortems on Enron and World Com?"

"Because Martinelli Global isn't just big and successful, it's how they do it. That's the story, John."

"You're suggesting there's something illegal going on? Got any real evidence to support that?"

"If you mean things like accounting machinations to hide debt, inflating revenues, no. Cheating investors, no. They may be, but that's not what I'm suggesting they do. I'm suggesting that Martinelli Global has a central strategy to do business in the most corrupt places in the world. That's got to be for a reason."

"Come on, Mark, that's not newsworthy. I'm willing to bet that a lot of the big guys have operations in some unsavory places. The oil companies do for example. So what makes Martinelli Global special?"

"John, Martinelli Global not only does business in some bad places but they're always the dominating economic force wherever they operate. They operate where there is a corrupt central government or dictatorship. We've got a fair amount of specific intel and a lot of antidotal evidence that the local Martinelli Global subsidiaries in all these countries court favor through bribery to the highest levels."

"That's illegal. Are you saying that Martinelli Global is engaged in bribing foreign government officials?" Fredericks asked.

"Of course I am. I just can't prove it. The Foreign Corrupt Practices Act was passed in 1976. Before that it was common practice for companies to bribe foreign officials. Since then, companies must go to some lengths to distance themselves when paying off officials. Companies sometimes get caught. Halliburton for example got fined in 2003 for bribing Nigerian tax officials. They paid the fine and fired some mid-level management. Just an operational cost. Christ, if you can influence the U.S. Congress through lobbyist's machinations, you can sure as hell do it overseas in these Third World countries."

Reynolds continued. "In Africa, Martinelli Global has extensive operations in Nigeria, Angola, Kenya, and Uganda. All are identified as some of the most corrupt countries of the world. In South America they're in Paraguay, Columbia, Venezuela, and Bolivia. Some rumor has it that they have an arrangement of convenience with major drug traffickers. In the last decade they got in on the ground floor in Russia as the former Soviet Union disintegrated and went public."

"You know, Martinelli Global is just not a prominent name," Fredricks said. "I wouldn't even know them as big, much less what they do. Sure you're not just fixed on these guys because of their connection to Agriproducts in Nigeria?"

"No, John, I just smell Martinelli Global as a story. You know, one of the reasons you don't know about Martinelli Global is they purposely keep a low profile. No ads anywhere. No brands. No philanthropy. However, the Chairman and CEO, Steven Martinelli is heavily connected politically. Martinelli Global's political funding is one of the highest among U.S. corporations.

"What they're good at is operating in foreign countries. Martinelli Global has perfected the art of using offshore corporations as a means of distancing themselves from their various foreign operations. I suspect there are other skeletons buried in those offshore records."

"Ok, Mark. Finish the series on African corruption. Conclude it with references to the influence of multinational corporations. Then let's see what kind of substance this Martinelli Global thing has," Fredericks said.

Mark Reynolds returned to his small office. It was close to lunchtime. He owed Rachel Stern a special lunch for all her work. Plus he needed to make a pitch for more of her research time as he dug deeper into Martinelli Global. Fredericks was clearly not yet on board with the idea.

Stern had a small staff of three. Technically she worked for John Fredericks, but in reality she was pretty much her own boss. Few people could do research as effectively. She intuitively understood the connectivity of data and could follow seemingly arcane paths to mine the targeted information. There were always more inquiries than could be handled. The majority of the work was fact-checking before a piece went to press. Her staff handled most of that work. Rachel tried to devote her time to new information discovery. To that end, she could be selective about where and to whom she devoted time. Mark Reynolds was her favorite reporter.

Stern readily accepted the lunch invitation. Reynolds chose an Italian restaurant in the Greenwich Village that he had not been to for some time.

"This is a wonderful place, Mark," Stern said. The restaurant was decorated in antiques. Exceptionally good paintings of Tuscan scenes hung on the brick walls. A CD with Andrea Bocelli singing Cont Te Partirò provided background.

"It is. The food is outstanding too. Plus, they have a great selection of Italian wines."

"So, you will ply me with wine until I do your bidding."

"Nope, this is just thanks for all the special work you did on the Nigerian story. Without you the story would never have come together. And, I would not have hit on the idea for a new story."

"Ah, now comes the real reason you invited me to lunch," Stern said. Reynolds might have detected a slight change in Stern's mood had he been more observant. "Are you expensing this?"

"Well, I guess. Why?"

"Well then, Mark, order us a good bottle."

Reynolds smiled. He ordered a 1997 Altesino Brunello di Montalcino. An old waiter with a spectacular mustache served them.

"My God, this is excellent, Mark. And this olive oil, oh my," she said dipping a crust of coarse ciabatta bread in the green oil. "This a place you and Denise come to often?"

"No. Denise has never been here. Been a while since I've been here. Seems a little out of the way from where we live. But I'm glad we came here today."

And he was. He liked working with Rachel but she was also a good person. She was pretty, but a little too conservative in her clothing. Trim, taunt figure, probably helped by the jogging. He thought she was about his own age.

"So am I, Mark," Stern said, giving Reynolds a warm smile.

"You really are a terrific researcher, Rachel."

Rachel looked at Reynolds for a long moment, enough to make him slightly uncomfortable before saying, "I appreciate that, Mark. And I appreciate you taking me to lunch at this special place. The company is good too. So enough of the compliments. Tell me about this new project."

"Well it started with what we dug up on Martinelli Global. Actually what you dug up. Taking it out of the context of this accident, Martinelli is an interesting example of how the largest corporations in the world influence third world economies. It's the supplier sweatshops controlled by Walmart, it's Microsoft sourcing programming in India, it's big oil in the Middle East. But Martinelli Global seems to have created a different strategic model that does business in some of the most corrupt places."

"It's going to be difficult to pierce their complex corporate structure and get any real evidence."

"There's no question that they must be paying off senior people in Nigeria. You simply can't do business there without greasing palms. I suspect that may be Martinelli Global's approach in other countries as well. That makes them a pseudo-government partnered with repressive regimes. My premise is that corporations are amoral, but Martinelli Global may be one of those that have moved beyond that kind of neutral label. Like an Enron, but in a wholly different way."

"Nothing new about reporting on big business taking advantage wherever they can. At the turn of the twentieth century you had Ida Tarbell's exposé on Standard Oil's monopoly of the early oil industry. Then of course there was Upton Sinclair's *The Jungle* and *Oil!*"

"Precisely. All the more reason that I can make Martinelli Global a twenty-first century Standard Oil story. Show how the crude practices of a hundred years ago are not that far removed when you place them in unregulated territory. It's the robber-baron concept of control in a modern international context."

They interrupted their conversation to order. It was one o'clock and they were both hungry. "I'll have the bistecca alla fiorentina. Medium, please," Stern said.

"I'll have the same, but make mine medium-rare. Good to see you're hungry, Rachel."

"Especially after that bottle of wine. Speaking of which, you seem to know your way around a wine list. How'd that come about?"

"I just like wine, I guess. To cultivate the habit, I naturally wanted to know something about it. I'm not an expert, but I know what's good."

"Does Denise share your passion for wine?"

"Not really. She drinks an occasional chardonnay, but doesn't care for the reds."

"So, what's next?" Stern asked.

"You mean the project?"

"Of course."

"Well, I need to understand more about these offshore corporations. How and why they're used by most large corporations. Enron showed how they could be used for all sorts of illicit purposes. My guess is that Martinelli Global is on the cutting edge of how to maximize the advantages. The question is, are they doing anything illegal or reprehensible? Clearly they were successful in creating a cut-out for corporate responsibility in the Agriproducts disaster."

"I can hunt down information, but I probably won't be of much help in untangling what it might mean, Mark," Stern said.

"That's ok. I have an old undergraduate classmate that's still a friend. I've used him to help me in the past. Harvard MBA. Now works for Goldman Sachs. Charlie's just the guy to give me an education in international business."

After the three-hour lunch, they left the restaurant to return to the office. Rachel kissed Reynolds on the cheek as they got into the taxi. "That's for the great lunch and the wonderful company, Mark."

Reynolds was a little embarrassed but gave her a warm smile. He enjoyed it as well.

CHAPTER 8

MANHATTAN, NEW YORK

T he next day, Reynolds arranged a meeting with Charles Todd at his Goldman Sachs office on Broad Street late in the afternoon.

"Mark, it's been a long time. How've you been?" Todd said as he shook hands with Reynolds. "Jesus, I read your articles about this chemical accident that killed those people in Nigeria. Sounds like you had a close call yourself."

"That's for sure. The guy I was with, a Nigerian journalist, may have been killed because of what we found. Most corrupt goddamn place I've been to, Charlie. Anyway, if you read my pieces, you can see I drew a bead on Martinelli Global. They had an interest in the Nigerian company but I could only go so far because of the connections through offshore corporations."

"Well that's one of the reasons corporations use them," Todd said.

"I'm researching for a project on large multi-national companies and their impact on developing countries. I need to understand how these offshore corporations work. So I thought of friend Charlie Todd, investment banker extraordinaire and an expert in the world of international business."

"Ok. I'll give you my patented business seminar on the subject and then you can buy me a drink. No, let's make that a couple of drinks. It's been a helluva day."

"That's a deal, Charlie."

"All right. First of all, what you're calling *offshore corporations* are more accurately described as foreign subsidiary corporations in tax-haven countries. These countries have minimal or no corporate taxes on profits. Profits made outside their countries of course. They make their money on company fees and bank licenses. The real benefit is the ancillary commerce and taxes that comes from a vigorous banking and legal community. After all, most of the better known tax haven countries have really no way to lure commerce to their shores. Most are recreational small places like the Cayman Islands, The Bahamas, Panama, Belize, Mauritius, Bermuda, San Marino. So they offer a place to hold profits without paying taxes there.

"For example, a Cayman Island corporation pays no taxes if the revenue is earned outside the Caymans. But taxes are paid by individuals, the bankers, the lawyers, the hotels, the restaurants, and such that earn income in the Caymans.

"If a U.S. corporation is making stuff at one of their foreign subsidiaries, they must pay taxes on profits when they report income on the sale of the goods. The whole point is to make stuff cheaply in one place then sell it at the highest profit possible. However, if that U.S. corporation incorporates an intermediate subsidiary in a tax haven country it can control its comparatively high U.S. taxed profits."

"Ok, so if you've got foreign operations making textiles in Indonesia, or mining minerals in South America, how does the offshore corporation in a Mickey Mouse place like the Cayman Islands come into play?" Reynolds asked.

"That's a good example. These offshore corporations work when you manufacture products in a low wage country which usually is a low tax country as well. The offshore tax-haven subsidiary is the legal owner of the low cost country subsidiary. It only pays taxes in the country producing the goods and of course no taxes in the offshore tax haven country which is why it's called a tax-haven. Remember, these goods are ultimately for shipment to the U.S. or the E.U. with their high taxation rates."

"Here's a basic scenario. The parent company sets up an offshore corporation in the Cayman Islands. It then sets up a production subsidiary in Thailand which is owned by the Cayman Islands subsidiary. The production subsidiary manufactures shirts which it invoices to the Cayman Islands subsidiary at a price that has little or no profit. The production cost for each shirt is $10 in Thailand. The Caymans subsidiary *buys* it for $11. The Caymans subsidiary then *sells* the shirt to the U.S. subsidiary for $45. The U.S. parent corporation sells the shirt to the retail customer for $50. U.S. taxes are paid only on the $5 paper profit that occurred in the Cayman Islands and U.S. transaction. Actual profit is really $39. The high U.S. taxes are avoided on almost 90% of the actual profits.

"The mechanism is called *transfer pricing*. Mind you, all the paperwork is executed onshore in the United States. The offshore Caymans entity is nothing more than a mailing address with no employees."

"And this is legal for U.S. companies?" Reynolds asked.

"In the broadest terms, yes. I have over simplified it, but the basis of having the tax-haven subsidiary is that profits are not taxed until they come *onshore* into the United States. There's a mountain of U.S. tax code to contend with, and companies regularly get their tit in a wringer with violations and wind up paying fines to the I.R.S. There's a whole industry of accounting and legal people that do nothing but manage and advise on transfer pricing, Goldman Sachs included."

"So why doesn't every company that buys foreign stuff do it through offshore subsidiaries?" Reynolds asked.

"Well my naïve friend, all big corporations do. But you can shit in your nest just so much. These tax laws come from heavy-handed lobbying in Washington. There has to be some quid pro quo to keep some taxes onshore."

"You know in the old days, the Cayman Islands and Bahamas were thought of like the Swiss banking system," Reynolds said. "Secrecy seemed the attraction. Most of us thought it was a mechanism for hiding illegal funds; Nazi loot, drug trafficking money, looted treasuries of Third World countries. But you're saying it's really to shelter profits from taxes."

"No, secrecy is a big part of offshore tax havens. It can be a place to hide illegal funds. But more importantly, it's a place for corporations to hide transactions. The lack of reporting requirements under these countries incorporation and tax codes may be as important as the tax incentive in some circumstances. Hiding information from the financial markets can be a compelling attraction for going offshore. That obviously makes it possible to engage in accounting practices that would be illegal in the U.S. Enron is the classic example. Enron had over 800 offshore entities. Most were in the Cayman Islands, but they used other countries as well."

"I assume there are differences in what these various tax-haven countries have to offer?" Reynolds asked.

"Absolutely," Todd said. "Most offer the same avoidance of corporate or capital gains taxes. Some are more secure in maintaining secrecy. The biggest difference is the level of cooperation with other governments and law enforcement agencies. You've got places like Vanuatu, a group of chicken shit islands in the South Pacific. This place offers everything. No taxes of any kind, and no release of any corporate or banking information to other governments or any of their law enforcement agencies. This place is so notorious that major corporations avoid it for fear of the implication they might be hiding something.

"Besides avoiding taxes, the lack of regulatory controls and secrecy create huge opportunities for enhancing a whole variety of financial elements; raising capital, hedging risk, manipulating revenue, hiding debt, hiding ownership. Then of course there's the criminal activity of laundering money, paying bribes, and just plain fraud."

"So what about Martinelli Global? How do they use offshore corporations?" Reynolds asked.

"Well, I should think that's obvious since your story wasn't able to pillory them like Bhopal did to Union Carbide. Avoiding liabilities for one. Just like intelligence agencies using cut-outs for security, the offshore corporation does much the same. You'll see what I mean if you try to go deeper into Martinelli Global's corporate structure." Todd answered.

"We already have. I know what you mean," Reynolds said. "Ok, so now I know something about how these offshore corporations work, tell me what you know about Martinelli Global."

"Ah, that is best done over strong drink. Let's get out of here to a proper watering hole. There's a place a few blocks from here called The Limerick. The waitresses have large tits and wear tight tops. Just what my tired eyes need. We'll beat the usual crowd by an hour."

Todd was right about the waitresses. The tall young thing that served them knew Todd by name. She flirted with both of them as she took their order. An obvious marketing ploy that nevertheless worked effectively on the male clientele.

Reynolds ordered a Macallan's Scotch, neat; Todd a Bombay Sapphire martini.

"Jesus, Mark, warm straight whiskey? Where'd you learn to drink like that?"

"Lot of places don't have easy access to ice. In my line of work you improvise and keep it simple. Besides, it's very good Scotch, not that hair tonic you're drinking."

"Well, I agree that straight gin is an acquired taste, but it's good for my soul."

"So tell me about Martinelli Global, Charlie."

Todd took a long sip of his martini and grabbed a handful of peanuts. "First of all, Martinelli Global performs very well financially. It has a fairly consistent net income of around ten percent and a very high return on equity. If you read their financial statements, it's not clear why they do so well. But that's not particularly suspicious. Goldman Sachs performs at the same levels and some wonder how we do it. With their performance numbers, they should have a higher price to earnings ratio. It's probably a reflection of the markets not totally trusting how Martinelli Global works.

"Their U.S. enterprises are principally involved in trading commodities. They also own all sorts of transportation operations, including shipping and even rail. They're invested in a wide array of logistics operations with not only warehousing but things like petroleum and natural gas storage complexes and various harbor facilities around the world. They operate the largest import-export brokerage firm in the world with offices literally in all major cities. Through their own financial subsidiaries they fund letters of credit transactions and provide other financial services such as hedging currency fluctuations and selling commercial insurance.

"But, like you already discovered, Martinelli Global does business in some nasty places. Not the sort of places a major multinational typically puts their money into. I'm not necessarily an expert on Martinelli Global, but I did a little research after you called me.

"Martinelli Global doesn't merely invest capital, they dominate a particular market segment where they operate. They even define this as a strategy in their annual report."

"What sort of businesses are they into abroad?" Reynolds asked.

"Pretty much the same as in the United States; commodities in the form of minerals and agriculture, transportation and logistics of course. But in their foreign operations they also expand into processing and even some manufacturing like this pesticide plant in Nigeria. But the key factor in their growth occurred in the 1990's when they invested in Russia."

"Yeah, our research showed that their Russian investments are pretty large," Reynolds said.

"Large? If you put all of their holdings together, the ones they officially report plus the ones that accrue through various offshore corporations, they are the largest foreign investor in Russia," Todd responded.

"You're the expert, Charlie, but our research didn't seem to indicate that kind of involvement in Russia."

"Ok, Mark. Now we're off the record. And I can only give you limited info. There are more investments hidden through multiple offshore structures than are reported in their SEC filings. I know this because Goldman Sachs did most of the deals. Our people assisted in architecting the offshore structure of connected companies. It was the first series of deals that caused us to establish an office in Moscow."

"That's legal under SEC regulations?"

"Absolutely. They're reported as loans in the form of bonds. Again through offshore corporations so their true origin is hidden, but all legal."

"Why would Martinelli Global only want a portion of their involvement made public?" Reynolds asked.

"Two reasons. The first is the Russians would have a shit-fit if they knew that a U.S. company had a direct investment in buying up assets of the disintegrated Soviet Union. Second, U.S financial markets would have felt uneasy. This is serious money, my friend. It's estimated that their Russian operations now account for over forty percent of Martinelli Global's earnings. Not necessarily directly, but that's how it washes out."

It was eight o'clock when Reynolds left the bar. He called the apartment but there was no answer. Denise did not answer her cell phone either.

Once home, he picked up the voice message from Denise saying she would be home later. Dinner was leftover cold pizza and a Perrier. His head hurt from all the Scotch he drank with Todd. He was pissed that Denise was not home but told himself to be on his best behavior when she did get in.

He was reading and falling asleep when he heard the door. It was eleven o'clock. He got up and gave Denise a hug and kiss. "How you doing?"

"Fine," Denise said. "Just a lot of work. Needed to complete a proposal for a new prospective client. Impossible deadline as usual."

Reynolds came up behind her as she was undressing and kissed her neck. There was a large irritated area on her neck. "What happened to your neck?"

She looked in the mirror at a red blotch the size of a quarter on her neck. "Shit, I don't know . . . it's been itching all day. Stress probably. Guess I irritated it. I'll put some cortisone cream on it."

"Let's make love," he said.

Denise turned around. "Must we? I'm pretty tired, Mark."

"It's been awhile. We've been on each other's nerves I know. I just want us to reconnect and enjoy each other. I'll make it worth your while."

"I'm exhausted, Mark. Perhaps tomorrow. I just want to take a shower and get to sleep."

"Sure." So much for a romantic reunion. He picked up a book and tried to read.

When Denise came out of the bathroom she kissed him goodnight then laid on her side with her back to him. He turned out the light but did not fall asleep for some time thinking about that spot on her neck. He was pretty sure what it was.

While Rachel Stern expanded her research, Reynolds pursued interviews with anybody that could offer information on Martinelli Global. However, all interview attempts with anyone at Martinelli Global were met with a polite refusal. Even middle level management outside of Corporate in New York would not grant interviews. Martinelli Global seemed obsessed about secrecy beyond anything Reynolds had ever encountered.

After spending hours talking to security analysts, a consensus profile developed. Martinelli Global had a long history of exceptional profitability even in the face of the seemingly higher risk of many of their ventures. An uneasiness about their strategic moves existed in the financial community. As Todd suggested, some felt this probably contributed to their stock selling at a lower multiple of earnings than would otherwise be suggested by their profitability. Martinelli Global was the lowest profile big corporation on Wall Street. Yet Chairman and CEO, Steven Martinelli, was broadly politically connected. That connection was not only with the White House and Congress, but with high ranking career staffers at the State Department and the CIA. This was inherently because of the extraordinary influence of Martinelli Global's operations in many trouble areas of the world.

Rachel Stern's research allowed Reynolds to diagram the essentials of the complicated Martinelli Global organizational structure. Charlie Todd contributed with an expert level interpretation. He also gave Reynolds confidential information on the many Russian associations. Unable to directly use some of

Todd's insider information, it still provided for avenues of investigation.

Making the case for the negative aspects of Martinelli Global's influence in Third World countries required more than what could be assembled through research alone. It needed the flesh and bones feel from the perspective of real people. Reynolds editor was at best only lukewarm about the project. No chance that Fredericks would spring yet for the time and expense to go abroad for another couple of weeks.

Reynolds laid out the key pieces of the project for John Fredericks.

"Could be newsworthy if you're able to uncover any really condemning stuff. If you couldn't tie them to complicity in the Nigerian pesticide disaster, what makes you think you can make a compelling story out of this?" Fredericks said after Reynolds pitched the outline of the project.

"Well in the first place some of these countries are so flagrantly corrupt that corporate collusion must take place by the simple fact they do business there. I'll be able to get enough facts to make the case, John. To add a real feel for the human cost, I'll use local journalists. We'll pay them modest expenses and allow them to share the byline for contributing copy and credit them for the photographs."

"Very modest expenses," Fredericks cautioned. "Ok, Mark. You seem bent on doing this. Do you have enough material now to do a few pieces?"

"Yes I do. The initial piece will define the worldwide situation in general terms."

"Which is?"

"That major multinational corporations are increasingly playing a major economic and social role in Third World countries. And in many situations they collude with repressive regimes for profit thereby perpetuating their hold on power," Reynolds said. "After that, I'll introduce Martinelli Global. I'll start with their beginnings a hundred years ago. No modern invention like an Enron, but an old-time company engaged in conventional commerce that has evolved with the times."

"You've got a real hard-on for Martinelli Global. Pissed you off with the Nigerian thing?" Fredericks asked.

"Maybe. But it still makes good copy, John."

CHAPTER 9

MANHATTAN, NEW YORK

M ark Reynolds' first article in the series of pieces titled *Are Multi-National Corporations Replacing Governments?*, set the tone for the project:

> The rise of mega-corporations that do business in many countries are a phenomena of the last few of decades. As all industries consolidate into several dominate players, these corporations continue to expand in size. It is no longer even meaningful to identify a corporation as being from a particular country. With the reach and economic power of these large multi-nationals, they increasingly weld greater political power. In some Third World developing countries that power may be to the same level as the ruling government itself. Since the Company's only obligation is shareholder value, there inherently exists a set of conditions ripe for corruption and excesses.

Rachel Stern had done an exceptional job in researching the origins of Martinelli Global. Beyond the facts, she had pursued obscure trails to piece together likely conclusions that put real flesh on the story. The hundred year old genealogy of the firm read like a novel.

BALTIMORE, MARYLAND – 1905

Stefano Martinelli immigrated to Baltimore, Maryland a year after the great fire, attracted by its newly rebuilt downtown and waterfront. He traveled by train from his ancestral home near the town of Spello in Italy's Umbria region, to the port city of Genoa. From there it was over two weeks to cross the Mediterranean and Atlantic in a second-class berth on a freighter. Once through Ellis Island in New York, he took the train south to Baltimore. Better equipped than most immigrants, he had the equivalent of $200 dollars when he landed. Better yet, he spoke passable English, the result of his school teacher mother's demands.

His family had been in the olive oil business for hundreds of years. Young Stefano, twenty at the time, was the youngest of three sons. The eldest was clearly going to inherit the management of the olive oil business. Stefano did not relish the idea of toiling his years in manual labor under the direction of his brother. The great wave of Italian migration to America beckoned with adventure and the prospects of starting his own business. Fearing she may never see her youngest again, his mother still promoted his move. Her son was too bright to waste his life in agriculture. She hoped he would go to a university in America.

La famiglia, the family, and *paesani*, from the same village, dominated the early Italian immigrants that settled in the twelve square blocks that became known as Baltimore's Little Italy. They were mostly Neapolitans, Sicilians, and Calabrese from southern Italy. Although Italian, being from the North of Italy set Stefano Martinelli somewhat apart.

The young Martinelli did not enroll in a university. Instead, he took a job with a small Italian importing business. He had his sights set on developing his own business in this thriving new country with boundless opportunities. Within a couple of years he was managing the Baltimore operation. He married the owner's daughter and became an equal partner in the business. The business thrived as the principle supplier of authentic Italian olive, wine, and Old World goods. He architected the consolidation of his family's business in Umbria and other olive oil growers into a cooperative. Buying their entire output for export to America, they were able to get a better price than offered by the domestic Italian market.

After the end of World War One, Martinelli expanded the business with branches in New York and Boston. Unfortunately, the Volstead Act, formally known as the National Prohibition Act of 1919, came into effect in 1920. The prohibition of any beverage with greater than 0.5% alcohol became not only the law of the land, but the eighteenth amendment to the Constitution. Martinelli's substantial trade in Italian wine came to an immediate end.

Importing goods into the ports at the time meant a percentage would be lost to theft on the docks. Italian organized crime controlled the docks, and payoffs to keep the losses manageable were just a cost of doing business. Martinelli therefore knew who ran things on the docks where his goods were unloaded.

Martinelli was aware that organized crime was taking advantage of Prohibition to smuggle liquor into the United States. He hit on an audacious plan to repair his lost revenue from Italian wine, while expanding his business.

In 1923, Joe Masseria ran the Sicilian Mafia in New York. Martinelli pitched his idea to a young Masseria lieutenant, Charlie Luciano. The idea was simple; Martinelli would set up a shipping company with a Panamanian corporation registry. U.S. owned cruise ships were changing to foreign registry to allow alcohol to be served on board. Martinelli would use the foreign identity for his new offshore corporation to hide the true ownership of the vessel. The Sicilian Mafia would put up the capital investment. Liquor would be shipped from various places in Europe to Italy; gin from England, whiskey from Ireland, Scotch from Scotland, vodka from Poland, wine from Italy and France. The liquor would be re-crated and labeled olive oil from a dummy Italian corporation. If discovered by U.S. Customs, only the goods would be lost but no link to his operations.

Luciano quickly embraced the concept and sold Masseria on the idea. Martinelli was astonished when Luciano informed him that not only was the plan approved, but three vessels had already been selected for purchase. Luciano wanted the operation to commence within sixty days.

This was the beginning of Martinelli's shipping empire, and a lifelong association with the Mafia. Martinelli made a fortune importing illegal liquor, both his and the Mafia's, until the disastrous Eighteenth Amendment was repealed by the Twenty-first Amendment in 1933, thereby ending Prohibition. By then, Martinelli Shipping was a major player in worldwide shipping.

Martinelli's business ventures expanded exponentially in the thirty years since the small olive oil and wine importing ventures. Martinelli was now a major commodities importer and exporter. Besides the ocean shipping fleet, the Company had their own rail cars and a number of regional trucking companies.

His only son, Fabrizio was playing an ever-increasing role in the business. Unlike his father, he did go to a school, graduating with a business degree from Columbia University in New York. With the United States entry into World War II, Fabrizio Martinelli enlisted with a commission in the Navy. Partly because of his expertise in logistics, and partly with the pull of his father through powerful government connections, the younger Martinelli served stateside for the duration.

During the War, Martinelli Group as it was now known, had tripled in size as measured by its revenue. They received lucrative contracts to supply all manner of agricultural products and vital war supplies. The merchant marine fleet and trucking operations expanded with the Government putting up the investment capital. New warehouses were built. Large special purpose storage facilities for oil and grain were constructed at key U.S. and Canadian ports. Overseas, similar logistics infrastructure investments were made in England, South America, and Australia.

After the war, Fabrizio took over greater control of the Martinelli operations. It was largely his idea to take the company public in the late 1950s. The move was not to take out a personal fortune for the family, but rather to raise capital for expansion. The huge windfall that was World War II could be leveraged into making Martinelli Group a major international corporation.

The elder Martinelli now devoted most of his business time to cultivating his vast network of government relationships. He was on close personal terms with a dozen of the most influential senators and congressmen on both sides of the aisle. He was a skilled raconteur and charming host. Stefano Martinelli had the knack of making anyone he was talking to feel the center of attention. Among the arrogant, self-important Washington political establishment, Martinelli was in his element. Had he not had his own vested interests, Stefano Martinelli could have been the consummate lobbyist.

Stefano Martinelli knew more about the power brokers in Washington than perhaps anyone. That was due to the simple fact that he spent millions on obtaining intelligence. Early on he understood the connection between information and power.

Martinelli viewed his business as one of movement of goods between major players, and not effected by the consuming public. Therefore, there was no need for advertising. Quite the contrary, it was better to keep a low public profile. What really affected his business was influence and information. Instead of advertising dollars, Stefano Martinelli expended equivalent sums on entertaining and information acquisition. Since information was power, Martinelli made sure he had the best available intelligence, legally or illegally obtained. He made no distinction, only that illegal cost more but was usually worth the price.

Martinelli employed a number of private investigative firms on retainer. Their reports came only to him or his son. No staff were involved. No paper or electronic trail existed. The edge in any negotiation is knowing what the other side really wants and what they are willing to give up. In the influence peddling trade, the edge is in knowing what the politician wants, so knowing *everything* about that person is leverage. The relationship was everything. It was an investment and Martinelli invested heavily. He was rarely disappointed with the return.

The elder Martinelli chaffed under the constraints of being a public company. He was wise enough to understand that his son was better equipped to manage the legal complexities of the vast enterprise that spanned the globe. Business had not changed, only the mechanics had become more complex.

Stefano Martinelli, senior died in 1966 when his namesake grandson was in graduate school at Harvard. The younger Stefano Martinelli preferred the Anglicized Steven to the ethnic Italian. Although too young to have been involved in the business under the reign of his grandfather, he nevertheless benefited from a unique business education that did not come with his Harvard MBA.

The elder Martinelli spent considerable time with his grandson, taking him on business trips during his high school and undergraduate years. The younger Martinelli showed an early aptitude for his grandfather's engaging style. He showed an equal aptitude for the intricacies of modern international business under the hand of his father. Even without the family influence, the younger Martinelli was clearly slated for greater things. In 1972, he married the daughter of a prominent Senator. By 1978, he had risen to the position of Chief Operating Officer of Martinelli Group. In 1982, he took over as CEO with the retirement of his father.

Steven Martinelli embarked on his own vision to expand the business of his grandfather and father. However, more like an Augustus to his great uncle Julius Caesar, he would not only build on the Martinelli legacy, but apply his own imprint.

MANHATTAN, NEW YORK

"How much of this stuff about the original Martinelli's involvement with Lucky Luciano can we corroborate?" Mark Reynolds asked Rachel Stern.

"Can't come right out and say they were in league together," Rachel answered. "Most likely they were, but the evidence is only circumstantial. At best you can say they knew each other. Martinelli served on the boards of several charitable organizations fronted by Luciano. Declassified World War II documents sight that both Luciano and Martinelli assisted Allied military intelligence by using their extensive connections in Italy. The Government of course reneged on their deal with Luciano and deported him. Martinelli got a presidential citation from Truman."

"And what about the illegal liquor trafficking?"

"Never arrested. Closest he came was a shipment that was seized in Boston on its way to a warehouse. Detected only because of a traffic accident according to our own archives. Martinelli was a partner in the distribution business, but the local managing partner took the fall. Stefano Martinelli had some good lawyers even back then. The Feds could not make an indictment."

"So where did you come up with all this shit that I can't use?" Reynolds asked.

"Hey. This is just like the CIA. Some intel is actionable, some is just another piece in the puzzle," Stern replied.

"Stick to the facts, Rachel, skip the philosophy," Reynolds said lightly. "Seriously, got anything even remotely interesting fit for print?"

Stern extracted a single sheet of paper from a file. "After the piece on the Nigerian chemical accident, you got a flood of e-mails denouncing Martinelli Global. You dumped the load over to me to see if there was anything to pursue. Most were the usual screwball fringe variety. A few disgruntled ex-employees. This one might be of interest though."

Stern handed him the sheet of paper.

"Former mid-level manager at Martinelli Global. Twenty-year employee. I confirmed that. Sent him an e-mail asking what he had to offer. Here's his reply."

Reynolds read the reply. "What's he mean about Columbian coffee? Doesn't sound terribly earthshaking, but I'll call him."

"Mr. Brown, this is Mark Reynolds of the New York Daily Press."

"Who?" the man responded.

"Mark Reynolds of the New York Daily Press. You sent me an e-mail. I'm doing a story about Martinelli Global Incorporated. You said you worked for Martinelli Global. You are Franklin Brown aren't you?"

"Shit. No. . . I'm sorry. . . I mean yes. I worked for Martinelli Global. Glad you called."

Wonderful. The guy sounded drunk. Reynolds was about to hang up when Brown said, "I've got some real juicy information for your newspaper. Tell you all about how Martinelli Global owned companies control the coffee trade in Columbia and a good deal of Brazil's too. I know all the details because I used to manage all the transactions."

"Well, that's interesting. If the story gets into those areas of Martinelli Global's business, I'll be sure to call you and check our facts," Reynolds said.

"No, you don't understand, Mr. Reynolds. I'm talking about laundering money. Major drug money."

Reynolds still wasn't buying. "That's a lot different than controlling the coffee market. Why'd you leave Martinelli Global, Mr. Brown?"

"Eased out. Early retirement."

"You were fired weren't you?"

Brown paused for a moment before answering, "Yes."

"For drinking?"

"No. That came after," Brown said. "Believe me, Mr. Reynolds, I do have valuable information. This is not whiskey talk."

"Ok, let's talk then. Where can we meet?"

Brown said he lived in Queens. He could take the subway into Manhattan. Reynolds suggested a Midtown bar the following afternoon.

Reynolds showed up at the bar at three o'clock. Brown was already there in a booth drinking a beer. Brown looked to be in his late fifties; overweight, balding. He was dressed in a wrinkled shirt with cuff-worn chinos. His jacket was slightly soiled. Reynolds was not hopeful. After brief amenities, Reynolds asked about Brown's background with Martinelli Global.

"Worked there twenty years. I'm an accountant. For the last three years before I left, I managed the accounting for Martinelli Global's coffee businesses in Columbia," Brown said.

"What businesses? I checked. My research shows only a subsidiary known as Grupo Columbia involved with oil. No coffee companies," Reynolds said.

"What about Americas Agarian Holdings or South American Products? One's a Panamanian corporation, the other is Belize?" Brown asked.

Reynolds consulted his notes. "No."

"What about Latin American Trading, another Caymans corporation?"

Looking at his notes again, Reynolds said, "Yes. They're listed in Martinelli's annual report. All sorts of agricultural products. Doesn't mention coffee."

"Right. Martinelli Global owns controlling interest in all four of the major coffee trading companies in Columbia through Latin American Trading. Latin American owns Americas Agarian Holdings, South American Products, and a couple of other shell companies which in turn own controlling interest in the coffee companies of Narion Coffees S.A., Grupo Medellin, República Agricola S.A., and Cordillera Este Brokers. You won't find any of that listed in Martinelli Global's annual report," Brown said. He motioned the waitress for another round.

"Martinelli Global buys virtually all the Columbian coffee crop through another Cayman Island company, South American Trading. South American Trading appears as a subsidiary in Martinelli Global's SEC filings and annual report. The offshore subsidiaries that own the coffee companies do not appear in any Martinelli Global public documents. Only Latin American Trading is listed as a foreign subsidiary on their books, but their actual purpose is camouflaged"

"Ok, so Martinelli Global owns these coffee companies through their offshore corporations. You're suggesting they have a monopoly on the Columbian coffee trade?" Reynolds said.

"Of course they do. They own 95% of the market. They collude to out-bid any other buyers. They're buying from themselves so they can set any price they wish. They control the market of the most important coffee production in the world."

"Fine. Adds to the case of Martinelli Global being a predator company. But what's this about money laundering?" Reynolds asked.

Brown took a long drink of his beer before answering. "Martinelli Global also has a Belize incorporated bank known as Latin Trust Group. Latin Trust provides the capital for South American Trading to purchase coffee. But the real thing here is the flow of drug money."

Brown lowered his voice and leaned toward Reynolds. "Drug money is deposited with Latin Trust Group. It then flows back into Columbia in the form of working capital laundered into coffee."

Brown laughed at his own remark. "Now because they have a monopoly on the Columbian coffee trade, Martinelli Global and their drug trafficking associates also make a profit on the coffee. Then they avoid the taxes on the profits by flowing it through the offshore tax havens. My estimate is that Martinelli Global makes 30% for the laundering, while the drug traffickers recoup some of that back by sharing in the legitimate enterprise profits."

Reynolds scribbled furiously in his note pad.

"And you were privy to these drug money laundering transactions?"

"Not directly. But I had my sources. Hard for any company this size to keep secrets. Everything gets recorded somewhere. Always somebody willing to share tantalizing information. Always somebody pissed-off."

"So what happened? Why were you fired?"

Brown grabbed some peanuts and took another drink of beer. "A stupid mistake. The operations manager at Cordillera Este Brokers, Santiago Mendez made a big clerical error in a purchase contract. Mendez is a good guy. Shit happens in business. Problem was I didn't catch the mistake. I should have, but I didn't. Cost Martinelli Global something like three hundred thousand dollars. My boss was pissed, but willing to move on. Not so with Redek."

"You mean Conrad Redek, the current chief operating officer?" Reynolds asked.

"That's right. Fuckin' prick. Called me in and chewed my ass. That afternoon, my boss let me go."

"So you want to get back at Martinelli Global? Why not go to the Feds with your information? Reynolds asked.

"It's just that; information, not evidence. I can't corroborate anything I've told you. If I went to the FBI then I'd just be caught up in a bunch of shit. My severance payments would stop. Why not let you guys do the work?"

"Why come to the Press now?"

"Because you're writing about Martinelli Global. You might be able to use this. Anyway there's no reason not to shit on them now."

"What do'ya mean?"

"My severance package included stock options annually for twenty years, contingent on my maintaining absolute confidentially about any corporate information."

"And you want to risk that?"

"Why not? I've got prostrate cancer. Doctor says maybe two years. Wife left when I was canned. No kids. What better way then to fuck-over Martinelli Global and Conrad Redek as my swan song?"

"That's too bad, Mr. Brown," Reynolds said. "So what can you tell me about this drug trafficking connection?"

Brown told him everything he knew, including the names of those at Martinelli Global Corporate where he got the information. He also gave Reynolds the addresses of the Columbian coffee companies.

"One more thing," Brown said. He handed Reynolds a piece of paper. "That's a letter I got from Santiago Mendez after we were both let go. That's his home address."

"Does he know about the money laundering connection?"

"I don't know. We never talked about it. But I don't see how he could not have in his position."

The next day, Reynolds was in his editor's office. He laid out what Brown had told him plus some new research.

"I can't confirm Brown's allocations, but we did turn up some interesting information. First, these four coffee companies do in fact control the Columbian coffee trade. We can't confirm Brown's take on the ownership, but what we have uncovered does not refute anything he alleges. Rachel is still digging further, but Columbia is not the U.S. Information is a little harder to come by.

"According to a Columbian journalist I talked to, two of the coffee company general managers have family ties to alleged drug trafficking figures. Another has an uncle who's a senior army general. The other guy is politically connected. According to the journalist, these companies all have unusual political clout. Beyond that, the FARC, the rebels, do not seem to target any of their operations."

"Ok, so you're leading to what?" John Fredericks said.

"I need to go down there, John. Probably just for a couple of days. I want to see if this guy Santiago Mendez will tell me anything. Plus this journalist guy that I've talked to may be able to share some more information."

"All right. Go ahead, Mark. This is interesting stuff if you can prove it has any substance. Frankly, you need to get something more than what you have. The piece so far doesn't have enough bite. It's way too complicated to grab the public's attention. But a major U.S. corporation implicated in drug money laundering might be something else. "

CHAPTER 10

BOGOTÁ, COLUMBIA

T hree days later, Reynolds was in Bogotá, Columbia. The flight approach into Bogotá was spectacular. The city of six million lay at the foot of a mountain range. The entire country seemed to be highlands blanketed in lush green vegetation.

The temperature was in the nineties. The pavement outside was still wet from a recent rain shower. His shirt was soaked with sweat by the time he got a taxi. Not quite as oppressive as Nigeria, but close.

His first stop was at the offices of the newspaper, El Espectador on the Avenida el Dorado. The street suggested a modern, prosperous city, not the capitol of a country dominated by drug related violence. But this impression was dispelled as he approached the entrance to the newspaper offices.

There were no windows, only a heavy steel door. A security camera was directed at the visitor. After pressing the buzzer and announcing himself, the camera panned the area behind Reynolds. He waited for over a minute before the door was released. The lobby was small with only the receptionist and two chairs. It too was an area with no windows.

Greeting Reynolds was a trim man of average height, perhaps in his forties with thick black hair and a thin mustache.

"Señor Reynolds. I am Juan Cortina. Please come this way."

Cortina was the newspaper's senior reporter Reynolds had spoken to. He was dressed in an open collar white shirt and dark slacks. His small office was neat with pictures displayed of his family. A single window looked out onto the street. The air conditioning could not keep up with the oppressive heat. Cortina showed no effects, while Reynolds was sweating profusely.

"Please sit down, Señor Reynolds. Can I get you something to drink?"

The two professionals exchanged pleasantries for several minutes. A young woman brought them coffee.

"To business as you say in English," Cortina said. "What you suggest about the collusion of these major coffee companies is interesting, Señor Reynolds. Your resources are much better than mine. So let me contribute to what I know."

"First, two of these people you have named, Carlos Fuentes and Miguel Vargas, have family connections to the drug trade. Fuentes has an uncle that is currently being sought on drug trafficking charges. It's a prominent family. Best guess is that the uncle is out of the country. The Vargas family is something else. They are like rabbits – the family extends everywhere. They are in senior government positions, senior army officers, and they have vast business enterprises."

Cortina handed Reynolds a thick folder of type written pages. "Here is all the information we have on those you have identified. Some are past newspaper articles."

Reynolds did a cursory scan of the documents. "Am I to assume you have not been able to corroborate a lot of this?"

"That is correct, Señor Reynolds. Even though we live in a corrupt Third World country, journalistic ethics still have a place. However, there is much we don't publish simply out of fear. I do not blame my editor. Physical danger is very real for anyone that challenges those in power here in Columbia. They can't do anything if you publish in the United States."

"I assume you would not want me to attribute you as the source?" Reynolds said.

"Unfortunately, that could prove unhealthy," Cortina said.

"What about this Manuel Ortega, the boss of Cordillera Este Brokers? Your information here paints him as a real monster, yet there are no articles in your paper?" Reynolds asked.

"Ortega is a monster," Cortina said. "But his uncle is the commanding general of internal security. We have all sorts of information on Ortega but it will never see print. For good reason. He is way too powerful. Bad things happen here and it's not all drug trafficking related."

"So why is Oretga such a bad guy?" Reynolds asked.

Juan Cortina leaned forward with his hands on his desk. He took a moment to light a cigarette. "Manuel Ortega likes young girls. He seduces and rapes girls in their teens. Then he pays off the parents. If they don't accept the money, there are consequences. The details of his alleged crimes are there in the copy I gave you. It is generally believed that Oretga is responsible for six murders – two young girls and two sets of parents. My sources say there is enough evidence to arrest Ortega, but that will never happen."

"And this manager of República Agricola. What's his background?" Reynolds asked.

"We don't have a lot of information on Pablo Reyes other than what is public. His father is the dominate financial force within the ruling party. Moneyed, old family. Married with two children. Forty-three. He was educated at Princeton in the United States. Runs not only República Agricola but the family land holdings. Perhaps the largest landholder family in Columbia. His is a different background from the others that run these coffee companies, I would say."

"Why do you think he's part of this illegal syndicate?" Reynolds asked.

"That is simple, Señor Reynolds," Cortina answered. "It is to protect those vast land holdings. Just because he comes from the upper class does not make him less of a criminal."

"You seem to know a lot about the dirty side of these business people, Señor Cortina. Isn't that dangerous for you?"

Cortina stubbed out his cigarette. "Yes, of course. I am a particular enemy of the drug traffickers and corrupt officials. When I leave this office, I have a bodyguard and an armored vehicle. I have moved my family to Venezuela. The United States does not like the Venezuelan government, but drug traffickers do not have a hold there. And since we are on that subject, I would suggest caution in your inquiries here in Columbia, Señor Reynolds. This can be a dangerous place for journalists of any nationality."

"What about this former Cordillera Este Brokers manager, Santiago Mendez?" Reynolds asked.

"I made some inquiries. He owns a small restaurant in a modest neighborhood. Here's the address. This also is not the neighborhood for a lone gringo. I would suggest you allow me to go with you, Señor Reynolds. How about if I picked you up at your hotel at ten o'clock tomorrow morning? We can talk to this Santiago Mendez over lunch at his restaurant."

Reynolds agreed then took a taxi to the Sofitel Bogotá Victoria Regia Hotel. It was rated four stars and a familiar international chain. Before having dinner, he read the file Cortina had given him.

There was much that Cortina could not corroborate, but there was also a wealth of material that could be published, at least in the United States. If he could make the link between Martinelli Global and these Columbian coffee companies, it would give his story one hell of a punch.

The next day, Reynolds rode with Cortina in his bulletproof Toyota SUV. His driver was a big fellow, made larger by his bulletproof vest worn under his shirt. A 9mm Glock was holstered on his hip. They arrived in a poorer section of the Bogotá, not the poorest but obviously still working class. The Mendez restaurant was a small affair between an auto parts shop and a second hand clothing store.

It was too early for the lunch trade. There only a middle-aged woman with an apron standing behind the counter.

"*Buenos dias, Señora,*" Cortina said to the woman. "*¿Habla Usted Ingles, Señora?*"

"*Si.*"

"*Bueno.* Is Señor Mendez here?"

"No, Señor. Who are you?" Her fear was evident.

"My name is Juan Cortina, and this gentleman is Mark Reynolds. Señor Reynolds is from the United States. We are both journalists. Would you know how we might get in touch with Señor Mendez?"

The woman's eyes darted around the restaurant nervously. "That man outside? Is he with you?" she asked referring to Cortina's driver. She was clearly anxious. "Who are you?"

"Of course, Señora. I apologize," Cortina said. "Please do not be frightened. As a newspaper reporter, it is necessary to have a driver that can protect me from certain difficulties. Sometimes my work takes me into dangerous circumstances. Now if you could tell me how to find Señor Mendez."

The woman stared at Reynolds and Cortina several moments before seeming to arrive at a decision. "I am Maria Mendez. My husband is dead. He died last year."

"I am very sorry, Señora. What was the cause of his death?" Cortina asked.

"A bullet to the head," she said. Her eyes were angry, not sad. "You see, my husband killed himself."

"Again I am very sorry, Señora Mendez. That is most tragic," Cortina said. "Being a reporter, it is my job to ask questions. Do you know why your husband took his own life?"

"Coffee?" Maria Mendez said. She placed three cups on the counter and poured what smelled like freshly brewed coffee. She offered no cream or sugar. Reynolds wasn't sure if that was the custom or just her preoccupation talking to two reporters.

"What did you want to see my husband about?"

"We wanted to ask him if he knew anything about Cordillera Este Brokers being financed by drug money," Cortina said.

Her face stiffened almost imperceptibly but revealed no other expression.

"We know your husband was in charge of operations at Cordillera Este Brokers. We know there was some sort of mistake that lead to his dismissal several years ago. Mr. Reynolds is researching a large international corporation that we believe controls the coffee market in Columbia. We are attempting to corroborate information that these companies engage in illegal enterprises."

Maria Mendez took several sips of her coffee before saying, "My husband took his life not because he lost his job. What destroyed him was what happened to our daughter. You see she also took her own life. Just two months before. She was so young. Her whole life was before her."

Maria Mendez paused and Cortina was about to say something when she held her hand up to stop him. "Señor Cortina, please allow me to finish. You must understand this is most difficult. You see, the problem was the boss of Cordillera Este Brokers, Manuel Ortega. First, it was his mistake that caused the financial loss, not my husband's. According to my husband, Ortega blamed it on him. Someone at the headquarters in the United States said my husband must be fired."

"Excuse me Señora Mendez, but why did your husband not protest to the corporate headquarters? He was a senior official and we understand he had important relationships there," Reynolds said.

"You mean Señor Brown? Yes, he was a friend to my husband. That was the worse part. What they did to my husband also cost Señor Brown his position, according to my husband. He had nowhere to turn."

"I'm not sure we understand what you're trying to tell us, Señora Mendez," Cortina said.

Maria Mendez poured more coffee. Fortunately no patrons had yet entered the restaurant leaving the three of them to continue their conversation.

"Manuel Ortega is not only corrupt; he's a monster – a monster that destroys people. He is powerful, and he has powerful friends. I believed my husband when he said that Ortega was the one who actually made the mistake. My husband was meticulous. He was experienced. Ortega is a stupid pig. He is not a businessman. He is a gangster."

"If what you say is true, why would your husband take his life several years after being fired?" Reynolds asked with Cortina translating into Spanish.

Maria Mendez' stern exterior seemed to crumble. Her lips trembled. Tears flowed. "He blamed himself for what happened to our daughter."

After a few moments, Mendez continued. "Patricia also worked for Cordillera Este. She was pretty - just nineteen. We found out that Manuel Ortega had given her gifts. She became angry when we asked her about Ortega. A week later she moved out of our house."

"Through a friend at Cordillera Este, we learned that she was living with Ortega. My husband attempted to see her at work. She worked in an office at one of the warehouses some distance from my husband's office. She would not talk to him. It was very difficult. This was perhaps a couple of weeks before my husband was dismissed."

"Then one night months later the Police came to the door. They informed us that our daughter had been killed. We had not seen her for some time, but knew she was still with Ortega. They told us it was a hit and run accident. But that was a lie. When we looked at our daughter's dead body, her face was full of bruises. We are not stupid. Anyone could tell these injuries were not from an automobile. She had been beaten."

Maria Mendez broke down sobbing heavily. Reynolds and Cortina said nothing. Two working men entered the restaurant and seated themselves at table.

Mendez composed herself. She called for her cook in the kitchen to come see to the customers.

"So my husband killed himself because he thought he was not man enough to protect his family. That is not what I feel, but that is what he said in a letter he wrote to me before taking his life."

"And you think this Manuel Ortega may have been responsible for your daughter's death?" Cortina said.

"Yes. He is that sort of animal. I have learned that there may have been other girls that he has killed,"

Cortina got up as if to take his leave. "Señora . . ."

"*Un momento, Señores,*" she said and disappeared into the back of the restaurant. Reynolds and Cortina looked at each other wondering what the woman was doing. She returned within a couple of minutes carrying a package.

"Here, take this. Perhaps you can make use of this. I do not know its importance, but my husband said to give this to someone who might inflict revenge on Manuel Ortega. I have saved this for the right opportunity. I hope that I am not mistaken."

Reynolds and Cortina thanked her and left. Once back into the SUV, Cortina opened the envelope. "Do you read Spanish, Señor Reynolds?"

"Afraid not."

Cortina leafed through a number of pages for several minutes in silence.

"*Mierda santa*! These are records of transactions involving drug money flowing into the business. There's also a list of what appears to be payoffs to government officials. We'll need to go over this material in detail. Odd how Mendez was able to get his hands on these. No, here's the answer. The last page. A name and address. There's a note to the reader. This is my second cousin. He is a brave man. He honors the family by providing this information. Protect him."

They returned to Cortina's office. Cortina made copies of the documentation and handed the originals back to Reynolds. They spent over two hours pouring over the details. Cortina translated and Reynolds made extensive notes. It seemed that Mendez' cousin was in the accounting department at Cordillera Este. The documents cited offshore corporations Reynolds had not discovered in previous research. The list of payoffs to senior officials was staggering in scope.

"Could you send another set of copies by FedEx to my office in New York?" Reynolds asked Cortina. "Just for insurance."

"Gladly. And what will you do with them?"

"Turn them over to the FBI. And you?"

"I would like to do the same. But I think not. It would come to no result. The corruption is just too pervasive here as you have seen by these records. It would simply be too dangerous to publish. Our newspaper is already a target."

"Can't imagine what it's like to work under those conditions."

"And what do you plan next, Senór Reynolds?"

"Well, I'll try to interview the managers of these coffee companies. Of course not about laundering drug money. I want to ask them about their connection to Martinelli Global. About their collective monopoly on the Columbian coffee trade. I don't expect much, but I want to get some response that I can use in the copy, even if they deny the Martinelli Global connection."

Cortina offered his assistance in attempting to gain interviews for Reynolds. The fabricated subject of Reynolds request was to obtain these large growers' position on the plight of the small coffee growers with the depressed world coffee prices and the more profitable alternatives of illicit cocoa production.

All four of the coffee company managing directors declined. Even the subsequent threat that articles were to be published in the United States that identified all four companies as being controlled by the large multi-national corporation Martinelli Global did not buy an interview. Cortina explained to the various executive assistants that the New York newspaper was going to publish a story suggesting that the four companies created a monopoly of the Columbian coffee market. This was their opportunity to comment.

Cortina made the calls on Reynolds cell phone. He identified himself only as an interpreter. There were no return calls.

Reynolds saw no point in staying on longer in Columbia. He arranged a flight to New York for the next morning. At the least, he owed Juan Cortina dinner for all of his help. He had taken a real liking to Cortina. There was a lot that reminded him of the Nigerian journalist, Abejide Ojukwu. Both men were intelligent and naturally friendly. Both did outstanding work under impossible conditions.

Cortina picked Reynolds up at the hotel that evening. Driver-bodyguard and armored SUV of course. Cortina selected the Pajares Salinas Restaurant on Carrera 10.

The Pajares was an institution in Bogotá serving traditional Spanish cuisine. Classically decorated, the dining room walls were lined with early twentieth century paintings. No New York restaurant could boast more beautiful women. Cortina pointed out several prominent government officials. Reynolds and Cortina wore sport jackets and felt underdressed. It was an elegant place and the food lived up to the ambience. They both enjoyed the evening, and each other's company.

Over coffees and cognac, Reynolds said, "I can't thank you enough for all your help, Juan. I wish I could acknowledge you in the byline."

"Maybe someday I'll come to the United States and you can help me find employment. But no, I joke. I would never leave. My country is too beautiful. The people are beautiful. We just have a terrible disease," Cortina said. Then added with genuine affection, "I have enjoyed working with you, Mark."

Using his cell phone, Cortina called his driver to bring the SUV around to the front. The driver checked the area critically before motioning the two men to get into the vehicle. He was serious about his job, hustling the two men into the vehicle all the time with his right hand on his weapon.

The Sofitel Hotel was only a short distance away. There was only light traffic in this upscale area of Bogotá at that late hour. The driver pulled out onto the street and accelerated rapidly.

At the intersection of the next block a delivery truck pulled out in front of them from a cross street. As they passed, a larger truck pulled out of the same street behind them. After a couple of blocks, the truck in front of them stopped at a red traffic signal.

Cortina's driver looked in his mirror and quickly scanned to either side. "*Esto es una trampa!*" he screamed.

Cortina turned his head to see the truck behind them barreling down at a speed clearly not intent upon stopping. "*Mierda*! Hang on!" Their driver jammed the accelerator to the floor and jerked the SUV from behind the stopped truck in front. The collision was avoided by only a couple of feet.

The larger truck hit the smaller stopped truck with a ferocious impact as Cortina's SUV sped away from the collision. Their driver backed off his speed and looked in his rear mirror, then abruptly accelerated rapidly. "Señor Cortina...*Otro desde trasero!*"

The pursuing vehicle was a dark Chevrolet Suburban with an equally experienced driver. Both vehicles accelerated to over sixty miles per hour through the city streets. The Suburban was attempting to overtake Cortina's Toyota. It had pulled up to the rear quarter panel as both vehicles approached another red traffic signal. There was no intention of stopping.

Reynolds was in the back seat on the left side. The Suburban's windows were down. For an instant he thought he saw a weapon protruding. Cortina's driver suddenly cranked the wheel to the right to avoid a small car passing through the intersection, sending the Toyota into a skid. It hit a curb at an angle, flipped, then skidded on its right side into the glass front doors of an office building.

As the car in the intersection braked to avoid Cortina's vehicle, the Suburban slammed into its front side. Spinning the smaller car away, the Suburban careened into a street light pole.

The top of the Toyota was crushed as it struck the building on its side. Reynolds was conscious but his right knee was stiff. "Juan! Juan! Are you ok?" He shook a groaning Juan Cortina.

"I think so. Pedro?" Cortina reached around the front seat to his driver. There was a cut on the driver's forehead, probably from the airbag. He was also conscious. All three men had secured their seat belts.

With some difficulty, they forced opened the doors and climbed out of the overturned vehicle. Sirens wailed from a distance but no emergency vehicles or police had yet arrived at the scene. All three men hurried toward the two mangled vehicles at the intersection. Cortina's driver had his gun unholstered.

Reynolds had a small digital camera in his pocket and began to take pictures. The small car had been struck on the driver's side by the heavy vehicle. The woman driver was crumpled in the collapsed wreckage. The body was recognizable only as a woman by the long hair.

Even after smashing into the small car, the heavy Suburban continued on, crashing into a metal utility pole. The speed was sufficient enough to cause two of the occupants to be ejected from the vehicle.

"Will you fucking look at this! That was a gun I saw. These assholes were trying to kill us," Reynolds said.

"You or me, Mark?" Cortina asked rhetorically.

Two men lay on the pavement to the right of the vehicle. Both appeared dead. The bodies were twisted at impossible angles. Blood pooled beneath both. Next to both men were assault rifles. Reynolds took dozens of pictures.

Police would arrive any moment by the sound of the sirens. Reynolds took out the storage memory disc from the digital camera and replaced it with a new blank one. He then took a quick sequence of more of the same photos.

Three police cars and a fire truck arrived two minutes later. There was a flurry of activity. The driver of the Suburban had been wearing a seatbelt. He was badly injured but apparently still alive. Everyone else was confirmed dead. Cortina's driver's weapon was confiscated. Cortina explained that the man had a permit to carry the weapon. He was a journalist with many death threats. The officer acknowledged that he knew of Cortina but made no show of deference. Cortina's driver was handcuffed and placed in a police car.

"Mark, I explained to the officer that you are an American journalist. He asks if you have pictures. If so, he must have the camera," Cortina explained. "Unfortunately we must go to the police barracks to answer questions."

Both Reynolds and Cortina were handcuffed and placed in the back seat of a small police car.

CHAPTER 11

MANHATTAN, NEW YORK

I t was ten o'clock in the morning in New York. Conrad Redek looked out his twentieth floor office window. It was a clear, bright day. The view was of Brooklyn across the East River. The large ventilation tower for the Brooklyn Battery Tunnel on Governors Island marred the otherwise pastoral view of the wooded landscape and the nineteenth century buildings.

Redek's office had full floor to ceiling windows facing to the southeast. The decor was modern; large glass desk, chrome plated metal furniture with white leather upholstery, indirect lighting. The walls were decorated with abstract art in brilliant colors. The impression was the art had been selected on the basis of the color impact not artistic merit. The effect was designer chic sterile.

Conrad Redek sat at his desk working on a notebook computer. A second notebook computer sat on the opposite end of the large desk. Medium build, in his mid-forties, with a dark complexion, he could be considered handsome were it not for his eyes. Some might describe them as cold, but threatening would be more descriptive. Coupled with thin lips, the overall impression was frequently menacing. With his blunt style and substantial power, Conrad Redek was menacing.

His intercom buzzed. The secretary announced, "Mr. Pablo Reyes from Columbia is on the line, Sir."

"The problem situation that originated in New York was unfortunately not resolved," Pablo Reyes said. Reyes managed not only the large coffee distribution firm, República Agricola, but was the senior Martinelli Global official in Columbia. His influence ran to the Columbian President's inner circle.

"That is unfortunate. It seemed like an easy task," Redek responded with a tone emphasizing the implicit criticism.

There was a pause before Reyes answered. "Yes. It should have been dealt with more efficiently. Steps are being implemented to correct the failure."

"Thank you. Please keep me informed," Redek said and disconnected the call.

Pablo Reyes was not used to such treatment. Redek was a gringo *pendejo* with no manners. He was coarse with no sense of culture. Reyes had only contempt for Americans, Redek especially. However, Redek was powerful and the partnership with Martinelli Global had multiplied the Reyes family fortune several times over. So he would ignore the disrespect.

BOGOTÁ, COLUMBIA

Mark Reynolds had been sitting in an office with barred windows for over an hour. There was no ventilation. The temperature was well over ninety. The walls were once white but now yellowed. Rust stains from the anchor bolts of the bars on the windows traced lines to the floor. The air smelled of old smoke and perhaps urine.

Eventually a police officer entered the room. "Señor Reynolds, this was a serious incident you were involved in. Two men and a woman were killed and another person may not live."

"What the hell are you talking about? Those guys were trying to kill us. Christ, didn't you see their weapons?"

"I suggest you calm down Señor Reynolds. There is much to sort out here. Your driver also carried a firearm. It is not at all clear what was going on. So perhaps you can tell me what you were doing this evening," the police officer asked. He lit a cigarette and inhaled deeply. The gesture signaled he was in no hurry to resolve this matter.

Two more hours passed. The alternating officers questioning Reynolds made no attempt to pressure him to reveal anything incriminating. Coffee and cigarettes were offered. After a time a more senior officer entered the room and told Reynolds he was being transported to police headquarters for further questioning. Reynolds' questions about Cortina went unanswered.

"I am a U.S. citizen, I must be allowed to contact my embassy."

"Your embassy has already been notified, Señor Reynolds. You were involved in a most serious incident. I am sure you understand that a thorough investigation must be conducted, no different than in the United States," the senior officer replied in good English. He opened the door and ordered two policemen into the room.

The police started to handcuff Reynolds. "If this is only routine, and I assume I am not a suspect in a crime, can we forego the handcuffs?" Reynolds asked.

The senior officer thought for a moment, then said something in Spanish to his men. To Reynolds he said, "Very well, Señor Reynolds. I will extend you that courtesy."

Reynolds was placed in the back seat of a Toyota Land Cruiser. In the front were two police officers and a third sat with him in the back. That officer was a young man in his early twenties, on the chubby side, also sweating profusely.

The SUV set out through the streets of Bogotá. The officer in the back seat kept looking around nervously, particularly to the rear of their vehicle. Reynolds looked to the rear and saw a black SUV behind them.

The traffic was heavy, moving at no more than twenty miles per hour. The police vehicle was in the right hand lane with another lane of traffic to their left. Parked vehicles were to their right.

Suddenly the police vehicle slammed on the brakes to avoid hitting a truck stopped ahead of him. The driver and the other officer in the front seat opened their doors and jumped out. The chubby officer in the rear was trying frantically to open his door. He could not find the button to release the lock. His eyes were wide in panic when he looked back at Reynolds.

Reynolds knew this must be some sort of a trap. And he must be the target.

As the officer finally found the lock release for the door, Reynolds grabbed the man's gun. It was a .357 magnum Colt revolver, an older police weapon. The man did not even register the theft of his weapon in his rush to exit the vehicle. As he stumbled from the high profile vehicle, he fell against a parked car.

From between two parked cars to the right, Reynolds saw a man with a weapon pointed toward him through the open SUV door. Reynolds slid to the floor of the vehicle as the man opened up with a burst of automatic fire from the compact weapon. Partly because of the high profile of the vehicle, the first rounds went high smashing the left side window but missing Reynolds. It was only a burst of little more than one second. In return, Reynolds held the heavy revolver in both hands and fired four times at his assailant. Two rounds caught the man in chest.

Reynolds scrambled up from the floor and opened the left rear door. A large truck passing on the left hand lane of traffic caught the door. The door was wrenched from its hinges. The truck halted. The police SUV's door was now wedged between the two vehicles. A man had come from the truck that had stopped in front of the police SUV. He brandished a weapon but could not get to Reynolds.

From the rear, the driver of the black SUV behind the police SUV exited his vehicle. He too carried a short automatic weapon. Closing his door, he was startled to find himself looking at Reynolds pointing the large revolver. His reflex caused him to raise his weapon. Reynolds' own reflex caused him to shoot this second assailant in the face.

Reynolds dodged between cars and then dashed for an alleyway. Somewhere behind him was at least one more attacker. With his adrenaline pumping, he ran full out for at least ten minutes, zigzagging from alley to alley. He still carried the large revolver.

Hiding behind a dumpster, he rested to regain his breath. He was drenched in sweat. After several minutes there was no indication that he had been followed. There were only distant sounds of police sirens. Looking at the revolver he flipped open the cylinder. Only one round remained. Not much of a defense. Worse yet was the liability if the police caught him with the weapon. He had just shot two men - probably killed them. Remembering the scene from the movie *The Godfather*, he wiped the gun thoroughly with his shirttail to remove any fingerprints. He dropped it in the first trash container he passed.

Reynolds walked another few blocks finding a modest commercial section. At a small hotel, the receptionist called him a taxi. He told the driver to take him to the U.S. Embassy. He hoped it was not far since he had only forty U.S dollars secreted in his sock. The police had kept his wallet and passport.

It took forty minutes of waiting before he could see a U.S. consular official. The man was in his late twenties, probably very junior in rank. They went into a small office with no windows, a steel table and a couple of chairs. It looked like any police interrogation room you would see on television. It did have decidedly better air conditioning than the Columbian police facility.

Reynolds told officials the basics of the first attempt on his and Cortina's life, then his transport by the police and the second incident. He omitted the part about shooting two of his assailants saying only that there was an attack on the police vehicle and he managed to escape in the gunfire.

"That's a hell of a story, Mr. Reynolds. First of all, how can we verify your identity?" the bureaucrat asked. He registered little emotion, obviously skeptical of Reynolds' fantastic story.

"First of all, I know my passport number. You can then retrieve my photo from your system can't you?"

"Yes we can. Let's do that right away. Who can we contact at your newspaper?"

The young man took the number and left the room. Returning after fifteen minutes, he said, "We verified your identity. It also seems that there was in fact some sort of violence involving you." The man was now clearly more interested. "We have a notification from the Columbian police that you are wanted for questioning in a murder, Mr. Reynolds. Just what have you been up to?"

"Fuck. The bastards are trying to set me up. Anything I did was in self-defense."

"Jesus! Are you saying you did kill someone?"

"Listen. I'm an American citizen. You can't turn me over to the Columbian police for christsakes! Those assholes were bribed to look the other way so someone could kill me."

The door to the room opened. A distinguished looking middle-aged man in a white shirt and tie entered. Behind him was a Marine sergeant with a holstered sidearm. The younger official jumped to his feet.

"Mr. Reynolds? I am Lorenzo Aznar, U.S. Ambassador to Columbia. Mr. Kramer, you and Mr. Reynolds will accompany me to my office."

The Ambassador's office could be described as official elegance in its style. The furniture was first-rate and two walls were comprised of bookshelves in expensive wood. But there was no art, just government photographs.

"Sit down, Mr. Reynolds," Ambassador Aznar said. The Marine guard and the junior consular officer remained standing.

"I had a call from a very senior police official, just ten minutes ago. They know that you are here. He requested that you be turned over to Columbian authorities. So, let's hear your story."

Reynolds recited the events again much as he had told the young staffer, except in this case, he did explain the full details of the police setup and his shooting of two men. He declined to explain the nature of the story that brought him to Columbia. However, he did indicate that he had information to share with U.S. law enforcement.

"That's very interesting, Mr. Reynolds. The police official that called me made no mention of what you describe as the first incident that lead to you being taken into custody. He claims you assaulted police and escaped custody as you were being transported to police headquarters. No mention of you shooting anyone either. According to him, you were being held for questioning in the murder of a Columbian journalist, Juan Cortina."

"What! You mean Cortina is dead? Shit!" Reynolds felt as if he had been hit in the gut. "Listen, Mr. Ambassador, look at this." Reynolds reached into his sock and pulled out the small digital storage card he had removed from his digital camera. "Do you have a way of downloading this to a PC?"

The Ambassador looked to the younger official.

"Yes, Sir. I can. I'll get a computer right away."

"So what did you tell the police official, Sir?" Reynolds asked as they waited for the junior official to return.

"Well, I told General Ortega that he would have to make a formal request. After that, I would take it under consideration. I am inclined to believe you Mr. Reynolds. I am not inclined to . . . This is off the record?"

"Of course, Sir," Reynolds said.

"I'm not inclined to believe General Ortega. My position precludes me from saying what I really think. My guess is the story you're researching has something to do with drug trafficking. What else? After all, this is Columbia. At any rate, Ortega is dirty. Again that's not a quote for attribution to me.

"I'm a former Congressman, obviously Latin, Spanish speaking. But you see, I'm also ex-FBI. Perfect choice to represent the U.S. in this pesthole. Don't get me wrong, this is a wonderful country, wonderful people, breathtaking scenery. But the drug trafficking dominates everything, even the diplomacy with the U.S."

The junior official returned with a notebook computer. He attached a device to allow the digital camera file storage device to load the photographs into the computer.

"These are the guys that were chasing us. Just luck that our driver swerved. These guys smashed into a car, killed the woman driving, and then slammed into a utility pole. See the automatic weapons?" Reynolds explained, however the photos showed the weapons clearly.

"And this shot. That's my colleague, Juan Cortina with the wrecked SUV in the background. Both Cortina and I were taken away by the police. Once at the police station, we were separated. That's the last time I saw him. If they're now talking about his murder then it's the police who are responsible."

"Interesting material. Not surprising. To say this country is corrupt is like saying Antarctica is cold. I have no intention of cooperating with the likes of Ortega. But that still makes you a real problem, Mr. Reynolds. So, I need to get rid of you. The longer you're here the more of a diplomatic headache you become."

"Kramer, get Mr. Reynolds something to eat and a change of clothes. It'll take a little time to put this together," Ambassador Aznar said.

Reynolds stood to go. "Thank you, Mr. Ambassador. I know this puts you in an awkward situation.

An hour later, Reynolds was back in Aznar's office.

"This is Special Agent Collins of the FBI. Mr. Collins is the agent in charge down here." Reynolds shook hands with the agent.

Aznar continued, "I don't know what you have to share with the FBI, but I have convinced Brian to consider you to be in U.S. custody. A material witness. That way when you are ·transported to the airport there will be no interference from Columbian authorities. One of Brian's agents will accompany you back to the States."

"I appreciate all you're doing, Sir. Too bad I can't write it up for publication," Reynolds said.

"It's not all altruistic on my part," Aznar said. "By the FBI's involvement, any flap the Columbians raise will not be an issue with my superiors at State. With you out of here, by the time Ortega can muster higher powered support from the Columbian President's office, you will not be a diplomatic issue I have to deal with. Now with that said, you do actually have information that will be of interest to give to the FBI, don't you?"

"Absolutely," Reynolds said, then looked at the FBI agent. "Not to be coy Agent Collins, but the information is in New York. It should definitely be of interest to U.S. law enforcement."

"Very well, Mr. Reynolds. I'm told that you must leave in the next few minutes," Ambassador Aznar said and shook Reynolds hand. "Unfortunately, there is just one more detail." Reynolds waited for Aznar to explain. "I'm afraid that to preclude any potential confrontation with the Columbians, you need to be handcuffed to the agent that will accompany you on the flight."

"The handcuffs will be removed once we're in the air, Mr. Reynolds," Agent Collins said.

"Wonderful," Reynolds said sarcastically.

Reynolds' entourage piled into the ubiquitous SUV for the drive to the airport. The junior consular officer Kramer and two armed security staff accompanied Reynolds, now handcuffed to an FBI agent. All but Reynolds had diplomatic passports. The Columbians could prevent the plane from leaving, but they would not dare to take Reynolds from U.S. custody. Besides that he was chained to a U.S. federal agent. The Ambassador was counting on quickly getting Reynolds out of the country before General Ortega could better organize a plan.

Nothing eventful took place. The worse part was the wait at the airport before the flight departed. People stared wondering what he had done to be taken back to the States in handcuffs.

CHAPTER 12

MANHATTAN, NEW YORK

"Oh my God, Mark," Rachel Stern exclaimed as she embraced Reynolds when he walked into the office. She kissed him hard on the mouth.

Both were a little embarrassed. Stern backed away, but still held Reynolds by his arms. "We're so glad you got out of there. John gave us only the broad facts. But Christ, they tried to kill you twice?"

"Yup. That's true enough. But it's worse than that," Reynolds said. "Listen, I've got to see John right now. Buy you a drink later?"

"I'll be here, Mark."

Reynolds made his way to John Fredericks' office.

"Goddamn. You'll give me a heart attack yet with your exploits, Mark," John Fredericks said after hugging Reynolds. "I've never lost a reporter. I don't want you to be my first. Scotch? I need one."

Fredericks poured drinks and both men sat down. For the next two hours Reynolds went over the investigation and the evidence provided by the Mendez woman.

"Well, I guess I owe you an apology. You've convinced me that Martinelli Global is something unusual. I thought you were on a witch hunt, but these guys are a potential real story. So, let's go with the next piece about Martinelli Global's monopoly of the Columbian coffee market. Expand on how this is disguised by their use of these offshore corporations. You're getting pretty knowledgeable in that area."

"What about the drug money investment? What about the money laundering, John?"

"The FBI will be here at three o'clock to pick up the info you agreed to give them. I want to see what they have to say before we expand the story with those allegations."

"John, I promised to give the FBI what we have. I didn't promise them not to publish."

"Mark, let's just see what the FBI has to say. Maybe they'll see a wider investigation. Maybe a bigger story."

"All right, John. Let's hear what the FBI has to say. But you know they'll want to suppress any publicity. It's classic. The press digs out this shit, and law enforcement wants to proceed with all due deliberateness. Their argument will always be to withhold publication so as not to impede the investigation."

Two FBI agents were shown into Fredericks' office promptly at three o'clock. After preliminary niceties, Reynolds handed over copies of the information that Santiago Mendez' widow had provided and he had wisely FedExed from Columbia before his narrow escape.

The senior agent skimmed through the documents.

"This is interesting material Mr. Reynolds. Would you care to tell us how you obtained this information?"

"No. I don't think so."

"Might assist in our investigation."

"And it might endanger certain people. Afraid I can't."

The agent did not press the issue. "This is pretty strong stuff if it proves true. The Bureau will undoubtedly open an investigation. Are you going to publish these money laundering allegations immediately?"

Fredericks answered. "Not right away. We need to conduct our own inquiries to corroborate before we go to print. We will advise the FBI when we are prepared to publish that aspect of the story."

After the FBI agents left, Reynolds asked Fredericks, "But we are going to publish what we know about Martinelli Global's ownership and associations with some of Columbia's more unsavory citizens? Right?"

"Partly right. We'll go with the story about Martinelli Global's monopoly of Columbian coffee. We'll not go into identifying business associates with alleged drug trafficking ties. I need to see more corroboration before we publish, Mark."

"Jesus, John, this is a hell of a story just about exposing Martinelli Global's control of the Columbian coffee trade. But their partners are real dirt bags. That's a real sinister slant. Why not publish who they're in bed with? I agree we need more before we go with the money laundering, but let's at least go with what we have."

"Not yet. I want to see some sort of corroboration to the Mendez documents before we go accusing Martinelli Global of partnering with drug traffickers."

"Christ, John, Cortina's research information is enough to paint these guys they're rubbing shoulders with as real criminals," Reynolds argued.

"Ok, I'll grant you that. But the information doesn't link them specifically as business associates of Martinelli Global."

"You're being too goddamn rigid on this, John," Reynolds said.

"Mark, humor me then. I want to see better evidence of the business connections. That's final."

Fredericks decided not to share the substance of an earlier telephone call from the Daily Press' publisher. The Publisher pointed out that he had received a number of calls from influential people that were upset with the Daily Press's attacks on Martinelli Global. He did not order Fredericks to desist, but made it clear that he needed to be on well documented solid ground with anything in the future. He commented that Reynolds was a first rate reporter, but clearly a renegade. He expected Fredericks to tightly control the integrity of future pieces.

John Fredericks got the message. It was the first time he ever had a publisher pressure him about a story.

Reynolds returned to his own office. He was pissed. Fredericks was being uncharacteristically cautious. Reynolds wanted to go with what he had and dig further for new material. Regardless, the next step was to explore how to investigate the structure of the offshore companies controlling the Columbian coffee companies. If he could corroborate the ownership of the offshores with the Mendez information, it would be easier to make the money laundering accusations. He would need Rachel Stern's expertise more than ever.

His phone rang. "Mark Reynolds."

"What the fuck is going on, Mark?" Denise yelled.

"What are you talking about, Denise?"

"I'm talking about your fucking crusade against Martinelli Global. It's affecting my job now."

"What the hell are you talking about?"

"I got a call today from the top guy at my largest account. Metcalf Communications. Joseph Metcalf himself. Never met him. He's the CEO and founder. I thought they were very happy with our new add campaign. Thought maybe this was a call to congratulate me.

"But that was soon dispelled. Seems that Metcalf is on the board of directors at Martinelli Global. Big stockholder too. He was not subtle. Told me that he was personally displeased with your unbalanced attacks on Martinelli Global. Gave me a whole spiel about how your articles were damaging Martinelli Global's stock price and how you were unreasonably maligning a venerable old company."

Reynolds interrupted, "Wait a minute. How the hell did this guy connect you with me?"

"I'm not sure. I probably mentioned it sometime to the Metcalf people I work with. I haven't made our relationship a secret, although I should have. Now your stupid crusade is affecting my career."

"Those miserable fucks. They tried to kill me in Columbia. Now they're trying a new tactic."

"What? Whatever. The point is I've had it, Mark. I think you know that it's not working anymore with us."

Of course he knew. "Yeah. You're not subtle, Denise. I almost get murdered and you're not even there when I returned from Columbia. Now you're blaming me for this pimp Metcalf."

"Of course I'm blaming you! I don't want any part of this." There was a moment's pause. "To hell with it, Mark. I'm leaving. In fact I'm leaving tomorrow. We can decide tonight about what's mine and what's yours. Oh, and by the way, don't worry about the Metcalf account. I told them we were no longer together so I didn't have any leverage with you."

Denise disconnected the call.

For several moments the impact of losing Denise gripped Reynolds. Was it loss or anger? Either way it wasn't rational. They had been at each other's throats for months. Love making had become just occasional sex driven by little more than biological need. Still, it was a several year relationship. Where had things so radically changed? Was it him or her? More like both. Just bad pairing.

For the next couple of hours he ranged from anger to resolving himself being without Denise. After a time he realized that he was not thinking of ways to dissuade her from leaving.

The next morning he was back at the office. The previous night had been difficult but there was a feeling of relief. He owed Rachel Stern an explanation so he went directly to her office.

"Sorry I had to leave early yesterday without telling you what happened in Columbia. Personal matter I couldn't avoid."

"No need to explain, Mark," Stern said.

"Denise and I broke up. That's the personal matter. She's moving out today. Probably for the best. We aren't good for each other. Probably never were."

"That's too bad, Mark," she said, but with little conviction. "I don't know if I should say I'm sorry or what. Maybe it's just good fortune?"

Reynolds smiled, not knowing what to say, or what Stern was implying.

She changed the subject saying, "So tell me about what happened in Columbia."

While Reynolds recounted the events in Columbia, Stern listened with little comment. Once he concluded, she said, "My God, Mark, you actually shot those guys? And the Columbians raised no stink?"

"That's right. The place is so stinking corrupt there's no official record of the guys I shot. There's only the trumped-up allegation that I killed my Columbian colleague, Juan Cortina. The place is deceiving. It looks like a modern society but under the surface it's a stinking mess. Any threat against those at the top of the food chain is met with swift reprisal."

"I can't imagine what you went through. Unfortunately you're making these life and death adventures a habit. First Nigeria and now Columbia. I'm glad you survived. I'm very fond of you, Mark," Stern said.

This was a different Rachel Stern. She looked him in the eye without qualification about her declaration.

Reynolds cleared his throat, then said, "Thank you, Rachel, I'm fond of you also." He paused for a moment taking in Stern's intense stare. "I owe you dinner. Are you free tonight?"

"Absolutely! That's wonderful. Pick me up about seven?"

"Fine. I'll need your address." He was a little anxious about where this might be going.

Rachel rescued the awkward moment. "I'll e-mail you. Now, back to the project," she said. "These offshore corporations are effective at blocking any access to ownership or financial information. Maybe the NSA can crack into their systems, but the information is just not out there in the public domain."

"Were you able to get anything?"

"Some. We can confirm the business partners for some of the privately held Columbian firms through Columbian government sources. We can identify executives of the publicly held corporations. It's tougher to get anything concrete about those individuals with alleged drug ties.

"We can access certain public domain information about trade transactions, both here and in Columbia. Gives you a sense of how transactions flow through these offshore corporations. Pretty arcane stuff. Tells us nothing about Martinelli Global's ownership. Doesn't prove a whole lot either. In reality, Fredericks was probably generous in letting you go with the monopoly story. We don't really have good evidence to back that up."

"Great. Got any ideas where we go from here, Rachel?"

"Number one, we've got to access who controls these offshore corporations if we ever intend to put some meat on the bones. I don't have an answer how to do that. Number two, we need somebody in DEA to feed us information on these drug guys we think are connected to the Columbian coffee business. Know anyone there, Mark?"

"Maybe. But I don't have an ideas about getting more information on these offshores."

Reynolds did have a source at the Drug Enforcement Agency. The guy helped out on story a couple of years earlier. Wouldn't probably reveal information about any investigations, but he might at least confirm the profiles of Martinelli Global's partners in Columbia.

A better idea was to talk to Juan Cortina's editor. He spoke with the guy a couple of times previously following up on any news about Cortina. The guy had been guarded. He was clearly reluctant to say anything critical about the Police or the Government. But he was worth another try.

As Reynolds expected, the call to Columbia was brief. Cortina's editor, Alfredo Rios said there was still no word about Cortina's fate. As to Reynolds inquiries about Columbians partnered with Martinelli Global in the Columbian coffee trade, he abruptly claimed that was an area in which he did not want to comment. With an apology, Rios disconnected the call. This time he sounded scared.

Minutes later, Reynolds had an e-mail from Rios. "Señor Reynolds – I apologize for my rudeness on the telephone. However, I have good reason to believe our telephone calls here at the Newspaper are being monitored. I am afraid that Juan must be dead. There are only rumors, but they're all bad. I will contact you if I hear anything reliable. As to your other questions about certain individuals, if you will send me the names, I will see what information we have. I also have contacts within the Government that might be helpful. I will e-mail you at the soonest."

Reynolds arrived at Rachel Stern's apartment that evening, a little late. He was in a good mood, satisfied with the piece he wrote. He was amazed at how at ease he felt about Denise leaving. He liked Rachel's company and was looking forward to the evening.

Rachel Stern opened the door. Reynolds was taken back by how she looked.

He had always thought her a good looking woman, but a little too conservative. Typically little makeup, glasses. Short hair tied up in back. Non-descript business attire. Always the professional at the office, except for her flirtations earlier that day. Standing in front of him was a transformation.

The glasses were gone. Her hair was done differently – stylish rather than practical, down to her shoulders. The makeup was professionally done. But it was the dress and what her body did to it that took him back.

He never thought about her body before, but he did now. She had on a sleek, form fitting, black silk dress with a plunging neckline. His eyes were drawn to the string of pearls falling between her breasts. Three-inch heels increased her height.

"Holy shit."

She was holding a glass of red wine. She smiled mischievously. "Does that mean you like the way I look?"

"You look terrific, Rachel."

"You look particularly handsome yourself."

She guided him into the apartment, then closed the door. Locking her eyes on his, she kissed him on the lips with her mouth wide open.

"Here, hold this," she said handing him the glass of wine.

Still standing close to him, she hooked her fingers under the shoulder straps of her dress and let it fall to the floor. She had nothing on underneath.

He was dumbstruck and more than a little aroused. She just stood smiling at him. Not a hint of shyness.

Rachel moved against him and took off his sport coat. "I've wanted you for years, Mark. Make love to me." Her voice was throaty. Her eyes were pleading. She had never risked so much.

He kissed her deeply. She pulled herself tightly to him. He ran his hands over her breasts, then eventually between her legs. She was so aroused that he could feel her wetness. He moved her to the bedroom.

They never went out for dinner.

CHAPTER 13

MANHATTAN, NEW YORK

The following day, Reynolds received a lengthy e-mail with all sorts of attachments elaborating on the various Columbians of interest. Reynolds had asked the Columbian editor Alfredo Rios specifically about information confirming these individuals' business connections with the four coffee companies. Rios had done a remarkable job. Reynolds took the package to Fredericks.

"Well, is that proof enough or what?" Reynolds asked.

Fredericks sat back in his chair and said nothing for several moments. "Very well, Mark, have at it." Thirty years of professional integrity outweighed the implied threat from the publisher. He reached for the bottle of Maalox tablets to quell the increasing pain in his stomach.

Reynolds spent the rest of the day and half the night writing the piece. John Fredericks approved the draft with only minor edits. It went into print the next day.

New York Daily Press – Byline Mark Reynolds:

> The vast enterprises of the large international firm of Martinelli Global have recently been revealed to include a monopoly of the Columbian coffee industry. Columbia is the second largest coffee producer in the world behind Brazil, and the largest producer of Arabica coffee,

considered the highest quality coffee bean. This newspaper has also come into possession of evidence that Martinelli Global has also partnered with certain Columbian nationals that are linked with drug trafficking, government corruption, and ties to right-wing paramilitaries.

Martinelli Global has majority control of the four largest coffee producers/exporters in Columbia, controlling over 95% of that country's coffee exports. That ownership control is exercised through Latin American Trading Corporation, a Cayman Islands company, wholly owned by Martinelli Global. Their control is then further obscured by other intermediate shell corporations to mask the monopoly of the Columbian coffee market. These same coffee companies are financed by another offshore financial company, Latin Trust Group, a Belize corporation. Latin Trust group is also wholly owned by Martinelli Global. Martinelli Global then purchases coffee beans through its Cayman Islands corporation known as South American Trading. This tangle of protected foreign offshore subsidiaries allows Martinelli Global to manipulate coffee prices and maximize profits.

Coffee is traded as a commodity on the world market, but Columbian coffee commands its own premium pricing based on the higher quality of its product. While world coffee prices have been depressed for most of the last decade, Martinelli Global has been able to sustain large profits. Martinelli Global keeps Columbian coffee bean prices artificially high and depresses the price paid to the growers which are largely small farmers.

The prevailing price paid to the growers is only 7% of the retail price for coffee, leaving the remaining 93%

for the exportering cartel, importers, roasters, and retailers. Martinelli Global takes profits in all these upstream supply chain operations. With their monopoly, Martinelli Global is able to fix profits at the expense of the growers.

Columbia has long been renowned for having an effective growers' association, the Columbian Coffee Federation, or FNC. However, two senior executives in the FNC are directly blood-related to senior partners in distributors controlled by Martinelli Global, making suspect recent FNC agreed decreases in prices paid to the producing farmers. These farmers have suffered the worse effects of declining world prices, while Martinelli Global's exporting, processing, and importing supply chain companies have sustained large profits.

Documented evidence reveals that Martinelli Global's Columbian operations have certain Columbian nationals as senior managers and partners in these enterprises that are alleged to have ties to drug trafficking and corruption.

Carlos Fuentes is the managing director of Grupo Medellin. Fuentes has an uncle currently wanted by the Columbian government on drug trafficking and murder charges.

Miguel Vargas is a principle stockholder in Narion Coffee. Vargas is currently under investigation on corruption charges and is alleged to have ties to a right-wing paramilitary group known to be involved in drug trafficking.

A third company, Cordillera Este Brokers is run by a Manuel Ortega. Ortega has frequently been investigated on numerous charges of murder and rape of young women. Ortega has successfully avoided serious legal consequences believed largely through the influence of his older brother who heads the national police.

The fourth coffee company controlled by Martinelli Global, Republica Agricola S.A. Republica is headed by Pablo Reyes. Reyes comes from old money Columbian aristocracy. His family is one of the wealthiest in the country with vast holdings in real estate and agriculture. Several Reyes family members are in senior posts within the government and military. Francisco Reyes, the family patriarch, is the financial power behind the ruling party.

Repeated inquiries to Martinelli Global headquarters in New York, as well as to these named Columbian companies, have gone unanswered.

The same day, the following story appeared in major newspapers around the world:

Associated Press - Caracas, Venezuela:

President Hugo Chavez announced plans to nationalize most of the petroleum upgrading operations currently operated by some of the world's largest companies in the Orinoco region of Venezuela. These operations process the heavy tar-like crude into lighter grades suitable for transport and refining.

In a major policy address, Chavez also announced another increase in crude oil royalties and income taxes, and placed particular emphasis on increasing penalties for delinquent taxes. A total of 23 companies owe Venezuela over $4 billion in back taxes. Chavez also pledged a more aggressive policy to collect those taxes. Backing that pledge, Chavez announced the nationalization of all operations and leases owned by California-based Chevron to pay back taxes. Chevron, like most of the other oil companies, had disputed the Venezuelan government's tax assessment.

The announcement sent shock waves through the oil industry as Chavez continues to move Venezuela toward socialism. Many of the world's largest oil companies have operations in Venezuela.

In spite of these pronouncements, foreign investment in Venezuelan petroleum production is not expected to slow according to Bloomberg petroleum analyst Robert Delaney. "Even with increased production costs and sharing profits with the Government, Venezuela is still the most attractive oil rich country for foreign investment. Most other countries with large undeveloped reserves severely restrict foreign investment making Venezuela still the best opportunity. Ultimately, Chavez needs the big oil companies to effectively manage Venezuela's oil supply chain. I believe there will be a point where equilibrium is reached." Delaney said.

MANHATTAN, NEW YORK

Steven Martinelli was seated behind his desk. He had just finished calling Ricardo Corrales in Caracas, Venezuela. Conrad Redek had just briefed Martinelli on the deal that Corrales had concluded with the Chavez government. Corrales had delivered handsomely.

Venezuelan Energy Resources, was an acknowledged part of the Martinelli Global organization, though technically it was owned by Latin Energy Group, a Belize incorporated company. Belize incorporation offered the same secrecy and minimal regulatory restrictions as other tax haven countries. Martinelli Global enjoyed strong political connections in Belize which lent a comfort level when doing business in South and Central America with their Latin partners.

Under the new agreement with the Venezuelan government, Venezuelan Energy Resources's taxes would increase thirty percent. In addition, bribes would amount to close to twenty-five million U.S. dollars per year. However, all of these increases would be more than cancelled out by the ability to raise prices on oil transported from Government-owned, or joint ventured operations. The deal included contracts to manage all refining operations owned by the Government at inflated management fees. These contracts also included the new Government-owned refining operations resulting from the recent wave of nationalization. Venezuelan Energy Resources replaced the lost expertise resulting from the dislocations of nationalizing complex operations. The net increase in Venezuelan Energy Resource's profits would be in the hundreds of millions of dollars. The partnership was profitable for both parties.

The successes in Venezuela represented the classic Martinelli Global approach; select a country with opportunity; understand the political dynamics and appetites; determine the leverage; then find a local national with the right stature and skills to manage operations.

"Are we expecting future expansions in nationalized Venezuelan oil? Can we trust those around Chavez? Can we trust Chavez not to turn on us?" Steven Martinelli asked.

"Yes to your first question. As to the second, I believe Chavez is onboard. The arrangement contributes to expanding his scope of economic control. Chavez needs money to expand his socialist state," Conrad Redek replied.

"My congratulations, Conrad. You brought us Señor Corrales. He has certainly proved to be an asset. I only wish affairs in Columbia were going as well. Pablo Reyes does not seem to have the same command over the situation there. These continuing articles in the Daily Press by that reporter Reynolds are very troubling. I'm getting uncomfortable calls from a couple of important allies in the government. The Speaker for one. Senator Haberstom for another.

"This latest piece about our Columbian coffee subsidiaries and our partners is in many ways worse than the Nigerian incident. There are way too many specifics. At the mention of drugs, our friends in Washington get nervous. How was it that this newspaper obtained such information?"

"We're looking into how the leak came about. Some of the information was only accessible by a limited number of people. Columbian internal security is investigating," Redek answered.

"I wouldn't hope for much success there. Do we have any new thoughts about blunting further media damage?"

"Not really. I've got some people working on it. Best thing is to stonewall and deny. It's unfortunate that our associates in Columbia did not contain Reynolds. Things would have been much easier had he not returned to the United States."

Redek measured his criticism since Martinelli was close to the Reyes family.

"You don't need to be delicate, Conrad. Pablo Reyes clearly blew it. This should have been a simple task. I believe his father would have handled the problem more effectively, but Francisco has turned operations over to Pablo. That is the reality we must deal with. Reynolds should have been eliminated. However, we need to move on. Is there any risk that Reynolds will be able to obtain anything that might link us to our less savory associates in the drug trade?"

"I think we are sufficiently insulated, Steven, but we're taking further precautions."

Redek was the principle architect of Martinelli Global's international business organization. This continuing attack in the newspaper was a personal frustration with no clear solution. Reynolds would be even more emboldened after the events in Columbia.

"I detect some uncertainty, Conrad. You think this could get worse?"

"As you know, our investment structure in Columbia as well as other places is complex. So complex, that it could be a model for the modern international corporation. It provides the ability for leveraging virtually any type of international business opportunity. Part of our protective insulation is that complexity. But that complexity could also provide opportunities for information leaks. We think that is how Reynolds got this information. The short answer is there are no absolutes."

Redek did not mention to Martinelli his additional concern that Reynolds might be in possession of even more damaging information. Redek had a report from Pablo Reyes that the local reporter Cortina had started to talk about some sort of documents. As evidence of further incompetence by the Columbians, Cortina died under torture by the police before he could be more specific.

"So what are these precautions you are pursuing?"

"Tightening computer security. Restricting information access further. New e-mail guidelines. And we have a high-tech security firm working on an elaborate software approach for continual screening of all electronic information. But for this immediate problem, Steven, the most effective remedy is to remove Reynolds as a threat."

Martinelli reflected a couple of moments, rubbing his jaw. "You're probably right. But that's an unacceptable risk here in the United States. We do not have the means without going outside our sphere of control. We cannot contract with the necessary people to eliminate Reynolds. This is not Columbia, Conrad."

"Not that crude, Steven. I mean we need to put some real pressure on the New York Daily Press. It may be time to call in some of your political currency. There must be some leverage that can be applied on the publisher. At the least, we need to find out everything about this reporter. I've already got Durbin's people working on it."

Martinelli Global was Durbin Security's only client. In reality, Durbin was a Martinelli Global subsidiary, removed by a double tier of offshore ownership. In the event that Durbin Security was ever accused of illegal activities, Martinelli Global could claim some distance as only being a client. William Durbin was ex-NSA and employed some of the best computer hackers in the world. There was plenty of illegal activity involved.

"Let's be careful, Conrad. If we can develop something substantive, something really damaging, it might be effective. But we don't want it to backfire. Which I suspect will be the result of that stupid old fart Joseph Metcaf's blunder."

"What do you mean?"

Martinelli recounted Metcalf's call earlier in the day about his pressure on Reynolds girlfriend.

"It doesn't matter, Steven. Reynolds will soon feel some real pressure."

CHAPTER 14

MANHATTAN, NEW YORK

"Good morning, Rachel," Reynolds said as he entered Stern's office.

He had not seen her the day after their love making. She had taken the day off by previous plan. Just as well. It gave him a little time to confront the awkward situation.

"Mark, hi. Coffee?"

"Sure."

Rachel turned to her coffee maker. Reynolds closed the door.

"About the other night, Rachel."

She turned to him and smiled broadly. "It was wonderful. Did you mind awfully? It was my doing."

"Well . . . no. I didn't mind . . . of course not."

"Mark, you're blushing." She amazed herself at how blatant she was and not blushing herself. The windows in the office prevented her from kissing him. "You don't have to say anything. It doesn't have to mean anything more than what it was; two people who like each other enjoying each other. I hope it happens again, but if it doesn't, then no regrets. Either way, we work well together professionally. So don't feel you have to say anything in particular."

She touched his cheek with her hand. "Now I've got something to show you."

Rachel Stern always knew when to back away, never to corner. Ever the professional; efficient and in control. The night with Mark Reynolds was totally out of character. She had mustered extraordinary courage to take the risk. Her fantasy had materialized. She had no intention of letting the opportunity slip away.

Reynolds had never before considered her from a sexual perspective. If he thought about it, he would say she was pretty. Fairly good body, although she did little to accentuate her assets by her conservative clothes. He just did not find her sexy even after the passion of the other night. The hormonal chemistry did not cause the expected reaction.

Yet he genuinely liked her. Liked her company. Great professional relationship. Intellectually she was one of the most interesting people he knew. Up to that night she felt more like a sister. Even so, he probably would commit *incest* with her again.

"So what've you got?"

"Look at these," Stern gave Reynolds a small stack of papers. "It's more about Martinelli Global's organizational structure, how they do business. I focused on more recent times from when the current Martinelli took the helm. Spent a fair amount of time with Bernie to get his take on these guys from a financial perspective. Gave him a whole pile of data to work with covering the last twenty years. He's got some pretty interesting comments. Look at page eight."

Bernie Poole was the newspaper's financial editor. According to his analysis, the Cayman Islands corporation known as South American Trading is acknowledged in Martinelli Global's annual report. Ostensibly dealing in agricultural commodities, there are no records of any purchases or sales on any of the commodities exchanges other than Columbian coffee. They also purchased the entire coffee bean output of that country. Based upon Martinelli Global's annual report, the company had transactions equivalent to four times the value of Columbia's coffee production.

Columbia's corporate financial reporting for taxes is crude by comparison to the United States. However, the basics were still there. While not public information, the newspaper editor Rios was able to provide full tax reporting details through a contact within the Columbian Government.

All four of the coffee companies had extreme levels of debit. So extreme, that the companies would be considered insolvent by any accounting standard. Each of the four companies had extensive holdings in land and various enterprises. The land had a value of less than one-third of what was collectively invested. The business investments all reported heavy losses year after year. There was continued borrowing and investing beyond any reasonable business justification. Funding for these investments was through loans from a Belize company, Latin Trust Group.

Poole concluded that if Latin Trust was owned by Martinelli Global as claimed by the former Martinelli Global manager, Franklin Brown, then these loans were clearly a mechanism for laundering money back into Columbia.

Since virtually all the Columbian coffee crop was purchased by Martinelli Global's subsidiary, South American Trading, prices always exceeded other world coffee market levels. Martinelli Global owned all the distribution and trading and controlled pricing to the small growers. Large growers were Martinelli Global companies or business partners. The losers in this supply chain were the small growers. They saw their profits slashed as world market prices for coffee beans fell during the last decade.

The conclusion was that the price paid for Columbian coffee was irrelevant since the transactions were all *intra-company*. Drug money in the form of cash found its way into Martinelli Global subsidiaries who returned it in the form of loans, which found their way back to the drug traffickers through bogus enterprises and land deals. Poole estimated that Martinelli Global subsidiaries probably retained 20-40% of the laundered drug money.

After reading Poole's conclusions, Reynolds said, "Poole doesn't equivocate does he? I'm impressed. What sort of foundation information did you provide him, Rachel?"

"A mountain of stuff. Most was public domain information. U.S. Customs importation data, Columbian export statistics, Commerce Department and State Department reports. In the U.S. if it isn't classified it's out there somewhere. Just have to know how to data-mine. For the Columbian stuff, I e-mailed that editor, Rios. He got me some data through his contacts in the Columbian government. That stuff was definitely not public domain info. Even so, Bernie took all these seemingly unrelated statistics and reversed engineered how these guys operate."

"That's impressive, Rachel. You're something else." They looked at each other for an uncomfortable moment. "I need to get in contact with Franklin Brown again. Maybe he can give us some more specifics. I also owe him a thank you for the info. The guy's dying and he should know that he's stuck a hot poker up Martinelli Global's ass."

"You can't contact Franklin Brown, Mark. He's dead."

"What! What do'ya mean dead?"

"I couldn't contact him with the phone and cell numbers we had, so I did a search. Police, hospitals. Franklin Brown was admitted to the emergency room of St. John's Queens Hospital two days after you left for Columbia. He was DOA. According to the police report, a victim of a hit and run. Two o'clock in the morning. Leaving a bar. No witnesses. Brown's blood alcohol was exceptionally high. He was dressed in dark clothing. The police report suggests he was drunk and wandered into the street."

"That's bullshit. That's just too much of a coincidence, Rachel. He may have been murdered."

Conrad Redek and Martinelli Global corporate counsel, Paul Belden, were in Steven Martinelli's office. Rain streaked down the windows obscuring the usually spectacular view. The day matched the tone of the meeting.

"Durbin reports that Reynolds' live-in girlfriend has moved out. Probably will not be a promising avenue for pressure," Redek said. "Parents are dead. He only has two uncles. A few cousins. Nobody close. Durbin is checking for any angles there that might prove helpful, but I have already written that off as a dry hole. Paul and I think there are only two promising options. The first being to resurrect the Columbian charge of murder against Reynolds, and seek his extradition back to Columbia.

"Paul has already contacted Pablo Reyes. Reyes will contact a Columbian deputy attorney general friendly to us. Serious money will change hands. Paul has outlined a plan that will use a well connected Washington law firm to assist the Columbians in navigating the process within the U.S. Justice Department and the U.S. Courts. The law firm is ostensibly being paid by this Juan Cortina's newspaper."

"Cortina?" Martinelli asked.

"He's the Columbian journalist that Reynolds' is charged with murdering," Belden answered.

"Do they have any evidence?"

"They're working on it."

"Sounds like a process that will still take some time to develop. In the meantime, we can expect more stories about Martinelli Global from the Daily Press. That's not acceptable," Martinelli said.

"Steven, the most effective approach is still more aggressive...direct action against Reynolds," Redek offered.

"Conrad, don't be so guarded. We're not virgins here. Are you suggesting we have Reynolds killed or at least incapacitated? Here in the United States?"

"I know there are risks, Steven. But it can be made to look like an accident. I even spoke to Nikolai. His associate, Feliks Garnitsky, could arrange it. Using Russian nationals. Professionals. Totally distanced from us."

"Oh I'm sure Nikolai could have it arranged. Seems a common practice in Russia to kill journalists. Little risk as long as you have the right political clout. I don't think the risk here in the U.S. is justified. What's the second option?"

"Well then, the only other way is to substantially increase the pressure on the publisher of the Daily Press. Paul?" Redek said.

"I know you already put some pressure on Thurston Enders, Steven. What was your read on that?" Belden asked.

Martinelli answered, "I don't know Enders personally so it was by reputation only that we know each other. He was somewhat surprised at the call. I told him that I thought his newspaper's attacks on Martinelli Global were biased, at the least not balanced. It appeared to be some sort of vendetta by his reporter Reynolds, or perhaps a way of publicizing his own personal exploits as news. I cautioned him against exposing the newspaper to the same sort of scandals experienced by the Times and the Wall Street Journal."

"What do you think was accomplished?"

"His promise to discuss the situation with the managing editor. Vague assurances that they would only print verified facts. At best he may have put the Editor on notice to be careful."

"Conrad and I think there are opportunities to up that agenda. Our Mr. Durbin has come up with a real gem. The financial editor of the Daily Press is Bernard Poole. Durbin has discovered that Poole is a large securities trader for his own personal accounts. Personally socializes with several partners of two large investment banking firms; Davis Capital and Feinberg-Tate. More than socializes. Takes luxury all-paid vacations. Expensive gifts. Durbin's research links highly favorable recommendations by Poole for IPO's and securities handled by these firms. Then there's a trail of correspondingly large personal stock purchases by Poole of those same stocks. Most of these buys are followed by quick sales once the stock price increased."

"Amazing. He's highly regarded on Wall Street. I even read Poole," Martinelli said. "Is Robert Tate, the Managing Partner at Feinberg-Tate involved?"

"Durbin's information thinks its only two partners at that firm named Frankel and Schulmann. Even if Tate is involved it doesn't change the plan of attack. Is he a close friend, Steven?"

"I see him and his wife socially on occasion," Martinelli said. "What are you proposing?"

"You contact Tate. Tell him what's going on. Impress on him the seriousness of what these guys were doing. Federal criminal offenses, SEC violations. It would ruin Feinberg-Tate. Since he now owes you, you ask him to contact the Publisher of the Daily Press who now has the same concerns as Tate. Both are going to be motivated to quietly get rid of the offending staff."

"How did Durbin get this kind of information? Is it absolutely reliable?" Martinelli asked.

Conrad Redek answered, "I asked him the same question. His answer was that his methods and resources are a trade secret. And yes, he feels certain the information is reliable. He showed me enough to convince me."

Martinelli rose from his chair and faced out the window into the gray expanse of the East River and steady rain. "And how do I tell Tate I came by this information?"

Belden answered, "Just tell him the truth. Martinelli Global was simply protecting its interests against this targeted attack by the Daily Press by doing its own investigation. Tell him we investigated all the key newspaper staff that might be involved in the series of articles about Martinelli Global. Since the stories heavily involve business details, we assumed that Poole might have a role."

"And therefore, in consideration for this information, I request Robert Tate pressure Thurston Enders to kill these stories about Martinelli Global," Martinelli said finishing Belden's scenario. "I don't have to make any threat; it's implicit. If the articles don't stop, we simply leak the information to the Justice Department. It won't matter if these guys have already resigned. Feinberg-Tate and the Daily Press are still vulnerable."

"Exactly," Belden said. He smiled in appreciation of how quickly Steven Martinelli picked up on the nuances of the scheme.

"This is excellent work, both of you. Can you get me a summary and enough back-up to convince Tate? I want to see him yet today. Face to face over lunch or drinks."

Conrad Redek handed Martinelli an envelope. "It's a scaled down version of Durbin's report. I personally edited it to excise any details that would indicate we obtained any of the information illegally."

"Excellent," Martinelli said. "And one other thing; continue to pursue the Columbian murder charge against this Reynolds. Even with the stories suppressed, I want Reynolds personally silenced."

CHAPTER 15

BALTIMORE, MARYLAND – 1942

Fabrizio Martinelli was born in 1915. He worked in the growing Martinelli business during the Depression years. The elder Stefano Martinelli had insisted on a first rate education for his only son. An undergraduate degree in business was followed with a degree in law from Columbia. Fabrizio Martinelli disliked the discipline of college. But he was a quick study which left ample time for a rich young man to experience the nightlife of New York City. After two hushed abortions, the elder Martinelli issued an ultimatum. Any further sexual indiscretions would be met with swift reprisal; removal from college and assignment to a job in some boring place outside of New York. Secondly, he must marry someone of social standing.

Fabrizio was head-strong but not stupid. He chose the obvious option laid down by his father. That course was easier given his genuine affection for his mother. In her own way she was a strong woman, but she avoided any involvement with her husband's business affairs. Although a first generation American, she embraced the traditional old world view of obedience to her husband as head of the family.

Within a year after the confrontation with his father, Fabrizio was playing a key role in negotiating the technical elements of international contracts. To the delight of both his parents, he married a beautiful socialite the following year. The union joined two powerful Italian families with many common business interests. It also produced a son and daughter in quick succession.

The ensuing years saw Fabrizio come into his own within the business. He had many of his father's skills. While not the olive-oiled smoozer personality of his father, Fabrizio had exceptional business vision. He intuitively identified opportunities and took commensurate risks. More often than not, those risks paid off with solid successes. Subordinates could not be said to *like* him, but they all respected his leadership. From his father, he had learned the fundamental tenant to developing key subordinates. Give them objectives, give them space, get rid of those that are mediocre, and compensate the performers very well. The model was strict meritocracy never autocracy.

By the time the United States entered World War II in 1942, Fabrizio Martinelli was a senior executive responsible for negotiating government contracts. But at only twenty-seven, he was still eligible for the draft. With political pull from his father he received a commission in the Navy. With his background and legal training he served stateside in naval procurement. Access to inside information allowed him to direct acquisitions and fix bidding prices favorable to Martinelli enterprises. He had learned well from his father.

By the end of the War, Martinelli Group had tripled in revenue. World War II made Martinelli Group a large international firm. They were also now extremely well connected in not only Washington, but in many foreign countries. Martinelli Group was a major beneficiary in rebuilding contracts in Italy after the War.

By the late 1950s Fabrizio Martinelli had assumed the helm of the Company. It was his decision to take the Company public to provide the capital for his aggressive growth plans. His father did not favor the move. Stefano Martinelli did not understand the legal complexities, nor did he like the additional government intrusion. However, he respected his son's abilities and understood that new methods were essential to compete successfully in the post-war world. Health problems were also diminishing his ability to actively participate in the Company's management.

Fabrizio moved corporate headquarters from Baltimore to New York City in 1960. The IPO for the newly named Martinelli Global Incorporated, stock symbol MGI, was a resounding success. Better still, the stock price slumped only slightly after a month-long run-up in price, recovered quickly, then continued to make steady modest gains. The elder Stefano continued his high level networking. His networking amounted to influence peddling as effective as any lobbyist. That considerable influence had its effect on the stock success of MGI.

NEW YORK CITY – 1968

Having received his law degree from Harvard, Fabrizio Martinelli's son, Steven was anxious to finally take a real position with Martinelli Global. Years ago he had adopted the more Anglicized Steven in favor of the Italian *Stefano*. His beloved grandfather, the Company founder had died two years earlier. His father, Fabrizio while an excellent chief executive, was a distant father, more so after the divorce from his mother. Steven was not close to the second Mrs. Martinelli.

The younger Martinelli had inherited differing traits from his father and grandfather. Both men were strikingly different. The only commonality was their intelligence. The elder Stefano Martinelli was a product of the old country with its ingrained tradition of family and social interaction. His son, Fabrizio was the product of twentieth century American enterprise with its fast-paced, bold financial maneuvering and reward system of success.

Like his father, the younger Martinelli embraced the complex world of international business. He also received a law degree from Harvard. It was not for the purpose of ever practicing law, but to get a firm grounding in the ever increasing complexity of international contracts as well as U.S. tax codes. While working at Martinelli Global, he completed an MBA at Columbia, his father's alma mater.

Steven Martinelli worked in the Company's contracts department initially. Soon he was participating in the highest level of negotiations. When interacting with the opposition, he was always gracious. It was frequently deceptive. His demeanor was always even-mannered, rarely displaying his real intent. Always having done his homework, he never entered a negotiation without understanding the other side's position; what they wanted and what they might be willing to cede. He understood timing; when to stall, when to press his offer. Like his grandfather, he understood that most negotiations were conducted outside of any formal meeting sessions. The deal was always concluded beforehand with the decision maker. It always came down to one on one.

While attending a lecture at Columbia graduate school, Martinelli was introduced to the newly growing corporate use of offshore tax havens corporations. The lecturer recounted the history of the Bahamas as a tax haven for personal wealth since the 1930s. The Bahamian holding companies catered to capital fleeing the United States because of the high tax rates during the Depression. But it was still not a widespread common practice for U.S. corporations to use offshore foreign subsidiaries as an integral basis for conducting international business transactions.

Things had changed by the late 1960s, both for the Bahamas as well as for international capital markets. Among the financial elite in the Bahamas, there was a growing concern for their continuation of running the tax haven for their benefit. With the election of a liberal Bahamian government promising to push for full independence from Britain, and an avowed redistribution of wealth, there was reason to believe that they would lose control.

Then in 1966, the Cayman Islands, also a British colony, enacted a comprehensive collection of banking and tax laws. The sum of these laws set up the perfect tax haven business environment; ease of incorporation, no regulation, absolute secrecy, and no taxes on profits made outside of the Cayman Islands. With the uncertainty of an independent Bahamas, there was soon an exodus of capital to the Caymans. The modern offshore foreign corporation as an integral international business structure was therefore born in the Cayman Islands.

Steven Martinelli sold his father on exploring how to use these offshore tax havens subsidiaries. It became his key project. A more difficult sell was his plan to pursue investment in the Columbia coffee trade.

"How can that be a sound idea, Steven? The damn place is in the middle of a civil war," Fabrizio Martinelli said.

"True, but coffee still gets grown and exported. I also have a pretty good idea of how business is conducted there. Few government controls, widespread corruption. That's opportunity. Anything you need done can be bought. The risk is balanced by the huge upside potential."

"And how do you come by these insights?"

"A friend I met at the university. The name's Reyes. Wealthiest family in Columbia. His father sent him to New York because of the University's name. Imagine that. Reyes is a smart guy. He expects to take over the helm of the family's enterprises one day. Amongst other things, his family is the largest coffee grower and processor in Columbia."

The senior Martinelli paused for a moment to consider his son. "You have a lot of your Grandfather's traits, Steven. You're good with people relationships. But I fear you may have some of your grandfather's pirate ways. Martinelli Global has moved beyond many of the extra-legal things your Grandfather did. He lived in a different time."

The younger Martinelli resented his Father's patronizing tone. "Grandfather did what was necessary to grow the business. Look at his legacy. They would now say he pushed the envelope."

The elder Martinelli wanted to avoid a quarrel. He knew his son admired his grandfather. "So what are you suggesting?"

"First, I would establish two Cayman Island corporations. One company will be created to purchase coffee beans from Columbia. The second company will engage in the purchase of a controlling interest in all the major coffee producers in Columbia. The objective is to achieve a monopoly of the world's foremost coffee producing nation."

The senior Martinelli understood the strategy even though he was not fully understanding of the benefits of offshore corporations. "So how do you buyout the existing coffee producers?"

"I don't, at least not entirely. You see they are key to making this work. They're the locals. They have the political connections and more importantly, the cultural connections. They become our partners. They manage the local day-to-day affairs. We're the senior partners of course; the people with the money and the international means. The beauty of this is, no matter the winds of civil unrest, even civil war, we still profit."

"What if the place goes communist, like that Allende that may become President of Chile? How do we protect our investments then?"

"Because of our partners. History shows that the moneyed classes almost always retain economic power. They adapt to new regimes and business goes on. Cuba was an aberration."

"And not in Russia. The Soviet Union dumped the aristocracy."

"And they were just that, aristocracy, not the real economic powers."

"They were the land owners. They owned all the agricultural resources. That was the economic power in Russia. How's that different from these coffee growers in Columbia?"

His father had a good point. Just because he majored in history didn't mean he could assume any gaps in his father's knowledge base of history and geopolitics.

"The insurgencies in Columbia will not result in a socialist government. I've discussed this with someone at the State Department. Someone that was close to Grandfather. Our Government isn't going to allow Allende to turn Chile socialist for that matter. Besides that, I projected recouping the initial investment within three years. Because of the civil strife, any investment is discounted. It's a bargain, Father. Isn't that how you grew the Company?"

The senior Martinelli had been slowly pacing around his office but now sat down behind his desk and looked at his son with interest. "How can you project such a return?"

"Let me explain how this works, Father. First, we set up several Cayman Island corporations. These are the companies that will own the individual Columbian coffee companies. The shareholders of these offshore corporations will be us and our Columbian partners. Therefore almost all the profits are sheltered. By that I mean outside of U.S. tax jurisdiction. We pay only insignificant taxes in Columbia and none in the U.S. The real profits are in the Caymans. No taxes of course owed there since the profits occurred outside the Cayman Islands."

"Is coffee profitable?"

"Well there's more to this. The short answer to that question is it doesn't matter. You see we set up one or more additional offshore corporations. We're the only shareholders. These corporations buy virtually all the Columbian coffee crop at whatever price we need to make whatever profit margins we set.

After all, we're just buying from ourselves, and we're controlling the price on the commodities markets. It's a giant shell game. We're moving money around by slight of hand, manipulating profits, avoiding taxes, and avoiding accountability."

Fabrizio Martinelli rubbed his chin and smiled. "How do you architect this takeover of the Columbian coffee business? Why are these Columbians going to sell to you?"

"Easy. We'll offer twice what their holdings are worth. The current problems with rebel insurgencies and drug trafficking actually work in our favor to depress values. They should see this as insurance. Allows them to get their equity out of Columbia and secure a future revenue stream."

"My association with Francisco Reyes already gives me entry into the power structure of the Country. The Reyes family also owns the largest coffee producing company in Columbia. If I can do a deal with them, the other owners can be persuaded. After all, they stand to multiply the value of their holdings several fold within a few years. They will still own a substantial interest in their businesses. It's kind of like going public for them. Just like you taking the Martinelli businesses public."

Fabrizio Martinelli now laughed out loud. He could see his son running Martinelli Global one day. "So how much is this going to cost?"

"Probably 200 to 300 million."

BOGOTÁ, COLUMBIA – 1970

Within two years Steven Martinelli had successfully achieved control of almost 90% of the Columbian coffee industry. Francisco Reyes turned out to be a strong ally. The two developed a strong personal relationship. Martinelli related to the familial attitude of the Columbians. There were many European traits, not the least of which was a strong reliance on relationships when doing business. Martinelli was accepted almost as a part of the Reyes family.

Developing this audacious project was critical to both Martinelli and Reyes. Each was vying to establish their leadership credentials to eventually head their respective family businesses.

Francisco Reyes became the perfect person to head Martinelli Global operations in Columbia. It was Steven Martinelli's first big success, establishing a blueprint for future ventures. The two became friends. Each attended the other's wedding. Both joked that even their marriages were good business moves. Martinelli married the daughter of a prominent Senator from Massachusetts, Italian heritage of course. Reyes married a daughter of another prominent land holding Columbian family.

By 1972, profits were ahead of projections. Martinelli spent most of his time now in New York solidifying his position within the Company. It was important to justify his capabilities to his father and certain key board members. He was looking for his next big project. Certainly it would be in some foreign country. The opportunities afforded by offshore corporations in tax haven countries were too compelling.

Francisco Reyes was Martinelli's equal in business cunning. He too was looking to advance his stature. One evening the two men were sitting on the veranda of Reyes' villa in the hills overlooking Bogotá. The night was warm. The view of the city's lights was spectacular. The very old cognac complimented the Cuban cigars. A uniformed maid came from the house and asked if they needed anything.

As she walked away, Reyes admired her figure. "Oh my. Isn't that something. She gives me many fantasies. But they must remain only fantasies. It would be foolish to pursue anything under my own roof. Camila is a wonderful mother to our children, but less than exciting in bed. Unfortunately that has always been the case."

Reyes sipped his cognac, then continued. "Do you know that I keep a mistress in Bogotá? Unlike Camila, she is very exciting in bed. So much so that I could not live with her. The physical demands would shorten my life."

Both men laughed.

"I trust that you and Regina still find each other interesting in bed?" Reyes asked, referring to Martinelli's wife.

"Actually we do. Besides, I would not dare stray. Things are different in New York. She's a very smart woman with a nasty temper and a lot of political clout."

Both men laughed again. Martinelli meant what he said but there were deeper reasons for his fidelity. He abhorred his own father's philandering and what it did to his mother. More than that, Steven Martinelli was simply devoted to his wife.

"We are much alike, Steven, even if we share slightly differing views on marriage," Reyes said. He poured more cognac from a crystal decanter. "I have an idea that might be of interest. The profit potential could be staggering."

"What's your position about drugs, Steven?"

"What do you mean?"

"I mean do you have any moral qualms about illegal drugs?"

"If you're asking would I be interested in getting involved in the illegal drug business, the answer is decidedly no. What are you suggesting?"

"Let me ask you this. If you were a Swiss banker, would you have taken in Nazi deposits?"

Somewhat off balance, Martinelli took a drink of cognac as he considered the question. "Probably." He mentally went though a series of rationalizations. The conclusion was he would have had no moral qualms about taking Nazi money.

"That's really all I am suggesting. Here's my thinking. I have connections to some very important people involved in the drug trade. Cocaine. It's Columbia's foremost export. These people have a singular problem in managing enormous quantities of cash."

"You're suggesting we get involved in money laundering?"

"Precisely, Steven. But let me show you how this works. First, we create a new offshore bank. The shareholders of that bank are the drug traffickers. Currently, our trading company, South American Trading is funded by one of our own offshore banking entities. We simply switch to the new bank. The drug cash is converted into a line of credit to purchase coffee. South American Trading continually repays the line of credit out of coffee sales. Since South American Trading is acknowledged as a Martinelli Global foreign subsidiary, we still preserve accounting transactional integrity. The money has now been laundered as coffee."

"And our profits?" Martinelli asked with evident interest in the scheme.

"We should be able to demand something like 30% as *banking fees*."

"And what does that amount to in dollars annually?"

"At least $400 million, maybe $500 million. The drug money is there. It's a matter of how much can be *converted* into coffee. The cocaine industry is much bigger than coffee. In fact, there are other outlets to reinvest the drug cash that might interest these people once we establish a relationship."

"From what I read, these people are thugs and murderers. Is that who you want to do business with, Francisco?"

"Certainly not. Those are the public faces of the drug business. Those are the guys that move the coca base from the fields and run the labs. They're the smugglers. They're the ones you see involved with all the violence. It's a tough business. No, I'm talking about those higher in the food chain, landholders, politicians, senior military officials. Some people even outside of Columbia."

Martinelli wondered if some of their current Columbian partners were involved in cocaine. The answer was probably yes.

"That's an interesting scheme, Francisco. But there's no way my father would go along with it. He becomes more conservative each year. Even the mention of drug related money would end the discussion immediately. I would be committing professional suicide if I attempted to sell him on this."

Three years later, Fabrizio Martinelli died suddenly of a massive coronary. It was 1973. By 1976, Steven Martinelli had consolidated enough control of the Board for them to name him CEO of Martinelli Global.

His first project was to resurrect Francisco Reyes' grand money laundering scheme.

CHAPTER 16

Manhattan, New York

Associated Press - New York:

The prominent Wall Street investment banking firm of Feinberg-Tate announced that two senior partners had resigned. The resignations were announced in the form of a press release. 'The firm announces the resignations of Karl Frankel and Aaron Schulmann. Their resignations resulted from differences with senior management over the strategic direction of Feinberg-Tate.' That was the entire text of the press release.

Both Frankel and Schulmann were well respected in the financial community and participated in many large projects and IPO's over the last decade. According to knowledgeable sources on Wall Street, there were no rumors about any conflicts among senior staff at Feinberg-Tate. The brevity of the press release raised speculation that something suddenly precipitated the shake-up.

Frankel and Schulmann could not be reached for comment. A spokesperson speaking on behalf of Robert Tate, Managing Partner of Feinberg-Tate, stated there would be no further comment on the departures beyond what was stated in the press release.

Reynolds wanted to strengthen his body of evidence implicating Martinelli Global in Columbian money laundering. He had new documentation from Columbia and he had Bernie Poole's financial analysis. If the Government had taken any action on the data he gave to the FBI that would add real weight.

He recalled a young attorney that worked in the U.S. Attorney's office for the Southern District of New York. The guy had been a source a couple years ago for an organized crime piece Reynolds had written. The attorney led a prosecution team in the trial of a mid-level Mafia figure charged with extortion. Reynolds mentioned the attorney's name several times in a favorable context. The attorney gave Reynolds information about the structure of organized crime in New York. The information was off the record, but it allowed Reynolds the framework from which to write a highly praised piece.

Reynolds called Deputy U.S. attorney Albert Thorne's office. "Mr. Thorne, this is Mark Reynolds of the Daily Press. Perhaps you remember me from a couple of years ago?"

Thorne of course remembered. The favorable mention of his name in those articles had not hurt his career. The information he gave Reynolds also stuck another stick in the eye of New York organized crime. "Of course I remember, Mr. Reynolds. How've you been?"

"Doing ok. Perhaps you've seen my series of articles about Martinelli Global?"

"Yes I have. Interesting stuff," Thorne answered. He wondered what Reynolds wanted.

"What you may not know is that I turned over some very incriminating information about Martinelli Global to the FBI. It implicated Martinelli Global, or at least their subsidiaries, in laundering drug money in Columbia. My problem is the FBI refuses to discuss if anything is being done to investigate these allegations. They don't even acknowledge if there is any sort of ongoing investigation. I'd rather know the lay of the land before we go to press with what we have. I want the story but I don't want to damage the Government's chances of nailing these guys. Could you see if there is anything you can comment on relative to Justice pursuing an investigation?

Thorne's immediate reaction was this was bullshit. Reynolds probably just wanted more ammunition for his story. "On the record or off?"

"Whatever you feel would be appropriate. I think the information you gave me a couple of years ago was important to get out to the public."

"Ok. I'll do some checking and get back to you."

Bernie Poole, the financial editor of the Daily Press walked into Rachel Stern's small office. Mark Reynolds was sitting there going through a stack of papers. Poole closed the glass door to the office. "Got a minute?"

"Sure, Bernie, what's up?" Rachel Stern asked.

Poole looked down at his shoes and bit his lower lip. He was a small slender man. Smart dresser, taken to wearing trendy suspenders. He wore glasses and looked every bit the picture of a prosperous Wall Street banker. Today however, he looked slightly disheveled. His white shirt was wrinkled. His hair was not neatly combed. His glasses were smudged.

"I just came to tell you that I'll be leaving the Newspaper."

"What? Why, Bernie? A better offer somewhere?" Stern asked. "Come sit down."

"No thanks. This is tough enough. Need to make it short. I can't tell you any of the details. I agreed not to."

"Sounds like you've done something wrong, Bernie," Reynolds said. "Can we help in any way?"

"No, but thanks for the offer. Yeah I did something wrong. But like I said, I can't say anything. That's the deal so this won't go any further."

"Criminal?" Reynolds asked.

"Probably."

"Did it have anything to do with the shakeup at Feinberg-Tate?" Reynolds asked.

Poole let out a sigh. "Maybe. But I can't talk about it, Mark. Anyway, I'll be leaving right away."

Poole hugged Stern and shook Reynolds hand. He left abruptly looking as if he might cry.

After he left, Stern said to Reynolds, "What do suppose Bernie did?"

"I have no idea. But it's a loss for us. We need his expertise as we continue to dig deeper into Martinelli Global. This is complicated stuff."

Reynolds answered his office telephone.

"This is Al Thorne," the deputy U.S. Attorney said. "First of all, anything I tell you is off the record. Second, I'm not going to tell you much."

"Ok. Whatever you can tell me I appreciate."

"Well, I discussed your call with a colleague that works white collar crime. I hit a nerve. Seems the FBI advised his office about the information you passed on. However, my colleague does not think there's an investigation going on. At least not that he is aware of. What he's pissed about is the pressure he got from Washington to suspend any further inquiries about the information you provided. According to him, that came from his boss's boss."

"What're you saying? Somebody high up in the Justice Department is preventing further investigation?"

"Could be. Or it might be that the information was just not compelling enough. I didn't see it so I can't tell."

"No way. If you saw what I gave the FBI, names, numbers, you'd have given your left nut to go after these guys. Fuck!"

Thorne paused before continuing. "I'm afraid I've got some more bad news, Reynolds. I came across it while checking up on you. Seems the Columbian government is pressing an extradition case against you. For murder. A fellow journalist. A Columbian. Know anything about that?"

"Christ. Yeah I knew about the allegation. It's bullshit. Juan Cortina may well be dead, but I didn't kill him. They tried to kill me. It's part of the same story, Thorne. Martinelli Global, drugs, coffee. Extradition? Can they do that?"

"Well they have to convince a U.S. federal judge. Do they have any evidence?"

"No. Unless they manufactured some. There's a lot of power being thrown around. No telling what sort of shit these guys will try to throw at me."

"It does seem like you stuck your hand into a hornet's nest. Hope you don't get stung, Reynolds."

Thurston Enders, Publisher of the New York Daily Press called John Fredricks very infrequently. This was the second call in two weeks.

"John, how are you?"

"Well, not so good to be perfectly honest, Mr. Enders. Bernard Poole came into my office this morning and announced he was leaving the Paper. Immediately. Literally today. I went round and round with him, but he wouldn't give any reason."

"I'm aware of Poole's departure, John. In fact I'm the cause. Now I'm going to tell you some things that must remain absolutely confidential. No one, including your wife is to know what I'm going to tell you."

Fredericks said nothing. He was stunned by Enders manner. The usually soft spoken old-money aristocrat was obviously struggling with what he was about to say.

"Poole was in league with those two partners at Feinberg-Tate that just resigned. Poole took money to print favorable recommendations on certain stocks and new offerings. There was insider trading and other criminal violations."

"And how did you come by this information, Sir?"

"Robert Tate called me. There's no question about what went on. Tate had a mountain of documentation. He sounded shaken. Been going on for years apparently. Just like Poole, when he confronted these two partners they offered their resignations immediately. These bastards created a fine mess. All of them are getting off lightly, including Poole. Should be going to prison, but we couldn't have that. The point is, these indiscretions must never come to light. It would cost Feinberg-Tate tens of millions, maybe more. Might even destroy them. As for the Daily Press, I shudder to think of what it would do to the Daily Press."

Indiscretions? Enders was asking him not only to keep the secret but to become part of the cover-up. "I wish you hadn't told me, Sir. Now I've got to subjugate my own ethics. Not only are you requesting I not write the story, but you are making me an accessory to their crimes. So are you for that matter, Sir. If I might ask, how did Robert Tate learn of these crimes?" Fredericks was not going to let Enders off easily.

"Well that's where it gets worse I'm afraid, John. The information came from outside Feinberg-Tate."

"From whom?" Fredericks asked.

"Martinelli Global."

"So I can guess the rest, Mr. Enders. In exchange for this information and their silence, the Paper ceases publishing Mark Reynolds articles."

There was a long pause. "Yes. You will simply inform Reynolds that these articles are beginning to lack objectivity and appear as a targeted attack on Martinelli Global."

"Jesus Christ. That's the worst goddamn thing I've ever been asked to do."

"Please curtail the profanity, John."

"No, Sir. This is clearly the time for profanity. What you're asking of me is an act of profanity."

"John, I understand perfectly. I too feel soiled by this sordid mess. But you must see that neither of us has a real choice. There is simply too much at stake. Not the least of which is the livelihood of all our employees. This is about the greater good. I'm asking for your cooperation as a personal favor, John."

It was a question with only a yes or no answer. Not only were his ethics at stake, but his very job. He was fifty-nine years old, at the top of his profession. The scandal on his watch would contaminate the prospects of any other job opportunities. Going along would assure his remaining years before retiring. Implicit in Enders request was more money.

"Very well, Sir. I'll tell Mark Reynolds that I am discontinuing his series on Martinelli Global. You might as well know that we may lose Reynolds over this."

"That would be a loss, but a risk we will have to take. I appreciate what you're doing, John. Believe me, I know how difficult this is."

John Fredericks sat frozen in his chair for several minutes staring at some indistinct point on the wall. No matter how he played back the rationalizations, he felt dirty. His was a profession that confronted difficult ethical questions daily. Years of constructing a personal ethical framework had just been abandoned in a single moment of crisis.

CHAPTER 17

MANHATTAN, NEW YORK

M ark Reynolds went to Rachel Stern's office the morning after Poole had told them about his leaving. "Rachel, I need you to read this. This is how I want to lead into my next piece on Martinelli Global. This is kind of a layman's explanation of how these offshore companies can be used to go beyond legal tax avoidance. Tell me if I've dumbed it down enough.

"The rest of the piece makes the case about the Columbian coffee industry being used as a vehicle for drug money laundering. By extension that makes Martinelli Global complicit. I'm going to take it to Fredericks. Your material and Bernie's work-up make the case to go public."

"Did you get any confirmation from the Justice Department about any investigation?" Stern asked.

"No. There's no ongoing investigation. Nothing I turned over to the FBI is going anywhere." He chose not to get into Albert Thorne's impression that there was high level pressure to block any investigation. He also did not mention Columbia's efforts to extradite him for murder.

"My source wasn't very communicative. Might not be telling me everything either. But it doesn't matter. After this piece, the Government will have to act."

"You think John will agree that you have enough? He's right about being cautious on this. Trashing these Columbian coffee companies is one thing, accusing Martinelli Global is a much more serious matter."

"That's still the weakest part of making the link between Martinelli Global and their Columbian coffee subsidiaries. So, I want to lay the foundation about how difficult it is getting even basic business ownership facts from a closed foreign banking system. I want to give the reader a context by which to judge the facts. This whole use of offshore corporations is a major corporate bullshit scheme directed at the U.S. public. Given the absolute secrecy of these offshore shelters, the temptation for corporations to hide all sorts of things has to be overwhelming. I want to prod stockholders and taxpayers to question what's going on."

"Nice speech. Not sure your instructor in journalism 101 would agree. Sounds more like editorializing," Stern said.

"Rachel, will you just read the copy?"

"The Cayman Islands is probably the best known and most widely used tax haven by major international corporations. It has all the basic elements of levying no taxes on gains for business conducted outside of the Caymans, absolute secrecy, and no regulatory reporting. Add to this a stable Western style parliamentary government that is totally committed to protecting and fostering its principle industry of tax-free commerce.

"A Cayman Island corporation is a unique creature compared to a U.S. corporation. It functions more like an individual rather than a collection of shareholders. It can conduct transactions and own assets that are not owned by its shareholders. In short, it can act as a proxy for real people who are doing business outside of the Cayman Islands, while under penalty of law, holding the identity of those real people in absolute secrecy from any foreign government prying.

"The Cayman Islands corporation is a simple architecture of legal paperwork. The multinational corporation creates a subsidiary in the Cayman Islands which becomes a foreign corporation. They build their product in some low cost country. The product is sold to the Cayman Islands corporation at little or no profit. The Cayman Islands corporation then sells the product to the high tax country at a high profit that is banked in the Cayman Islands. The profits were produced outside the Cayman Islands, therefore there are no Cayman taxes. The parent U.S. corporation takes delivery of the product directly from the low cost producing country at a transaction cost many times higher then the real production costs. The parent U.S. company shows artificially higher costs and books the real profits in its no-tax Cayman Islands subsidiary.

"The beauty of this is there is no functional entity in the Cayman Islands, just a mailing address. The product never goes to the Cayman Islands. All the paperwork is actually done by the parent U.S. company in the U.S. Taxes are only paid on the modest profits realized when selling the product to the U.S. entity because of the fictitious cost. And all this is legal under U.S. tax code."

Stern finished reading Reynolds' draft. "Ok. Good explanation of how these offshore tax-haven corporations work. Our average reader will understand. But the rest about Martinelli Global's use of these secret corporations to launder drug money is still not founded on strong documented fact. Nothing here really substantiates Martinelli Global's ownership of these corporations."

"I know that, Rachel. But this is the best we can maybe ever get. We've got a lot of circumstantial evidence. I think it's enough. We have to approach this like proving a murder without delivering the body."

"I agree with your argument, Mark, but John may not."

"He's got to, Rachel. This is good material. John is just being unreasonable about covering our backsides on this because of the clout Martinelli Global wields."

Before Reynolds could arrange a time to meet with Fredericks, Fredericks himself called asking Reynolds to come see him.

"Shut the door, Mark," Fredericks said as Reynolds entered his office.

Reynolds had a copy of the next piece that he had just discussed with Stern. Fredericks was old-school and preferred to read paper rather than an electronic file.

"What's up? I was just about to come see you anyway. Wanted to go over my next piece."

"About Martinelli Global I assume?"

"Right. Just read this, John. This is some really good material. Martinelli Global's dirty and we have enough here to defend our position on the story."

Reynolds dropped the pages on the desk in front of Fredericks.

Fredericks looked at paper-clipped pages, but did not pick them up.

"Mark. I'm killing the so-called Martinelli Global story. This started out . . ."

"What! What the hell do you mean, killing the story?" Reynolds interrupted, leaning forward in his chair.

"Because this seems like a personal contest now between you and Martinelli Global. It's no longer objective."

"Why? Because they tried to kill me twice? I should think that gives me some reason to dig under their rotten skin."

"That's what I mean, Mark. You don't have proof that Martinelli Global tried to have you killed. You're in these shithole Third World countries asking unwelcomed questions to the locals. It's dangerous work. But it doesn't mean Martinelli Global is pulling the strings."

"Locals that work with or for Martinelli Global," Reynolds said.

Fredericks sighed with resignation. "Mark, listen to me. I've had reservations about the quality of your information on Martinelli Global from the start. You're probably right about them being dirty. But we just don't have good enough facts to publish that allegation."

"John, you haven't even read this copy. It makes the case."

"Mark. Listen. There's more problems with this story. I'm not sure I fully understand Bernie Poole's deduced conclusions from all that technical crap Rachel dug up. But Bernie was convinced. Now he's left. I'm not going out on a limb with this complex financial stuff without someone like Poole to vet the technicalities. Second, there's this problem of the Columbians wanting to extradite you on murder charges."

"Christ, you don't believe that shit do you?"

"Of course not. But continuing to have you write stories alleging Martinelli Global is mixed up with money laundering in Columbia while you're wanted there will become a story in itself for other papers. There's no solid link there to Martinelli Global. None we can print anyway."

"That's bullshit and you know it, John."

"Goddamn it! I'm tired of your arrogance. Who the fuck do'ya think you're lecturing? You've lost all prospective on this Martinelli Global thing. The story is dead. I'm pulling the plug on this story. Move on to something else."

Reynolds stood up from his chair. For a moment he said nothing; too surprised and angry. "I expected more support from you, John. We've been friends for a long time. I've respected your work. But I think you've lost your backbone. Maybe you're too concerned about your retirement years now to make strong decisions."

Fredericks shot out of his chair. His face flushed with rage. "You fucking bastard! I'm not going to listen to your stupid insults. Get the fuck out of my office."

"No fucking problem, John. I'll do better than that. I quit."

"Your call, Mark."

Reynolds turned and left without saying anything further.

John Fredericks slammed his office door shut then sat down at his desk. He rubbed his eyes. Some tears flowed. He felt ashamed. Reynolds was on to something with this story. He let Enders pressure him without much of a fight. There was a time when he would have told the publisher to go to hell.

Reynolds went back to his own office. Did he mean what he told Fredericks about quitting? Yes he did. It was personal now. The only way to fight Martinelli Global was to write about them. He couldn't do it from the Daily Press anymore. He was not about to back away from this.

Rachel Stern opened his office door and came in. "Hi. Don't tell me. By the look on your face it didn't go well." She closed the door and stood beside his desk. "Mark, talk to me."

"John killed the story."

"Well, I told you there were some problems there."

"No, no. I mean he killed the whole series, anything having to do with Martinelli Global. Told me I'd lost perspective. There's more going on here, Rachel. I've never seen him so critical about corroborating facts as he's been on this."

"That does seem a little extreme to kill the whole thing," Stern said.

"I have my own extreme issue, Rachel. I just quit."

Stern looked as if she had just been slapped across the face. If Reynolds left the Paper she knew she would lose any chance of getting closer to him.

"Oh my God, Mark, no. You can't leave. I . . . ," she trailed off not knowing what to say.

"Listen. I'm going to download my files, then get the hell out of here. Maybe tomorrow you can have my books boxed up and sent around to my place. Maybe go through my desk and send any personal things you find. There shouldn't be much. I travel light. I really don't want to come back in and have to explain to everyone."

"Mark . . . sure I will. Tell you what. I want to talk to you. Maybe there's some way out of this."

"Rachel, I don't think so."

"Well I want to talk with you anyway. I want to see you. You're in pain. I'm in pain. Can I come over later? We'll go to dinner. Please? For me?"

Reynolds looked at her. Tears were running down her cheek. He felt guilty that she was hurting so much. He also felt guilty that he did not share the same level of romantic attachment she obviously did.

"Sure. I'd like that, Rachel. We'll go somewhere nice." Reynolds stood up and came around from behind his desk. They hugged. Stern kissed his cheek still crying.

Steven Martinelli excused the people in his office to take the call from the Speaker of the House of Representatives, Dennis Adams. "Dennis, how are you?"

"I'm fine, Steven. And you?"

"Very good actually. Business is good and we've got some interesting projects in the works."

"Excellent. I hope these articles in the Daily Press don't grow into a problem though. My chief of staff has briefed me. He raised some troubling concerns. This isn't headed for some major scandal is it, Steven?'

Martinelli knew the Speaker's concern wasn't for Martinelli Global. Over the years, Martinelli Global had been a major campaign contributor to Adams. Martinelli had also steered Adams into several lucrative personal investments. They saw each other socially; expensive trips, dinners, cultural events; ultimately all on Martinelli's tab.

"No, Dennis. Nothing to worry about there. There's no substance to these allegations. Just goes with the territory. Martinelli Global has always been on the leading edge of international business. This reporter's whole thrust is to build a story around the use of foreign offshore corporations as some nefarious mechanism of big internationals. You know yourself that every major international corporation uses this legal architecture for tax management and legitimate commerce. All within the bounds of U.S. statutes and IRS regulations."

"Still, it must make you uneasy that the Daily Press has made Martinelli Global the poster child for the practice," Adams said.

"Granted we'd rather not be in the spotlight, but we'll weather it. To be honest, I don't think the general public grasps the concepts, or even cares. Way too complicated. After all, these allegations don't point to the kind of things that titillate the public like the escapades of Enron, World Com, or Tyco. Martinelli Global has been around for a hundred years. Its business practices may use all available legal options, but they are still solid. At any rate, I believe all that unpleasantness is behind us."

"What do you mean?"

"I have it on good authority that the Daily Press will not be running any more stories about Martinelli Global. Seems that the powers-to-be at the Newspaper determined that this reporter was a loose canon. Seems to have been his way of personally advancing himself. At any rate, there won't be any more stories."

"That's good news, Steven.

"By the way, Dennis, I just heard your son made partner at his law firm. Pretty good at his age."

"Yes it is. He's a real talent. Couldn't be prouder," Adams said.

"On another note, Delores has been prodding me to get away for a couple of weeks to our place in Tuscany. She's thinking about next month. Should be good weather. Any chance that you and Mary could join us, at least for a few days? We'd get you and Mary over there on the Gulf Stream. Promise you some great food and great wine."

"You always do that, Steven. I certainly would welcome a few days away from Washington. I appreciate the offer. Let me get back to you on that."

"Wonderful. In fact, just pick a date in May and we'll build around that."

Rachel Stern arrived at Mark Reynolds' apartment at six pm. She was dressed casually but took great pains to look her most attractive.

"What's in the bag?" Reynolds asked as he showed her in. She was carrying a grocery bag.

"Dinner. Actually the makings of dinner. I got a great Bordeaux too. At least the wine guy said it was. I'm going to cook us dinner. I didn't want to go out. Do you mind?"

He didn't mind. He also knew what she intended. He didn't mind that either right now. With all the things swirling out of control with his life right now, being with Rachel was comforting. She was always good company. Making love with her tonight seemed like a pretty good idea.

CHAPTER 18

MANHATTAN, NEW YORK

Steven Martinelli genuinely despised the periodic calls from securities analysts. It was much like what the President of the United States endured during press conferences. The analysts only expressed interest if there were potentially negative or positive issues they wanted clarified by a corporation's senior management. For a company like Martinelli Global that went to great links to keep a low public profile, these calls were particularly intrusive.

Martinelli sat at a table in a small conference room in the Martinelli Global office building. With him were his chief lieutenants, Conrad Redek and Paul Belden. On the speaker telephone were analysts from three major brokerage firms. Two of the analysts were friendly to Martinelli Global, the third had a reputation for being aggressive in his questions.

"These stories in the Daily Press paint Martinelli Global as a predator corporation," one analyst said. "We're concerned about what amounts to a continual flow of negative press directed at Martinelli Global."

"And this coming on the heels of the disaster in Nigeria," another analyst said.

"Gentlemen, first of all, that incident in Nigeria cannot be blamed on Martinelli Global. The Nigerian government has repeatedly called it an act of terrorism. No responsible government has disputed that finding. Our own investigations lead us to the same conclusion," Martinelli answered.

"The tone of these articles, Mr. Martinelli, suggests that Martinelli Global is engaged in activities that might border on illegal," this from the analyst with the reputation for hard questioning. "With the examples of Enron and Parmalot there are naturally concerns when we hear these kinds of published allegations."

"Allegations? I was not aware that the Daily Press had made any allegations of wrongdoing by Martinelli Global," Martinelli said.

"Perhaps not, Mr. Martinelli, but the tone of these attacks on Martinelli Global are implicit in their meaning."

"Gentlemen. Too much is being made of a reporter looking for a headline. The entire thrust of these articles is about the use of foreign subsidiaries."

"Tax havens. Shell corporations," the analyst said.

"Those are the kind of provocative terms the Press chooses. You know as well as I do that every major international corporation uses foreign subsidiaries. The U.S. tax code is quite extensive on the subject. Martinelli Global abides by all U.S. tax statutes and SEC regulations in that area," Martinelli responded.

"Martinelli Global, like other corporations, has extensive foreign subsidiaries in those countries where it does business. I wouldn't pretend to lecture you gentlemen on the necessities of foreign corporate structures to legitimately do business internationally. It is essentially not only to seek the most favorable tax circumstances, but just to facilitate the flow of commerce."

"Mr. Martinelli, the Daily Press directly alleges that Martinelli Global owns the Columbian coffee industry – a virtual monopoly to reap profits at the expense of the small growers."

By now the other two analysts simply listened, letting this other guy be the pariah.

Steven Martinelli was soft spoken and not easily provoked. However, he could not be bullied. "Gentlemen, I will not get into company confidential areas. Beyond acknowledging that Martinelli Global does have foreign subsidiaries in South America, as noted in its SEC filings. I categorically refute the unproven allegations that we have a coffee monopoly in Columbia."

"And the associations with Columbians involved in drug trafficking?"

"Mr. Boucher, I resent your question. In fact, I resent your entire line of questions this morning. This conference call is to provide you information in order to make informed recommendations to the financial markets about Martinelli Global Incorporated. It is not a forum to act like a newspaper reporter looking for scandal. Our discussions are for the sole purpose of evaluating this company's financial performance and investment worthiness."

"Well, on that note, Mr. Martinelli . . ."

"Please do not interrupt until I'm finished. Martinelli Global stock prices have continually risen over the past decade. After only a slight dip with the unfortunate terrorist incident in Nigeria, the stock recovered quickly. During these slanderous articles in the Daily Press, Martinelli Global stock has not suffered. No Government investigations have grown out of all these wild newspaper speculations. The Market clearly is not responding to the publicity.

"Add to that, a strong record of consistently strong profit performance over decades. Which I might add, I am projecting to be up twenty-five cents a share for the next quarter solely on margin improvements in a number of markets. Frankly, gentlemen, you are focused on the wrong questions."

There were several moments of uncomfortable silence. Martinelli smiled slightly to his staff at the conference table. Eventually, one analyst who had said little during the interview spoke up.

"Mr. Martinelli, I for one want to apologize for any questions that may have been taken as accusatory. That is certainly not our job. But you must understand that we had to raise certain issues."

Martinelli responded, "I understand. But you must also understand our sensitivity here at Martinelli Global. These articles were a witch hunt by a discredited reporter. I have been informed that the reporter, Mark Reynolds, is no longer with the Daily Press, nor is their financial editor who we understand contributed on these series of stories."

"You mean Bernie Poole?" the abrasive analyst asked, clearly surprised. The news had not yet been announced. Poole was well respected in the financial community.

"I believe that's his name," Martinelli said.

"And you're saying that Reynolds and Poole were fired over the Martinelli Global stories?"

"Certainly not. I don't even know if they were fired. I'm only saying the Daily Press staff that were central to these attack stories are no longer with the Newspaper. I might also add that the Columbian Government is seeking to extradite Mr. Reynolds back to Columbia to face murder charges."

The remaining discussions were brief. The analysts were only too happy to extricate themselves from the conversation. Martinelli had the right numbers and the right answers. This whole issue of bad press had indeed not hurt Martinelli Global.

Martinelli disconnected the call then smiled at his staff. "At the risk of being crude, that turned out pretty fucking well."

Martinelli Global's annual board of directors meeting was scheduled for the following week. Martinelli had summoned Nikolai Krasin to come to New York. The principle new business item was the proposed acquisition of the Russian state-owned petroleum pipeline company, Transneft, and Krasin's proposed expansion in Caspian Sea oil reserves.

Prior to the celebrated business scandals of the last decade, board of directors were frequently just rubber stamps of the CEO and senior managers. Apart from the public noise level about governance responsibilities and Sarbanes-Oxley, little had actually changed. Martinelli Global's Board was no different. Steven Martinelli had firm control. Not only was he the largest single stockholder, but board members were also lavished with extensive perks beyond their atypically high salaries.

Nonetheless, Martinelli's control was not absolute. None of the Board members were privy to any illegal activities. Few if any of them would be complicit if they had known. All were successful in their own right. For differing reasons they served on the Martinelli Global's Board, but typically for the influencial networking connections that accrued from the association.

Martinelli also had to be careful to shield the Board's audit committee from any of the Company's tangled down-stream affairs in the Third World and places such as Russia. Martinelli Global maintained a cozy relationship of understanding with the major auditing firm of Kellogg-Tyler. But even the auditing firm was not privy to all of Martinelli Global's operations. It was an elaborate financial architecture that shielded the outside auditors and the Board's Audit Committee from anything much beyond what was reported in Martinelli Global's SEC filings.

There were several Board members that remained outside the sphere of Martinelli's control. Two were there at the insistence of a group of institutional investors that controlled twenty percent of the voting stock. They were certainly not antagonistic to Management, but could not be assumed to just blindly follow all Management's proposals. Another Board member was clearly a potential problem.

Tyler Ashcroft had become a member of Martinelli Global's Board some years before at the request of Martinelli Global's principle banking partner, Manhattan Commercial Bank. Steven Martinelli had a personal relationship with Manhattan's CEO, but the professional relationship with the Bank carried certain strings. That string was Tyler Ashcroft, nephew to the Bank's CEO.

Ashcroft was a senior vice president with Manhattan Commercial. An old-money Brahmin, he possessed only a light-weight intellect and an outsized collection of dissipative personal excesses including alcohol and sex. Because of his position of personal wealth and inherent arrogance, he did not bend to Martinelli's influence easily. Martinelli disliked Ashcroft and therefore was not able to seduce him to his sphere of control.

The selling of the Board on the Transneft deal and the Caspian Sea venture was not an assumed fait accompli. Martinelli could bully Board approval, but there would be real negative ramifications if they did not embrace the moves. Therefore, selling these strategic plans to everyone on the Board was important. Krasin came over from Russia expressly for that reason.

Krasin was a real plus. Martinelli Global's acquisitions in Russia and other former Soviet States had proven highly profitable. Krasin was their man in Eastern Europe. He was a first rate executive possessed with an Old World charm. Western educated, urbane, spoke excellent English.

Conrad Redek had brought Krasin into Martinelli Global and was intimate with the technical aspects of the Russian ventures. Together, they made a powerful team.

Martinelli himself was an expert in international finance, but his chief operating officer, Conrad Redek was an absolute genius. It was Redek who had designed Martinelli Global's elaborate international business structures. He was perhaps the highest compensated COO in the country - worth every dollar he was paid. He had the inclinations of a modern day Machiavelli possessed with the ingenuity of a brilliant technician. He was the consummate hired gun.

Conrad Redek came to Martinelli's attention sixteen years earlier. In a causal conversation at a social event, Martinelli mentioned that he was looking for new talent with international business experience.

"Steven, I've just the guy for you," an attorney sitting next to him at a fund raising dinner for the Metropolitan Opera said. "One of my clients was putting together a number of foreign acquisitions. But more than acquisitions, they wanted to move products between countries in such a way as to increase margins and minimize taxes. We were doing the legal work. I'm no slouch at international work and I've got some of the best international business attorneys on my staff, but I tell you, this guy is brilliant. He came up with a business model that was truly impressive. Blew my team away with his ideas."

"What was so impressive?"

"This guy seemed to be an expert on taxation law for every known country in the world. Understands their banking laws as well. What he designed was an integrated strategy to continually take advantage of different markets as conditions changed, manipulate currency transactions, and move virtually all the taxes out of the U.S. and Europe. The guy is a genius with how to use subsidiaries in tax haven countries."

Martinelli's interest was piqued. "You're right, I would be interested. What's his name?"

"Conrad Redek. Works for the consulting firm of Habour-Klein."

CHAPTER 19

MANHATTAN, NEW YORK

N ikolai Krasin arrived at JFK on an Air France flight from Paris. With him was the internationally celebrated opera soprano, Malika Domokos. Domokos was Hungarian but had been the principle soprano at the Moscow Opera for several years. She had been Krasin's companion for almost ten years. She was younger than Krasin, but in the twilight of her career.

Domokos had insisted they stop over in Paris for a couple of days on the flight from Moscow. She had some serious shopping to do. That was fine by Krasin. He loved Paris. Coming from comparative privilege, he had studied at the Sorbonne for a graduate degree after completing a degree in economics at Moscow University.

His privilege came from his father being a high ranking Communist Party official. In the Soviet Union wealth accrued from privilege and privilege could only accrue from stature within the Government or the Military. His father was a skilled politician. Government was the fastest track to success in the Soviet Union. From that came the best apartment, access to the best food and luxury goods, the best education, and most of all, power. Power equated to access to wealth.

Leaving the insulated, provincial gray world of Moscow for Paris was life changing. For a smart, handsome, impressionable man from behind the Iron Curtain, Paris was the face of the decadent West that had been instilled into his upbringing. If this was decadence, Nikolai Krasin fully embraced it.

He returned to Moscow three years later. More fundamental than the ability to speak French fluently, he had an entirely new perspective on the world. Clearly the Soviet Union was an isolated concept. It survived only as some form of autocratic dictatorship of a small group of people. The West would clearly win eventually. Their economic concepts drove the world, not the state-controlled economies of the world's Communist states. Nikolai Krasin's graduate degree in international business from the Sorbonne gave him an understanding of Western market-based economics.

The Soviet Union would eventually fail economically. That was a given. As that happened, those that understood the West would be in the best position to profit. Two things would happen; first, the Soviet structure would dissolve, opening vast opportunities. Second, the vacuum would bring in Western investment.

Paris was therefore always a welcome stop. He felt himself partly Parisian. Malika Domokos also liked Paris. If you were part of the world stage, Moscow could only be considered a backwater.

Nikolai Krasin and Malika Domokos arrived at the classic French restaurant, La Grenouille on East 52nd Street in Manhattan. Krasin was dressed in a light gray Armani suit with a light blue shirt and gold tie. Domokos was dressed in a cream colored sheath, offset by her raven black hair, a black pearl necklace, and a mink stole.

"Nikolai, it's so good to see you," Martinelli said as Krasin and Domokos approached their table. He embraced Krasin in the European style.

"Ah, Malika. You look positively stunning." He kissed her offered hand. "May I introduce my wife, Anita."

Anita Martinelli, although older than Malika Domokos, was equal in elegance and a naturally classic beauty. She was the CEO of her father's non-profit foundation that funded the arts. From all perspectives she was the perfect partner for Steven Martinelli.

Krasin took Anita Martinelli's hand and gave it a brushing kiss. "It is a sincere pleasure to see you again, Anita. May I introduce Mademoiselle Malika Domokos."

"Such a pleasure to meet you Miss Domokos. I attended your performance of La Traviata some years ago at the Met. Your Violetta made it truly an evening to remember."

"Thank you Mrs. Martinelli," Domokos said in halting English. "I enjoyed New York City that time much. Pardon my bad English."

"*Parlez-vous Français*, Malika?"

"*Oui. Et vous?*"

"*Mais naturellement. Le Français de* Steven *n'est pas aussi bon.*"

"*Merveilleux!*"

"*M'appeler veuillez*, Anita."

Anita Martinelli engaged Domokos in French for the remainder of the evening. Steven Martinelli spoke French only haltingly, but he could see that Domokos was enjoying herself. Anita was every bit his equal at charming people.

The conversation was light and social throughout dinner. When the ladies excused themselves to go to the powder room, Martinelli took the opportunity to turn to business.

"I think it is important for you to address the Board directly on this venture, Nikolai. Since this is your creation and you're there in Moscow, it will make everyone more comfortable to get to know you."

"You're not expecting any difficulties are you?"

"No. I just want the investment community to feel comfortable. We'll start with our own Board. And I want full funding support from Manhattan Commercial. I expect them to be the lead source of financing for the project. Unfortunately, Manhattan's CEO might listen to that idiot nephew of his who he stuck on our Board."

"Is his nephew a problem?"

"Not necessarily. But since we do not like each other, he can be unpredictable."

"Perhaps I can pay particular interest in winning him over. What kind of man is he?"

"Arrogant. Only an average intellect. Investment banking background, although I suspect it was only in figurehead positions. He's not liked by the other Board members. Mostly postures and obstructs."

"What are his pleasures?" Krasin asked.

Martinelli grunted. "I believe alcohol and women. We know quite a lot about Mr. Ashcroft's sordid sexual escapades." Redek had extensive dossiers on all the Board members assembled by Durbin's investigative firm.

"Does that not ultimately give you leverage if he should become a problem?"

"Possibly. But however irrational he might be, his uncle at the Bank treats him with deference. Treats him more like a son which he never had. So the outcome is uncertain if we revealed his excesses. Not sure the uncle would even care. I prefer to keep the Bank as a firm ally and not introduce any distraction."

"Who are the others on the Board?"

"Two members represent a group of large institutional investors. Good guys. Smart. One's a banker, the other is a retired executive. Of course their loyalties are in a different direction. They tend to avoid any perks that might compromise their independence.

"As for the others, they will generally vote with me. Most are there because of me. They have a nice arrangement and enjoy the advantages that come with being on Martinelli Global's Board. The key here is that the Board knows very little beyond what is public information. Certainly none of our *real* secrets. If we don't report it to the SEC, then we don't tell the Board. That way we don't risk someone having an attack of conscience and feeling compelled to exercise their governance responsibilities."

"It is so much more complex here, Steven. It is a contest between you and the Government. In Russia it is much more a relationship of cooperation."

Martinelli smiled and took a sip of wine. "Cooperation if you know the right people and you make sure they are adequately *compensated*."

Nikolai Krasin smiled as well. "But of course. That is the nature of business in Russia. It has always been so. Just a cost of doing business. And in the end, we make good profits and all are happy."

"I agree my friend. You are an excellent partner. We are very pleased with our Russian holdings. That's why we want to increase our investments there. I trust we have support from the right people in the Government?"

"To be assured. The cost of that support is within the projected budget amount. I believe you would say it's a done deal," Krasin said.

"I see the ladies are returning. We can resume business tomorrow," Martinelli said.

Two days later Martinelli Global's Board of Directors convened a special meeting to discuss further investments in the former Soviet Union republics. Steven Martinelli opened the meeting with an introduction of Nikolai Krasin. Krasin had met only a few of the Directors when he first became associated with Martinelli Global eight years previously.

Krasin had sold controlling interest in his energy company, Far-North Oil & Gas to Martinelli Global. Far-North was a cobbled together company assembled from former state-owned assets at the collapse of the Soviet Union. It boasted impressive profits. It had long term lucrative contracts with the Russian government and other regional companies. Far-North had an array of subsidiaries involved in transportation, warehousing, equipment leasing, and maintenance.

The profitable contracts were secured through kickbacks and bribes funded through Krasin's private equity firm, Moscow Capital Partners. In a country ripe with such graft, Krasin was as successful as any of the other emerging business oligarchs. He was well connected within the government and careful to spread his largesse across all factions. Krasin avoided taking any political position of any faction.

Krasin teamed with Martinelli Global to take his businesses a quantum leap ahead of the pack. Martinelli Global gave him access to unlimited Western capital. It added international opportunities with a new level of credibility. Martinelli Global also had an appreciation for how business was done in Russia. They also let him run things with minimal interference.

Martinelli concluded his introduction of Krasin. "For some of you new to the Board, I would point out that under Nikolai Krasin's leadership our Russian holdings have quadrupled in revenue since we invested in Far-North Oil & Gas Company eight years ago. Profit margins have kept pace with this growth, and the return on our investments has substantially exceeded expectations.

"We are looking today to get Board approval on two bold new ventures in the region. The first is the acquisition of the Russian state-owned pipeline company Transneft. The second is a strategic expansion into the energy-rich Caspian Sea area. That expansion will provide new revenue opportunities for the former Transneft and open new opportunities that will create a synergy with many other operations under our control. With that introduction, I will let Nikolai Krasin expand on the details. Nikolai?"

"Thank you, Steven," Krasin said. He shook hands with Martinelli and took the podium. A staffer lowered the lights and switched on the digital projector. "This is a brief introduction to Transneft and how it plays a strategic role for Martinelli Global's holdings in the region."

The video was professionally produced with audio narration. There were aerial shots of pipelines crossing Siberia tundra and Russian steppe. There were refineries and storage facilities. Maps were interspersed and statistics displayed.

Once the video concluded, Krasin resumed his comments. "Conrad Redek's team prepared the hand-outs that are being given to each of you. Conrad, perhaps you might wish to discuss the financial details."

Conrad Redek joined Krasin at the podium and began walking the Directors through the financial work-ups.

One Director asked, "I assume there's the understanding that the Russian Government *wants* to sell Transneft?"

"Of course. You perhaps recall the reports that appeared a number of weeks ago in the financial media about the speculation of the sale," Krasin answered.

"But how can you be assured that the purchase price of $5.1 billion U.S. dollars is going to do the deal? Aren't there others interested?"

"There have been others. For various reasons no other company has made a concrete offer, or at least anything close to our offer," Krasin said.

"Our offer?" The same Director said. "You mean we've already entered into negotiations?"

"Of course we have," Conrad Redek said. "More than that, the deal has been concluded."

"Concluded?" Tyler Ashcroft said loudly. "You went ahead and did the deal without even consulting the Board? I assume you are assured that the funding will be no problem. I can tell you that Manhattan Commercial will have issues with this venture until we have thoroughly studied it."

"Well we are not going to be constrained by a goddamn. . ." Redek's comments were interrupted by Krasin.

"Mr. Ashcroft, let me explain. There was no intention of excluding the Board from this decision. But you must understand the situation is different in Russia. Most importantly, the persuading of the Government to sell a state-owned asset was necessary to even establish if the venture was possible. The valuation alone does not follow the normal considerations of an acquisition as they would here."

"I appreciate that the situation in Russia is different from here in the West. No personal offense, but I for one view Russia as an unpredictable corrupt environment. I can tell you that Manhattan Commercial is going to have a lot questions," Ashcroft said.

"Mr. Ashcroft, I would disagree with your characterization of my country. Granted it does not have the financial and government infrastructure that you have in the United States. But isn't that a fundamental business strategy of Martinelli Global? And as Steven has pointed out, our operations in Russia have grown with substantial profits. It is Hollywood that makes us out to be a land of cowboys as you say here in the United States."

Another director asked, "You mean the Russians are willing to sell a state-owned asset to a company with a majority U.S. ownership?'

Conrad Redek answered, "No. A new corporation. We have formed a new Russian corporation, TransEnergy. Far-North has only a modest stock position. The remaining stock is owned by a number of Russian shell corporations sufficient to satisfy the Russian government. Those shell corporations are owned by various Martinelli Global offshore corporations, each with a minor Russian partner. Those *partners* are all prominent business men necessary to access Government contracts and operating permits. Their participation made the deal possible. It made the deal acceptable to the Russian Government."

One director voiced the concern of several others. "No offense to Mr. Krasin, but is there something illegal in this?

"Not in either the U.S. or Russia," Redek answered for Krasin.

"That's because there are no real laws in Russia. That's my point. We become unreasonably exposed financially," Tyler Ashcroft barked. "Besides, this sounds like more fodder for continued media attacks in the Daily Press? Is this more of Nigeria? More of Columbian coffee?"

Martinelli stood up and slowly took the podium. Krasin stepped aside. "Let me first say that these series of unflattering articles in the Daily Press are at an end. The reporter and the financial editor responsible for these stories have been fired. The Publisher has given personal assurances that there will be no more of this witch hunt.

"Secondly, the strategic business model of Martinelli Global has always been to invest in higher risk, higher return environments. We have been successful in this for decades. We understand how to do business in foreign countries that may lack regulation, that may have less than stable governments. The key to that success is to partner with the right people in those countries and allow maximum autonomy from Corporate. Nikolai Krasin is the brilliant example of how effective this strategy has been. This Board should understand that. Our history of profitability and stock performance validates our strategies.

"Thirdly, we obey the laws of the United States. We also obey the laws of those countries where we do business. If those laws are lax, we take full advantage of the opportunities. We use tax haven foreign corporations extensively like every other major international firm. We use the best legal talent to ensure that these structures comply with all laws.

"And lastly, as Chairman, I am personally offended by Mr. Ashcroft's continued attacks. They are unproductive and disruptive. To my memory, Mr. Ashcroft has never contributed anything constructive to this Board. I question whether Mr. Ashcroft has ever contributed anything constructive to anything."

Ashcroft was stunned by Martinelli's attack and about to lash back when Martinelli continued. "You are here only at my sufferance. I've tolerated you because of your uncle and the close association between Martinelli Global and Manhattan Commercial. The time for you to leave this Board is probably at hand."

"Fuck you, Martinelli!" Ashcroft yelled. Getting up he knocked over his glass of water on his notes. "Fuck." He tried to blot the water up with his handkerchief to little effect. "You can consider that Manhattan Commercial will not be participating in your commie adventure."

Ashcroft stormed out of the boardroom.

"Gentlemen, my apologies," Martinelli said. "That has been brewing for a long time. It is sometimes necessary to clear the air. Speaking of which, let's take a thirty-minute break before we get back to business."

Martinelli, Krasin, and Redek adjourned to Martinelli's office and closed the door.

"Well gentlemen, that did not go well. It's not often I lose my temper like that. Never gave you a chance to charm him did I, Nikolai?" Martinelli said.

"I believe his mind was already made up." Krasin answered.

"Fuck the little prick. Better that he's gone," Redek said.

"Ashcroft's uncle is no fool. He won't necessarily dump lending to Martinelli Global just because of his nephew. But he will listen to him. Knows we don't like each other. Probably assumes he hears the most negative slant on things from his nephew. The Old Man will not like the subterfuge implications on the Russian Government though, or the bribery implications."

"They know that about other deals as well," Redek said. "They've always rubber stamped us as long as they don't know too many of the details. Plausible deniability. These guys are not virgins."

"It would be helpful if Ashcroft was discredited. Can we do anything like we did with that reporter?" Martinelli asked.

"Let me work on it, Steven," Redek said.

There was some further discussion about the Transneft deal when the meeting resumed. Besides Ashcroft, a couple of Directors appeared less than enthused about the acquisition, but offered no real opposition. Then Martinelli turned the discussion to the broader investment in the Caspian Sea.

"We want to leverage the Transneft acquisition and become perhaps the dominant player in the last significant undeveloped oil and gas region in the world, the Caspian Sea. I will let Nikolai explain."

"Unlike the sensitivity of the state-owned Transneft purchase, we propose to expand the reach of Caspian Enterprises. Caspian as you may recall is a Russian corporation wholly owned by Martinelli Global, principally through our Cayman Islands corporation, Eastern Industries. So for the Transneft purchase we could not do a purchase by either Far-North Oil & Gas, or Caspian Enterprises. But Eastern Industries already owns a Georgian corporation, Tbilisi Industries. We identify all these holdings in our public reporting. Unlike the Russians, the Georgians embrace U.S. investment so there is no need to hide it.

"A great number of countries have interest in the region. Not only those that border the Caspian Sea, but the European Union, the Balkan states, and of course the United States.

Kazakhstan and Turkmenistan want the oil and gas revenues. Georgia and Azerbaijan want to control pipelines through Turkey as an alternative to routing through Russia. Of course we have covered the Russian option with the Transneft acquisition. Now we want to control any other alternative routes as well.

"The Americans need to make friends with the Muslims in the region. Nobody wants to allow the Iranians any control. And everybody wants the oil and gas. Therefore, we propose a vast investment in the region. We have several smaller Martinelli Global controlled energy related companies already in place in the region besides Caspian Enterprises and Far-North Oil & Gas. These are in Ukraine, Belarus, and Azerbaijan. They give us a starting infrastructure in those countries. We are working to develop important contacts within Kazakhstan and Turkmenistan. Collectively, we can assemble a consortium of regionally based companies with strong nationalistic foundations that will win concessions from their various governments.

"With Martinelli Global funding through our subsidiary financial companies, we have the means to be the dominate force in developing Caspian Sea petroleum and natural gas resources."

Conrad Redek passed out the thick prospectus on the project. Phase one of the project required an investment commitment of $12 billion dollars.

The discussion went on for three hours. Surprisingly, the Board's reception was more favorable than the Transneft purchase. While complex in structure, it was seemingly more conventional without the implied illicit financial structure of the Transneft deal. Krasin and Redek had elaborately laid out the project in such a way as to hide the massive bribes and kickbacks that would lubricate the venture.

Redek and Krasin dined alone together that evening.

"Business is so much more difficult here, Conrad. Having to put up with the charade of this board meeting is a waste of time. So much simpler in Russia," Krasin said. He was sipping a scotch.

"I agree, Nikolai. But we all have our cultural difficulties. Do you have any suggestions about dealing with Ashcroft?"

"I suppose simply killing him is not an alternative?"

"That's a riskier proposition here. Might not achieve our objective if it were to backfire. Better to discredit him if we can. That will still allow for retaining relations with Manhattan Commercial."

"Is Manhattan Commercial that important?"

"Only that they've financed major Martinelli Global ventures for many years. If they severed the relationship that could cast doubt among other capital sources."

"I believe you know this Ashcroft's habits? Steven mentioned he drinks heavily and likes women."

"That's right. We know a lot about Ashcroft. He has an addiction to both, particularly women."

"Does he use prostitutes?"

"Yes. Call girls. The very exclusive kind. The ones that don't look like hookers. Takes them to the best restaurants and the theater. He keeps a small apartment uptown that his wife doesn't know about. Probably doesn't even care. She does her own thing. The threat of making his sexual escapades public probably doesn't have leverage value."

"I think I understand the situation, Conrad. Perhaps some people I know in Brighton Beach could assist in removing this Tyler Ashcroft as a problem."

Brighton Beach is on the southern tip of Brooklyn, a half mile from Coney Island. It is otherwise known as Little Odessa because of the large population of Russian émigrés. It is also the center of Russian organized crime in the United States.

Tyler Ashcroft got out of the taxi a little wobbly from all the alcohol he had consumed that evening. It was a warm evening. It was two o'clock in the morning. He took the hand of his companion. As she got out of the taxi, her skirt slid up to reveal she was not wearing underwear. The sight was not lost on Ashcroft, or the doorman. He exchanged grins with the doorman and tipped him a twenty.

The woman was drop-dead gorgeous. Tall, long blond hair, long legs, large breasts, face of a model. After they entered the building, the doorman shook his head. To himself he wondered why a woman who looked like that would have to be a prostitute and screw the likes of old guys like Ashcroft.

Two hours later a homeless man urinated on the building only a hundred feet from the front door, in plain sight of the doorman.

"What the fuck? Get the hell out of here!" the doorman yelled then chased the man a short way down the street. Behind him, two large men slipped through the front door unseen. They took the stairs to the eighth floor.

One man put his ear to the door of apartment 812. Hearing nothing, he knocked softly.

The blond woman opened the door. She touched her finger to her lips. She was wearing only a robe. "Let's get this done," she said.

One of the men pulled a digital camera from his jacket pocket.

Tyler Ashcroft was sprawled face-down on the bed. He was naked. There were semen stains on the bedspread. The woman took off her robe. Both men stared at her breasts. She gave them a threatening look.

In Russian she said, "So help me turn him over. You have to get his face and cock in the picture. Wife needs to recognize him. Keep my face out of the picture. And be careful not to wake him."

Ashcroft would not easily be awakened. After the alcohol at dinner, the sex, then more alcohol, he was passed-out.

The two men positioned Ashcroft. The woman turned on her side and positioned Ashcroft's hand between her legs. Her breast spilled over his shoulder. She positioned her head next to his.

Both men were transfixed by her magnificent body.

"Well what the fuck are you waiting for? Take the fucking pictures!" the woman said in a muted voice.

The man with the camera moved to the right to frame the photograph. The second man moved to the left out of the way. The camera clicked several times.

From the left of the room, the second man approached the bed. He crushed the woman's skull with a heavy Waterford whiskey decanter. Whiskey spilled onto the woman's body and the bed. Ashcroft continued to snore.

The man with the camera just shook his head. Wearing latex gloves, the killer laid the decanter on the floor, and then touched the woman's neck to feel for a pulse. He nodded slightly to his colleague.

The two men left down the stairs. They exited the rear of the building unseen through a back one-way service door.

CHAPTER 20

Manhattan, New York

Associated Press – New York:

In a telephone interview earlier this week, the Columbian Consul General in New York confirmed a report that former New York Daily Press investigative reporter, Mark Reynolds, 43, was being sought on charges of murder. Consul General Javier Rivas Delgado stated that the Columbian Ministry of Justice is seeking Reynolds' extradition to Columbia to stand trail for the murder of fellow journalist Juan Cortina several months ago. Rivas stated that formal legal steps have been initiated with the U.S. Department of Justice.

Reynolds is an acclaimed investigative reporter and author of two books on international subjects. Reynolds had been on the staff of the New York Daily Press for eight years, resigning only recently.

Reynolds was reportedly in Columbia researching material for a series of featured articles in the Daily Press. A number of articles were published in June alleging that the Columbia coffee industry was a monopoly controlled by the large multi-national corporation, Martinelli Global. The article further alleged that Martinelli Global had partnered with various Columbian nationals tied to drug trafficking.

Reading from a prepared statement, the Columbian Consul General stated that Cortina and Reynolds were working together on researching material for a story about the Columbian coffee industry. According to a source at Cortina's newspaper, there was a dispute between Cortina and Reynolds regarding where the investigations were leading. That dispute allegedly became violent after much drinking, resulting in the death of Cortina. The cause of death was reported as blunt force trauma from a blow to the head with a liquor bottle. Reynolds left Columbia before authorities linked him to Cortina's death.

The U.S. District Attorney's office for the Southern District of New York would only confirm that the Republic of Columbia had filed a petition for the extradition of Reynolds. They declined to comment on any details included in the petition.

Reynolds left his position with the New York Daily Press only weeks ago. The reason for his abrupt departure is unknown. It is also not known if there is a connection to the equally sudden departure of the Daily Press's financial editor, Bernard Poole. Poole was a respected media professional in the financial markets. The managing editor of the Daily Press declined any comments as a matter of policy regarding personnel related matters. Neither Reynolds nor Poole could be reached for comment.

And there wouln't be any comment now or at any other time Reynolds said to himself. As a reporter he knew there was nothing to be gained by speaking to reporters. After reading the article on page four of that morning's Daily Press at a coffee shop, Reynolds returned to his apartment. He let the phone ring and the messages pile up. He deleted most and noted calls from a couple of friends. He returned the call from Rachel Stern.

"Hey, how are you?" Reynolds asked.

"Oh my God, Mark. I read the AP piece. Does that mean they're really going to pursue this extradition thing in U.S. Federal court?"

"Might appear so."

"Are you worried?"

"Some I guess."

"But they have no evidence. How can they convince a federal judge?"

"I don't know. Make it up probably. Trumped-up witness affidavits. I just don't know. What worries me is the possibility of some other hand working things behind the scenes. Like Martinelli Global. They have real clout. Remember Thorne's information about pressure from Washington to not pursue the information I gave the FBI. Maybe they can push this extradition thing. I don't know."

"You should find a lawyer just in case, Mark."

"I guess," Reynolds responded with resignation. Things were really coming apart.

"What are you doing the rest of the day?" Stern asked.

"Working. Picking up e-mails and phone messages. Plus trying to figure out what I'm going to do about a job."

"Anything promising the last few days?"

"Too early to tell. Everybody has been sympathetic. Told them I left because of editorial disagreements. That's certainly the truth. There're a couple of possibilities that might develop into something."

"Can I come over tonight?" Stern asked.

Reynolds could sense the thinly veiled anticipation in her voice. He wasn't really in the mood, but he felt obligated.

"Sure. We'll go out somewhere."

"Wonderful. See you at six, Mark."

Shit. He shouldn't be taking this affair with Stern any further. It was too tough to get out of it though. Didn't want to get out of it all together. Certainly didn't want to hurt her. He genuinely liked her, but it wasn't going to lead to something permanent. She hoped otherwise. He felt guilty. He would share her company and her body again tonight. They were seeing each other about twice a week.

The last couple of days of his job search networking had been discouraging. The possibilities were limited. A couple of major newspaper editors had expressed guarded interest. Washington D.C., and Chicago. He didn't like either city.

Beyond that was the headache of settling into a new work environment with a new set of organizational bullshit. He wasn't yet over the blow-up with Fredericks. Three weeks of goofing off and boozing hadn't tempered his anger.

Still more depressing was the accelerating decline of the newspaper business as more people turned to the Internet for news. Even the major papers were down-sizing their news staff. Print journalists were an endangered species. He should perhaps think of a different career path.

Reynolds answered his telephone. "Mark, this is Francis."

"Francis, how are you?"

Francis Kline was his literary agent. She was a great help in both the editing and selling of his two previous books. Thirty-five years in the business. She was blunt speaking, smoked, drank whiskey, and had little time for small talk.

"I'm fine. How are you fairing? Did you quit or get fired?"

"Quit. Journalistic integrity. The editor refused to go forward with my story about Martinelli Global's misdeeds."

"You mean you got pissed off and walked out."

"Something like that."

"I read your pieces on Martinelli Global. Are those people as bad as you make them out to be?"

"Probably worse. For a publicly traded company, Martinelli Global is damn good at hiding what they do. They're at least connected to major money laundering from Columbian drug trafficking. That's what the final argument was about that lead to me leaving the Daily Press."

"And what's this about a murder in Columbia? Are they seriously trying to extradite you?"

"Maybe. The thing is trumped up. The guy I was supposed to have murdered was a journalist. We became friends actually. He and I were working together on the same story. We were both arrested together. I escaped, he didn't. The bad guys killed him, not me. Frankly, I think Martinelli Global is behind this. Just like in Nigeria. They certainly have the political juice in Columbia."

"So what're you going to do?"

"About the charges?"

"No. You'll get a good lawyer. Americans are not extradited to banana republics. What I mean is what are you going to do about working?"

"Don't know yet. Still looking for options."

"What about doing a book? You've painted Martinelli Global as a real monster. Do you have enough material for a book?"

"No. It needs to go further for a book. I need to get deeper inside what they do."

"But you've got plenty for a book proposal. This is timely stuff, Mark. With all the corporate wrongdoing over the last several years, Martinelli Global fits perfectly. Enron, the Italian giant Parmalot, the sub-prime mortgage debacle, now Martinelli Global. This stuff about big corporations using offshore subsidiaries to avoid taxes also hits the hot button of globalization."

Reynolds considered the idea for a few moments. If he hadn't been so blindly angry, it would have been obvious. It could be a way to continue pursuing the Martinelli Global story as freelance. Martinelli Global was more than a story now. They had made it personal. Chances were that another newspaper would not have any great interest in pursuing the story. It's too technical. Not enough blood and sex. Martinelli Global was really the subject of a book rather than a newspaper series. That's where it was always leading.

"Interesting thought, Fran. Think you could negotiate a respectable advance?"

"Possibly. Write me a topnotch proposal and I'll sell it. We did pretty well with your *Nuclear Threats for Our Time*. That was only three years ago. You're still credible. You've got the right credentials."

Instead of drinking scotch that afternoon, Reynolds set to work on this new project.

He was in an exhilarated mood by the time Rachel Stern arrived at his apartment. She was delighted when he kissed her passionately then made love to her in the living room. Over dinner, he explained the book project.

She was enthused. It was a perfect idea. He now had real work he could sink his teeth into. It had already lifted him out of his depression. More than that, she could continue to do research for him. The perfect way to stay connected.

Stern certainly liked the benefits. Reynolds made love to her again that night after they returned to his apartment from dinner.

Two weeks later, Reynolds had completed a draft of his book proposal. *Shell Game* was to be an expose about Martinelli Global. In a wider sense, Martinelli Global would illustrate the ugly extremes of the unchecked financial power of large multinationals. It was good material. Martinelli Global was the perfect villain. He had a list of various experts willing to assist with explaining the complexities of international business.

It would read like a novel. The history of Martinelli Global starting in the early twentieth century as an immigrant success story was now into its third generation of the Martinelli family. The alleged criminal associations during the early years followed by liquor smuggling during Prohibition would make an interesting historical backdrop. This would be followed by showing the shadowy involvement of Martinelli Global in the post World War II decades in troubled places in South America and the Middle East.

That history would lay the foundation for exposing the present day multi-national Martinelli Global. He would show how Martinelli Global became an early pioneer in the use of elaborately structured tax haven foreign subsidiary companies. How those structures were used for criminal purposes. His personal experiences in Nigeria and Columbia would add the color of a genuine adventure story.

Francis Kline, was enthused as well. She had a few suggestions. "Have you run some of these more complex financial maneuvers you've tried to explain in layman language by any financial experts? No offense, but that's not necessarily your area of expertise. Any editor will vet this with their own experts so you want to be spot on."

"I have. My interpretations will stand up, Fran."

"The other thing, I'd like to see you do more to show that these very same business practices used by Martinelli Global, are common among big corporations. Paint the whole spectrum using examples from legitimate business practices, to greed, all the way to criminal. After all, your premise is that Martinelli Global abuses these practices because they operate in unregulated and corrupt countries. Aren't you making the case that other corporations could do the same, but simply choose not to commit excesses quite like Martinelli Global?"

"Well, my guess is that to varying degrees, many multinationals commit some of the same abuses as Martinelli

Global. However, most have not embraced such a comprehensive business model of corruption like Martinelli Global. But you're right, the book is meant to convey that premise as well. I'll work on bolstering that theme."

CHAPTER 21

MANHATTAN, NEW YORK

R eynolds had just completed a revised draft of the book proposal. He was concluding his final edits when he received an e-mail addressed to his old Daily Press address. Ever since he resigned, he had continued to access his e-mail account at the Newspaper through the Internet. It had never been removed, probably just an oversight.

The e-mail was from someone calling themself Rasputin. Odd that the spam filter software had not quarantined the e-mail. The subject however drew his attention: *Martinelli Global Articles.*

"I read your stories about Martinelli Global with much attention. They are very good writing. Martinelli Global is like a cancer. They need to be destroyed. Why have you stopped writing stories about Martinelli Global?"

Reynolds responded to Rasputin, "I agree with you – Martinelli Global is a disease. It was the Newspaper that stopped the series on Martinelli Global. I am no longer employed by the New York Daily Press. Thanks for the support."

Minutes later, Rasputin responded, "That is terrible news that you are no longer reporting on Martinelli Global. There is much new information I can provide. Martinelli Global has many businesses in Russia. Many are not known by public. They are involved in all types of corruption in Russia. Much bigger corruption than places you wrote about. They have powerful partners in Russia. It is bigger story. Perhaps you will find another newspaper? Perhaps you will go after Martinelli Global again?"

Reynolds replied, "What kind of information do you have? Are you Russian? I am still researching Martinelli Global."

If this was some kind of Martinelli Global ploy, let the fuckers know that he hadn't gone away.

After thirty minutes waiting without a reply, Reynolds went back to work on finishing the book proposal.

The following day, Reynolds opened his Daily Press e-mail account again. There was a new message from Rasputin. "I have very confidential information on many things about Martinelli Global business in Russia. Things they would not want known. Things that could damage them in Russia, maybe damage them also in America. Why are you still interested in Martinelli Global if you are not writing for the New York Daily Press?"

"How do I know you are not working for Martinelli Global – trying to trap me? They tried to kill me twice. Maybe you are a trap."

Rasputin answered, "I have my own reasons for hating Martinelli Global. Actually it is their Russian partners I hate. I suffered personal loss because of these people. If Martinelli Global is destroyed, their Russian partners will also be destroyed. You will have to trust me, Mr. Reynolds. You should trust me because we have same enemy."

Reynolds considered his response with mixed concerns. Ultimately, his reporter instincts won out. "Very well. I am still pursuing Martinelli Global because I intend writing a book about them. I have written two other books so I expect that someone will publish this one. If the book has enough facts, the pressure could bring down Martinelli Global. Is your information that damaging? How did you come by this information?"

"I shall also trust you Mr. Reynolds. Yes, the information is very damaging. Here in Russia, that kind of information can get you killed. No newspaper in Russia would print the information I have. Reporters have been murdered for much less. Publishers would be threatened. The only way this information can be made known is outside Russia. I got this information from computer databases. Databases thought to be very secure. You see Mr. Reynolds, I am what you call a hacker. Actually I am very accomplished hacker. Perhaps one of the best. My information is more damaging than anything you published about Martinelli Global in your newspaper."

Sonofabitch. If this was not a Martinelli Global trap, it could be the mother lode. Reynolds answered, "Ok. You have my attention. Can you tell me what Martinelli Global is doing in Russia that is so terrible?"

"Corruption, bribery, monopolies. Partners with organized crime. Money laundering. Government contracts through bribes. Purchasing state-owned assets with special deals. Russian companies that are partly owned and financed by Martinelli Global are very big players in all parts of Russian energy industry. They even process nuclear materials. Run everything with big profits. They have more power than you can imagine. People have been killed that have tried to go against them."

"Nuclear materials? What exactly do they do?" Reynolds replied.

"Something to do with reprocessing spent fuel from nuclear reactors. They are also involved with what is called weapons grade nuclear materials with the military. I know little about this technology."

Reynolds interest was aroused with the mention of nuclear materials. He knew a great deal about the subject. His book, *Nuclear Threats for Our Time*, was devoted in part to the legacy of the Soviet era. It dealt with their antiquated design nuclear power plants, epitomized by the devastating failure of reactor #4 at Chernobyl in the 1980s. Then there was the enormous inventory of nuclear warheads. Both of these civilian and military applications were supported by a vast industry engaged in processing and reprocessing nuclear fuels. For Martinelli Global to be involved in such a sensitive area was alarming.

"Is Martinelli Global doing anything illegal with respect to nuclear materials?"

"I do not know. It would take much more of my study, but I am also no expert. Martinelli Global involvement in Russian nuclear industry is not known by public. I have accessed internal e-mail communications of Russian subsidiary companies that shows they want to hide Martinelli Global investment."

Reynolds e-mailed, "So what do we do next, my friend? I assume Rasputin is not your real name? Are you Russian? Do you live in Russia?"

"Rasputin is my handle as you say in English. I prefer not to use my real name for obvious reasons. Yes, I am Russian. For anybody hacking into our e-mails they could identify you, but not me. My IP address is obscured by a false proxy each time I send a message. As to what to do next, I will first tell you that I have researched you extensively. You are good writer. As a reporter you are what is called a hard case. Never give up on the story. Believe you must piss people off but are much respected. Therefore I shall trust you and be your partner. Problem is how to share the information I pulled from these databases. Most is in Russian. Do you have someone you highly trust that can translate?"

Reynolds did not. He could obviously find someone, but at what level of trust? He answered Rasputin, "I see what you mean. No I do not have anyone I know who is fluent in Russian. I will need a few days to consider who I could use. I will be in touch soon. And thank you. If your information is what you say it is we may be able to bring down Martinelli Global and their Russian partners."

The following morning, Reynolds had another e-mail from Rasputin. "My friend, I may have solution to the language problem. I know a Russian journalist. Much like you. Has written articles critical of Russian business and government corruption. The person was good friends with Anna Polikovskaya. Polikovskaya was the famous journalist murdered in 2006 because she angered the Government with her writings about Chechnya. This journalist is much the same as Anna. I have given this journalist some of the same materials about these Martinelli Global subsidiaries in Russia. She could not use for publication because of government censorship and fear of reprisal. There is much information of corruption with high level Russian Government officials. Polikovskaya's murder made my friend very cautious. I can ask if this friend would be willing to collaborate on our project. Advise if I should pursue."

Reynolds replied immediately, "Of course. I would welcome the collaboration. Without the help of colleagues in Columbia and Nigeria, I could not have assembled the story on Martinelli Global so far. I should also warn you and your friend, both these people were murdered. I want no one else to die for this story. Let me know what your friend says."

Rasputin replied, "Can you come to Russia? Soon?"

Reynolds hadn't considered that but it was the only obvious course. Not only to facilitate the translation of Rasputin's material, but to ask questions and see things first hand. He could not write this chapter on Martinelli Global from a distance. He was still wary of this newfound source however.

"Of course I can come to Russia. But it is also time to establish trust. If I am to come to Russia, I cannot do so blindly. Your journalist friend must identify himself. I must know who I am dealing with. He must trust that I will tell no one of his identity. As soon as I hear from him, I can be there in a couple of days," Reynolds replied.

"I understand. I take no offense. We all must be cautious. I will discuss with my friend. If agreed, my friend will contact you."

Three days passed without further e-mails from Rasputin, or his journalist friend. At three o'clock in the morning on the third night, Reynolds telephone rang. Half awake, he answered, "Yes?"

"Is this Mark Reynolds?" the caller asked. It was a woman. The accent sounded East European but the English was good.

"Yes it is. Who is calling?"

"My name is not important. I am calling for a friend of Rasputin's. I was told to arrange for you to speak to this person. You will need to write this telephone number. You will call this number in two hours time from a public telephone. Do not use this telephone or your mobile telephone. Are you prepared to write this number?"

"Wait a minute. Why can't we communicate by e-mail? And why can't we talk right now?"

"It is a matter of security. E-mails are not secure. Your telephone may not be secure."

"Rasputin used the e-mail to contact me."

"And Rasputin's identity cannot be traced. He is very good computer specialist. He never used his friend's name. Security must be maintained. Can you call in two hours?"

"Christ it's three in the morning. But yes, I can call. Give me the telephone number." Reynolds said sharply. He scribbled the long number with its international calling codes on a scratch pad having the woman repeat it twice because of her accent.

Reynolds turned on the coffee pot then dressed. The caller had jarred him with these seemingly over-reacting precautions. Is it possible that Martinelli Global might actually be monitoring his communications? Absurd was his first reaction. Was it? They had tried to kill him. They were after him on this trumped-up charge of murder in Columbia. Did they have that kind of reach? Was he important enough? The answer was probably yes to both questions.

He called for a taxi. Twenty minutes later he was at an all-night diner he knew of. There were a few patrons, a couple of NYPD officers and a couple of off-duty hookers. He ordered breakfast to kill the remaining time before making the call from the public telephone on the wall.

The same female voice answered on the third ring. "Hello?"

"This is Mark Reynolds. Are you the person that called me a couple of hours ago?"

"Yes. Are you calling from a public telephone?"

"Yes."

"Very good, Mr. Reynolds. It would appear that we both have an interest in Martinelli Global. Both of us have been doing work in different parts of the world. Our mutual friend Rasputin believes we can work together for a big story."

"We? Are you the journalist?"

"Yes. My name is Katerina Nikolaevna Avramenko. I work for the Московский Журнал Весточки. In English that is the Moscow News Journal. You can verify. Rasputin is a special source for confidential information. He is what is called a computer hacker. I cannot use much of this material here in Russia. Too many powerful people involved. I need someone like you to publish outside Russia. Are you interested?"

Reynolds paused for moment. "Yes. I'm interested. What do you suggest?"

"You must come to Russia. I can translate and we can understand how these companies do illegal business here."

"Why do you find it necessary to use public telephones?"

"I am fairly sure that my calls are monitored. I do not know about your calls so I am cautious."

"Who would be tapping your calls?"

"Tapping?" Avramenko asked.

"Listening into your telephone conversations."

"Criminals, police, politicians. I have made many enemies. They have powerful resources to do these things. I had a friend that was also a journalist. She was murdered. There have been others. This is Russia, Mr. Reynolds."

"Ok. I will come to Moscow. How do I contact you? Do you trust e-mail?"

"No! Mr. Reynolds, if Rasputin can get into secured computer networks, e-mails cannot be safe. Rasputin has never used my name has he?"

"No, he was careful to avoid identifying you."

"Good. Call me two days from now at the same time. Use public phone. Call the following number," Avramenko said giving him a different number. "Advise your flight number and the day you shall arrive. I will take care of hotel arrangement. Is that satisfactory?"

"That's fine. How will I recognize you?"

"I am sure you will check me out. Google the Moscow News Journal. There will be a photograph of me in the staff section of the website."

"I will call you in two days then," Reynolds said and disconnected.

Reynolds was anxious to check out this Katerina Nikolaevna Avramenko. But once back at his apartment, he hesitated to go on-line to check the Moscow News Journal website. If someone were monitoring his e-mail, then they would logically be monitoring his Internet activity. It was probably paranoia on his part, but better to take the extra precaution.

He showered and left his building to find an Internet coffee shop. He had some research to do, and airline tickets to purchase.

"How'd you get this stuff? And who the fuck is this Rasputin?" Conrad Redek said to Bill Durbin, the head of Martinelli Global's security subsidiary. Durbin had brought his report personally to Redek's office.

"A Russian hacker. Has a bit of a reputation in the hacking world. A self-styled do-gooder. Disrupts things for political reasons. Left-leaning. Environmental causes, anti-globalization, that sort of thing. The Russians and some European governments would like to get their hands on him."

"Is he good enough to have hacked into our Russian systems?"

"Can't say specifically. From the hacker chat rooms he has a certain level of respect. In that world, that comes only from exploits. We should assume he may have accessed our Russian subsidiary systems," Durbin said.

"What about our systems here?"

"Doesn't appear so."

"What does that mean? Would we know?"

"Yes, we would know, at least once we've completed a thorough investigation. Even the most elegant hacking intrusion will leave some sort of electronic tracks. I've got two of my best people working with your IT Department."

"Does Krasin know that confidential data may have been compromised?"

"I doubt it. I haven't informed him of this Rasputin's claims. I assumed I should leave that to you. If you want, we can work with his Russian IT staff to investigate. My people are better suited to this type of work than normal computer professionals. After all, what we do is the same thing that this Rasputin does."

"Any idea who this journalist might be?"

"Not yet. I've got someone working on trying to identify a list of journalists that might be candidates. Looking at reporters that might be considered anti-government, anti-corruption.

Crusaders against organized crime. And of course friends and acquaintances of Anna Polikovskaya."

"Are you having Reynolds watched?"

"After we monitored these e-mails from this Russian, I put a team on physical surveillance. We've had his phone tapped for some time, including his cell phone."

"He got a call from a woman. Didn't identify herself. Warned Reynolds against using his phones. Had him go to a pay phone. Took a while to trace the number he was to call. Turned out to be a public telephone in Moscow. If he goes to Russia, how do you wish to handle it?"

"Oh, I hope Reynolds does go to Russia. That will open up new options for dealing with him. I'm going to telephone Nikolai Krasin as soon as it's morning in Moscow. He needs to know about this computer security problem. I'll get you a contact name over there so you can coordinate efforts to plug this hole. This is top priority, Durbin."

CHAPTER 22

MOSCOW, RUSSIAN FEDERATION – 1993

B y the early 1990s, the former Soviet Union was coming apart as a governmental entity. They simply gave up the arms race as too costly. The Soviet totalitarian system was bankrupt both financially as well as a social experiment. The very fabric of its socio-economic structure was undergoing one of the most radical changes in history. The Gorbachev years of modest transition in the 1980s notwithstanding, the former superpower was morphing into something radically different in a short span of time. The last gasp was the failed military coup in 1991, thwarted with Boris Yeltsin's famous confrontation atop a tank.

From a Western business analogy, the entire economic structure was undergoing restructuring. A less charitable view was decomposition. The most volatile element of that process was the privatization of formerly owned state enterprises. That privatization was a collective liquidation of assets at a fraction of their real value. Sales were secured through massive bribes to government officials authorizing the sales without any defined structure. Those in the private sector with capital and connections, and their partners within the Government, divided former state-owned assets valued in the tens of billions of dollars for a fraction of that invested amount.

By the mid-1980s, Nikolai Krasin was a senior officer at the Bank of Moscow. He was Western educated at the Sorbonne in Paris, a perk of being the son of a ranking Party official. He understood Western financial mechanics. He understood opportunities offered by capital investment in market driven economies. More importantly, he understood the limitless opportunities offered by the early stages of the disintegration of the Soviet Union.

Rigorous Soviet state control over all economic institutions was abruptly stripped away even before the final collapse of the Soviet Union in 1992. No effective market-based regulatory controls were created in their place. What little regulation did evolve was rendered ineffective through corruption. The post-Soviet judicial system had no investigative teeth, nor were there even laws to cope with complex financial crimes.

Krasin was ideally equipped to this period of unprecedented opportunity with his broad expertise. He knew the West and he knew Russia. He was well connected politically, intelligent, and without ethical inhibitions. Beyond that, Nikolai Krasin was Russian street-smart tough.

There was a rising tide of organized criminal activity resurgence with the collapse of the Soviet state. Enormous sums of money were involved. Krasin understood that this flow of money needed banks as a conduit. He was not the only Russian banker to understand this, but he was the most successful.

Russians historically were wary of commercial banking during the Soviet era. Arranging loans with state-owned banks was difficult. Even if successful, the process took so long that the opportunity afforded by the capital had long passed. Checking accounts were unheard of. The fear that some future government action might jeopardize their investment made attracting both domestic and foreign legitimate investors a difficult sell. As a result, capital from criminal enterprises was to varying degrees an important revenue source for Russian banking. Krasin had his share of illicit investor clients.

Krasin left the Bank of Moscow in 1989 to found his own bank, NVK Commercial Bank. His initial capitalization was a modest 3 billion rubles. Within a year, that had grown to 30 billion rubles. Krasin had successfully taken many former Moscow Bank clients over to his new bank. He offered high-return opportunities for investment and did not question the origin of the invested funds.

"This is the deal Pavel Yevgenivich; NVK Commercial Bank will secure the 54 billion rubles necessary to fund the purchase. Moscow Capital Partners will invest 5 billion of its own funds and receive an additional 20% of the initial offering shares for underwriting," Nikolai Krasin said.

He was seated at the head of a large conference table at NVK Commercial Bank. They were on the eighth floor with a commanding view of the Kremlin. There were a dozen other men seated at the table.

Pavel Yevgenivich Mikoyan was in his mid-thirties, the same age roughly as Krasin. Like Krasin, he wore a well-tailored dark gray suit. Several of the others at the table were not as well dressed.

"With no disrespect, Nikolai Mikhailovich, that seems like a deal intended to enrich everyone except my investment group. Besides making excess profits for itself, why is Moscow Capital Partners necessary to the deal?"

Moscow Capital Partners was a venture capital group headed by Krasin himself. Moscow Capital Partners was the brainchild of Krasin. Numbered among his other associates within the investment group were an impressive list of senior government and military officials. For a token investment, with funds typically loaned by Krasin's bank, these officials received returns as multiples of their investment. Official bribery was cloaked as good investments by officials embracing newfound capitalism. For that bribery, all manner of things became possible; no-bid contracts awarded, purchase approval of state-owned assets facilitated, sealed bids revealed prior to closing, licenses approved preferentially, red-tape expedited, regulations ignored.

"That is simple, Pavel Yevgenivich," Krasin answered. "Moscow Capital is essential to architecting this deal. In short, without Moscow Capital, the deal will not be approved by the necessary people within the Government." He cast a glance at two older men sitting at the end of the table.

"I would suggest that you consider instead the enormous gains you will make by acquiring these two shipyards. Consider that not only are you acquiring the assets at a fraction of their real value, but also the assurance of continued lucrative government contracts."

Krasin knew that Mikoyan was shocked by the cut Moscow Capital was demanding to architect the deal. But that was Mikoyan's problem. Much as Mikoyan may not like the split, the deal would still make him a fortune.

"I am not as polite as my partner. You and your bank are thieves. This deal is shit. You're just a fucking thief," said the husky man sitting next to Mikoyan. He stuck out from the other better dressed men at the table. His cheap suit was ill-fitting. His shirt was rumpled, his tie too short over his large belly. Mikoyan had introduced him as his investment partner.

Krasin knew all about Grigory Lakovlev Seleznyov. He was a gangster, his money came from smuggling and drugs. Seleznyov was a fourth generation criminal, trying to adapt to new opportunities but still clinging to old ways.

Krasin was unruffled by Seleznyov. "Well, if I'm a thief, then you should feel comfortable doing business with me, Grigory Iakovlev. You yourself are one of the biggest thieves in Russia."

Seleznyov glared back at Krasin. He was clearly not used to being confronted in this manner, much less by a banker.

Krasin continued, "Look at it this way. You'll be able to launder your money while gaining a handsome return on that money rather than suffering a discount trying to launder it through other channels."

Seleznyov looked around the table uncomfortable with Krasin's crude framing of his profession.

"No need to worry. No one here is a virgin, Grigory Iakovlev. We all intend to make money from this project. Each must do it differently. Each has a role to play in facilitating deals such as these."

Turning to Mikoyan, Krasin said, "May I suggest we adjourn for lunch. In the adjacent room, we have set out an excellent selection of food and drink. After lunch, perhaps you and Grigory Iakovlev would like to discuss our proposal privately."

Both Mikoyan and Seleznyov nodded. Everyone moved to the lavishly catered spread in another office. Main entrees of fresh seafood and prime rib were flanked by Beluga caviar, French cheeses and foie gras. There were vintage first-growth Bordeaux wines and hundred year-old Cognac, along with vodkas for the more provincial taste.

The luncheon was not only for Mikoyan and Seleznyov, but for the several government officials present at the meeting. They were already on board for the deal, but Krasin's lavish entertaining was part of their expected perks.

Mikoyan stayed in the hallway making cell phone calls. Seleznyov availed himself of the food, gorging himself but avoiding any conversation with others. No one seemed eager to talk to him anyway.

After lunch they reconvened, except for Seleznyov.

"Your associate Mr. Seleznyov will not be joining us?" Krasin said to Mikoyan.

"No. However, I spoke with him before he left. I also spoke with my other partners. We agree in principle to your terms, Nikolai Mikhailovich."

The deal was concluded four months later. Two months after that, there was an attempt on Nikolai Krasin's life. It was a clumsy attempt. Two gunmen with assault rifles fired on Krasin's car as he drove out the gate of his walled dacha. The Mercedes was armored. Krasin's driver was trained in evasive driving techniques.

Two weeks later, Grigory Seleznyov and two bodyguards were gunned down in front of his house before he could enter his car.

Soon after the death of Seleznyov, Mikoyan's group of investors was persuaded to sell Seleznyov's shares to Moscow Capital Partners. The shares gave Krasin control over Great Northern Shipbuilding.

Nikolai Krasin was seated at his usual table on the second floor of the Café Pushkin. The restaurant was in the very center of Moscow on Tverskaya Street. Krasin liked the second floor "Library Room" with its décor of telescopes, globes, and old books. The style was intended to be Russian nineteenth century with high ceilings and rich wood paneling. Apart from well prepared Russian cuisine, the Pushkin had an excellent wine list.

The restaurant was a favorite of upscale business people. As usual, it was full of well-dressed mostly younger business types. Krasin's table was at the rear of the room in front of a window. It was a gray Moscow day outside.

Krasin's luncheon guest strolled through the restaurant in tow by a waiter in period dress. Krasin recognized the man from a photo. He noted the slightly out of place appearance of the man with his leather coat and longish hair style.

Feliks Alekseev Garnitsky looked every bit the Russian criminal he actually was. Krasin had requested the meeting with

Garnitsky through another investment partner in Moscow Capital Partners.

Krasin stood up and shook hands. "Borya Lazutkin speaks highly of you, Feliks Alekseev. It is good to meet you."

"My pleasure, Nikolai Mikhailovich. Borya has been able to invest substantial funds for me with your Moscow Capital."

Krasin was well aware of the illegal sources of Garnitsky's money. Moscow Capital had provided a convenient avenue to launder funds gained through a range of his smuggling enterprises.

"Very good. We also see your investments as an important source of capital. Some wine?"

Garnitsky nodded his approval. Krasin poured him a glass of a good Petrus Bordeaux vintage. "I wished to meet you and extend my compliments for your assistance with resolving that disagreeable business with Seleznyov."

It had been Garnitsky's muscle that assassinated Seleznyov. Mikoyan paid by losing a finger to Garnitsky's thugs. He was thereby *persuading* to relinquish control in the shipbuilding venture to Moscow Capital Partners by selling Seleznyov's shares to them at well below market price.

"Glad to be of help."

"Is the wine to your liking? They prepare an excellent Boeuf Bourgogne here. Made to go with Burgundy, but I still prefer Bordeaux."

"Sounds fine with me," Garnitsky said. He had no idea what the French dish was. As to the expensive Bordeaux, he would prefer vodka or beer.

They talked about business only in general terms while they ate lunch.

"That was very good," Garnitsky said. He expected that Krasin would finally get to why he really called this meeting.

Krasin ordered coffees and Cognac.

"Let me be frank with you, Feliks Alekseev. I am here to suggest a merger. I believe that a joining of our respective enterprises would greatly profit both of us."

"You flatter me, Nikolai Mikhailovich. My enterprises as you call them are really trucking companies and warehouses. I make my money by investing in all sorts of commodities, then selling them for profits in better markets using my trucks."

Krasin smiled. "You are too modest. I am well aware of the origin of your funds. You are one of the most successful smugglers of petroleum in Russia. My sources also tell me you are well connected in arms dealing and drugs."

Garnitsky was quiet for a few moments. "You are well informed, Nikolai Mikhailovich. Other than investing money into your Moscow Capital Partners, how would my business interest someone such as yourself?"

"I am seeking to expand investments into the energy sector. You are already in that business. I believe that you also have strong connections in the Caucus region. That would prove beneficial for investments we are considering there."

"This would seem an odd alliance. Your business is high finance, big deals with the Government, foreign investors. Mine is more . . ."

"Criminal? That is just a label your enemies use. Both of us are successful because we see opportunities and apply resources to make profits. I break as many laws as you do. You are successful because you are intelligent and very good at organization. I have need of such skills."

"That's a compliment indeed coming from Nikolai Krasin."

"I understand that you were formerly with the KGB."

"That's right."

"Which brings me to the other reason we should join together. Your skills developed with the KGB could prove invaluable in many areas. I also believe you still have strong ties with Russian Intelligence as well as senior military people."

"You are the businessman, Nikolai Mikhailovich, I'm used to doing simple buy and sell deals. What are you proposing?"

"I'm proposing to buy your businesses for a handsome price. You can still run them, but I actually want you to work on projects where your expertise can be of greater use. You'll become a senior executive and move in the highest circles."

"How much?"

"What do you mean?" Krasin asked.

"How much to buy my businesses?"

Krasin already had a number in mind having done enough research to approximate Garnitsky's profits. He took out a gold pen from his pocket and wrote a number on the napkin.

"Eighty? Million?" Garnitsky asked as he looked at the two digits.

"Yes. Dollars, not rubles."

Garnitsky was astounded at the sum. "Christ, that's an impressive sum. Tell me more about what I would be doing in your employ."

Krasin took note of Garnitsky's reference to employment rather than alliance. It was important that he understood the hierarchy of their new relationship.

"What you do best, Feliks Alekseev - run your own intelligence department. I have some good people who do research. I find out what I need to know. But we're getting larger. The task is more complex. Information is at the heart of what we do. My guess is you have a network of *agents* and Government employees on your payroll. I need more than intelligence. I need someone that can execute the equivalent of intelligence operations. You seem to have the skills and experience. It will be just like your KGB days except this is for profit."

"Operations like Seleznyov?"

"Sometimes."

Two months after that conversation, Krasin's Moscow Capital Partners had purchased Garnitsky's operations. Since it was essentially a criminal enterprise, Krasin structured the new acquisitions to insulate the rest of his enterprises from any future problems.

Krasin explained the organizational machinations to Garnitsky.

"We set up a new corporation in Liechtenstein called Eastern Investments. The shares of Eastern Investments are owned by Moscow Capital Partners. But that information is not available to any government. That's why we do business in places like Liechtenstein.

"Eastern Investments owns all the shares of a new Russian investment bank we formed called Moskva Commercial. Moskva Commercial funds the new corporation created from your former businesses which is now known as Smolensk Logistics.

"Lastly, Smolensk will be highly leveraged with loans owed to Moskva Commercial. Shareholders will have a negative net worth."

"Excuse me, Nikolai Mikhailovich, what is meant by *highly leveraged*?"

"That means that the shareholders own little of the business, or in this case, nothing. The Bank effectively owns everything because of the debt owed by the Company."

"Who are the stockholders?" Garnitsky asked.

"The employees. Your senior guys that run things are the largest stockholders. Actually, they won't even know that they are stockholders."

"So what's the point to all this complicated business organization?"

"The point, Feliks, is that if there are any legal difficulties, we are insulated on several levels. First, Smolensk is a Belarus corporation doing most of its business outside of Belarus.

Second, ownership is disconnected through the Bank which in turn is owned by a foreign tax haven corporation."

"How am I connected?" Garnitsky asked. He was amazed at the complex nature of Krasin's corporate architecture.

"You're an executive of Moscow Capital Partners. You are also a consultant to Moskva Commercial Bank. You are not directly connected to Smolensk Logistics. In reality of course, you still run it, you still give the orders.

"If there should ever be any serious problems, your employees take the fall. Even Smolensk's assets are all secured by our Bank."

"I am impressed. You would have been a great success in the intelligence business, Nikolai Mikhailovich."

"Perhaps, but not as rich," Krasin remarked.

CHAPTER 23

SMOLENSK, RUSSIA – 1995

F eliks Garnitsky's former companies had been just the starter set for what was now a major logistics enterprise. Smolensk Logistics operated throughout the former Soviet republics. Profits exceeded expectations even for the legitimate business. For the illicit business, profits were off the scale.

Smolensk Logistics had become the conduit of choice for the flow of all manner of goods. Much of the legitimate commodities business such as petroleum, metals, and lumber involved smuggling to avoid taxation. Their clients ranged from major international corporations to small companies.

For handsome fees, Smolensk would manage the entire transportation deal for their clients. Smolensk's span of operations reached from the Caucus to the Baltic, to the Black Sea. Their network had institutionalized bribery to a scale impressive even by the corrupt standard of the region. In practice, corrupt officials interfered only with the small smugglers for public effect. Smolensk was left alone.

Clients could shift all responsibility and risk to Smolensk. They were a full-service third party logistics provider to the Russian illegal enterprise market.

Drugs and arms smuggling grew as Smolensk expanded. Garnitsky exploited his newly found capabilities. Not only were drugs smuggled using Smolensk trucking, rail, and air, but expanded services for laundering money were offered. Krasin had established a bank in Estonia called Baltic Capital. Estonia was a principle conduit for smuggled Russian goods. Monetary transactions between Moskva Commercial and Baltic Capital made for the perfect money laundering structure. For Russian drug traffickers it was one-stop shopping.

Russia was the perfect conduit for drugs to come out of Central Asia and pass through to Europe. Since the fall of the Soviet Union, Russia itself became a growth market in the use of narcotics. Severe government repression against narcotics under the Soviet state gave way to ineffective law enforcement after its collapse.

ROME, ITALIA – 1998

Garnitsky arrived in Rome on a flight out of Krakow, Poland in the afternoon. He had flown from Moscow to Krakow, then spent the night there. It was a precaution against announcing his presence in Italy. He did not know if he was known to Western police organizations, but it was better to be cautious. Since he also carried a false Polish passport, he could enter Italy as a citizen of another EU country.

The person he was to meet had booked him at the Hotel Locarno. The Locarno was a quaint old hotel near the Piazza del Popolo. It was not the typical five-star hotel frequented by some organized criminal figures. Garnitsky made it known that he did not want his presence in Italy connected with anyone from the Russian Mafiya. He thought of himself now as something of a hybrid - more businessman than common criminal. However, Boris Stepanov Lebedyenko clearly fit the persona of an organized crime figure.

Lebedyenko entered the small bar just off the hotel's lobby. Garnitsky was sitting alone at the bar.

"Feliks Alekseev, how have you been?" the barrel-chested short man greeted in Russian, then hugged Garnitsky.

Lebedyenko was dressed in a white brocade shirt, worn outside his trousers. A large gold watch and heavy gold chain around his neck marked him. In contrast, Garnitsky sported a light-weight, black leather jacket over a pale blue shirt, with light gray slacks. His shoes were an expensive Italian designer label. His only jewelry was a gold Rolex watch.

"I apologize for being late. What are you drinking my friend? Looks like a pussy Western drink."

"Vodka martini, Boris. Very good vodka. French, not Russian. Not that horse piss you like."

"Ah, bartender, give me one of those French vodkas like my friend. And give him another." Lebedyenko said in broken Italian. "We will take our drinks in the garden."

Lebedyenko lead Garnitsky to the small outside patio area. It was a rare amenity for a Rome hotel. The October day was warm, but comfortable at this hour. They were the only people outside.

"I was late because I took more than my usual precautions to make sure I was not followed. I used two cars, two drivers, but it is still an inconvenience."

"Are you usually followed?"

"Not usually, but it has happened."

"Who?"

"The Italians. They don't like own Mafia types much less a Russian. However, I am very careful. Besides, I would not wish my good friend Feliks Alekseev to become of interest to the Italian police."

Lebedyenko was connected with a major Russian criminal organization. His brother ran operations in Russia, Boris operated in Europe. They moved substantial quantities of opium out of Afghanistan and Kazakhstan. From the golden triangle of Southeast Asia, they brought opium by ship through Iran. They were well connected with traffickers in Iran who then moved the product through Azerbaijan and Georgia in the Caucus region. They were an important client to Smolensk Logistics. Moskva Commercial and Baltic Capital facilitated the financial transactions and laundered the money.

"You said you wanted me to meet someone from South America, Boris. Someone in your line of work."

"Yes. I did not want to communicate any more details except in person. I am perhaps overly cautious about all methods of communication. These fucking Muslims have made it difficult for us. I read about how the Western intelligence agencies intercept cell phone calls. And this e-mail shit. I do not know computers, but I would never write anything to anyone. So it is necessary to travel. But this is Rome. Much fucking better than Moscow is it not?"

"The weather certainly is. So who am I to meet?"

"His name is Pablo Reyes. Columbian. Old landowning family. They're well connected."

"What's he want?"

"Reyes is representing a syndicate of drug traffickers."

"You mean one of those cartels?"

"Not exactly. Those old-school cartels from Medellin and Cali are history. The leaders are mostly in prison or dead. Reyes describes his group as a syndicate."

"What's the difference?"

"According to Reyes, the old cartels were gangs at war with the Columbian government. The Medellin Cartel was a bunch of greedy thugs. That Pablo Escabar that was killed a couple of years ago was the last of that group. Then the Cali Cartel ran things for a couple of years. They were smarter than the guys from Medellin, but eventually their leadership was arrested."

"So who does this Reyes represent?"

"As he describes it, what was left of the Cali cartel and a bunch of new groups came together. They're well connected with Columbian officials. The payoffs go up to the highest level. They're also heavily connected with the Columbian Military. According to Reyes, they do business with both the right-wing paramilitaries and the leftist guerillas. Reyes says that all Columbian drug traffic is now under the control of this syndicate. Says they're like a shadow government."

"Uh. Good for them. What's he want to see me about?"

"Laundering money. Your operations, Feliks, are the best for converting great sums of illegal money into legal money. That's why we use you."

"You do business with these Columbians?" Garnitsky asked.

"Да. We purchase some of their cocaine for our European market."

"When do we meet?"

"Tomorrow, my friend. For lunch. But tonight, Feliks, you and I will have an outstanding dinner. I have a wonderful place. And even better, two young woman will join us. Much better than dessert."

"Whores, Boris?"

"Ah, you wound me, Feliks. You are a connoisseur of women. Would I give you whores? No, my friend. These two work for me. They like expensive gifts and partying. Bodies like goddesses."

"Sound like whores to me, Boris. Are they pretty?"

"Gorgeous. But you be the judge my friend. If I am wrong, may my dick shrivel."

OZERSK, SOUTHERN URALS, RUSSIAN FEDERATION – 2000

Nikolai Krasin and Feliks Garnitsky, along with several key staff, flew from Moscow on a military VIP aircraft to the city of Ozersk. Ozersk is located east of the Ural Mountains, a thousand miles from Moscow. This was not a location anyone would venture to without a compelling reason. The area has the singular distinction of being the most polluted place on Earth. Worse yet, that contamination stems from decades of deposits of nuclear waste. The background radiation is far higher than contamination levels around Chernobyl.

Within a hundred mile radius of the city of Chelyabinsk is an array of cities that represent the former Soviet Union's nuclear industry. Many of these cities were never identified on any maps until only recently. Until the mid-1990s, Ozersk was known only as Chelyabinsk-65. Here were the fissionable material processing plants and the nuclear weapons assembly plants. And here also were the inadequately designed storage facilities for nuclear waste. Unlike in the West, nuclear waste management was secondary to achieving production goals. This was Stalin's Soviet Union. Safety was a security concern not a human welfare concern.

The Soviet Union's nuclear weapons program started here after World War II. The Mayak Chemical Combine at Chelyabinsk-65 was the site of the earliest facilities built for the production of weapons-grade plutonium and reprocessing spent nuclear reactor fuel. During the 1940s and 50s, highly radioactive nuclear waste was simply dumped into nearby rivers and lakes.

Two weeks previous to this trip, Krasin had been summoned to the office of the Minister of Defense, General Oleg Basilevsky. The General told him directly that the President had requested he speak to Krasin.

The meeting was held in the Minister's large office. The office had only two tall, narrow windows. The gray, cloudy day offered only frail light penetrating the thin curtains. The wood paneling added to the dark effect. Dour military portraits adorned the walls. The only color was the Russian flag.

Only General Basilevsky, Krasin, and another high-ranking general were present.

"Nikolai Mikhailovich, let me introduce General Konstantin Stepanov Sobolev," General Basilevsky said to Krasin. "General Sobolev is the chief of all nuclear weapons programs for the Ministry of Defense. Please, let us be seated."

The three men sat in comfortable chairs arrayed around a small table set with coffee and mineral water.

"Let me first thank you for making the time to come here, Nikolai Mikhailovich," Basilevsky said. "Let me also say that you have important friends high in the Government, including the President's office. Your companies currently have a number of important contracts with the Government. You are also successfully engaged in a diverse range of business enterprises."

Krasin had no idea where this was going. Was this intended to be some sort of official warning? Did the General have his hand out for kickbacks? Why the nuclear weapons chief?

Basilevsky continued. "What do you know about the status of the Russian nuclear industry, Nikolai Mikhailovich?"

"Only what is public information. I believe we have a greater arsenal of nuclear warheads than the Americans."

"No, what I meant was the broader elements of the industry. That includes not only manufacturing weapons grade nuclear material, but reprocessing spent fuels from reactors, and of course managing our nuclear arsenal. From all of this, the most problematic part is dealing with the contaminated waste. General, perhaps you can explain better," Basilevsky said to Sobolev.

"Yes, Sir. Perhaps you have read something about our contamination problems in the Southern Urals?"

Krasin nodded affirmatively.

"It has been a subject of world concern since we became a federation." Sobolev avoided the more direct statement of *since the fall of the Soviet state*. Before that, the nuclear facilities in the Urals were a closely held state secret. The cities themselves did not publicly exist.

"However, what has been made public is not an accurate assessment of the potential for future catastrophe. The reality is much worse.

"The problem with any nuclear program, whether for power generating reactors or weapons, is always dealing with the waste. Waste of course that remains toxic for decades, some even forever. It's a problem in other countries as well. Containment of nuclear waste has reached a crisis point here in Russia. We essentially have no further storage capacity. Worse yet, those inventories of existing waste are not static. They require constant maintenance. Current maintenance is nowhere near adequate.

"Each year another 10 million cubic meters of radioactive waste is dumped into already overfull reservoirs. These reservoirs are contained by dams. Unfortunately the damns are deteriorating. They already are suffering leakage."

"Where does this leakage go?" Krasin asked.

"Theoretically it could reach the Arctic Ocean through a succession of rivers. The more serious issue however, the more immediate concern, is the limitation imposed upon our strategic nuclear programs."

"Those problems of managing nuclear waste represent the cause of a greater strategic problem for Russia," Basilevsky interjected. "It jeopardizes our own nuclear needs and it hampers a key trade industry. Russia is the world leader in constructing nuclear reactors and reprocessing nuclear fuel. It is perhaps our most strategic industry. It is vital to Russian national security."

"As the General said, this is of vital national interest," Sobolev said. "The problems are not technical. Like everything else, it's money. Insufficient funding has been a chronic problem for the last ten years. The effects of the crude waste disposal practices of the 50s and 60s greatly aggravate the situation today."

"Let me get to the point of why we asked you here today, Nikolai Mikhailovich." Basilevsky said. "Why the President himself has authorized what we are proposing."

"I am flattered that the President thinks I could be of help," Krasin said.

Basilevsky nodded. "We need the resources of your various enterprises. Your businesses span a wide range of industries including banking, transportation, and energy. That is one of the reasons we believe you can help. I am not expert in these areas, but I am advised that all your enterprises are very successful. We need that business expertise. More importantly, Russia needs your investment in its nuclear industry."

"I must confess, that I know little about the nuclear industry," Krasin said. "If I might be so blunt as to ask; are there profits to be made that would justify the investment?" Krasin hoped what they proposed was not some patriotic pitch.

Sobolev sighed. "There is the difficulty, Mr. Krasin. The short answer is no. The Russian customers, including the Government cannot pay prices that are profitable. The foreign customers will go elsewhere if we do not invest in new facilities."

"I trust you are going to explain why I would entertain an investment with no profit potential."

"Most certainly," Sobolev said. "But first let me assure you that there is profit potential. Substantial profits I might add; just not directly. I believe only someone like yourself can appreciate those potentials in what can only be described as complex.

"I am also not an expert in the area of business. But I will attempt to give you a general idea what our own financial experts have constructed. While cash-poor, Russia is wealthy in natural resources. It is with these resources that we will fund our nuclear industry.

"Simply put, your company, or companies, will be given oil, gas, and mineral rights that will more than compensate for losses within the nuclear business itself."

"Why do you need my involvement in this? Why not just sell these rights and use the proceeds to fund the nuclear industry?"

"Yes. That was considered first of course. But our economic experts advised that such an approach would be extremely difficult to accomplish. It would require far too many senior officials to be involved. It would take too long, even if it could be successfully organized. Lastly, it would be politically unsound. It would point out to the world that the Russian nuclear industry is not economically sound. That it needed artificial subsidies. That it was not competitive."

All of which was true. Krasin said to himself. "So by privatizing, investing in new infrastructure, you create a favorable marketing impression."

"That is a fair assessment, Mr. Krasin," Sobolev said. "It is not inconceivable that the industry itself could become profitable in the future with this new investment. Your firm would also be given the work of decommissioning nuclear weapons under our agreements with the United States. Funds from their so-called Cooperative Threat Reduction program would go to your company. I am advised that by itself, this is profitable work."

The economic projections by the Ministry of Defense were compelling. Krasin's own people confirmed that. But the viability of the nuclear industry was yet to be fully understood. Krasin was therefore making the trip to Ozersk with a select team of his best people.

Feliks Garnitsky also made the trip with Krasin. Through his contacts at the Federalnaya Sluzhba Bezopasnost, the FSB, Garnitsky developed a select list of current managers and scientists employed by the Mayak Chemical Combine. Mayak had operated the Soviet Union's nuclear fuels processing in the Urals since 1948. The personnel intelligence was necessary to understand who they wished to talk to. Krasin could not accept the Government's data and interpretations without independent validation. Additionally, he would pirate the best people away from Mayak for his own operations.

Accompanying them from the Ministry of Defense was General Sobolev's head of operations for nuclear weapons, General Pavel Dyachenko. Dyachenko was a technical expert in his own right, holding a doctorate in nuclear physics. More importantly, Garnitsky had obtained the classified dossier on General Dyachenko from his contacts in the FSB.

It seems Dyachenko was known to have strong appetites for luxury items. During the trip, Garnitsky made sure that Dyachenko understood the *opportunities* that could accrue from working to the benefit of Krasin's enterprises.

CHAPTER 24

MANHATTAN, NEW YORK

I t was seven o'clock in the morning at the Cyberspace Coffee Café on Eighth Avenue. Reynolds found the last vacant table and booted up his notebook. The others tables were occupied by an assortment of teenagers nursing lattes or cold coffee concoctions. Reynolds felt a little silly with Avramenko's security paranoia. Not silly enough to ignore it though.

Reynolds did an online search of the Moscow News Journal with the English translation. Under the staff section there was a brief curriculum vitae and small photograph of the newspaper's reporters and editors. Katerina Nikolaevna Avramenko looked to be in her late thirties, maybe forty, dark hair, intelligent face - beautiful face. He would have no difficulty picking her out of a crowd.

He spent the next couple of hours researching Avramenko. He read some of her stories that made their way into the foreign press. Much of it was controversial. Her beat was the messy stuff, chiefly the epidemic Russian climate of corruption.

She asked difficult questions of government officials. That pretty face probably seduced many an official into making indiscrete comments. Her stories were hard-hitting. They documented well-researched facts then delivered well argued conclusions. Avramenko was not hesitant about naming names.

She would have enemies had she been a reporter even in the West. In Russia, those enemies would be far more dangerous.

He was on his second cappuccino when he saw a middle-aged man in a cheap gray suit come into the coffee shop. There was nothing particularly unusual about the guy, just a businessman on his way to work. But something appeared not quite right. Probably imagined whatever it was. Just his instincts being on alert after talking with Avramenko.

No one else in the coffee shop was older than early twenties. All were dressed in trendy, sloppy styles. Reynolds himself looked out of place if for nothing else than his age. The guy in the suit was decidedly out of place. Probably did not know the neighborhood. Neither did Reynolds for that matter.

The man ordered a regular coffee and a newspaper. Reynolds watched him fiddle at the cream and sugar counter. Then the guy found a chair close to Reynolds and opened the newspaper. He could not see Reynolds' computer monitor from the position of his chair but Reynolds was still uncomfortable.

Reynolds decided to move to another open table to complete his on-line tasks. He had made the decision to go to Moscow. He needed to buy airline tickets. If someone was monitoring his communications, might they be also be following him? As preposterous as it seemed, he might as well act out his paranoia by trying to see if he was being followed.

Reynolds abruptly closed down his Internet session and left the café. He walked briskly, zigzagging every block, stopping after turning a corner. Stopping to look in store windows, he tried to identify anyone out of place or someone seen earlier. Nothing. All this bullshit tradecraft was learned from reading spy novels.

After forty-five minutes of this farcical exercise, Reynolds concluded he was not being followed. He found himself close to the public library at Bryant Park. The library also provided Internet access. He went inside and booked a reservation on Air

France for the following week. It was a 5:00 p.m. flight from JFK, connecting in Paris. He would arrive in Moscow at 3:15 p.m. the next day.

There were quite a few people in the library this morning. If he was being followed, there was no way to tell. As he left the library, he passed a man just inside the main front doors wearing a baseball cap and windbreaker. For some subconscious reason Reynolds noticed the man's pants. They were gray dress pants. They didn't conceptually belong to the otherwise casual attire. The shoes however did belong; black oxfords with heavy rubber soles. But that was what had been wrong with the earlier scene at the coffee shop . . . the shoes!

Reynolds kept walking, stifling the urge to turn around for a longer look. Shit, this was the same guy! Wrong shoes! Suit guy wears glasses, no hat. Windbreaker guy dons ball cap and sheds glasses. Unless you're very observant, you would not make the connection. But the shoes were the giveaway. Wrong for the suit attire. Difficult to change shoes if you're working a tail on somebody. Read that somewhere too.

He returned to his apartment. After pouring a Scotch he sank into a chair and stared out the window. If Martinelli Global was determined enough to have him followed, then they certainly could have his telephones bugged. Might even have his e-mail accounts hacked. Maybe his personal e-mail account, but it would seem unlikely that his New York Daily News account would not be secure. Martinelli Global had the resources though. Reynolds had not appreciated just how determined they were in silencing him.

This Columbian murder accusation was a Martinelli Global effort. He would have to see a lawyer as Rachel suggested. Speaking of Rachel, he would bring her up to date when he saw her this evening. Better it was at her apartment. He no longer trusted that his was not bugged.

Reynolds took a taxi to Rachel Stern's apartment at six o'clock that evening. He couldn't spot any tail, but then he guessed that it wouldn't be that easy. Anyway, they would already know about Stern so there was no point in trying to sneak to her place unseen.

"High stranger," Rachel greeted him. She embraced him and gave him a passionate kiss. "Oh, I needed that." Then she kissed him again. She made no attempt to contain her arousal.

Reynolds returned her kisses. His hands stroked her back then slid to her buttocks. It was easy to give way to her unrestrained passion.

Rachel Stern had become totally uninhibited in her sexual assertiveness. She moved her hand to stroke his crotch and felt his growing erection. Disengaging from the embrace, she quickly undid his belt, unzipped his fly, and then pulled down his slacks and underwear. Dropping to her knees, she took his erection fully into her mouth. She worked him with obvious delight accompanied by her own small groans of pleasure.

Reynolds wondered where she had acquired such skill at fellatio. After some minutes of her vigorous attentions he was close to climax. He gently pulled her head back. He was breathing heavily. "Any more of that and I'll end too quickly."

She pushed him to the sofa on his back. Dropping her skirt, she climbed on top of him, resting her weight on her knees. She wore no underwear, obviously planning for the lovemaking.

Somewhere in her riding him, her blouse and bra were discarded. He gripped her hips and pulled her hard against him as they both reached orgasm.

"You are one horny woman, Rachel."

Stern smiled in the warm afterglow of coitus. She was laying with her breasts on his chest and her cheek against his. He was still inside of her.

"I've never made love like I have with you, Mark. I never was this uninhibited before. Must be because of you."

Dangerous ground. He hoped she would not steer this into something more serious. He sensed she wanted to say she loved him. But then that would require some response from him. She perhaps did not want to confront that risk. Guiltily that served his purpose.

Stern excused herself for the bathroom. Reynolds dressed and poured Scotch for each of them.

Stern came out in a robe. She kissed him. "That was grand." Reynolds just smiled. "So, are we going out for dinner? Should I fix something?"

Reynolds handed her a drink. "Dinner can wait. I need to tell you about some things that have developed over the last few days."

"Good developments? A new job?"

"No, it's about Martinelli Global. First, I'm pretty sure I'm being followed."

Reynolds told her about the day's events with the shoe guy.

"You still can't be sure. Mark. That sounds kind of thin. And why would they follow you anyway?"

"I'm making them nervous, Rachel. That means there's more to the Martinelli Global story. It might also validate the other important new development. My Russian sources might be right about my phones being tapped, maybe even my e-mail."

"Russians? What are you talking about?"

"Perhaps like Woodward and Bernstein, my equivalent to Deep Throat. Could lead to something that might blow the Martinelli Global story wide open."

"That's great! What've you got, Mark?"

"It appears I've got access to confidential stuff. Stuff about Martinelli Global's wrongdoing in Russia; money laundering, bribery, organized crime. Incriminating internal e-mails. How Martinelli Global has invested in Russia. How Martinelli Global operates over there."

"Sounds like more of the same. We know Martinelli Global's dirty in most everything they touch. Their Russian operations are very profitable so it stands to reason they're paying people off. What's so special about this Russian information?"

"Nuclear. This source says that Martinelli Global is heavily involved in the Russian nuclear industry. Their annual report and SEC filings make no mention of investments in the Russian nuclear industry. Petroleum, gas, ship building, transportation, banking, but no mention of nuclear. If the source is accurate, here is a U.S. publicly traded corporation conducting operations with national security implications in secrecy. Could be that it's hidden from the Russian Government as well."

"Hold on, Mark. Who is this source?"

"A computer hacker. Calls himself Rasputin."

"How'd he contact you?"

"E-mail."

"Ever talk to him?"

"No."

"Mark. This could be anybody. Could even be Martinelli Global. Now that's a scary thought."

"I thought about that too. But I don't think so, Rachel. He had someone else contact me by phone, a Russian journalist."

"Or someone posing as such."

Reynolds understood the logic of Stern's skepticism. Her more objective questioning of the circumstances sent a shiver through him. Was Martinelli Global that committed? Were they that cunning? Was this the equivalent of an old KGB honey-trap? Were Martinelli Global's Russian people luring him into a trap? Recounting his conversation with Avramenko, his instincts told him otherwise. But he was less certain now than before.

"I know what you're saying, Rachel. The reality is that I have to go. It's too important to pass up."

"Go where?"

"Russia. I'm leaving in a few days."

"What?" Stern was shaken by Reynolds pronouncement. Selfishly she wanted him close to her. She was in love with him - had been for years. Now that they were together it was a bitter disappointment to be separated, not to mention the danger of such a trip.

"I'm going to Russia. Have to. I need to meet with this Rasputin. Need to see what he's got. I'll need an interpreter if it's what he claims. That's where the Russian journalist comes in."

"Do you know the journalist's name at least?"

"Yes. Her name is Katerina Nikolaevna Avramenko. I talked to her briefly. She speaks English. She's an investigative reporter. Focuses on Russian corruption. I did a little research on her. She must have a fair understanding of business by the nature of her pieces. At any rate, she has access to Rasputin's information."

Stern was shaken a second time. Not only was Reynolds leaving the country, but he would be working with a female colleague. There was the instant stab of jealousy. It also made her feel as if she was being replaced professionally. Not an objective view, but still an emotional blow.

"Oh, I need a favor. I think I should talk to a lawyer about this Columbian Government request for extradition. I don't think it has any weight, but I would feel more comfortable if I heard that from a lawyer."

Stern was quiet for a moment. It hurt doubly that he did not see how this news affected her. It took some willpower to focus her thoughts. "Sure. That makes sense. I'll try to get you a couple of names of lawyers specializing in international criminal law. When do you leave for Russia?"

"In five days. Tuesday."

They went out for a late dinner on the Upper East Side. Stern was uncharacteristically quiet. The conversation was somewhat strained throughout the rest of the night. Reynolds declined to stay the night. Stern did not try to change his mind.

The next day, Reynolds purchased a new cell phone and opened a new e-mail account. He sent Stern an e-mail to her personal address, avoiding the newspaper's e-mail system just in case it might be compromised.

The e-mail read, "Hi. I enjoyed last night, Rachel. Don't be angry. You know I need to do this. You also must know I need your help on this project. Without you I would never have gotten this far with the story. Anything on lawyers? Note the new e-mail address. Mark."

Later in the day, Stern answered. "I'm not angry, just worried about you going to Russia, especially after you told me you're being followed. Sounds like Martinelli Global means to stop you. Promise you'll be careful. Promise you'll come back to me. Promise you'll not forget about me? You must know how I feel. Here are a couple of heavyweight lawyers. Love you. Rachel."

Two days later he had an appointment downtown with Matthew Solomon. Solomon was a criminal attorney specializing in international law. He had represented every type of client from white-collar crime American fugitives to foreign nationals accused of terrorism.

"Good day, Mr. Reynolds. Have a seat," Solomon said as he closed the door and ushered Reynolds to a chair. "Since you called, I did a little research on your situation. Did some research on you as well. Like your work. Seems you've made a powerful enemy in Martinelli Global."

"No question there. Not through with them either. What I need to know is what kind of leverage they have with this murder charge."

"First, tell me what you know about this Juan Cortina."

Reynolds told him about the events in Columbia.

"Well, you don't seem like the kind of person to kill a colleague. Besides, the U.S. Government helped you leave Columbia. The Ambassador apparently believed you. Taking at face value what you say, the Columbia Government should have no credible evidence."

"Unless they trumped stuff up, like bogus witnesses," Reynolds interjected.

"True. If this is a move by Martinelli Global as you say, they would have to have something tangible to bring to the Justice Department. However, it's not quite that easy for them. First of all the Columbian Government is considered to be riddled with corruption. Ties to extra-military human rights abuses, ties to drug trafficking. In short, Justice knows them to be a banana republic. Your claims provide a plausible scenario to their attempts to silence you."

"Are you saying they won't get anywhere with the Justice Department?"

"Well not necessarily. First of all, Columbia is a *friendly* nation. They even extradite their own citizens on occasion, usually kingpin drug traffickers, to the U.S. for prosecution under U.S. laws. The Justice Department can't just ignore them. Under international law, a country cannot be compelled to extradite a citizen of that country by a foreign country. Obviously a country can choose to do that, just like the Columbians do for their own reasons. But that's a very rare occurrence in the United States. In lieu of extradition, the United States would almost always choose to prosecute the defendant within the U.S. for a crime committed abroad."

"Would there be a case against me?"

"I can't say. I don't know what evidence they claim to have. By what you say, they can't have anything solid beyond witness affidavits and circumstantial stuff. It would take the same level of evidence as for any criminal preliminary hearing in a U.S. Federal Court."

"Christ. Are you saying this may go that far?"

"No, no. I'm not suggesting anything. That's way too premature. Before anything could possibly happen, the Justice

Department would have to initiate an investigation. Before they would even do that, the Columbians would have to present prima facie evidence to support the murder allegations."

"So what do you recommend I do next?"

"Retain me as your attorney. Then I'll check with the Justice Department to understand where this might be going. My advice is that it's too soon to worry."

"Any problem if I leave the Country?" Reynolds asked.

"What? You mean you're planning to leave the U.S.?"

"Business. Perhaps for a few weeks."

"Where are you going?"

"Russia."

Solomon did not respond immediately, rubbing his chin.

"Is there a problem with that?"

"Can't say without knowing more details about the Columbian's allegations. The problem could be if they were to get an Interpol Notice against you."

"What's an Interpol Notice?"

"You see, Interpol is essentially an international police intelligence agency. They send out information to all member countries about things ranging from fugitives to missing persons, to criminal procedures. There's a so-called Red Notice which serves as an international wanted notice. Many countries will act on a Red Notice as if it were an arrest warrant."

"Could the Columbian's get a Red Notice on me?"

"Possibly. Depends again on the evidence. The point is if you're not in the U.S. then you could be vulnerable. I would recommend against leaving."

Reynolds left Solomon's office with assurances that Solomon would notify the Justice Department that he was representing him. He would also monitor any activity involving Interpol.

Wonderful. Reynolds had hoped to hear Solomon reassure him that the Columbian bullshit murder charge was just that.

Now this Interpol factor added a whole new concern. But not sufficiently troubling to stop him from going to Russia though. It was too important.

On his new cell phone, he called Avramenko. "I will arrive in Moscow on Tuesday. Air France flight 1644 from Paris. Arrives in Moscow at 3:15 p.m. You'll meet me?"

"That is good. Yes, I will meet you. I will arrange hotel. It will be good, Mark Reynolds. We will exchange information. Create major international story about international corruption. Martinelli Global is very big all over world. Nikolai Krasin is very big in Russia. All are criminal partners."

"I hope you're right Miss Avramenko. I will see you in two days."

The day before his flight, he had dinner with Rachel Stern. He chose a small Italian place in the theater district he'd been to a couple of times. Not pretentious, but excellent food with a very good wine list. The atmosphere felt like a genuine Northern Italy trattoria.

"This is very nice, Mark."

"It is. And the food's outstanding. Maybe my last good meal for a while. Probably borscht and cheap vodka in Russia."

Both were quiet for several moments. Stern broke the uncomfortable silence. "I wish you weren't going, Mark. I think this could be dangerous. Especially in Russia. Martinelli Global has a heavy presence there."

She was also jealous of him working so closely with another woman, especially one that looked like Katerina Avramenko. Stern had also looked up her picture. She also knew a display of jealousy would make matters worse.

"Well Russia's not as lawless as Nigeria or Columbia."

"And you were lucky to have escaped both."

"I've got to do this, Rachel. Could be the kind of information that would make this a bigger story than Enron. You see, Enron was a few arrogant executives that thought they had invented a whole new business model. Martinelli Global is even a bigger corporation, and these guys are more insidious criminals. They have a unique business model also. This is what one could imagine the Mafia evolving into if that leadership hadn't been populated with mental inferiors. At its heart, Martinelli Global is a criminal organization."

"Goddamn it I know that, Mark. Can't you see I'm concerned because I'm in love with you?"

Tears ran down Stern's cheeks. That's not what she wanted to say. She did not want to spoil their last night before he left. She did not want to corner him.

"Rachel . . ."

"Mark, don't say anything. You don't have to say anything. I'm not expecting you to say you love me. I don't believe you do love me. Like me? Yes. Love me? I don't think so."

"Listen, Rachel . . ."

"I've said way too much. I'm leaving before I really lose it." Tears flowed fully now. She got up. "I've got to be alone right now. I'll get a cab." She left abruptly, evading his grasp as he tried to stop her.

She was already out the door while he hurriedly settled up with the waiter. In a rare Manhattan occurrence, she hailed a vacant taxi immediately. By the time he exited the restaurant, the taxi was pulling away. She looked at him through the window.

Shit. He knew it must eventually come to this. He liked Rachel Stern, actually more than just liked her. But he wasn't in love with her. He was a stupid, selfish shit for letting sex get into the mix.

CHAPTER 25

MOSCOW, RUSSIAN FEDERATION

The Air France flight was on time into Moscow's Sheremetyevo Airport. Unfortunately, the early afternoon arrival coincided with a number of other European flight arrivals. Reynolds queued in line for over an hour before getting through passport control. After retrieving his luggage, it was another forty-five minutes getting through customs.

He looked around trying to locate Avramenko among the people waiting for arriving passengers. He kept scanning the crowd for fifteen minutes. Before he could become more disgusted about being stood up, his cell phone rang.

"Yes?"

"It's me."

He recognized Avramenko's voice. "That's nice. Where are you? I'm here at the airport."

"Yes. I am so sorry not to be there to greet you. Please take taxi. Instruct driver to take you the Medea Hotel. Very good hotel. Do not let taxi driver overcharge you because you are American. Pay only 750 rubles. That is with tip," Avramenko said.

Reynolds was a little put out by Avramenko not being there to greet him. "When do I meet you?"

"I will meet you in a couple of hours at the hotel."

"Ok. Fine. The Medea Hotel. See you later." This was not starting out well.

Outside the terminal it was a cold October day. The sky was overcast. The pavement was wet from a recent rain. It took several tries to find a taxi driver that understood some English. Several more minutes were consumed with haggling over the fare. Reynolds generally hated the ritual of haggling, but he was sufficiently pissed off to be a worthy opponent. He settled the fare at 800 rubles.

The drive took forty minutes. To Reynolds pleasant surprise, the Medea Hotel was located on an attractive street in the center of Moscow. It was on the opposite side of the Moscow River from the Kremlin and Red Square. Most of the buildings appeared to be from the nineteenth century. It was an area not unlike what might be found in many prosperous European cities.

At least there was a reservation in his name. The Medea was small, but modern. The clerk spoke good English. Avramenko had made a good choice.

After tipping the bellboy, Reynolds stretched out on the bed to test the mattress. Not bad. A nap would be nice but no telling when Avramenko would show up. There was a small bar off the lobby. Better to have a drink and wait for her there.

After using the lavatory, Reynolds had just finished washing when there was a knock at the door.

He opened the door.

"Mark Reynolds?"

The woman was recognizable from her photograph. "Yes. And you are obviously Katerina Avramenko. Please come in."

Avramenko moved past him into the room. Reynolds knew only the pretty face. The whole of Katrina Avramenko was a head-turner. Tall with dark long hair, she carried herself like a model. She wore a fashionable wool coat over a tight-fitting sweater, with a knee-length skirt, and calf-length black boots; the perfect vision of Russian fashion.

"I must apologize for not meeting you at the airport, Mr. Reynolds."

"That's ok. It was no problem getting here."

"You see, Mr. Reynolds, I was being cautious. I wanted to see if you were being followed."

Reynolds frowned. "Followed? And was I?"

"Yes."

"How do you know that I was followed?"

"Because I followed you and the man following you. Look out your window. Across the street is a white Lada. There are two men. One older than other. Black leather jackets. The older one followed you out of airport. Watched as you argued with taxi drivers. Once you departed, the other one picked up older man and they follow your taxi."

Reynolds went to the window. There was a white sedan parked on the opposite side of the street. There were also a number of other parked cars on the street. "I can't see anybody inside. Are you sure?"

"Yes. I am sure. It is same men, same car as followed you from airport."

"Ok. So what's the plan?"

"Plan?"

"What do we do?"

"Ah yes. We go to different hotel. But we leave unseen out back way. It is how I entered Hotel. I have a car parked not far on next street."

"What about this room? I gave them a credit card," Reynolds asked.

"It is no problem. I shall call hotel and say you have emergency. Must return to United States. Tell them to charge you for one night."

Reynolds and Avramenko exited the rear service entrance of the Medea Hotel unseen and walked the block to her car. It was a black Lada. Avramenko might be chic, but not so for her car. By western standards it was a certifiable piece of shit. Reynolds couldn't tell the age, but it had more than a few years evident by the scratches showing rust. The interior was Spartan. The manual transmission sounded unhealthy as the gears gnashed.

Avramneko drove only a short distance to another small hotel, the Sretenskaya, on a quiet street in central Moscow.

"I have also made you reservation here. But only for one night. Martinelli Global has many resources here in Russia. If they wish to find you it would not take long."

"And tomorrow?"

"We shall decide that tomorrow."

"Wonderful. Right now I'd like a drink and something to eat. And we need to talk."

"That would be nice, Mr. Reynolds."

"How about calling me Mark?"

"Yes. I will call you Mark. And you may call me Nicky."

Reynolds looked a little puzzled.

"It is what my friends call me. My name is Katerina Nikolaevna. Nikolaevna is after my father. That is Russian custom. He always called me Nicky. He said I had the temper of a Nicky not a Katerina."

"Then Nicky it is. Let me check in and dump my suitcase in the room."

Twenty minutes later they were at a small quiet restaurant. Nicky said she wanted to introduce him to Russian food.

After asking Reynolds a few questions about his food preferences, Nicky insisted on ordering.

"We shall start with *pochki v madere*. It is kidneys cooked in wine and butter sauce. It is bad for you, but very good."

It tasted exceptionally good, especially paired with the ice cold vodka.

"What is this soup?" Reynolds asked as the waiter placed a bowl for each of them.

"It is called *botvinia*. Very simple, just green vegetables with fish," Avramenko said and took a spoonful. "Ah, this is with sturgeon. Much better than with salmon."

Reynolds was not fond of fish, but this wasn't too bad. There was the sharp taste of horseradish which he was fond of.

Reynolds and Avramenko made small talk as they ate. She mostly asking about New York, he about Moscow.

"Now we continue healthy dinner. This is called *tushenaia kuritsa pod sousom iz chernosliv*. It is chicken with a prune sauce.

Prune sauce? Reynolds tried a piece and liked it. Not as much perhaps as a steak, but very interesting. He wasn't sure what to expect of food in Russia. This meal certainly gave a good accounting of Russian cuisine.

Finishing his chicken, Reynolds said, "I enjoyed that. Your choices were excellent, even if they were the healthy choices. You must know a lot about food?"

Avramenko smiled, "No. I just read menu and know what I like. Perhaps some dessert?"

"Not for me. Perhaps a cognac though. Would they have good cognac here?"

"I am sure. I will join you. I rarely have dessert myself."

The waiter cleared the dishes then brought their cognacs and coffee.

"What do you know about our mutual friend, Rasputin?"

Avramenko hesitated, seemingly trying to find the right words. "He is good person. He has given me much material on political corruption. He is what is called a computer hacker."

"I know that. Do you know him?"

"No. I have never met him. I do not know even his name."

"Do you know anything about him?"

"He sounds young."

"So you have spoken to him?"

"Oh yes. We have talked on telephone many times. Usually he sends e-mails though."

"Has his information in the past been credible?"

"I am honest journalist so I check all information. I try to confirm by other sources. Rasputin's information has always proved accurate. There is some information that I cannot use even if I could confirm."

"What do'ya mean?"

"This is Russia, Mark. Most business involves some cooperation with government officials. That means favors and bribes. The bigger the business, the more senior the government officials that must be paid off. I read Western newspapers about your white collar crime. That is something rarely published in Russia. Corruption is way of business here in Russia."

"What about these billionaires like Berezovsky and Khodorkovsky that are jailed or were forced to leave Russia?"

"I do not know if they committed any crimes. But I know they were removed because they became a problem for someone with more power. It is never justice at work in Russia."

"For a Russian, you have a pretty low opinion of Russian society."

"Not Russian society, only for Russian government and powerful people. Russian people are good people. We have a rich culture. But Russians suffer an eternal history of being ruled by tsars or dictators. What is called democracy here is only since 1991. And it does not work. All history before was feudal. Even the twentieth century was little different than nineteenth."

"Is it dangerous for journalists in Russia?"

"For some. If you write damaging stories about powerful people then yes, it is dangerous."

"Rasputin said you were friends with the famous reporter Anna Polikovskaya."

"Yes. Anna was great journalist, great friend. She was tough and smart but she angered very important people with her stories critical of the troubles in Chechnya. So even someone as famous as Anna Polikovskaya was murdered. That story died away within weeks."

"How about you? Your work is more about business and corruption, not politics. Does that put you in danger as well?"

"Yes. I threaten those that make a lot of money. So I am careful."

"Anna Polikovskaya must have thought herself careful as well."

Avramenko paused for a moment. "Anna was my friend. She knew the danger. She was very brave. But Anna was how you say, arrogant. She was not enough careful. She thought her reputation would protect her. Her murder was made to frighten other journalists. It did. So I am more careful now. I carry a gun in my purse."

Reynolds just nodded. Christ, a gun! "Nicky, a gun? That's not going to help against professional killers."

Tears welled up in Avramenko's eyes. Reynolds said, "What's the matter Nicky?"

"Mark. Understand that I know what are the dangers. Violence has touched me more than with just Anna Polikovskaya's murder. Even closer. My own colleague, Sergi Astapkovich was destroyed by these people."

"What happened?"

"He was writing a story about Caspian Enterprises. It destroyed him."

"What do'ya mean?"

Avramenko paused to compose herself. "They beat and raped his wife. Right in front of him. She never recovered, mentally at least. She had to be put in an institution. Months later he killed himself."

"I don't know what to say. We don't contend with that in the West. I'm sorry, Nicky."

"Mark, Caspian Enterprises is run by Nikolai Krasin."

"Jesus Christ! You mean they've already come after reporters?"

"Yes. I wanted you to know that I understood the dangers, Mark."

Reynolds was humbled by what Avramenko just told him. It also gave him a new appreciation for Avramenko's precautions.

"From the West's perspective, Russia is economically important, but it's seen as a lawless frontier. Strong-men rule here just like a Third World country. That's of course why Martinelli Global is here. This is their type of environment. So speaking of Martinelli Global, how do you know about them?" He wanted to bring the conversation back to a professional footing.

"About Martinelli Global? Only what I read in Western newspapers like yours. And of course this new information discovered by our friend Rasputin. Mostly I know about the Russian billionaire, Nikolai Krasin who runs those Russian corporations. I know much about Krasin's businesses."

"Yes, I know a little about Krasin from our research."

Avramenko ordered more coffee and cognac. "Let me tell you how I came to know Nikolai Krasin's corporations. It started perhaps a year ago. Much of my work has been to investigate business and government corruption. In Russia, that also means organized crime.

"Before collapse of Soviet Union, criminals, organized criminals made their money with things like extortion and smuggling. Smuggling has always been the way for Russian criminals to make money."

"You mean drugs?" Reynolds asked.

"Always drugs for sure. But many other things; cigarettes, gasoline, even Levis. All things that were in short supply. But these opportunities changed when Soviet Union was gone. New opportunities suddenly became available, not only smuggling but other things for making illegal money. Certain very smart criminals took advantage. Many corrupt government officials also took advantage. There were sales of government-owned factories, even military equipment. Many important officials made much money. Criminals became their partners. I have focused my investigations on exposing these people."

"I have read about this problem for several years. The Western press alternates between portraying Russia as something like the United States a hundred years ago, to the newest frontier for investment opportunity. Which is it?"

"It is both. Things like poor Anna's murder are really not commonplace. The real criminals are now more sophisticated. You see under Soviet Union traditional organized criminals were part of subculture. Black market activities have always been important to Russians for hundreds of years. During Tsarist times and Soviet times the Government was always the enemy. Most old crime bosses spent time in prison. After fall of Soviet regime, smarter criminals have come into control.

"One of those new criminals is Feliks Garnitsky. Garnitsky is now high ranking executive with Moscow Capital Partners. That is Nikolai Krasin's company."

Reynolds interrupted. "You mean Moscow Capital Partners is part of the Martinelli Global subsidiary, Martinelli Global Europe, Ltd?"

"Yes. But this Garnitsky started out as a criminal. He is new Russian criminal, more sophisticated than old criminals. He was with KGB for many years. His father was KGB under Stalin. Garnitsky was in what you call operations; those that committed acts like murder. He served in KGB at same time as former President Putin. Now he works with Krasin."

"Is he connected to Putin?" Reynolds asked.

"That I do not know. But I know he is now connected to very powerful government officials. His name is frequently associated with many allegations of corruption. There are rumors that certain enemies of Nikolai Krasin have met with violence because of Feliks Garnitsky. It was probably Garnitsky that arranged the attack on Sergi and his wife."

"So how did he come to be connected with Krasin?" Reynolds asked.

"Krasin wanted to expand into the energy market. Garnitsky controlled large trucking operations engaged in smuggling oil. Garnitsky had many contacts in the Caucus. Garnitsky also had many politicians on his payroll."

"But Krasin is a major figure in Russian business. He's a banker. You're saying this Feliks Garnitsky is now a senior executive in Krasin's businesses?"

"Yes, that is what I am saying."

"You're saying that a major Russian criminal is now a senior executive with a subsidiary of Martinelli Global?"

"Yes."

"Tell me about this Feliks Garnitsky."

Avramenko motioned the waiter to bring them more coffee.

"Feliks Garnitsky did much business with a major criminal gang run by the Lebedyenko family in the southern city of Volgograd since the 1990s. The Lebedyenko criminal enterprise was headquartered in the former Stalingrad, close to the smuggling routes through the Caucasus region. Garnitsky moved smuggled oil and drugs for the Lebedyenkos, and laundered their money.

The Lebedyenkos were challenged by a rival Ukrainian gang that teamed with a Chechen group. There was much bloodshed all around. Garnitsky resolved the problem for the Lebedyenkos by arranging the assassinations of the entire leadership of the Ukrainian gang. They were eliminated in one stroke. This was in 2001. Garnitsky became even more feared and powerful after that."

"He stills sounds like just an organized crime boss. A Russian Mafiya don. How does he connect with Krasin."

"You are right, Mark. I believe Feliks Garnitsky's control over highly placed politicians may have been his value to Krasin. Maybe his strong ties to KGB. KGB became FSB, but it is still same. Many former KGB officers are in positions of power in the Russian Federation. I believe that it could still be a network for someone who can pay generously. Krasin has such money."

"I'd like to use your material on Garnitsky in my book about Martinelli Global. That alone is powerful material. Is Garnitsky's background well documented?"

Avramenko's expression suggested she was affronted by Reynolds' questioning the quality of her work. "I will give you my research on Feliks Garnitsky. I believe you will find it up to Western journalistic standards."

Reynolds quickly try to back-peddle. "I wasn't questioning your work, Nicky. I only meant are there public records that could substantiate some of your allegations?"

"I believe so. But you can judge for yourself."

Wanting to smooth the waters, Reynolds asked, "I have researched some of your pieces before I came over here. You've done some really fine work. How have you been so successful in exposing bad guys?"

The imagined slight had passed. She leaned forward with both elbows on the table. "That is easy in Russia. There is so much crime and corruption. All these bad guys have enemies. Most of their enemies are also bad guys. If you know who's against who then you can use this knowledge as leverage to get information."

"You play one side against the other. Is that it?"

"Yes, exactly. Each bad guy wants to harm his enemy, or someone wants to gain power. I find sometimes the means to offer information for trade to get information I need."

Reynolds laughed. "And I bet you're good at that double-dealing."

"*Double-dealing*? I am not familiar with that phrase?"

"Ah. Well, it's doing something for a deceitful reason," he said, instantly regretting the characterization.

But Avramenko smiled. "Yes, that is what I do. I am double-dealing these assholes. Is *asshole* the right word?"

Reynolds laughed. "Yes, asshole is the right word for bad guys."

Reynolds hoisted his cognac in a mock salute.

"How about our mutual friend, Rasputin? He's not one of the bad guys is he?"

"Oh no, Rasputin is a good guy. Like many other of my sources. I not only get information from bad guys, but from good people too. Many government workers, even some politicians that hate corruption. I get much information from these types of sources. Sometimes they incriminate their own superiors. I am good at finding all manner of people with reasons to give me information."

Reynolds felt the time was right to get down to the purpose of his visit to Russia. "Rasputin said that he had very sensitive information on Martinelli Global's activities in Russia. He implied that you might assist me by translating and explaining the materials."

"Yes. That is correct."

"Forgive me for asking in this way, but why would you not just use this information for your own newspaper?"

"I might. But if Rasputin is correct about some of this information, I am not sure my editor would publish. It could be too dangerous. Nikolai Krasin and Feliks Garnitsky are very powerful. Both have strong ties even to the new President. Besides that, the bigger story is about Martinelli Global. That will be bigger story in the West."

"So where do we start?" he asked.

Avramenko looked around the restaurant. She reached into her purse and pulled out three small USB storage devices displayed in her opened palm. "We start with these. They're from Rasputin. I've taken a brief look at the material. There are hundreds of pages."

"What kind of information?"

"Contracts, letters, accounting records, e-mails. It will take some time just for me to read them. Then I have to translate for you. Most are of course in Russian. We will need at least two weeks to examine them."

"Two weeks!" Reynolds exclaimed. And that would be just the beginning. From Rasputin's information, he expected to identify other courses to pursue. He could be in Russia for quite some time. "Can you get that much time away from your job, Nicky?"

"Yes. It is all arranged. My editor has allowed me to take two weeks holiday. We shall make it a holiday at least a little bit. Your book publisher is paying your expenses to come here to Russia?"

"Well, sort of." He didn't want to reveal that his literary agent had not yet concluded any deal with a publisher. Therefore, there was no advance to finance this Russian venture.

"Good. Then we shall vacation on the Black Sea. It will be safer there. I have rented rooms at a resort in the Crimea. It is beautiful place outside the small town of Yalta. That of course is in the Ukraine. We shall travel by train to town of Simferopol in the Crimea. Then we rent car to make the short trip to Yalta."

"In Ukraine?"

"Yes. I have selected the Hotel Katrin outside of the town. The photos on the Internet show wonderful views of Black Sea. We shall work undisturbed. I have false papers for both of us. We shall not be followed to Yalta by Martinelli Global spies."

False papers? What the hell had he gotten himself into?

CHAPTER 26

MOSCOW, RUSSIAN FEDERATION

As arranged, Avramenko picked up Reynolds at his hotel at eight o'clock. They drove straight to the Kievsky Train Station, but only to purchase tickets. The train to Simferopol did not depart until 3:30 p.m. It would be a twenty-two hour trip.

Reynolds was still skeptical about why they had to go to the Black Sea to review Rasputin's material. Moscow was a large city. They could easily avoid being followed by Martinelli Global. He suspected Avramenko might just be using the excuse to go to a resort. That issue aside, he protested why they could not fly instead.

"Because airports are watched by many people. People we might wish to avoid having knowledge of our movements. The false papers are good enough for train and hotels, but would not pass airport security. We have fear of terrorists in Russia also. Besides, the train is much more enjoyable. You relax. Get to see beautiful Russian countryside."

"Tell me about these false papers. Do you mean false passports?"

"Yes, of course."

"Of course? Isn't that dangerous?"

"Only little. As I said, they are not thorough on the trains. And they are not thorough with people moving between Russia and Ukraine. It is what I understand border is like between United States and Canada."

"So who am I?"

Avramenko smiled. "You are Peter Duncan. Here is your passport."

Reynolds took the burgundy colored passport. It read the *United Kingdom of Great Britain.* Opening to the photograph, there was the face of a man obviously several years younger. The hair was the same color, but with a noticeably longer hair style.

"Shit. This doesn't even look like me. This is supposed to pass a security check?"

"It will pass. All passport pictures are not good likeness. You are now older. Cut your hair shorter now."

"How did you get this?"

Avramenko appeared to blush slightly. "It was from an old boyfriend. He was with the Reuters News Bureau in Moscow. He apparently lost it in my apartment. Months after he was transferred from Moscow, I found it in a pocket of a jacket he left."

Reynolds also noted that the visa was still current. The *old* boyfriend was not from that long ago. "By now, he's replaced it. That means it's no longer valid."

"Yes. But security people for trains do not check passport numbers with any databases. They will not check. That is why we are taking train."

"What about when we enter Ukraine?"

"It is same. They do not check computer database. It is ok."

"I'm not sure that is very comforting, Nicky. And how about you? Are you traveling under a different name too?"

"Of course," Avramenko said, then handed him a Russian Federation passport.

Reynolds examined the photograph and uttered a groan. "Nicky, this photo is worse than mine. Doesn't remotely look like you. You're much more . . ."

"Better looking?" Avramenko offered with a mischievous smile.

"Much. This looks like a police booking photograph of someone else. Who the hell is this anyway?"

"A close friend. I have used it before when I do not wish my identity known. I have never been questioned when I have used it. Do not worry, she knows how I use it. It too is no longer valid. She reported it lost. If I am ever caught, she can claim no knowledge."

Reynolds could only think that this whole Russian adventure was spinning out of his control. "Ok. I guess I have to trust you on this. At least with this damn long train ride we can start working on the Rasputin material."

"Yes, perhaps we can. But we should also enjoy the trip."

Since they had most of the day before their train left Moscow for Simferopol, Avramenko asked Reynolds if he would like to see some of the Moscow points of interest before their train departure.

"No offense, Nicky, but I'd rather get into the work I came here to do. How about we go to a coffee shop. We've got a lot of background work to cover before we get into the stuff Rasputin provided."

"Very well, Mark. I understand."

Avramenko drove to the Coffee Bean on Tverskaya. It was not the American chain, but equally as good. Over several coffees, Reynolds recounted what he already knew about Martinelli Global's Russian subsidiaries, Moscow Capital Partners and various banks.

"There's no public record of any Martinelli Global holdings involved in Russia's nuclear industry. What has our friend Rasputin uncovered?" Reynolds asked Avramenko.

"I have not had chance to look into documents he has given me. That is what we will do together. Rasputin claims not to understand all details, but he has told me some facts that are very interesting.

"Well tell me about what he says about this connection to the Russian nuclear industry."

"Rasputin says that Krasin became involved with Russian nuclear industry in 2001. Made large investments."

"What area of the nuclear industry? Nuclear reactors, fuels?"

"I am not sure, but Rasputin mentioned weapons. We must research Rasputin's material to understand better."

"I have some technical knowledge on the subject from some previous work I did on a book I wrote. What seems suspicious is why Krasin, and by extension, Martinelli Global, would want to invest in Russia's nuclear industry."

"Why not? They are well connected with the Government. There must be much potential for profits."

"Obviously. But the Russian nuclear industry is a financial disaster. The Soviets set up secret cities in the Urals back in the forties and fifties. They were run as military installations to develop weapons and process nuclear materials. Profits were not a factor.

"Environmentally these sites became disasters. Even today, the problem continually gets worse. Remedial efforts of containment have astronomical costs. Krasin would not invest out of any patriotic motivation. He must have gotten extraordinarily strong financial inducements from the Government to invest."

"I know of these cities. Like Ozersk. We learned of these places in the 1990s after fall of Soviet Union. It is still restricted military area," Avramenko said.

"Ozersk used to be known as Chelyaabinsk-65," Reynolds said. "Employment is still dominated by the Mayak Chemical Combine. Krasin's investments must now compete with them. Do Russian citizens know about the accident in 1957?"

"I have read references to a problem like what happened at Chernobyl."

"Probably worse. This was long before Chernobyl. They had a non-nuclear explosion that released enormous quantities of radiation. Killed hundreds of people. Contaminated hundreds of square miles for decades, maybe even for centuries. They've had other accidents as well."

"I see what you mean. No one would invest there unless there is very important financial motivation."

"What else did Rasputin say about Martinelli Global?"

"Rasputin said that he has documents from a company called Rusatomic Industries and another that I don't recall the name. These companies are owned by a holding company. That company is controlled by Nikolai Krasin."

"And how does this tie into Martinelli Global?"

"Rasputin says he has evidence that Martinelli Global is a partner with Krasin in these operations through companies that eventually lead to the Cayman Islands."

"That would fit. And is this criminal associate of Krasin, this Garnitsky, involved in these nuclear operations?"

"I am sure he must be. He works for Krasin. Very senior person. Very powerful."

"If our friend Rasputin is right, then Martinelli Global, a U.S. based corporation, is secretly operating Russian nuclear facilities. Maybe Martinelli Global's investment is even hidden from the Russian Government. And, there's the involvement with this major criminal, Garnitsky. If Rasputin's documentation supports this, this is one helluva story."

Reynolds suggested Avramenko show him the corporate offices of Krasin's Moscow Capital Partners before going to the train station. It was on a reasonably quiet street populated with similar buildings.

"This was street of homes of wealthy aristocrats before Revolution. Moscow Capital Partners was originally home to a first cousin of Tsar Nicholas II," Avramenko commented as she drove slowly past the building. "Now it is offices of most successful businessmen."

There were no markings to identify the building. Two large ornate wooden doors did not suggest a commercial enterprise. Reynolds took some digital photographs.

"They don't advertise their presence do they?" Only a small bronze plaque identified the occupants, but with letters too small to read from the street.

Avramenko parked the car at Moscow's Kievsky Train Station. It was a large neo-classical building with a clock tower and a large modern sculpture outside. They crossed the spacious waiting lounge area to the platform area with its large-span arches. Reynolds was pleasantly surprised having expected some dreary bus terminal-like facility.

They found their train and boarded. A severe looking heavy-set woman in a uniform checked their tickets and passports. She exchanged words with Avramenko, then gave a scowl toward Reynolds. His immediate thoughts were concerns that the attendant was questioning his identity after looking at the fake passport. However, she abruptly turned and led them to their first class compartment with no comment.

Reynolds was again pleasantly surprised. There were two bunks, one on each side of the compartment. There was a small table and two chairs. The window had curtains.

"This is called *spalny vagon*. It means first class. It costs twice as much as *kupé* which is second class. *Kupé* has four bunks. This is better, no?"

"Certainly. Very nice." He couldn't deny that he was pleased to be sharing a compartment with such an attractive woman. "Was there a problem out there with the attendant?"

"The *provodnitsa*? No problem. She asked if we were traveling together. Probably because you are British."

"She looked like she didn't like the idea that we were rooming together."

Avramenko was puzzled for a moment. "Oh, I see. But, no, in Russia, men and women stay in same train compartment, even strangers. It is common."

An hour after the train pulled out of Kievsky Station, Reynolds needed to use the toilet. Avramenko directed him to the end of the car corridor. He returned only minutes later.

"Jesus Christ. The restrooms sure as hell aren't like this room. Smells like something died in there. And from the stains in the toilet, that's where it must have died."

"Yes, that is a problem. Russian train toilets often smell bad."

"How about we start looking over Rasputin's material, Nicky?"

"Very well. We shall work for a time then have dinner in the dining car?"

Avramenko unpacked her notebook computer and booted-up. Reynolds also powered up his own computer.

"Rasputin organized the information by sources and categories," Avramenko said.

"How has he labeled the sources?"

Avramenko displayed the file folders. "There're more than twenty folders."

Reynolds digested the information as Avramenko translated. Rasputin provided a summary of the information he had cataloged. Avramenko then identified Rasputin's folder names. "Ok. Let's look at the Rusatomic folder. That's what Rasputin has identified as the principle business involved with the Russian nuclear industry."

For the next two hours, Reynolds directed Avramenko as she pulled up financial records. Reynolds was interested in establishing the Martinelli Global connection that Rasputin alluded to. "Scan through the documents and tell me the subject matter of each. Then we'll see what is most important to translate first."

It was a slow process, but they found the documents that supported Rasputin's claim that Martinelli Global was involved in the Russian nuclear industry.

"Ok, here's what these documents point to; Rusatomic is wholly owned by RusEnergy, a public corporation traded on the Moscow Stock Exchange. RusEnergy is a holding company that controls a number of other corporations besides Rusatomic. Not clear yet what all they're into. We'll need to explore that further. But according to this info that Rasputin uncovered, the Martinelli Global connection comes from how RusEnergy is funded. It seems that Martinelli Global finances investment and operating capital through a number of offshore corporations. In short, Martinelli Global, a U.S. corporation is financing Russian production of nuclear fuels, and maybe even nuclear weapons work."

Reynolds shook his head at the magnitude of the thought.

The source of Rasputin's information was largely financial reports and e-mails. None of this was public information. At the least, Martinelli Global's withholding of this information violated SEC regulations. Since they went to great lengths to hide their involvement, it must violate a host of other U.S. laws. Reynolds wasn't sure of the exact legal context, but he was sure that covert financial funding of a foreign power's military nuclear infrastructure must violate U.S. national security statutes as well. And it must also violate Russian law.

"Rasputin didn't exaggerate. This stuff already is enough to topple Martinelli Global," Reynolds said. "Rasputin has access to some very deep secrets. If this is from computer hacking, our friend is truly gifted. How long have you known him?"

"I told you, I don't know him, Mark. If you mean how long has he been giving me information, perhaps for two years. The first time was to provide me information on a company called

Smolensk Logistics. His material showed it was a former business owned by Feliks Garnitsky, now owned by Nikolai Krasin. He said he noticed my stories about corruption. Said he wanted to help."

Reynolds suggested they explore the folder titled *Corruption*. They worked for another hour. The folder contained mostly e-mails. Avramenko translated by Reynolds prompting her to either translate the full text, or to move to another document.

"Who is this Chernienko," Reynolds asked in response to Avramenko's translation.

"That is *Admiral* Chernienko, the head of the Defense Ministry procurement."

"These e-mail exchanges are not specific but they suggest contract awards to various Krasin enterprises. What do you make out of the one about nuclear fuels to the Navy?"

Avramenko answered, "It suggests that Rusatomic is being awarded a broad contract to service all Russian Navy reactors; repairs, new fuels, re-processing spent fuels. It suggests that Rusatomic set the price."

"Interesting procurement twist."

Avramenko looked up from the computer. "Are you hungry? I am. Can we have some dinner in the dining car?"

"Sure. I'm hungry too."

Reynolds could see this was going to be a long laborious process. Going to this resort outside of Russia now made better sense.

The dining car was a pleasant surprise. He supposed it was as good as any in the West, but he had never dined on a train before. The menu was short. Avramenko ordered. Surprisingly, they even offered a couple of French wines. Avramenko asked Reynolds if he preferred the wine even though it was very expensive. The Bordeaux was not a particularly good label, but it was better than having the ubiquitous vodka.

After dinner, they ordered coffees and brandy. Diverted from the project, Reynolds allowed himself to fully appreciate Avramenko's physical charms. Apart from her figure, accentuated with a blouse showing cleavage, it was her face that drew him. It clearly suggested intelligence laced with a strong sexual component. Not a classic beauty with her slightly too long nose and high cheek bones, but all together a captivating face. With intensely dark blue eyes, her tendency of direct eye contact made it feel as if you were being pulled into a vortex.

They talked on for the better part of an hour. Avramenko was intensely interested in all things American. Her questions spanned every conceivable subject. Why didn't people travel by train in America? How widespread were these great shopping malls she read about? Did most women have their hair and nails done each week? Why was there so much poverty and crime in a nation so wealthy? Why were there so many murders? Was it really a dictatorship of the wealthy? What was New York like? Was living in New York better than living in California?

Reynolds found himself enjoying her questions about America. In spite of being manipulated by Avramenko since he arrived in Russia, he liked her company. Besides her looks and intelligence, she possessed a lively wit.

In reply to Reynolds comments about America's addiction to fast food, Avramenko said, "But you say this food which is unhealthy tastes very good. Here in Russia much of our food is unhealthy, but it also tastes bad."

Commenting about America's problem with violent crime, she said, "It is perhaps because there is too much religion and not enough sex."

"American society does have a lot of hang-ups about sex."

"Those are from the older generation? From the peasants? Do you call them peasants?"

Reynolds laughed. "No, not peasants. Usually they're just identified as from rural communities. They're typically the more religious part of American society."

"Like the old peasant women we call *babushkas*. They cling to the old ways. I think old peasant men would like to see pretty naked women just as much as young men do."

Reynolds was intrigued with all these references to sex. "You're right. It's a small group that represses sexual expression. Advertisers push the envelope as far as possible. It's kind of a game to see how far they can go."

"Perhaps when we have completed the project I can come to America for visit."

"If I get the book published, I'll pay for your trip."

"I would go to New York where you live, but I wish to see California too. Why do you live in New York not California?"

"Well, it's the place to be if you're a journalist. Plus, I like it there. At least in Manhattan, you can walk from where you live to everything; restaurants, coffee shops, bookstores, theaters. In California you have to drive. It's a different lifestyle."

"American movies are mostly filmed in New York or Los Angeles. It always shows Los Angeles as warm. Is that so?"

"Warmer than New York, at least in the winter."

He found himself yawning. The coffee did not buffer the effects of the wine and cognac. "Let's call it a night," he said.

"*Call it a night?* What does that mean?" Avramenko asked with a slight smile.

Reynolds didn't know if she was serious or flirting. "Just means it's been a long day and it's time to get some sleep."

"Yes, it is time we go to bed."

They returned to their compartment. A little awkwardly, Reynolds said, "So which bed do you prefer?" Both were identical, on opposite sides of the compartment.

"It does not matter. You may choose. I am going to the toilet." She took a small bag and left the compartment.

Reynolds was at a loss as to the protocol. There was no privacy in the compartment. He never wore pajamas. He decided just to remove his shoes for the time being. Once Avramenko was in her berth and the lights were out, he would shed his shirt and pants leaving on his underwear.

Fifteen minutes later, Avramenko returned to their compartment. Reynolds must have stared too long. "What is it?" she asked.

"Nothing. Ah, nothing."

Avramenko was wearing blue silk pajamas. He didn't know they made tailored pajamas, but her figure was abundantly evident. Maybe it was just a size too small. The effect was stunning. The whole scene was like that old Claudette Colbert and Clark Gable movie.

"I'm afraid I didn't pack any pajamas."

"That is not a problem. Sleep as you like. I am not a prude as you say in English. Good night, Mark. You will enjoy Black Sea. We shall make a good project together."

It was some time before Reynolds fell asleep. He was not thinking about the project. He was thinking about Nicky Avramenko in her blue silk pajamas.

CHAPTER 27

YALTA, CRIMEA, UKRAINE

Reynolds woke to the smell of hot tea being prepared by Nicky Avramenko. She was still dressed in her pajamas.

"Russian trains always have samovar with hot water. I prefer coffee, but tea is easier to make in compartment." She set out some raw sugar and a small bottle of cream.

"Tea is fine." He was still under the covers wearing only his underwear. After a couple of moments he threw aside the bed linen and pulled on his pants and shirt.

"Give me a couple of minutes to shave and brush my teeth."

He slipped on his shoes. No way was he going into that pigsty of a toilet barefooted. The thought of even doing his morning toilet in the place was daunting, even more so when Avramenko handed him toilet paper to take with him. Wonderful.

When he returned, Avramenko was dressed. Her hair was done; makeup fully in place. For his part, he felt a little disheveled. She had made tea and drawn the blinds back on the window. It was a sunny day as the train rolled through the endless wheat fields of the breadbasket of Mother Russia. The gentle rocking of the car and clacking of the rails made for a relaxed atmosphere. For a few moments it did feel like they were on holiday.

There was a knock on their compartment door. A man said something. Avramenko opened the door. The man was in uniform.

"Please get your passport. He is with Ukrainian Customs," Avramenko said to Reynolds. "We are crossing now into Ukraine."

Reynolds nearly dropped his cup of tea. This was it. He had a fleeting thought of some rat infested prison, cold, damp, fed only cabbage soup and stale bread.

But as Avramenko said, this was not a serious security check. The middle-aged man merely glanced at the passports, not even looking up to compare the photographs. He handed back the passports, gave Avramenko a smile, and left.

For the next several hours, Avramenko pulled up accounting records. It was a laborious process deciphering which documents were of the most interest, then even more tedious translating the details. Fortunately all of the documents seemed to have some intelligence value. Their friend Rasputin had been discriminating in his selection.

After a break for lunch in the dining car, Reynolds outlined a new plan to attack the data. "There is so much information here that we need a more organized approach to understand the bigger picture. We've been skipping around to various folders that Rasputin has labeled as financial records, corruption, government deals, etcetera. It's told us that our friend has hit a gold vein of insider information. But now we must put some structure to the research.

"From our work this morning, I've got enough notes to attempt to map out Martinelli Global's and Krasin's operations. How about you focus on identifying everything associated with this Rusatomic?"

"Very good. We shall commence our work accordingly once we get settled at the hotel," Avramenko said. The train was scheduled to arrive in Simferopol within the hour.

"I shall hire car to drive us to Yalta. Actually we are staying in small resort village of Miskhor. It is south of Yalta. Drive will be only 90 minutes."

The front of the Park Hotel in Miskhor was promising. It was a pretty white building with balconies on most rooms. A grove of tall trees surrounded the hotel. A uniformed attendant opened the car door. Inside, the lobby was polished wood. It could have been a beach resort in any place in the world. Only the Cyrillic lettering suggested Eastern Europe.

While Nicky Avramenko checked in at the desk, Reynolds let his imagination wander as he looked at her. He could already sense the sexual tension on the train ride. The prospect of spending two weeks together sharing the same room already caused a sense of arousal.

A bellboy, or whatever they were called in the Ukraine, managed their luggage down a long hallway. "You are Englander?" he asked.

"Yes. British."

"That is good. I am allowed to practice my English with you," the young man said then unlocked the room door. "This is nice room. You and your beautiful woman will enjoy here."

Reynolds followed Avramenko into the room. It was not lavish, but well appointed with good furniture. She looked into the bathroom to check the amenities. Reynolds looked at the single large bed before his attention was drawn to the bellboy opening the doors to the balcony. "You have beautiful view of Black Sea."

Reynolds followed him outside. It was a great view. The Black Sea was a few hundred yards away. The day was sunny. The bellboy continued to ramble on about the resort amenities. He learned that Miskhor was the warmest of the Crimea resorts. Reynolds gave him a generous tip to get rid of him.

"I hope you do not mind the arrangements," Avramenko said.

"Certainly not. This is an excellent place. Magnificent view."

Avramenko smiled broadly. "That is good. Is it so that Americans are bothered about things sexual?"

"Probably not any more than any group."

Nicky Avramenko came up close to him and looked straight into his eyes. Reynolds did not avoid her intense stare.

She laid the palms of both hands on his chest. "You have wondered about the sleeping arrangements with only the one bed?"

"The thought had crossed my mind."

"I think you are very handsome man. I believe you find me attractive also. We have many days together. We should not have anxiety of wondering what might happen." She then slid her arms around his waist and kissed him aggressively with her mouth open.

Reynolds held her head with both hands and returned the passion. After some moments, Avramenko disengaged and pushed Reynolds onto the bed. He kicked off his shoes then started to unbutton his shirt.

"No, wait, Mark. I have seen you looking at me the last two days. Do I arouse you?"

Reynolds grinned. "Very much so."

"Then let me undress first so you can become more aroused."

He simply nodded and settled back on his elbows on the bed.

Avramenko removed her blouse first. She then dropped her skirt to the floor and stepped out of it. Reaching behind her back, she unfastened her bra. Before exposing her breasts she smiled at Reynolds.

She stood before him with only her panty hose, still in her heels. She put one foot on Reynolds knee. The motion drew his attention to her exposed sex, obscured only by the sheer fabric of the panty hose. He removed her shoe. She repeated with the other. Without taking her eyes off Reynolds, she removed her panty hose slowly.

Standing on her toes naked, she asked, "Do you like what you see, Mark Reynolds?"

Reynolds motioned for her to come closer. She obeyed then began unbuttoning his shirt. He caressed the underside of her breasts.

After removing his shirt, she unbuckled his belt. She unzipped his fly. His erection strained his underwear, even more so when she rested her hand on it.

Then slipping her hand down the waist band of his underwear, she gripped his cock and pulled it free. "I believe you do like what you see."

Avramenko quickly removed his pants and underwear. She knelt on the floor in front of him and took his cock into her mouth. She was gratified with an immediate groan of pleasure from Reynolds.

While she worked him with her mouth she looked up at him with those deep blue eyes. He cupped her breasts with his hands.

After several minutes, Reynolds pulled her up and laid her across the bed. He buried his face into her soft pubic hair. She was equally aroused as he gently probed her with his tongue and lips. He was intent on protracting her pleasure. But within only a few minutes her stomach hardened and convulsed as she climaxed in waves.

She muttered some words in Russian as he entered her. Minutes later she cried out more loudly as she came again in response to Reynolds' own orgasm.

After her breathing returned to normal, she said, "Now you see, we can work and make love without anxiety. Do you not agree this is good start?"

They made love again the next morning before going to breakfast. It helped Reynolds ability to concentrate the rest of the day without continually having sexual fantasies.

"Do we have an Internet connection here at the hotel?" It appeared there was a data connection on the desk but the instructions were in Russian.

"Yes. But we need to call desk and have them turn on. They will charge for use."

"Fine. Make the call. I need to send an e-mail to my colleague in New York."

"Colleague?"

"Yes. Her name is Rachel Stern. She's a researcher with the New York Daily Press."

"But you are no longer employed by the newspaper. She must be good friend to help you."

"Yes she is." He felt a tinge of guilt as he typed an e-mail. It was brief. He told her he had arrived in Moscow. After meeting up with Avramenko they left Moscow for a location that felt safer. Nothing to worry about, just a precaution. Had she anything new to report? He signed *Love, Mark.*

Avramenko looked over his shoulder with no self-consciousness. "You sign with *Love*? She is perhaps more than just a colleague?"

"A friend, Nicky."

"Not a lover?"

Another twinge of guilt. "No."

What qualified someone as a lover? Rachel would like to think she was. Was she that to him? She at least had been a lover for awhile. Was he being unfaithful?

"Are you jealous?"

Avramenko turned him around in the chair and kissed him fully with her open mouth. Then she sat on his lap facing him. Her skirt rode up high on her thighs. Her breasts pressed hard against him. For the next hour, she made him think only of her.

There was a return e-mail from Rachel the following morning; "Nothing new to report. I am still very worried about your safety, Mark. Finish and leave there as soon as you can. Hope Miss Avramenko is proving to be worth the trip. Rachel."

"She sounds like a lover," Nicky Avramenko said.

CHAPTER 28

MOSCOW, RUSSIAN FEDERATION

"What the fuck do you mean you lost him?" Feliks Garnitsky said into his cell phone, startling his lunch guest, an assistant deputy minister of the Industry and Energy Ministry. Garnitsky excused himself and stepped outside the restaurant. It was a cold Moscow day with a slight breeze.

Once outside, the caller told him that Reynolds had arrived the previous afternoon at Moscow's Sheremetyevo Airport. "He met no one at the airport. Had one brief cell phone conversation then took a taxi to the Medea Hotel. He received no visitors. Didn't leave the hotel. Our people got suspicious by around noon. They used their FSB credentials to have a maid open the door to Reynolds' room. He wasn't there. No luggage in the room. Bed was not slept in."

"Goddamnit, Stanislav, Reynolds was gone five minutes after he arrived at the hotel. Didn't your people get suspicious that he hadn't eaten for almost 24 hours? Didn't your idiots put somebody to watch the rear of the hotel?"

"No sir. And yes they are idiots. They've been dealt with for their stupidity. I've got a lot of people out there looking for Reynolds. Spreading a lot of money around to informants. I'm sure something will turn up soon," the man called Stanislav said.

"Don't be so sure. Somebody is helping Reynolds. He wouldn't have even known how to escape surveillance much less get around Moscow by himself. I'll make some calls. Keep me informed of anything you find out."

Fuck. What a stupid fuck-up. He would have to excuse himself from finishing lunch with the assistant deputy minister in order to call Nikolai Krasin with the bad news. That would be unpleasant.

As anticipated, the call to Krasin did not go well. "I don't understand, Feliks. This was a simple task yet your people fucked it up. I expect it to be resolved quickly. I trust that you will see to this personally. Is that too much to ask?"

"I will see to it personally, Nikolai Mikhailovich. Reynolds will be found. And once he is, what is to be done?" Garnitsky said sarcastically.

Krasin hesitated. "My choice is to get rid of him. No body to be found. No inquiries. No stories. Something you're good at, Feliks."

The fucking arrogant weasel, Garnitsky thought. "Fine. I'll see to it." Krasin was an aristocrat, a giver of orders. He didn't know what it was like to get his hands dirty. He'd never seen someone tortured. Never felt the desperation of someone clinging to life. Never the one to extinguish that life.

"We may have to temper that, however. I said that was my choice but Steven Martinelli seems uncomfortable with that option. He's too American I'm afraid. He's still upset about how that situation with the board member Ashcroft was handled. Although it achieved what we wanted, he thought it too heavy handed. Wants to be sure about what Reynolds may have before disposing of him. Martinelli has a bigger risk with Reynolds' stolen information than we do, so it's his call. Things are much more difficult in America. Martinelli can't circumvent things like we can here in Russia. Yet he still avoids the obvious solution.

He doesn't want to consider that we can extract from Reynolds whatever he knows before killing him."

"So what's that mean? Do I get rid of Reynolds, or not?" Garnitsky said.

"It means that I need to call New York. Bad enough that we lost Reynolds. But Martinelli's got to be part of the next step. Otherwise we become responsible for the consequences. When you locate him you grab him and let me know."

To Garnitsky, doing business in the United States was something truly foreign. According to Krasin, everything had to be hidden from some government agency. Those same agencies demanded all sorts or recordkeeping so it was difficult to avoid incriminating paper trails. Direct bribery was rarely an option. Everything had to be second, third, or even fourth removed.

Garnitsky followed his call to Krasin with a call to an old KGB associate, now a colonel in its successor ministry, the Federalnaya Sluzhba Bezopasnost, or FSB. The FSB was responsible for internal security of the Russian Federation.

Given the fact that the Colonel was on Garnitsky's payroll, he had a direct telephone number to the Colonel's desk. A meeting was arranged at FSB headquarters in Lubyanka Square within the hour. It was the same building that housed the old KGB, still ugly and ominous.

The meeting was brief. The Colonel would issue an order to locate and detain Reynolds on suspicion of threatening Russian state security. The basis of the charge was sufficiently vague. The Colonel was not curious as to Garnitsky's real reason for locating this American. For the equivalent of $10,000USD in Russian rubles, it didn't matter. Garnitsky also instructed the Colonel to continuously monitor for the issuing of an Interpol Red Notice on Reynolds. That would provide a legal basis for the Russian government to detain and deport Reynolds to Columbia.

"When we locate this American, what then?" the Colonel asked.

"Simply place him into custody. Perhaps with no record of his arrest would be best. That will leave our options open. I will take care of the men that arrest him with generously rewards. There will be no problems. Just contact me immediately when you locate him."

YALTA, CRIMEA, UKRAINE

Over the next days, Reynolds and Avramenko settled into a routine of making love each day. The daily regimen satisfied their sexual appetites, freeing their concentration the rest of the time to work on Rasputin's files. After four days, they had amassed a considerable list of damaging information on Martinelli Global and their Russian partner, Krasin.

Reynolds and Avramenko were relaxing on their terrace overlooking the Black Sea. The sun was low in the western sky maybe an hour away from sunset. They were enjoying a good bottle of French Bordeaux. The setting was idyllic. The scene was two lovers on holiday.

Reynolds thought how incongruous it was to their real purpose. It was important they stayed focused. "Let's summarize what we know so we can determine our next course of action."

Avramenko exhibited a false pout. "You are a much driven man, Mark Reynolds. We have been working hard for days. You need to learn how to turn off work. You should enjoy life more."

"I am enjoying you," he said, then leaned over to kiss Avramenko. "And you are a good reporter too."

She hit him in the shoulder playfully. "You are good reporter too. Not too bad lover either." Her tactic worked. They made love and then had a late dinner.

Back to the project the next morning, Reynolds said, "As I was saying last night before you seduced me and I succumbed to your hedonistic pleasures."

"What is *hedonistic*?"

"Hedonism is the self-indulgence of pleasure."

"Yes, that is what we do when we make love."

"And when we drink wine and look at sunsets in beautiful resorts. So back to business. This is work time."

For all her joking and flirtatious behavior, Reynolds knew Nicky Avramenko was a serious journalist. She understood Russian business. She had ferreted out a wealth of rich information from Rasputin's documents.

Reynolds summarized. "So we know Martinelli Global owns a majority interest in a whole host of Russian companies. Only some are recognized in their public reporting, mostly energy related companies. Nikolai Krasin controls all of their Russian companies. Many of these companies were founded by Krasin, including his flagship Moscow Capital Partners. The whole segment of Martinelli Global's acknowledged holdings in Russia and the other former Soviet states contribute significant profits. We get some juicy insider stuff from Rasputin, but generally Martinelli Global being invested in Russian business is public knowledge. Nothing newsworthy there.

"On the dark side, we have Martinelli Global invested in undeclared enterprises that deal heavily in a sea of corruption and even criminal activity. That's the real stuff."

Avramenko added, "Yes. Martinelli Global would wish to hide Feliks Garnitsky and his Smolensk Logistics. He is total criminal. Drugs, smuggling, money laundering. Murder."

"True enough. But the real master criminal here is Nikolai Krasin. His crimes are on a grander scale. He has co-opted high ranking government officials and senior military officers. Krasin's reach spans into almost all sectors of at least the Russian government and at least some evidence of Ukraine and Georgia as well.

"Krasin's various banks engage in practices that might not be illegal in Russia, but would be criminal anywhere else. That's why Martinelli Global buries their investments through several layers of offshore subsidiaries.

"So just the evidence we have of Martinelli Global hiding ownership in foreign enterprises and engaging in international criminal activities should be enough to drive a stake into their heart. But then we have this whole involvement with the Russian nuclear industry. That would be more than just business news. That exposure would collapse all of those Russian companies, especially if it becomes known that an American company is financially involved. Nikolai Krasin and Feliks Garnitsky would just disappear."

"That would be very good for Russia," Avramenko said. "That is what Rasputin hopes to accomplish."

"Well, before we can cause that to happen, we need more information on how that whole nuclear deal works with the Russian government. It's not clear yet how Martinelli Global is involved. Maybe they're not. We've still got a lot more Rasputin files to plow through, but we should try to think of some other avenues to probe.

"Speaking of Rasputin, when was the last time you heard from him?" Reynolds asked.

"Not since you arrived in Moscow. I e-mailed him after you arrived. I told him you were followed. I e-mailed him that we were going to a safe place to research his documents. He has sent me no reply."

That changed the next day.

"Mark, Rasputin just sent me an e-mail," Avramenko said.

Reynolds came over to her notebook computer. The e-mail was of course in Russian. Avramenko translated.

"Have discovered something new. It is extremely serious. Extremely urgent. I must meet you and Mark Reynolds face to face. Information is sensitive. Must be delivered to the West. Are you safe? Where you are?"

"Shit. I don't believe this. At the least, I don't like it. This guy goes to great lengths to hide himself. Knows people are trying to keep us under surveillance. You've never seen him. You don't have any idea who he is. This e-mail could be bogus. If he can hack into secure systems then someone else could have hacked into the e-mail provider and sent this message. Could be just a way for Martinelli Global to locate us." Reynolds said.

"They don't know I am helping you."

"I hope that's still the case." He was not that confident.

"Do I answer him?"

Reynolds thought for a moment. "Reply for him to tell us where he is and we will come to him."

Avramenko sent the e-mail. They both sat transfixed to the computer screen waiting for Rasputin's reply. They waited only a couple of minutes.

"Very good, Nicky. I see you and Mark Reynolds are being cautious. That is good. I will be in Kiev in two days. Can you and Reynolds meet me there?"

Reynolds looked at Avramenko. Kiev was in the Ukraine. They came through Kiev on their way south to the Crimea. It was several hours by train.

Avramenko replied, "Yes. Day after tomorrow. Will arrive by train. Will advise time. How do we meet?"

Rasputin replied immediately, "I will meet you at train station. I can recognize both of you."

CHAPTER 29

BAKU, AZERBAIJAN

F eliks Garnitsky was sitting in the lounge at the Park Hyatt
Hotel in Baku, Azerbaijan. Baku is the capital of Azerbaijan
lying on the Western side of the Caspian Sea. It is a city of mixed
impressions. The old walled section is a picturesque collection of
medieval buildings that could be anywhere in Western Europe.
South of the old city is the architecture of the early twentieth
century. The fine old mansions now housing museums were the
product of the early oil boom of that time. Beyond the old walls
the city spreads with the typical Soviet era planning. The new oil
industry of the twenty-first century has funded a skyline of ugly
high-rise structures.

Baku is petroleum. At the turn of the last century, half of the
world's oil came from Baku. The World War II Battle of
Stalingrad to the north was fought largely for control of the Baku
oil fields. Petroleum brought Garnitsky to Baku as well. At the
beginning of the twenty-first century, the Caspian Sea has the
largest undeveloped petroleum reserves in the world.

Garnitsky was there establishing business relationships for
Krasin's Caspian project. The two other men having drinks with
Garnitsky were executives of a large oil extraction equipment
manufacturer. It was late in the afternoon in the spacious hotel
bar lounge.

Garnitsky was startled to see a familiar face sitting across the room looking toward him. His old KGB training concealed any indication of surprise to his guests.

The slender, dark-skinned man across the room stood and walked to where Garnitsky assumed the toilets might be. Garnitsky excused himself for the same reason and followed the man into the toilet.

A brief survey by both men confirmed they were alone in the toilet. They embraced and kissed each other on both cheeks.

"My dear, Feliks. I must say you are looking well," the dark-skinned man said in badly accented Russian.

"And you as well, Farzad. It is certainly a surprise." It was definitely not a coincidental meeting.

"I have something of importance to discuss, my friend. I preferred that we meet somewhere away from Moscow. When I learned you would be in Baku I seized the opportunity."

"I do not advertise my travel plans. Your intelligence is very good."

Farzad Savi smiled. "Since you must return to your guests, could we agree to meet tomorrow perhaps?"

"Of course. Where do you have in mind?"

"There is a small café in the old town section called The Azeri Cafe. It is located two blocks north of the Boulevard, just behind the Maiden's Tower. Perhaps noon would be a suitable time?"

"I shall see you tomorrow, Farzad," Garnitsky said, then left the restroom.

Farzad Savi was now a colonel in the Iranian Ministry of Intelligence and Security, or MOIS. Garnitsky knew him from the 1980s during his own time with the KGB. Their respective intelligence agencies had cooperated in trying to assess the extent of the nuclear technology proliferation of Pakistan's A. Q. Khan. Iraq's Suddam Hussein had been a recipient. Iran had also been a recipient of Khan's sharing of nuclear technology among

Muslim nations. Iran and Iraq were engaged in a protracted war at the time. The Soviets had their own concerns about an Iraq with nuclear weapons so there was a level of cooperation between the KGB and MOIS.

Garnitsky had gotten along well with the Iranian. Savi was not a wild-eyed revolutionary. To the contrary, he was a shrewd pragmatist. He had been an operative in the former Shah's feared secret police agency, the SAVAK. Most operatives fled Iran after the overthrow of the Shah in 1979. Savi had worked undercover against leftist dissident groups. Seeing the imminent fall of the Shah's police state, Savi saw his opportunity. He simply found the means to change sides by playing on his leftist connections. His skills were in demand in the new regime. All this he told Garnitsky one night in Moscow after too much vodka.

Savi was a talented intelligence professional. He was smart and resourceful in adapting to all manner of circumstances. Apolitical and pragmatic, he was able to manipulate Iran's otherwise politically driven organizations. Savi was a chameleon who thrived in the Shah's secular police state, then successfully adapted to the fanatical religious zeal of the Iranian post-revolutionary state. Personally, Savi had no religious feelings. Since he predominately worked outside of Iran, he was free to indulge in all things non-Islamic.

Garnitsky liked Savi. Both were intelligence professionals. Both enjoyed their pleasures. Garnitsky saw fundamentalist Islam as untrustworthy as Soviet Communism. Ideologues could never be trusted. Garnitsky trusted to human greed and the pragmatic social order of thieves. He knew Savi was not a believer in Islam, regardless of the religiosity of his country.

Garnitsky assumed Savi knew him equally well. So tracking him down to arrange a meeting in Azerbaijan must have significance. Garnitsky's curiosity was acutely aroused.

Garnitsky arrived at The Azeri thirty minutes early. Actually he was some distance away outside a small art gallery. Ostensibly he was looking at the paintings displayed in the window. His real purpose was to observe the arrival of his old acquaintance. Did he have people with him? Old cautions died hard.

Farzad Savi arrived alone at five minutes before the hour. He took a small table outside. If there was someone with Savi, they were not obvious even to Garnitsky's trained eye.

"Are you alone?" Garnitsky asked as he approached the table.

Savi smiled. "You took up a surveillance I presume?"

"Of course. I have not spotted anyone. So that means you are alone or he, or she, or they are very good."

Savi laughed. "Over there. The one selling theater tickets."

Garnitsky turned to look at the guy in period custom. He had been hawking tickets when Garnitsky had first arrived to take up his own surveillance.

"Very good. Why is he needed for this meeting?"

"Only to make sure you are not being watched, my old friend. You are a very important man, Feliks Alekseev. Who knows who might have interest in your movements? It is best if we are not connected."

They ordered cheese and bread, along with a bottle of wine. While they waited, they each lit a cigarette.

"You have done very well my friend," Savi said. "You are perhaps very rich by now?"

"I'm doing well. Not sure about rich. Besides, you can never be rich enough."

"Exactly! I have followed your career with some interest over the years. You were always keen to try a venture that held the promise of much profit. Now you are a trusted colleague of the billionaire, Nikolai Krasin."

"Do you have a dossier on me, Farzad?"

Savi smiled broadly. "But of course. I am in the intelligence business. We have dossiers on everyone of importance."

The waiter brought the food and a bottle of wine. Once the ritual of opening the wine and tasting were concluded, they resumed their conversation.

"And what interest does the Iranian MOIS have in me?"

"Your talents. Your organization. Your connections. And your access to certain places of interest."

"Sounds as if you want to steal something, Farzad."

"That is precisely what we want. Something so valuable that we are prepared to pay an enormous sum to get it. So much money that even someone of means such as you will be interested."

"How much?"

Savi paused to light another cigarette. After taking a sip of wine, he said in not much more than a whisper, "600 million Euros."

Garnitsky said nothing for a several moments while he as well lit a cigarette. Even to Garnitsky, it was a staggering sum.

"To steal what?"

"Nuclear weapons."

Garnitsky was shocked into pausing for a moment before lighting his cigarette. The implication was as staggering as the amount of money involved.

"From who?"

"From the Russians."

"You're fucking mad. We Russians are not some half-assed nuclear state like Pakistan. You work for religious lunatics. I would have thought you had better sense, Farzad. No one could pull off such a theft. Even if they could, they'd never get away with such a thing. The Russians and every Western intelligence agency would be after you."

Farzad had expected Garnitsky's reaction. "Come my friend, you know me better than that. I admit it is bold beyond all imagination. But I assure you, it can be done. You see, I head the team that devised the plan."

"And what would my part be in all of this?"

"You are involved in Nikolai Krasin's company Rusatomic. Among other work for the Ministry of Atomic Energy, Rusatomic is engaged in dismantling Russian nuclear weapons. It stores nuclear materials and reprocesses fuels. You have unique access to these facilities as a senior executive for Krasin. You also have strong ties with your former associates in the KGB. You ex-KGB people control Russia now. This new FSB is nothing more than a new name for the old KGB."

Savi was correct. The new FSB and their partners such as Nikolai Krasin and Feliks Garnitsky, controlled the Russian economic sector. The old KGB had evolved into a state within a state. Economic control had replaced the Soviet style police-state control.

Foreign intelligence and internal counter-intelligence became secondary priorities with the collapse of the old Soviet state. The fifty years of contesting with the United States changed overnight. With economic and political control of the Russian state, the FSB had replaced the Communist Party. In Russia, fundamental things do not change, they just adapt to new realities with new names.

"No, no, Farzad. I don't have access. I go there infrequently. Less lately. Besides, these Rusatomic facilities are secured by the Ministry of Defense. The Military guards everything. The security is not sloppy."

"I am aware of the details of the security arrangements. But I hardly need tell you that any security system can be breached."

"I would guess that you have informants within Rusatomic. So what do you need of my services?"

"My friend, before I go into greater detail, I must understand your interest in this venture."

"Venture? It's the theft of all time! It will change world politics. Are you saying if you tell me more and I refuse, you'll have to have me killed? Would you not do that anyway with what you've already said?"

"You exaggerate our abilities. I do not suppose that killing Feliks Garnitsky would be easy. However, the realities are such that I would not attempt this undertaking without your special contributions. If you do not join with me, then the project will be abandoned."

"Then tell me more of the details, Farzad. It will depend upon how good your plan is."

"Very well. The plan is this. I have two Russian Army officers that work at two different Rusatomic facilities. They are well paid. They have provided detailed information on procedures and security. Even photographs. Without going into all the fine points, the plan is to hijack the functional parts of several nuclear warheads from Rusatomic's Ozyorsk reprocessing plant following disassembly at the Trekhgornyy facility."

Garnitsky interrupted, "That transportation is done by the Military in specially secured trucks. If you hijack the truck you'll never get far."

"Of course not. I used the term hijacked only as a metaphor. The Military will transport the intact warheads to the reprocessing facility. Normally this would only be the fissionable material cores, but these will be the fully intact warhead assemblies. The transport personnel will not know that of course.

"Your services are required after that. We need you to arrange for your own people to impersonate soldiers and to establish a false military installation. Again with orders, the Military will transport the warheads from the reprocessing plant to your sham facility. All this is necessary because the security is much less at the reprocessing plant. It will also add to the complexity of the audit trail of these warheads.

"Your people will need full security documents. The sham military facility must be convincing. These are all details we are contracting for you to provide. You have access to these Rusatomic facilities, and you have special relationships with high ranking military. For that, we are paying 600 million Euros for the delivery of three warheads to Iran. 200 million each."

"Farzad, I believe you are over-simplifying these tasks."

"Bear with me, Feliks. I can explain down to the smallest detail how this can be accomplished. But let me first flesh out the full scenario. Once your people have the warheads, you will smuggle them through the high country into Northern Iran. I am well aware that you have extensive connections among Kurdish smugglers. Guns, drugs. Even Iranian oil. You already have an indirect relationship with Republican Guard factions."

"I have seen these bombs at the Trekhgornyy Plant. They're too large to easily smuggle, especially through the mountains."

"You will not be smuggling the bombs, only the operational part. They are essentially spheres. They're placed in secure boxes. The whole package will weigh less than 200 kilos. They can be lifted by as few as four men. We are seeking only modestly sized warheads." Savi chuckled at his own black humor.

"All right. So let's say all of this is successful. First, the Russian Military will discover the theft. They're not incompetent. That puts me at risk. Second, the theft will get tracked to Iran. Who else? Next thing, Israel bombs the shit out of you before you can reassemble these warheads into bombs. The Israelis would have no other option."

"You are right. Secrecy is absolutely essential. But that's not the end of the plan. We have devised a way to account for the missing material by changing past records. When they take their next semi-annual inventory and discover the discrepancy, it will be reconciled when they dig back through the records and discover the *errors*. Our key asset is a senior Russian Army officer, a full colonel who heads the auditing team. He is paid very well."

"Well that all sounds interesting, Farzad, but there's still a major problem. There are too many people involved. Why are they spying for you? If you pay them some great sum of money they'll spend it and become targets of suspicion. There are no cut-outs. Everything leads back to theft of Russian nuclear weapons and the whole world goes fucking crazy."

"All these people think they're working outside the normal chain of command under orders from some high-ranking general. They think that because our Russian Army colonel has shown them *secret orders*. Ostensibly, these officers have been made to believe they're working under direct orders from the High Command, and the President himself. The ploy being that the Russian President wants to circumvent U.S. monitoring of Russian nuclear weapons inventories.

"These lesser officers also receive monies to make their deceit more palatable. The Colonel, he's just a spy, doing this for a lot of money. His female companion is also one of our assets. We can monitor his reliability closely."

"That's not very reliable with so much at stake, Farzad."

"That's where we need your other special services, Feliks. There's surprisingly few people needed for the plan to work. Once concluded, we need all of these smaller functionaries disposed of quickly. It must be accomplished in such a manner as to not raise suspicions. That is why you are vital to this operation. You need to accomplish this to insulate yourself from involvement. We need that to secure sufficient time."

"Why is Iran willing to take the risk of this failing? It would seem to cause worse problems for you. The World believes you are pursuing your own nuclear weapons program. Assuming that is true, why not just continue down that path?"

"Because our leaders have no political sense. Especially the clerics. They scare the rest of the World with their fanatical ravings. They threaten the World. Mostly they threaten Israel. It is openly speculated that Iran conceals uranium enrichment activities that would generate weapons-grade fissionable material. Any Iranian nuclear program that advances to any significant degree of achievement will provoke an Israeli attack.

"Possession of actual functioning warheads would provide those I work for greater influence within the government. It would change the dynamics in the Middle East by leveling the playing field with Israel. These weapons are much more advanced than any initial Iranian program could ever hope to produce. This is not Pakistani level technology. These are weapon designs of the most advanced type. The yields of these weapons will rival anything the Israelis might have."

"Let's assume everything goes according to plan. The theft is never discovered. The warheads are assembled into operational weapons by the Iranians. At some point you have to make the threat known to the rest of the World. To make that threat credible, you have to suggest the origin of the weapons. How do I escape that?" Garnitsky said.

Savi smiled. "That is why I came to you Feliks. You are a master at hiding and smuggling, at bribing and getting around legal obstacles. I would assume that you could devise a plan that removed you from suspicion. The Military is ill-paid and corrupt. Your enterprises have taken advantage of that corruption. You architected that part of Krasin's business empire. This will require use of the Military."

"I must give this considerable thought. I will only agree if I can devise a way to insulate myself. Once this becomes known, it would be the end for anyone involved. Might even be the end of Iran. Have you thought about, Farzad?"

"I would then have to find another country."

Garnitsky said, "I shall contact you in one week. How do I do that?"

"Here is a cell phone number," Savi wrote a number on a fake business card.

Garnitsky rose to leave. Savi rose and embraced him.

"If I do accept, Farzad, the price is 900 million Euros. There will be certain large expenses."

Savi shrugged. "Life is a negotiation. With crude oil prices continuing to rise, I believe that we can agree to that figure."

CHAPTER 30

MOSCOW, RUSSIAN FEDERATION

G arnitsky replied to Savi with a call five days after the Baku meeting.

"I accept the contract. Are we agreed upon the 900 million Euros?"

"Yes. For three devices of course."

"Of course. The Terms?"

"450 million to be placed on deposit. Just advise me the bank and account number. Balance of the funds upon delivery of the weapons."

"One more detail, Farzad. My people shall run the operation. I need the names of these officers you are controlling. I also need the ability to directly access your control agents."

"My dear Feliks, would you seek me to turn over my entire intelligence network? You are a partner in this, but I cannot relinquish all control."

Savi's career would be made with this coup. He could become head of the Iranian MOIS. If he failed, it would cost him his head. This was not something he could subcontract.

"I mean that I need everything you have. This will be a complicated undertaking. There must be no mistakes. If I don't control all the pieces then the possibility of failure becomes unacceptable."

Savi was silent for a moment. "This is too important not to proceed because of organizational disagreements. Perhaps we can find an acceptable compromise. Can we meet in Moscow?"

"Very well, Farzad. We can meet."

Savi cringed at Garnitsky's security slip of using his name on the cell phone call. The entire conversation made him uncomfortable. He was aware of the United States National Security Agency's vast eavesdropping capabilities.

"That would be best. This is of too much importance. I shall ccontact you."

Garnitsky had accepted the deal after giving much thought on how he could insulate himself. Savi's plan for stealing the warheads was elegantly simple. With the level of poor military pay and scarce resources for security, it was a wonder that it hadn't been tried already. As it was, the Russians had hundreds of pounds of weapon grade fissionable material that were unaccounted for. The real task was insuring he was personally insulated from complicity once the Iranians went public.

To accomplish that, he had to limit his connection to only a couple of people. Secondly, there had to be a plausible alternative group on which to shift suspicion. The basic plan inherently got rid of the majority of players. The killings of these would be blamed on the same group ultimately to be implicated in the theft. Who other than Chechen separatists? The perfect motivation by striking a blow at Moscow while getting funding from Iran to continue their struggle to free the province from the Russian Federation.

That left only who would remain to connect him to the event. Farzad Savi would know, but he was Iranian with no motivation to reveal Garnitsky's participation. Obviously, Garnitsky would have to personally co-opt a high ranking army officer in the 12th Directorate to issue false orders for the bogus transfer of the warheads. And one more person was essential; the person on the scene that would direct the operation. That would clearly be Garnitsky's right-hand man, Yuri Antonovich Dratshev.

Dratshev was only in his mid-thirties but a proven asset. His rapid rise among Garnitsky's staff was a result of his inordinate organizational abilities. Not only could he assimilate complex variables into a plan, but he could quickly make adaptations to changing circumstances.

As the son of a mid-level bureaucrat Yuri Dratshev was afforded a good education, receiving an advanced degree in mathematics. Dratshev's father regularly took bribes from Garnitsky. Dratshev quickly saw a faster track to success with the criminal-business elite represented by people like Garnitsky.

"Yuri Antonovich, you have proven to be an outstanding asset to me," Garnitsky said to Dratshev. They were in a small restaurant seated in a secluded corner.

"Thank you, Feliks Alekseev. I appreciate your confidence."

"I have something of great importance to share with you. It is an opportunity of a lifetime. It would be a private matter. Not something to do with our work with Moscow Capital or Smolensk Logistics. You would have the opportunity to make a great deal of money, a very great deal of money. There is only one catch to the offer."

"And that is what?"

"Once I tell you, you become committed. It would not be possible to back out."

"I think I understand."

"How much money is involved?"

"10 million Euros."

Dratshev's eyes widened. "How much would I personally get?"

"10 million. That is your take for managing the project."

Dratshev was silent for a moment as he digested what he had just heard. It was an unbelievable amount. What he would be asked to do would be commensurately difficult and dangerous. But if he refused to accept the offer, it would be career-limiting, probably life-limiting. You can't turn down a promotion. It really was not an *offer*.

"I thank you for your confidence in me, Feliks Alekseev. For such a sum you can count on me to do whatever is required."

"Excellent. I never thought otherwise."

Dratshev speculated on what Garnitsky wanted him to do for such a sum. Assassinate a major head of state? Eliminate a political party? Start a war?

"We are going to steal three nuclear warheads," Garnitsky said.

Dratshev was stunned. Starting a war may not have been that far off. "Do you know this to be even remotely possible?"

"Very much so. I will tell you the broad outline of the plan. I shall rely on you to supply the minute details and for directing the actual operation. Only you, Yuri. No other staff is to know about this."

Garnitsky explained the plan. Dratshev interrupted only occasionally to ask questions. He concluded that the plan was indeed workable, but the implications were still staggering. He internally shuddered at the implications of a nuclear armed Iran with their fundamentalist theocracy and unstable leadership.

"One final thing, Yuri. Do not commit anything to paper. Do not use e-mails. Keep this deep and dark. You will have to supervise this first-hand from the Urals. I want to avoid e-mails. No records of any kind as a trail. As much as I hate to, we will have to communicate by cell phone. We must be cautious there as well. No direct references to the project."

"When is this to take place?"

"That depends upon my convincing of General Ryndenko for his assistance," Garnitsky said. "I would think we could put this together over the next 90 days if I am successful there."

Oleg Ryndenko was a major general in the 12th Main Directorate of the Ministry of Defense, officially named

Glavnoye Upravleniye Ministerstvo Oborony. The 12th GUMO was the directorate responsible for Russian nuclear weapons. Ryndenko had been the liaison between Krasin's Rusatomic and the Ministry of Defense from the inception. He was the one who arranged the agreed upon offsets that made Krasin's investment in the Russian nuclear industry profitable. Non-bid contracts and preferential government business were directed to another Krasin enterprise, Advanced Technologies. Ryndenko assembled the deals, and then fixed the audit trails. He was a clever bureaucrat.

As the chief of all nuclear weapons programs for the Ministry of Defense, General Sobolev appointed Ryndenko to the position after architecting the deal with Nikolai Krasin years before. These illicit deals with the Government were Garnitsky's principle area of involvement with Rusatomic and Advanced Technologies. Ryndenko's association with sanctioned corruption made him a prime target of Garnitsky. What better way to get the better deal than to bribe the fixer. Garnitsky simply paid much better than the Military.

Ryndenko had fallen so deeply under Garnitsky's control over the last several years that his lifestyle was one of dependency; a better apartment, newly remodeled with western furnishings; a cook; expensive wines and liquors; jewelry for his wife; Black Sea vacations; education for his daughter in Paris; dining at the best restaurants; a mistress with her own apartment. All this provided by Garnitsky.

Then of course there was the matter concerning the death of Leysa Varvarinski. Garnitsky had covered up the incident. Ryndenko's career was saved, much less having avoided a possible prosecution for manslaughter. There were incriminating photographs.

Ryndenko was the reason Garnitsky accepted Savi's proposal. Ryndenko had the means to do this, and Garnitsky had control over Ryndenko. Ryndenko could hardly refuse. If he did refuse, he could not do anything about it. He could not inform his superiors without his own ruin. More than that, he would be paid such a sum that avarice would win out over fear.

"What if Ryndenko balks? Maybe he might not have the balls," Dratshev said.

"In that event, Yuri, the General will be a liability that will need to be removed. But I do not think he will refuse. Let's remain positive."

"For now I need you go to Trekhgornyy and Ozersk right away. I need you to become familiar with all of the physical aspects of the operations of the warhead disassembly and the reprocessing operations. We need a full understanding of the security measures at both locations. Most of all get a look at these warheads. What do they look like? How big are they? I will get you the necessary access."

Farzad Savi arrived in Moscow two days after Garnitsky dispatched Dratshev to the Urals. They met at the same café.

"Let us not haggle about running this operation. It is of too great importance," Savi said.

"I am not haggling, my friend. I need to have control. I need to understand all of the players. Can they be relied upon? Will they keep quiet? It is my neck on the line if this should fail."

"I fully understand. Of course you need to know of these officers to construct the remaining details of the plan. But I do believe that my intelligence penetration has provided me with a better understanding of the internal security mechanisms. Even though these are Rusatomic plants, it would take you some time and at some risk to gain the same knowledge. You have been in intelligence. You know that it is highly risky to change control of operatives."

"I was not planning to exclude you, Farzad. However there must be no misunderstanding that I shall dictate the operation. You will work with my key man, Yuri Dratshev. He will be the one actually in control.

"And I shall be kept informed on all details by Dratshev and yourself?"

"Yes. But you must find a good cover. You cannot pass for Russian. Your accent is terrible. I do not want your presence to compromise the operation."

"Feliks, you wound my professional pride. I am not a virgin at this. After all, my network penetrated the most sensitive area of Russian nuclear arms. Now, since I believe we have an understanding, there's just one other thing."

"And what is that?"

"A small matter of my payment. You see I have approval for a total sum of one billion Euros. That is your fee of 900 million plus 100 million for me. Since I am in the employ of the Iranian government, I am only entitled to my salary. It just didn't seem fair. With your extensive international financial transactions I am sure you could deposit my fee in a secret numbered account somewhere secure."

"Not very patriotic of you, Farzad."

"Patriotism is a very complex thing. I do not think that my properly earned remuneration for delivering such a great service to my country conflicts with my patriotism. It is entirely right that we should both prosper handsomely from this, my friend."

CHAPTER 31

General Oleg Ryndenko arrived at the elegant Grillage Restaurant near Red Square at 8:00 p.m. Garnitsky had called the previous day. Said there was something of importance to discuss. He suggested they could conclude business then enjoy an excellent meal.

Ryndenko arrived on time. He wore a well-tailored civilian gray suit. He understood that Garnitsky would frown on him wearing his military uniform. "Feliks Alekseev, so good to see you." They embraced and kissed each other on both cheeks.

"Good of you to join me, General. I am having a very good Scotch. Single malt, twenty years old. You should try it."

They were seated at a table in the back that afforded almost complete privacy from being overheard. Garnitsky had chosen the Grillage because it would impress Ryndenko. Krasin had introduced Garnitsky to the restaurant but he was not a regular himself. It was more Krasin's style with its rare books and world-class wine cellar. Garnitsky rationalized that it was the kind of place that made Krasin feel less like a criminal.

As they enjoyed their Scotch, Garnitsky said, "How long has it been since we have been doing business, General?"

"I believe it has been four years now."

"And a good four years. For both Rusatomic and for you as well."

Ryndenko tensed slightly. Where was Garnitsky going with this? "Yes, it has been a most successful working relationship."

"Let me be frank, General. I believe that your personal work has delivered to Rusatomic even more than the Government committed to. That is why we have seen that you were properly rewarded. The pay of a major general does not begin to compensate you for the high level of responsibility you carry. Such is the lot of those in government service I fear."

"That is true, Feliks Alekseev. The pay does not allow for even the basics required of one's position."

"Tell me this, General, where do you see your career in a few years?"

Ryndenko took a strong gulp of Scotch. That was a question he asked himself repeatedly. But he had no good answer to himself much less for Garnitsky. "I still have many years of military service. Like any good officer, I expect to be promoted. I have reason to expect my second star by perhaps as early as next year."

"And well deserved too. Much overdue. Your skills exceed your office. And meaning no offense, your appetites exceed the pay of even more senior general officers."

Ryndenko knew he was hired help, but he was still a general in the Russian Army. "All of what you say is true. Therefore I hope there is no problem. What is it you wished to discuss?"

"Certainly not about a problem, General. It is rather an opportunity. One of those opportunities that occurs only once in a lifetime. It is bold. It offers you the type of wealth to indulge all your appetites."

Garnitsky leaned over. Ryndenko leaned closer as well. In barely an audible whisper, Garnitsky said, "We need your assistance to steal three nuclear warheads."

Ryndenko physically recoiled backwards. His face drained of color. "What? That is madness? Why do such a thing? Isn't there enough profits in these special arrangements Krasin has made with the Ministry of Defense? I am a general. Do you expect me to be a traitor? You go too far, Feliks Alekseev. I will hear no more on this."

"Calm down, General. I can well understand your initial reaction. I'm prepared to convince you that this is a practical endeavor. But you have not asked the most important question."

"Which is what?"

"How much you would be paid for your part."

"It doesn't matter. There is no amount of money worth the risk of a firing squad."

"What about 10 million Euros?"

Ryndenko was stopped again. This time he drained his Scotch. "Euros? That is over 300 million rubles. That would be my fee?"

"Yes. Foreign numbered account. More than that, you could retire from the military and become an employee of Rusatomic. Three times your general's salary, and you would still get all of the current perks you receive. Your job would be to work with your replacement at the 12th Directorate on behalf of Rusatomic. When you eventually retire you can live anywhere in the world in style. Live off the interest discreetly and no one will ever know about the source of your wealth."

Ryndenko signaled the waiter for another drink. Garnitsky could see he had sunk the hook.

"Is this for some terrorist group?"

"No. There's no terrorist group that has that kind of money. They wouldn't have the capability to make use of such sophisticated weapons either."

"Then it's a state. What state?"

"Does it matter?"

Ryndenko speculated. It had to be North Korea or Iran. Probably Iran.

"It matters because of what kind of aftermath takes place."

"Your involvement will be entirely concealed. There will be no evidence pointing to you. Once I explain the plan, you will understand."

"How many others will know of my involvement?"

"Only two others besides me. Yuri Dratshev which you know. And the foreigner paying for the weapons. We have other army officers working within the facilities that we have enlisted. They think they are working on secret orders from the President to conceal these decommissioned weapons from the American inspectors. Once the operation is completed, all the records will be altered to conceal the theft. Any records implicating you will be destroyed. Once that is completed, these officers will be eliminated, seemingly in an accident."

"And why would I not also be eliminated?"

Garnitsky smiled. "No need, General. There is no reason you would tell anyone. Besides, your death would raise suspicions. Your rank, your sensitive responsibilities. We also have future needs for your skills."

"What is it that you would require me to do?"

"The details are being worked out, but essentially you will be issuing orders. You will issue orders to relocate three specifically designated warheads from the weapons disassembly plant in Trekhgornyy to the fuel reprocessing plant in Ozersk 180 kilometers away. That of course is a normal event. The fissionable material from the decommissioned weapons is reprocessed for use in reactors at the Ozersk plant.

"The difference is these warheads will not be fully disassembled. I know little about the technology, but I am told that the warhead consists of uranium or plutonium, or both, but surrounding the actual bomb material is a complex assembly."

"Very complex," Ryndenko said. "Precision machined components. There is shielding to reflect back the neutrons to increase the yield. Outside of that is a sphere of conventional chemical explosives."

"Are you familiar with the technology of how the bomb works?" Garnitsky asked.

"Yes. I have a basic understanding. When the outer shell of explosives is detonated, the imploding force uniformly compresses the fissionable material. The compressed core reaches a state of uncontrolled chain reaction by an ever increasing neutron bombardment of the nuclei of the uranium and plutonium atoms.

"At some point the atoms of the fissionable material give up their binding energy and you have a nuclear explosion. The whole assembly looks like an oversized soccer ball with wires that connect to the electronic arming controls."

"I'm impressed, General. You know more about the technology than I do. Never have seen the guts of one of these, but I'm told it does resemble a soccer ball.

"At any rate, these three warheads will not undergo the normal disassembly to extract the fissionable material. Instead, they will be placed in special crates for shipment to the reprocessing facility. All of this will require orders from you, General."

"But warheads are fully disassembled before the fissionable material is shipped to the reprocessing facility. It's only the nuclear core that goes to the reprocessing facility. What is the purpose of transporting the entire warhead assembly there?"

"Because the tightest security is at the disassembly facility. After all, that's where the fully operational warheads are stored. That's where the American inspectors account for the decommissioning of each warhead to satisfy the nuclear disarmament treaties between Russia and the United States.

Little chance of falsifying records there to cover a theft. But security is much less rigorous at the reprocessing facility."

"But the transfer of complete warheads to the reprocessing facility will violate procedure. It will be too obvious."

"I do not believe so. First of all, only one officer at the disassembly facility will understand these warheads are destined for the reprocessing facility. He is under our control. He is the one that will destroy your orders. Then he will falsify the records to account for the transfer of the appropriate amount of fissionable material.

"The transport personnel are simply following orders to move material. The crates will just be larger than typical. For all they know, they're just from larger bombs.

"Now once the warheads are at the reprocessing facility, another shell game is played. Again on your orders, the warheads are transported to a highly secret military installation. That location was a former facility operated by those idiots at Mayak Chemical. It stored nuclear material at one time but has been closed for years. My people will be in army uniform with the appearance that this is a functioning military facility. They simply take delivery of the warheads."

"How is that part of the audit trail concealed?"

"Another officer, also under our control will destroy any records related to the shipment to this phantom military site. That includes your written orders as well. Like the other officer, he also thinks this is part of a high-level ordered military maneuver to conceal weapons from the Americans."

Ryndenko shook his head slowly. "You still have the problem of unaccounted weapons grade fissionable material. A lot of material. Physical inventories are conducted every six months."

"We have a third asset that resolves that problem. A colonel. He's in charge of auditing the inventories at the reprocessing facility. He will substitute an earlier receiving record with one that shows lower quantities. The difference is equal to the fissionable content of these three warheads. So when the physical inventory comes up short, an audit of the records will identify the discrepancy as being from a prior transaction error. The substitute documentation will be meticulous."

"My God. You've bribed the whole fucking Russian Army. I feel like I am swimming in shit, Feliks Alekseev. We once stared down the mighty Americans. Now we scavenge for scraps by taking money from criminals."

"Criminal? Is that what you think I am, General?"

"I did not intend offense, Feliks Alekseev."

Garnitsky smiled to dismiss any sense of hostility. "I understand your anxiety, General. But you must look to the huge reward of this project."

Ryndenko let out a long sigh. "And what is the next step?"

"Dratshev will be in contact with you. He will manage all the details. Now let us enjoy a superb dinner."

Throughout dinner Ryndenko was uncharacteristically quiet. He was trapped. Always had been ever since his association with Feliks Alekseev Garnitsky.

Garnitsky ordered cognacs and coffees after the waiter cleared the dishes away.

"General, you must relax. Cheer up. All will go well. Perhaps the two women walking this way will divert your thoughts."

Two women made their way among the other tables of diners. Heads turned. One was fair and blonde, the other was darker with black hair.

"The dark one is named Elena. Looks Middle Eastern, but she's Georgian. A belly dancer. Wonderfully strong body. She will be your companion tonight."

Ryndenko's gloom receded somewhat.

CHAPTER 32

MANHATTAN, NEW YORK

C onrad Redek walked into Steven Martinelli's office and shut the door.

"Good morning, Conrad."

"It was until I got a call from Moscow a few minutes ago. It was from Nikolai Krasin. About our problem, this reporter Reynolds."

"So what's happened?"

"Reynolds arrived in Moscow on a flight out of Paris. Apparently he didn't meet anyone at the airport. Took a taxi to a small hotel. According to Nikolai, Feliks Garnitsky had a team of three people doing surveillance. After almost 24 hours, Reynolds had still not left the hotel. The surveillance guys had FSB credentials. That's the new KGB. Eventually they had a maid open the door to Reynolds' room. He was gone. The maid said the bed was never slept in."

"Garnitsky?" Martinelli said. "Oh yes. I met him a couple of times over there. He's Krasin's muscle. Probably the architect of that clumsy fiasco with Ashcroft."

"That was crude, but you'll have to admit that it proved effective. Among other things, Garnitsky is ex-KGB. Still well connected with his old colleagues. Half the damn Russian government is ex-KGB. He's usually very effective. Krasin relies heavily on him. But it looks like his people screwed up this time."

"So these KGB agents let a reporter get away from them? Like everything else in Russia it's second rate. To think we feared these keystone cops at one time. So what's Garnitsky doing about it?"

"Full court press. When I said Garnitsky was well connected within the Government, I was not exaggerating. He managed to get the FSB to issue an arrest order for Reynolds on charges of suspicion of espionage. That means that Reynolds can't move around. Can't stay at a hotel using his passport. Can't travel easily."

"Somebody's obviously helping him then. Reynolds is not navigating around Moscow without assistance. That in itself is even more troubling. Do we assume he has met up with this computer hacker calling himself Rasputin?"

"Possibly. Maybe that's even better. The FSB will find Reynolds. Russia still has the structure of a police state. Maybe they'll find Rasputin with him. Contrary to those goons that fucked up the surveillance, this is still one of the world's best intelligence organizations."

Martinelli turned his chair to face the large window overlooking the East River. It was a beautiful sunny day. He turned back to Redek.

"Conrad. I would feel better if you went over to Moscow and got a first-hand assessment of the situation. The security breach has not been located according to my last conversation with Nikolai. He has some so-called experts that have been working on it for over a week. I think we should send some of Durbin's people over to assist. Now there's this unresolved loose end of Reynolds."

Redek wasn't enthused about going to Russia. He'd been there too many times when he put the merger together with Nikolai Krasin's corporations. He hated everything about

Moscow; the weather, the food, the culture. "Nikolai won't like that."

"No, but he'll live with it. That's why it must be you. You and he obviously get along well. It was you who architected our Russian investments after all. Besides, he would consider it an insult if anybody else went. I'll call him today. When can you leave?"

Redek sighed in resignation. "Day after tomorrow. I'll call Durbin and line up his best computer geeks."

Nikolai Krasin was not pleased. The intrusion by so-called American computer experts was unwelcome. But Garnitsky's failure with the surveillance of Reynolds was an embarrassment. On balance he thought it best to refrain from voicing a real objection.

"I feel that is unnecessary, Steven," Nikolai Krasin said. "I am told by our experts that they have discovered tracks where the hacker accessed the system. They have assured me that they have enhanced our security to prevent unauthorized access. Redundant firewalls have been put in place."

"I'm sure you have first-rate people working on this, Nikolai, but just the same, I'd feel better if we brought in some additional people. From what I'm told, this hacker may even have accessed our databases here in New York through our connections with Moscow. That internal linkage must be thoroughly secured. Bill Durbin has done exceptional work for us over here. He has people that are particularly expert at understanding this whole business of computer hacking. He even has hackers working for him."

"And why is Conrad coming over?"

"Just to get a top level assessment. It's been a while since he was last in Moscow. He understands computer systems. This debacle by this hacker stealing information is unsettling. Simply repairing our computer security is not enough. I want Conrad to propose a whole new level of protection corporate-wide. Our information has to be made as secure as any government intelligence agency."

"Fair enough, Steven. Conrad is always welcome. I'll enjoy seeing him."

Martinelli paused before touching on the more immediate problem. "Nikolai - Where is Reynolds?"

"We're not sure, Steven. That's temporary I assure you. The entire Russian security apparatus is alerted. Just a matter of time. Feliks Garnitsky has assured me it will be sooner rather than later. He understands our disappointment in how this was handled. Once Reynolds is located the problem will be eliminated."

"I believe an Interpol Red Notice will be forthcoming very soon. I understand that will obligate Russia to extradite him to Columbia once he is in custody."

"Steven, I was thinking of a more immediate solution."

"A trial in Columbia for murder will go against Reynolds. It will be a vehicle to cast doubt on any of his past stories."

"I would suggest it would be safer to let Garnitsky deal with the problem over here, Steven. Too many things might go wrong if we bring governments and the legalities of extradition into this. Better to just let Feliks take care of Reynolds."

"Like he took care of keeping an eye on Reynolds?"

"I'll admit that Feliks bungled this. Actually his staff was at fault. Nothing wrong with Feliks' instructions. We've all had those management problems. I assure you, he has remedied the problem. Besides, Steven, this type of solution in Russia does not get the same level of scrutiny that you have in the United States."

"I understand the differences, Nikolai," Martinelli said with evident sarcasm in his voice. "Tell me this, what happens if the State security people take Reynolds into custody?"

"They'll contact Garnitsky and follow his instructions. No records. Reynolds will simply vanish."

"Except there will be more people knowing what happened. There's the possibility that Reynolds' death while pursuing his investigation of Martinelli Global would only lead to more scrutiny. Let's leave the decision as to what to do with Reynolds open until he's found. At the least we need to understand all that he knows."

"Very well, Steven. But remember, Reynolds represents a danger to us here in Russia as well. He's a danger to all of us. He can't be allowed to endanger all that we've built."

MOSCOW, RUSSIAN FEDERATION

Conrad Redek arrived in Moscow in the afternoon on Martinelli Global's Gulfstream executive jet. A limousine picked him up at the airport. He was allowed time alone to rest in his hotel suite before meeting Nikolai Krasin for dinner.

At Krasin's private club, Redek was shown to Krasin's table. The two men embraced and kissed each cheek in the Russia manner.

"Conrad, it's been a long time since you were here. It's good to see you. You've been well I trust. You certainly look fit. How's Janet? And I guess I should ask how Margaret is as well?"

Janet was Redek's long-time mistress. Margaret was his blue-blood wife.

"Janet's fine. Made partner last year at her law firm. Margaret is still Margaret. Still a lush. Still daddy's girl. Not aging well, except for her net worth."

Redek was not the best in a social situation, but Krasin liked Redek's plain talk. He also recognized Redek's exceptional business abilities. Redek was the matchmaker that merged Krasin's enterprises with Martinelli Global. The structure of the deal was exceedingly complex, a brilliant piece of work. Beyond his business genius, Conrad Redek had street-smart instincts.

After fifteen minutes of exchanging what constituted pleasantries, Krasin said, "What kind of a threat does this reporter Reynolds pose?"

"Not sure Nikolai. He's already brought us unwelcome attention. Made some of our high-level political friends very nervous. What we're worried about is the stuff this hacker suggested he has that enticed Reynolds to come over here. Anybody's internal databases will have all sorts of things that could not be made public. I suspect yours even more so, Nikolai."

"The problem is worse for you in the United States I fear."

"You're probably right. The U.S. is a maze of laws. But then again, I don't know what sort of information might be found in your computer systems."

"Krasin took a sip of Scotch. "Same kind of information found in any corporation's electronic files."

"Nikolai, we're business partners and friends. I know all the things you're into here in Russia. The question is how damaging any stolen information might become if it fell into the wrong hands."

"Conrad, what do you think we do, make a computer entry every time money changes hands with a politician?"

"Of course you do. Everything winds up as a computer entry somehow. It's a question of how well it's disguised."

"Let's not argue. I agree we need to stop Reynolds. I'm confident that the leak in security has been repaired."

"I'm sure it has been. But it won't hurt to have these two guys I brought along with me take a look. Believe me, they're very good. But the more pressing issue is Reynolds. Tell me where we stand."

"I'll have Feliks in the office tomorrow. He can provide more details. But I'll give you an overview. First, the FSB is searching the entire country. Feliks has personal friends there.

He's provided incentives so it's getting attention. That means hotels and all forms of transportation will be alerted."

"Nikolai, someone's helping him. He's not at a hotel. He's not taking public transportation. What is Garnitsky doing to really get a line on Reynolds?"

"Easy my friend. Feliks can give you a better report tomorrow. Suffice it to say, there's a lot of resources being put on this. Reynolds will be located soon."

Krasin hoped so. This was not his area of expertise. He too was frustrated with the lack of progress. By all accounts, Reynolds should have already been located.

"We I am concerned, Nikolai. This Reynolds is no pro. He shouldn't be able to elude the Russian internal security service. These are ex-KGB guys for Christ sakes."

The following morning, Conrad Redek was being escorted around the Information Systems Department at Moscow Capital Partners. The department head was a woman in her thirties named Raisa. She was a stereotypical female version of a geek; utilitarian hairstyle, no make-up, pants, flat shoes. Spoke English. Redek got the impression she knew her stuff.

"This is Ilya Varvarinski. He's our systems administrator," Raisa said.

The tall lanky Varvarinski stood and shook hands all around. "Welcome to Moscow. We will appreciate your assistance. This is very troubling thing to have intruder into our systems."

Varvarinski moved away from his cubicle to an adjacent area. Two men there were furiously working their keyboards and looking over an array of monitors. Varvarinski got their attention and they stood up to shake hands. Raisa introduced the two American computer specialists to their Russian counterparts. It was obvious that the Russians resented the intrusion.

"These are two security specialists that have been working with us on this problem," Varvarinski said. "I will try to explain simply what it is they found."

In more computer jargon than Redek could follow, especially delivered in Varvarinski's accented English, he at least got the main points. Only after much searching were *tracks* discovered of unauthorized entries into the system. The entries were disguised as legitimate log-in accesses. Once inside, the hacker planted simple, but very elegant programs to run search routines. Hits to the searches resulted in exporting those data files to some unsuspecting outside servers.

Tracking down the servers proved a dead-end. The receiving server moved the files to another server and so on. All of the servers were legitimate servers, unaware that they were being used as platforms to move tramp files. At some point the data was downloaded and erased from the servers. Once the bandit program concluded its work, it self-destructed. The tracks were minimal and subtle. This hacker was very skilled.

Varvarinski was tasked by Raisa to get the American computer specialists set-up with workstations and the necessary systems access.

Raisa escorted Redek back upstairs to Krasin's top floor office. Feliks Garnitsky was seated there talking to Krasin. He rose and greeted Redek in Russian. They shook hands. Redek responded in the little Russian he knew.

Krasin motioned for both of them to sit. He told his secretary to bring coffees and small sweet cakes.

Garnitsky spoke only Russian so Krasin was forced to translate. "Conrad is of course interested about the details of what is being done to find Reynolds."

Garnitsky spoke for almost two minutes before Krasin raised his hand to stop and allow him to translate to Redek.

"Apart from what I told you last night, Feliks says both the FSB as well as our own people are investigating this reference to a journalist. That's a lot of people Feliks says. They're also showing Reynolds pictures to all Moscow taxi drivers and railroad ticket people. Of course all airports are being monitored."

"That sounds like a difficult process. A lengthy process. What else?"

"Credit cards. The security service has excellent computer specialists. They can see Reynolds credit card transactions when they are posted at the banks," Krasin said after Garnitsky told him in Russian.

"You mean they've hacked into U.S. banks?"

"According to Feliks, they have that ability. But I'd guess it's more like Russian banks. I'm not sure, but I'd guess these transactions probably go through Russian affiliated banks."

"Has Interpol issued a Red Notice yet on the Columbian murder charges?" Redek asked.

"Not yet. Feliks' friends at the FSB will notify him as soon as they receive notification. If it is issued that is."

"What do you mean?"

"Feliks says a ranking FSB officer had contacted Interpol. Told them they had a direct request from the Columbian Government to detain Reynolds. Russian security wanted to know the status on the Columbian's request to Interpol. Seems there are issues with the quality of the evidence presented to Interpol. It's still under review."

"So what happens if you find Reynolds and there is no Red Notice?"

"Whether there is or not, I told Steven that I recommend that Reynolds simply vanish. This extradition to Columbia carries too much risk. What do you think, Conrad?"

"I'm inclined to agree with you. But Steven's concerned about fallout if Reynolds goes missing. I don't think his disappearance will cause that much of a flap. He's a well known journalist, but not that big a figure.

"However, we don't know what information Reynolds has already collected. I'm more concerned about that. It might be in the custody of someone with instructions to send it to some newspaper, or the Justice Department. That's what I'd do."

"When we find Reynolds we'll find out what he has and where it's at," Krasin said. "Feliks is good at that." He translated in Russian to Garnitsky who nodded his understanding.

Redek looked at Garnitsky. He knew his criminal background. There was no doubt that he would be as ruthless as necessary. "Who snatches Reynolds? The FSB or Feliks' people?"

Krasin and Garnitsky conversed in Russian for a few moments.

"Feliks says the FSB will notify him when they've found Reynolds. Feliks has people waiting to move immediately. If it's somewhere remote, Feliks may have the FSB capture him. That will not be a problem. There will be no record of his arrest. They'll turn him over to our people as soon as possible."

"Ok. Let's play it this way then, Nikolai; when Reynolds is captured we'll count on Feliks finding out what all Reynolds knows, where the information is kept, and who else is involved. Depending on what we find out, that will determine what we do next. If it makes sense to kill Reynolds immediately, I'll sell that to Martinelli."

Redek devoted the following day to reviewing general business issues with Krasin. He would have liked to have spent more time with Garnitsky, but the language barrier was a problem. The topics for discussion could not involve an interpreter, therefore it fell to Krasin to act in that capacity. That also meant he learned everything only through Krasin. Garnitsky was heavily involved in many of Krasin's/Martinelli Global's operations in Russia and surrounding republics. It would be useful to question him directly.

"It's difficult to assess the overall profitability of the Rusatomic venture, Nikolai." They were alone in Krasin's office.

"Just the legitimate income statement looks acceptable in itself. But the offsets should be where the real value is. I know all of the major pieces but I don't know enough of the details to construct an accurate picture."

"That's not a problem, Conrad. I'll have one our best people put together a report. He works for Garnitsky. His name is Yuri Dratshev. He's most familiar with our nuclear related business. He's down in the Urals right now. For yours and Steven's eyes-only of course."

"Is Garnitsky heavily involved with these nuclear plants?"

"Not so much with the operations, but with the offsets the Government offered as part of the deal. Feliks is well connected, especially within the Military. Those offsets are run through Advanced Technologies and Smolensk Logistics. Advanced Technologies was formed expressly for that purpose. Smolensk was already well established. You know that Garnitsky founded what became Smolensk."

"Of course. Smolensk Logistics is the most successful smuggling operation that I could envision. Only in Russia is something on that grand a scale possible. I agree that Garnitsky knows his business. So this Yuri Dratshev speaks English?"

"Certainly."

"How about I meet with him? And Garnitsky of course."

Krasin had no problem with Redek meeting with Dratshev, but Garnitsky would resent the interference. Garnitsky generally resented the American connection. America was still an enemy regime to his background.

"It would mean that Dratshev would have to fly back here to Moscow. Is it that important, Conrad?"

"What about a meeting with you and Garnitsky, then we have this Dratshev join us by phone?" Redek offered.

"Fine. I'll talk to Feliks and set it up for tomorrow."

"Goddamn these Americans. It's not enough they make good profits from our businesses here. I don't like them knowing everything. And why this interest in our nuclear business with the Government?" Garnitsky said to Krasin.

"Probably because their investment must be totally hidden from the U.S. and Russian governments. That means they are not kept informed of details. Since the details are complex and the profits are buried within these offsets, it makes them nervous."

"I still don't like it. In the intelligence business, we operate on a need-to-know basis. Our American partners don't need to know the operational details of how we make them money."

"Just give Redek details on where we generate the majority of profits with the business flowing through Advanced Technologies and Smolensk. Dratshev can give Redek an overview of the nuclear operations themselves. Be thankful that Redek didn't insist on Dratshev flying back to Moscow to meet directly. By the way, why is Dratshev in the Urals? Any problems there?"

"No, not at all. It had been some time since he had been to the plants. I thought he needed to look things over first-hand."

Garnitsky was relieved that Dratshev would only have to conference in. He was still in the process of removing all traces to the warheads theft.

CHAPTER 33

YALTA, CRIMEA, UKRAINE

A vramenko had the hotel purchase first class tickets to Kiev and arrange for a car to take them to the train station in Simferopol the next day. Reynolds and Avramenko were anxious to see what Rasputin had discovered, important enough to bring him out in the open. Both were disappointed that their *holiday* was cut short.

They worked on Rasputin's files the next morning. They had most of the day at the resort. The daily train to Kiev did not leave until 5:30 p.m. The sun was out with some high clouds over the Black Sea. It was a postcard day. After lunch on the restaurant terrace, they returned to their room to pack.

Avramenko came to him and put her hands to his face. She kissed him. "I am sad that we cannot continue our work in this beautiful place. I am scared that we must now return to reality. Make love to me, Mark. Right now."

They spent two hours in bed then showered before their car arrived. It would be another grueling train ride, arriving in Kiev at 9:00 a.m. the following morning.

During the trip they drank tea and strategized what they would do once they arrived in Kiev. Reynolds was more apprehensive than Avramenko. She harbored the view that her association with Reynolds was still not known to those after him. He was more wary.

"You still have your gun?" Reynolds asked.

"Yes."

"Let me see it."

Avramenko took the small pistol from her purse and handed it to Reynolds.

He had shot a few times but didn't know guns all that well, but knew enough to check the magazine then the chamber. Avramenko had wisely not chambered a round. The safety was on.

"Rather small. Guess at short range it could still do damage." The engraving labeled it as a Walther PPK .38 caliber. It weighed less than a pound and a half. He slipped it into his jacket pocket.

"Here's the deal, Nicky. When we arrive in Kiev you're to walk up through several of the train cars. You'll get off the train a long way away from me. Keep me in sight, but stay a hundred meters away. I will look for a coffee shop or a stand. Watch to see if I am approached by anyone. If I am and I think it is ok, then I will scratch the back of my head. Don't come to me unless I give you that signal."

"And if you do not signal me?"

"Then return to Moscow. If I am still ok, I'll get in touch with you by e-mail."

Avramenko reached for Reynolds hand. "I'm afraid, Mark. I did not know you a few days ago. This was just another story then. Now you are more than a story."

"I'm just being cautious, Nicky. As long as this is really our friend Rasputin it will be all right. Rasputin has proven to be a very clever fellow to get this information. He'll be careful. As long as it's Rasputin that's meeting us."

Reynolds slept fitfully on the train. There were too many conflicting thoughts. Most of all, he didn't feel in control. Not with having to avoid whoever was following him. Not with this rendezvous with Rasputin, and not with this emotional entanglement with Nicky Avramenko.

The only thing certain was that he had one hell of a story. There was already enough to bring down Martinelli Global. Just the information from Rasputin's file they already reviewed ensured that. It would be bigger than Enron. Enron was corporate smoke and mirrors; financial manipulations the average person could not understand; arcane white-collar crimes. Martinelli Global was money-laundering, drug trafficking, murder, and colluding with corrupt foreign governments; stuff anyone could understand.

That was just what he already knew. Apparently Rasputin had something even more incriminating. Reynolds made up his mind to leave Russia as soon as they concluded their business with Rasputin. He would return to New York to finish work on the book. Avramenko would join him. He would ponder how to deal with that later.

KIEV, UKRAINE

The train pulled into Kiev on time at 9:00am. Reynolds sent Avramenko forward on the train to disembark some distance away from him. They kissed before parting.

Reynolds stepped down from the train and looked around. No one seemed to be looking at him. He walked to the terminal. There was a coffee bar next to a newsstand. No customers at either place. He ordered a coffee by pointing to the dual language sign in Russian and English.

A tall gangly young man dressed in jeans and a windbreaker approached after the clerk handed Reynolds his coffee.

Reynolds sipped his coffee and looked around the station. No one seemed to be looking at him. He hadn't yet spotted Avramenko. She was following instructions.

"Mark Reynolds?" the young man said.

Reynolds jerked around to face the man. "And you are?"

"You know me as Rasputin."

Rasputin was in his early twenties. His hair was unkept. He had a broad smile revealing uneven teeth. He had the look of a computer geek at least.

Rasputin offered his hand. Reynolds shook it.

"Just so that I know you are really Rasputin, tell me a couple of things you sent me."

"Very well. It is ok. I understand your caution. Let me see. I sent you an e-mail from Nikolai Krasin to Steven Martinelli that confirmed the arrangements with Rusatomic and the Government. I sent you an invoice from Smolensk Logistics to a Fyodor Kautsky for consulting fees. Kautsky is of course big criminal in Russia. I sent you an e-mail from Yuri Dratshev to Feliks Garnitsky confirming that someone named Dyakonov, had been taken care of. The death would be ruled a suicide. Dratshev works for Garnitsky. Oleg Dyakonov was the Managing Director of Transneft, discredited in a scandal involving young girls."

"Ok. I'm convinced," Reynolds said. "So what's your real name, or do I call you Rasputin?"

"My name is Ilya Sergeyevich Varvarinski. Please call me Ilya. And where is Katerina Avramenko?"

Reynolds scratched the back of his head. "She should be joining us soon."

Avramenko walked up a few moments later with her rollaway suitcase.

Varvarinski introduced himself. "It is good of both of you to come. I have important information I must show you."

"What kind of information?" Avramenko asked.

"Please. It is better to explain in place where we can talk. I have made arrangements for room at good hotel here in Kiev."

"Why are we here in Kiev?" Reynolds asked.

"This is my home. I work in Moscow, but this is my home. I am Ukrainian. My father lives here. It provides excuse for me to travel here."

It was only a ten minute drive to the Impressa Hotel located on the bank of the Dnieper River. Ilya Varvarinski's faded blue Lada sedan was not in much better shape than Avramenko's Lada back in Moscow. The hotel was small but very stylish.

Reynolds and Avramenko registered under their false passport names. All three went to the room. It was spacious with two stuffed chairs and a small desk.

Varvarinski set up his notebook computer on the desk.

"Before you start, Ilya, tell us why you are doing this," Avramenko said.

"And just exactly who are you?" Reynolds said.

Varvarinski sat down on the desk chair. He leaned forward with both forearms on his knees. "I work for Moscow Capital Partners. I am a computer specialist. I am in charge of information security." He grinned broadly. "That is joke, no?"

Reynolds and Avramenko understood the irony, but their stress didn't allow for humor.

Varvarinski shrugged. "It is true. That is what I do. I am real hacker also. Very good also. Rasputin has reputation in world of computer outlaws."

"So you didn't really need to hack into Moscow Capital Partners databases; you had total access?" Reynolds asked.

"That is only partly true." Varvarinski's tone suggested that he felt compelled to defend his skills. "It was necessary to leave very small tracks so that suspicion would fall to an outside hacker. I was also able to invade Martinelli Global's own databases in the U.S. Since Moscow Capital Partners system communicates to Martinelli Global's system, I created a very elegant Trojan horse there. It has not yet been discovered."

"What is Trojan horse?" Avramenko asked.

"It is way of sneaking into a system to place concealed code that will execute specific tasks. I did same to other systems that Moscow Capital Partners talks to."

"And this has not been discovered by Moscow Capital Partners, or Martinelli Global?" Reynolds asked.

"Partly. You see they were monitoring your e-mails so they read my e-mails to you. So they sent computer security experts from United States. They have been in our department for almost two weeks. They discovered the false tracks I left in the system. They installed new firewalls. Two Americans are now in our department. There were also other people that questioned all information systems staff for many hours. They were probably Garnitsky's ex-KGB associates. I do not believe I am under suspicion. They think it was a hacker."

"You know how dangerous this is, don't you?" Reynolds asked.

"Yes."

"Why do this?"

Varvarinski rubbed his hand across his face. It was several moments before he answered. "I have revenge to inflict on Feliks Garnitsky and his boss, Nikolai Krasin. It is revenge for my sister Leysa. They are responsible for her death.

"It is very sad story. Leysa was my older sister. There were just the two of us. We were very close. When my mother died I was only eight years old. Leysa became more than a sister to me. People only saw her as beautiful woman, but she was much more."

Tears ran down Varvarinski's cheek. He wiped both eyes with the backs of his hands. "She encouraged me to go to university. Was so proud when I graduated from Kiev Polytechnic Institute . She got me job with Moscow Capital

Partners. Very good pay. Found me small apartment in Moscow."

"How was she connected to Moscow Capital Partners?" Reynolds asked.

"She wasn't. She was connected to Feliks Garnitsky. It was Garnitsky that got me my job. My sister was a model. Very beautiful."

Varvarinski produced a photograph from his pocket and handed it to Avramenko. Leysa Varvarinski was gorgeous. Avramenko said so in Russian.

"She did advertising modeling. I believed that she was very successful. She had beautiful clothes, jewelry, expensive apartment. She was seen with wealthy men. But I was naïve. No matter how beautiful Leysa was, there were just as many others as beautiful. Her life style did not come from modeling."

Reynolds and Avramenko did not say anything, waiting for Varvarinski to continue.

"She was a prostitute. Garnitsky's whore. Perhaps a very special one, but still that is what she did. I learned that only after her death. It was a terrible blow. I kept that knowledge from my father."

"What happened?" Reynolds asked.

"I was told that it was an intruder. Broke into her apartment, stole her jewelry, then strangled her. That is what the police report stated. But that was not what happened.

"When I viewed her body, her face was badly swollen. There were cuts around her eyes. Her nose was clearly broken. I looked at her neck. There were no marks. I am not a doctor, but I thought there should be evidence of bruising if someone was strangled.

"When I confronted the police inspector with this question, he became angry. Said I was just reacting badly to my sister's death. He said I was no expert. The pathologist had declared her death was caused by strangulation. The killer had obviously beaten her before strangling her he said.

"I was still troubled by the police report I was shown. It described all details about the crime scene. It described how my sister's body was found. It said she was strangled by hands to her throat. There was no mention of her being beaten.

"So the following day I went back to the morgue. I found the same attendant. For a bribe, he showed me Leysa's body again. I looked at her neck closely. There was no bruising there. I asked the attendant what he thought. He said he had heard the pathologist comments. For another bribe he told me. The doctor said she had died of trauma to the brain. He also said she had been raped."

"So how do you connect Garnitsky and Krasin to her death?" Reynolds asked.

"For the next several months I played detective. I learned what Leysa really did. Where she went, who she saw. I learned about some of the men she entertained. All of them were connected to Garnitsky or Krasin in some way.

"Then I found a friend of Leysa's. She was terribly upset and afraid to talk to me. She admitted that she and Leysa dated important men. Said she believed it was one of these men that killed Leysa, not a thief. She pleaded with me not to pursue my inquiries. I of course continued, but I used methods that would not arouse suspicion.

"I shall not go into all the details, but I began researching information in the e-mail systems of Moscow Capital Partners and Smolensk Logistics. Most of Garnitsky's e-mails originate from the Smolensk system. Anyway, it was a long process, but I was obsessed with discovering the truth.

"Eventually I pieced together what probably happened that night. Most of the incriminating material I found was between Garnitsky and his right-hand man, Yuri Dratshev. They did not particularly attempt to hide the circumstances, other than to identify the killer only as the *General*. Garnitsky even commented that they now had the *General* totally under their control. I am still working on trying to identify the *General*."

"I'm very sorry about your sister, Ilya. I'm not sure why you are so interested in Martinelli Global. Seems Garnitsky is the one you want to pay for her death," Reynolds said.

"Yes it is true that I want my revenge on Feliks Garnitsky. But he is just a criminal working for the billionaire Nikolai Krasin. My sister entertained important men for Krasin. I want to bring Krasin down as well. Best way is to bring down Martinelli Global.

"You see, Mark, none of that is possible in Russia. Krasin is too powerful. Garnitsky has important friends in the FSB. No matter the evidence, nothing would happen in Russia. Only I would be killed. That would happen. So I use connection with Martinelli Global in the United States to reach Krasin and Garnitsky in Russia. If Martinelli Global is destroyed because of Krasin and Garnitsky, they will then be destroyed. It will be good to destroy Martinelli Global as well, no?"

"Most certainly. Martinelli Global is a bunch of real assholes."

"Yes, assholes. That is good American word to describe these people."

"Now why did you come out of hiding to meet us? What is so important, Ilya?"

Varvarinski paused for a moment to apparently gather his thoughts. "Let me tell you what information I have and see if you come to the same conclusion.

"With the increased security, I have not dared to attempt to access anymore data. Only the e-mail accounts remain accessible to me. I am still amazed at how people think their e-mail is secret. They think an e-mail doesn't exist if they delete it."

"How is it you can access the e-mail so easily?"

Varvarinski smiled. "A long time ago I inserted a virus onto those e-mail accounts I had interest in. The virus program simply directs a copy to me of any incoming or outgoing messages from these addresses. It is a very well hidden code. The e-mails are routed through three different e-mail systems, all with false e-mail addresses."

"And you are sure you will not be found out with these experts looking into your computer security?" Avramenko asked.

"These asshole American experts will not find me." The last was said in Russian with Avramenko translating for Reynolds.

"Ok, so tell us what you have, Ilya," Reynolds said.

"First, I confess I am not as smart as I think I am. I suddenly have this brilliant idea that I could hack into Feliks Garnitsky's cellular telephone calls. It was so obvious I should have done it long time ago.

"It turned out to be very difficult. The wireless networks have very good security and encryption protections. But after much work, I am able to implant code within wireless system that records all of Feliks Garnitsky's calls into a computer. Just like the e-mails I'm looking at. But this is beautiful part; his calls are recorded on the wireless provider's own servers. I access them when I wish. I am totally insulated."

"Ilya, just tell us what you found out."

"Yes, of course. Garnitsky has a lot of calls. I became good at recognizing which calls to listen to based upon who he was speaking to. First call of interest came from Iran. I could tell after checking the call routing. Garnitsky called him Farzad. It was about a great sum of money. Both men were cautious to avoid saying anything incriminating so it is not clear what they were talking about.

"There were lots of calls between Garnitsky and Dratshev. Dratshev works for Garnitsky. Dratshev spoke about Rusatomic's Trekhgornyy plant and their Ozyorsk Plant No. 2.

The Trekhgornyy plant disassembles nuclear warheads. The Ozyorsk Plant No. 2 reprocesses nuclear fuel. I am not sure what *reprocessing* means."

"In this case with weapons grade fuel the plant probably is converting the fissionable material into reactor fuels," Reynolds said. "Is Garnitsky much involved with these nuclear operations plants?"

"No. That is also reason that I became interested. Also Yuri Dratshev is not involved. He is usually in Moscow close to Garnitsky. I wondered why he would be in the Urals for weeks."

Varvarinski turned on his computer. "I have assembled some of the more interesting conversations. Would you translate, Nicky? Your English is much better."

Varvarinski pulled up a file. These were audios of Garnitsky's telephone conversations. Varvarinski had edited many of the conversations down to selected portions then strung them together into a sequence. He separated each with his own recorded date of the call.

"...August 5th - Dratshev: I was introduced to Colonel B. by his controller. Controller is Chechen. Colonel B. thinks he's working for rogue faction of Russian Military."

"...August 29th - Dratshev: Everything is set. All critical arrangements are in place. Items are scheduled to move from Trekhgornyy on the fifth of September. Removal from Ozyorsk Plant No. 2 will be on the ninth. Garnitsky: And the facility on Zukov Street? Dratshev: All set. I shall send you photos through cell phone. Garnitsky: The means for transporting the items; how is that being managed? Dratshev: They shall arrive in their special transport crates, just as they were packaged in Trekhgornyy. Garnitsky: And arrangements in Astrakhan? Dratshev: Departs on the fourteenth. I will remain until ship sails."

"...September 5th - Dratshev: Packages are in route."

"…September 7th - Dratshev: Packages have arrived at the Ozyorsk Plant."

"…September 9th - Dratshev: All three packages have arrived at Zukov Street. Sending photos. Will complete reassembly tomorrow."

"Did you capture these photos from the cell phone?" Reynolds asked. He could see why Varvarinski was spooked by these conversations.

"Of course. Here are the ones Dratshev referred to as from Zukov Street."

"What does that say?" Reynolds asked looking at the first digital photo.

Varvarinski zoomed in on the photo. "It identifies the building as an Army facility. Gives its battalion and division numbers. But there is the problem."

"What's that?"

"There is no such army unit. I checked."

"Oh shit," Reynolds said.

Avramenko said, "Show the other pictures."

"Yes. This is why I had to meet with you urgently."

The first picture showed a wooden crate. It had no lettering, only a collection of numbers, plus the universal danger symbol for radiation. The second picture showed one side of the wooden crate removed. Inside was a cylindrical object appearing to be maybe 24 inches in diameter. Wires came out of the cylinder uniformly about the surface. The pixel resolution did not allow for reading the printing on the object's surface.

"I think I know what the second picture shows," Varvarinski said.

"So do I, Ilya. It's a fucking nuclear warhead. Not just the fissionable nuclear core, but the whole fucking assembly! Shit!"

"What does that mean, Mark?" Avramenko asked.

"It means that it's already a bomb, a high-yield bomb. All it needs is the triggering circuitry. That's an easy step to make it operational. If it was just the fissionable core, then it would need a lot more sophisticated work to make it into a real weapon."

"I do not recognize the piece of equipment in this other photo," Varvarinski said.

Reynolds looked at the third photo for a few moments. It was a piece of equipment mounted on a steel base about 8 ft x 10 ft. It appeared to be a diesel engine and a large tank.

"Zoom in on the photo," Avramenko said in Russian. She translated the writing on the side of the equipment into English.

Looking over her shoulder, Reynolds said, "It's a compressor with an accumulator tank."

"Here is the rest of the phone calls," Varvarinski said.

". . . September 14th – Dratshev: The ship has sailed. Will arrive on the seventeenth."

"Astrakhan is a Russian port on the north coast of the Caspian Sea," Varvarinski said. "I checked. Two ships sailed that day. Both bound for Baku, Azerbaijan. One was to return to Astrakhan. The other was bound for Iran in the south after Baku. Both were manifested as carrying petroleum drilling equipment."

Reynolds let out a long sigh. "Yeah. Compressors. Compressors with nuclear warheads concealed inside the tanks. Iran now has the *bomb*."

Varvarinski added, "It would appear they have three."

"Right. And it's worse than that. These are state-of-the-art warheads, not crude low-yield devices like Pakistan and India. Iran just joined the major leagues. You see, the real task of making a high yield nuclear weapon comes from very sophisticated work on how the fissionable material is caused to have a chain reaction. The yield is increased through the level of technology of the weapons construction. Advanced software design is required along with precision manufacturing techniques. Iran just jumped over all that."

"What is this *yield*?" Avramenko asked.

"The yield is how big an explosion you get – how much energy is released. Before you can get a nuclear explosion you must cause the fissionable material to achieve what is called critical mass. The explosion comes from an uncontrolled chain reaction of the enriched uranium or plutonium core. What happens is the core is bombarded with neutrons by a trigger called an initiator. These neutrons bombard the heavy nuclei of the uranium or plutonium core. These nuclei split, releasing more neutrons and energy. The result is a runaway chain reaction of neutron bombardment that leads to the release of immense amounts of energy that is the nuclear explosion.

"To achieve this, you need to compress the fissionable material core under great pressures. You do this by detonating conventional explosives arrayed around the nuclear core in a perfect sphere. This is necessary to get a uniform compression on the fissionable material. That takes very advanced engineering designs, and the components require highly sophisticated machining techniques. Beyond that, weapons designed by Russia and the U.S. have design advancements that boost the explosive yields even higher using comparatively small amounts of fissionable material."

"You sound like expert," Varvarinski commented.

"Not really. But I did research on a book I wrote a few years ago. *Nuclear Threats For Our Time* was about the dangers of nuclear materials in Russia falling into the wrong hands after the collapse of the Soviet state. That's unfortunately a reality now. Worse than the fears of just losing the radioactive fissionable cores. These are entire warheads of the most advanced design. They're easily made operational."

"So my fears are correct?" Varvarinski said.

"Unfortunately, yes. You're also correct that we must get this information to the West."

Reynolds produced several large capacity USB storage devices to load copies of all Varvarinski's incriminating files. He would carry one set, the two others he instructed Varvarinski to send via FedEx to Rachel Stern in New York and another to his lawyer. He wrote brief notes of instruction to Rachel Stern and Matthew Solomon and gave Varvarinski the addresses.

The first order of business was to get out of the Ukraine and back into Russia. They could try to leave for the West by air from Kiev. That would require using their real passports. The problem was there were no entry stamps into the Ukraine. Would that be discovered? It was too great a risk. They were in Ukraine illegally.

They looked at flight options from Russian cities other than Moscow. If Martinelli Global's or Krasin's people were looking for them, they might have surveillance there. Unfortunately, most western bound flights connected only with Moscow or Saint Petersburg. Saint Petersburg was many hours north of Moscow by train. There was probably no reason to believe that they might not be discovered there as well. There was Rostov to the east, but there was no direct train there from Kiev.

"I have idea," Varvarinski said. "You take train north from Kiev back into Russia, but you leave train at first stop once inside Russia. Do not take express train. Other trains make more stops. You buy return tickets to return to Kiev using correct passports with proper entry stamps into Ukraine. You can fly from Kiev to Europe, then on to the United States."

The train left Kiev at 10:42 p.m. Avramenko got first class reservations for that same night. The best flight option proved to be a Ukraine International Airlines flight to Berlin leaving Kiev at 4:30 p.m. the day after next. That was the best they could do with the time necessary on the train to leave Ukraine then return back to Kiev. They would spend the night in Berlin, then visit the U.S. Consulate the next day to get Avramenko a visa. At least they would get some rest before continuing the journey to New York.

The three of them had dinner. Later, Varvarinski drove them to the railway station. "I will leave you here," he said as he parked at the curb while Reynolds took their bags from the trunk.

"Thank you, Ilya for all you have done for us. This is important work we are doing. Russia needs these truths," Avramenko said in Russian. She hugged and kissed Varvarinski on both cheeks.

"You are a brave man, Ilya," Reynolds said. "Your files will bring down Krasin and Martinelli Global. I hope the fallout will crush this Feliks Garnitsky. I believe you will have your revenge." He hugged and kissed Varvarinski on the cheeks as well. "Goodbye, my friend. Be careful."

BRYANSK, RUSSIAN FEDERATION

It was 5:00am the following morning when the northbound train from Kiev pulled into Bryansk. Bryansk was 70 miles north of the Ukraine border. The city was a major crossing of trunk lines for the Russian rail system.

Avramenko booked seats on the returning train to Kiev. Unfortunately, that train was more than twenty-four hours later. The railway station building was an elegant old building but was lacking in amenities. There was one restaurant serving basic fare and a bar. It would be a long day and night.

Even though there was a pleasant green area with trees outside the station, it had turned quite cold and rainy. They were confined to the station. Reynolds and Avramenko spent the time working on their materials. They dosed for a couple hours with their heads on each other's shoulder.

They were both still fatigued when their train pulled in at 7:00am. They hoped to get some rest on the six hour trip back to Kiev.

"I know we must get this information to the American government. Iran with nuclear bombs is huge story. Whole world will go crazy. But I must confess I am excited about going to America with you."

Reynolds liked that prospect as well. He kissed her.

"Will I be able to stay there once this is over?"

Conflicting thoughts ran through Reynolds' mind. Was he that serious about his affections for Avramenko? Did he want a new relationship? After what they would expose, it was doubtful she could ever return to Russia without risk to her life. Did that make him responsible? What about Rachel Stern?

"I think so, Nicky."

Reynolds felt more comfortable using his legitimate passport as they arrived back in Kiev. It had been stamped by a Ukrainian official on the train as they stopped at the border. They were out of Russia where he assumed there was the greatest danger of discovery. In a couple of hours they would be on a flight to Berlin.

Arriving in Kiev, they lugged their bags out of the old English Gothic 19th century passenger train terminal to the taxi queue. It was cold here as well, with a steady rain.

Their coats were soaked by the time they got into a taxi. Avramenko instructed the driver to take them to the airport.

CHAPTER 34

MOSCOW, RUSSIAN FEDERATION

Garnitsky telephoned Krasin immediately upon hearing news from his FSB contact. It was midnight. "Nikolai, a credit card transaction was just posted for Reynolds. It was a cash advance at a bank ATM."

"Where?"

"Simferopol?"

"In Ukraine? In the Crimea? How did he get there without your friends in the FSB tracking him?"

"I don't know, Nikolai. Whoever is helping him I assume. We'll soon find out. I'm sending down some people today. Obviously the FSB can't operate openly there, but my contacts there assure me they have assets in Ukraine that can be of help."

"What's he doing in Ukraine?" Krasin said rhetorically.

"My guess he's meeting with someone. Probably this journalist that was mentioned in the hacker's e-mail to Reynolds. Maybe even this hacker too."

"Anything more on who this journalist might be?"

"Not yet. The FSB is working on it. There's more journalists in Russia then you would imagine. They've developed a manageable list of about forty names. Reporters and editors that have been anti-business, or especially antagonistic to any of our businesses. All of them knew Polikovskaya. Seems she had a wide range of professional acquaintances. I've asked them to check to see if any of these people have been away from their places of work for the past several days. We should have that information within a couple of days."

"I guess that's good news. Better if we'd have found him though. Get it done quickly, Feliks. I'll inform Redek tomorrow. Goodnight."

Redek was using a small conference room as his adhoc office. The more senior of the two American computer specialists Redek brought to Moscow knocked and entered. "Do you have a moment, Mr. Redek?"

"What is it?"

The man closed the door. Redek did not invite him to sit.

"We can't be sure, but I think there's a strong possibility that these security breaches were an inside job."

"What suggests that?"

"Without going into arcane technical explanations, let's just say that the hacker's tracks don't seem to account for all the breaches. Not enough tracks. They're too random. Don't follow a consistent pattern. We should be seeing a lot more of the same repetitive kind of evidence. Why would the guy change his hack program if it was working well?"

"Maybe he got wise that he was leaving tracks as you call them," Redek said.

"I don't think so, Sir. The footprints aren't as subtle as they appear. A really first rate hacker wouldn't have left this sort of evidence. My colleague and I both agree."

"Why haven't these Russian computer experts picked up on the same thing?"

The middle-aged balding man grinned, "Because they're not as good as us, Sir."

"So who could pull this off internally?"

"Only two people; the plain broad who's the IT boss, and the tall skinny guy. They're the only ones that have full admin access."

"How sure are you?"

"Ninety percent."

"Fuck. You're not to discuss this with anyone. No one. Especially no one back in the States. Tell your partner. Got that?"

Shit. Not even a thanks for a good job. But Conrad Redek was not someone you wanted to cross. The man nodded. "Yes, Sir."

Garnitsky joined Krasin and Redek in the conference room the following morning. Yuri Dratshev joined them via telephone. As instructed by Garnitsky, Dratshev explained the actual nuclear related operations to Redek. His English was almost as good as Krasin's.

"Our nuclear businesses are principally involved in reprocessing fissionable fuels. All levels of fuels, from Russia as well as other countries; spent reactor fuels, and high energy uranium and plutonium. These are what are called weapons-grade fuels. As part of that, we operate a weapons disassembly plant. Along with all that comes the ever present issue of nuclear waste. We manage a number of waste sites. That of course was why the Government sought our investment."

"I'm well of aware of all that background. Give me a brief summary of where and how profits are generated," Redek said.

"The reprocessing work is very profitable. Rusatomic has exclusive contracts from the Russian Military as well as civilian power reactors. Our newer facilities and capacities have allowed us to obtain lucrative contracts with other countries as well."

"The reprocessing accounts for how much of Rusatomic profits?"

"About 80 percent," Dtarshev answered. "The weapons disassembly process generates moderate profits, accounting for the remaining 20 percent. The issue of course is the waste management. We inherited 50 years of poor management and poor funding. That part of the business still operates at a loss."

"Which of course brings us to the offsets that apparently make the whole thing work," Krasin said.

"Yes, Sir. I understand much of this, but Mr. Garnitsky is the most knowledgeable in that area."

It was Dratshev's way of deflecting those questions to Garnitsky. Garnitsky had already prompted him not to divulge any more than necessary to Redek.

Krasin was acting as translator for Garnitsky throughout the conversations.

"The Government provided offsets fall into two groups. The first involves Advanced Technologies. The foundation of Advanced Technologies was based upon assets of previously state-owned enterprises that were given to Advanced Technologies. These businesses were in various industries. We produce precision machined nuclear weapons components, precision CNC machine tools, oil and gas drilling equipment, conventional explosives, and industrial lubricants. Many of these products are closely associated with the nuclear weapons industry so the Government easily awards highly profitable contracts to Advanced Technologies to offset losses in the core nuclear business operated by Rusatomic.

"Perhaps Mr. Garnitsky could better explain offsets that flow through Smolensk Logistics," Dratshev said.

Krasin agreed and translated for Garnitsky.

"Smolensk Logistics acquired a whole new range of lucrative transportation and logistics contracts as a result of the Rusatomic deal. We operate vehicle parts depots for the Russian Navy and Army. We manage the entire supply chain for Aeroflot. We purchase grains under cost-plus contracts with the Military. We manage jet fuel storage facilities. The list continues," Garnitsky said.

"And smuggling?" Redek asked.

"Smuggling? The Government doesn't need to smuggle, Conrad," Krasin said.

"No, but they're in the position to turn a blind eye. Is that part of the deal?"

Krasin nodded to Garnitsky to answer. "Yes. We have that understanding."

"What is smuggled?"

Reluctantly, Garnitsky answered through Krasin. "Petroleum. Lumber. Gold. Other commodities as the opportunity presents itself."

"Does this generate more income than the Advanced Technology enterprises?"

"Almost twice as much," Krasin answered.

"This should not be taken the wrong way, Nikolai, but how do we audit our investments once this gets laundered through the offshore corporations?"

Only a slight narrowing around Krasin's eyes belied his reaction to the question. "I assumed we were providing sufficient detail in our quarterly reports to New York. Is that not the case."

"No it's not the case actually, Nikolai. The line item information consists of only vague summaries. It's not possible to associate expenses with particular revenues. We'd like to see the reporting more like the other subsidiaries where we've invested publicly."

Martinelli could be a difficult partner at times, but Conrad Redek had always been tough from the beginning. Krasin struggled to contain his irritation. "You and Steven are not suggesting we're withholding information are you?"

Redek wanted to avoid a confrontation but he was not the type to dance around an issue. "Not at all, Nikolai. We're just seeking to get a better idea of the revenue stream. After all, we are your partners in this."

Krasin thought to himself that this was the downside to having American partners, even partners like Martinelli Global. They were from a different world. They wanted precise accounting of what were illegal transactions. A country of bean-counters. They didn't understand the wisdom of not committing certain things to records. Yet it was just these records that could prove legally problematic in a country like the United States.

"Do you have any further questions for Yuri, Conrad?" Krasin asked curtly.

"No. You have been most helpful, Yuri. Thank you."

Krasin spoke in Russian for the benefit of Garnitsky. He thanked Dratshev and disconnected the telephone call.

"Very well, Conrad. You must understand our reluctance to commit some business details to written records. But given that you want something more, I will arrange a different reporting structure, one that will present a more comprehensive picture. I trust that you will treat this with special eyes-only security for just you and Steven?"

"Of course. That's all we're looking for, Nikolai."

"Shall we have some lunch?" Krasin said, signally an end to the meeting.

"There's something else, Nikolai," Redek said. "It's about the computer system security breach."

Krasin sat back down in his chair. "What do you mean?"

"The people I brought with me already have an opinion."

"Opinion? What's that mean?"

"They're sure that it's someone inside your IT Department, not some outside hacker."

Krasin was stunned. He translated for Garnitsky.

"What evidence do they have?"

"Technical computer stuff. I don't pretend to understand it, but I trust these guys judgment. The guy they work for says they're the best there is. And that guy has done exclusive work for us for years. Even if they're wrong, we must rule out the possibility."

Garnitsky sat forward in his chair after Krasin translated.

"My experts tell me it's most likely your IT director, Raisa what's-her-name, or the tall skinny guy. They're the only ones that have all necessary levels of administrative access. That's apparently the key."

"I'm not sure that I'm convinced," Krasin said, then asked Garnitsky in Russian, "What do you suggest, Feliks?"

"I'll get some people on it right away," Garnitsky said. "We'll find out."

Garnitsky put the IT department head, Raisa, and Ilya Varvarinski under continual surveillance within an hour of the meeting. The following day, as they were both at work at Moscow Capital Partners, both apartments were expertly searched. Nothing overtly incriminating was discovered. Address books, letters, bills, everything defining one's life was photographed. Both had computers at their apartments. One of the searchers was a first-rate computer specialist.

Garnitsky assigned a number of ex-KGB people in his employ to investigate the contacts suggested by the materials obtained from the apartments. It took another day to assemble a list of people that Raisa Pastukhov or Ilya Varvarinski might be working with.

Garnitsky asked his subordinate Stanislav for a report the next morning.

"The computer guy is working on the stuff he copied from Pastukhov's and Varvarinsky's computers right now."

"When will he be done?" Garnitsky said.

"Well, Sir. There's lots of files to look at. He's gone through Pastukhov's files. Nothing to suggest she has anything to hide. Her computer security was typical. Varvarinsky's files are a problem though. The computer guy says the hard drive access was very secure. Says the files themselves are highly encrypted."

"What's that mean?"

"I'm no expert, Sir, but he says they're in some sort of code. He's trying to decipher it."

"How long?"

Stanislav hesitated while trying to frame an answer to his boss. "Not sure, Sir. But he thinks he can crack it. I can have him see you to explain if you wish, Sir."

"No. But tell him this is absolutely important. Have those American experts work on it too. I need to know what's in those files."

Three days later, Ilya Varvarinski requested an unscheduled personal leave. His father was ill with a heart condition. He must return to Kiev for a few days.

Garnitsky's people reported that Varvarinski's father had no medical record of heart disease. A team of three men were dispatched to follow Varvarinski to Kiev.

CHAPTER 35

KIEV, UKRAINE

The surveillance team on Varvarinski reported to Stanislav that they were watching Varvarinski who was at the Kiev railway station. An hour later they reported to Stanislav that Varvarinski was at that moment making contact with a man and woman. The description of the man matched Reynolds. Stanislav realized he had neglected to arm the team with a photograph of Reynolds. No matter, who they described had to be Reynolds.

"Sir. We've found him. Reynolds. He's meeting with Varvarinsky. Kiev railway station," Stanislav said to Garnitsky via cell phone.

"Get your strike team down there right away, Stanislav. Charter a plane. Get down there immediately. I want to hear that you've got them in custody by the morning. Figure a way to get them out of Ukraine. Is that understood?"

Stanislav and a team of three men arrived at Kiev's Borispil Airport on an executive jet at midnight. He called his surveillance team leader's cell phone. "Where are they?"

"Reynolds left over an hour ago on the train to Moscow. He's traveling with a woman. I'm on the same train right now. I left my two men to watch Varvarinski."

Stanislav was disappointed over missing the opportunity to capture Reynolds with his team. At least he should get credit for locating him. They would take him when he got off the train in Moscow. Stanislav called Garnitsky.

Varvarinski returned to his father's home after seeing Reynolds and Avramenko off on the train. Stanislav called his two watchers. They were soon joined by the capture team for a long cold night of watching the apartment house.

Ilya Varvarinski left his father's apartment at 7:30 the next morning. Walking down the street, two men forced him into a car at gunpoint.

North of the Ukrainian border, Reynolds' train pulled into the Russian city of Bryansk at 5:00 a.m. Stanislav's man on the train was alert and knew his tradecraft. He stepped off the train just as a precaution. To his surprise, Reynolds and the woman left the train with their luggage. The man followed them into the railway station.

Reynolds went to the ticket counter. After he left the counter, the man showed an FSB identification to the ticket clerk. The intimidated clerk told him the previous customer had purchased two tickets to Kiev. After purchasing his own ticket, the man called Stanislav.

Reynolds and Avramenko disembarked the train upon its return to Kiev the following morning. It was cold with a steady rain. At the taxi queue, Avramenko instructed the driver to take them to the airport.

Less than a mile from the railway station, a large Mercedes sedan came up quickly behind their taxi and flashed its headlights repeatedly. The taxi driver uttered an expletive in Ukrainian and then turned his head to face his two passengers.

"What is this?"

Ukrainian was a Slavic language closely associated to Russian so Avramenko understood the question. "We do not know. Who are they?"

Before the taxi driver could answer, the Mercedes pulled around along side the taxi. The passenger in the driver's seat was yelling and holding up what appeared as some sort of identification. The taxi slowed then pulled off the highway onto the shoulder. The Mercedes followed, coming to a stop after crossing in front to block the taxi.

Three men approached the car. None were in uniform. Two opened both rear doors and pointed pistols at Reynolds and Avramenko. A third man yelled something to the driver through his rolled down window.

Reynolds and Avramenko were told to get into the Mercedes. One of the men removed their luggage and notebook computers from the taxi to the Mercedes. No one answered Avramenko's questions about who they were or what was going on.

One man sat in the front with the driver. Reynolds and Avramenko were cramped uncomfortably between men on either side in the rear seat. The Mercedes accelerated with a spinning of tires leaving the taxi and its frightened driver on the side of the highway.

"What did they say to the taxi driver?" Reynolds asked Avramenko.

"They identified themselves as Ukrainian Security Service."

The man next to Reynolds elbowed him hard in the chest, and then yelled something in Russian to Avramenko.

The Mercedes with Reynolds and Avramenko was joined by an identical black Mercedes that fell in behind them. The two cars sped through the ancient city of Kiev eventually working their way into a warehouse district near the river. The driver slowed the car as he and the other man in the front seat appeared to be looking for an address.

After a couple of blocks, the driver braked and stopped in front a large door to an industrial building. He got out of the car and entered the building through a adjacent personnel door. From inside he raised the large roll-up door.

The two Mercedes drove inside. It was a warehouse. There were stacks of boxes occupying the majority of the floor space. There was an office area just to the side of the roll-up door. All five men exited the cars, leaving Reynolds and Avramenko inside the Mercedes. They were not restrained.

"Why the Ukrainian Security Service? Is Garnitsky connected even here in Ukraine?" Reynolds asked Avramenko.

"I don't know. Maybe. But except for speaking to the driver, these men have been speaking Russian. Lots of Ukrainians speak Russian. But perhaps they're Garnitsky's men, or even Russian FSB."

Two of the men stood guard over the Mercedes. Their weapons were drawn. No chance for escape. The other three men entered the office.

The warehouse was unheated. Reynolds could see the men's breath. After ten minutes the Mercedes windows were clouded over with condensation.

"Listen, Nicky. Whatever they want to know, tell them. It's not worth being hurt. We've sent our materials back to the United States. They should be safe there." With Martinelli Global's reach, that was not a surety. "But for God sake, don't tell them we know anything about the nuclear theft. They'd have to kill us for sure if they knew we knew. And only tell them we sent the files to my attorney, Matthew Solomon. Do not mention Rachel Stern. Understood?"

"Yes. I understand. But I am also very afraid, Mark. We are dangerous to these people. To them it is better we are dead."

"You may be right. All we can do is just keep our heads and see what they're planning," Reynolds said.

"Shit! I almost forgot. Where are the USB drives?"

"In my purse."

Reynolds opened her purse and looked inside. "Well I'll be damned," he said and withdrew Avramenko's small handgun.

"These idiots haven't even searched your purse yet. Can you hide this on your body where they might not find it?"

Avramenko took the gun. She thought frantically for a moment, biting on her lower lip. This might be their only chance. "Yes!" She pulled up her skirt then opened the waistband of her pantyhose. She slid the weapon down the front to a position on the inside of her right thigh. With the skirt arranged back into place, the gun was not visible. She wasn't sure if the pantyhose would grip the weapon tight enough, or if it would slide down her leg when she stood.

"I hope they will not search me between my legs."

Reynolds gave a pained expression. "The USBs?"

She lifted the hard bottom liner of her purse and handed Reynolds the two USB drives. One duplicated the files on their computers and the other contained the Garnitsky telephone intercepts of the nuclear theft. Fortunately, they had not saved the telephone recordings on their computer hard drives. That would be a death sentence if discovered.

Where to get rid of the small USB drive with Garnitsky's calls? Couldn't trust Nicky's panty hose. If they found her gun, they were no worse off. If they found the USB with Garnitsky's calls, they were dead. The answer suddenly struck him as obvious.

It was a tight squeeze to push his hand in the space between the car seat and the seat back. He pushed both USB devices well down in the recess of the rear seat. Even the USB device with the same files that existed on their notebook computers was best abandoned. No point in suggesting that any copies of anything existed. The USB devices would not be discovered unless the seat was ever removed.

After spending half an hour in the car, Reynolds and Avramenko were escorted into the warehouse offices. They were taken into a room which looked like a break area for the employees. It was filthy. The grimy tiled floor was littered with food wrappers. The walls were scarred. A single fluorescent light fixture with one missing bulb hung from the ceiling. There was an eight-foot cafeteria table with some grossly stained white plastic chairs. A soft drink vending machine occupied one corner.

The man in charge they overheard called Stanislav put his gun to Avramenko's head and barked an order. One man pulled Reynold's arms out in front of him then bound his wrists with duct tape while another man held a gun to his head. Avramenko's wrists were then bound as well. Reynolds pockets were emptied. Avramenko was not searched beyond the pockets of her coat and her purse.

Their luggage and notebook computers were brought in and placed on the table. Two of the men proceeded to dump all the contents of the bags onto the table. Everything was thoroughly searched. Toiletry containers were emptied into the pile of clothing. Avramenko's makeup was destroyed. The interior pockets and liners of the luggage were cut out down to the frame.

After finding nothing in the luggage, Stanislav left the room taking the two computers, their passports, and their credit cards.

The day passed with Reynolds and Avramenko forced to sit. They were given only bottled water and escorted periodically to a filthy toilet. The smell of food carried in from an adjoining office. Their captors were eating but they were offered nothing.

Light faded from the warehouse skylights as day turned to night. They had been held now for over twelve hours. Reynolds and Avramenko dosed uncomfortably sitting upright in the plastic chairs over the next several hours. Their empty stomachs growled.

When one of the other men came into the room to relieve the other, Avramenko overheard part of their conversation.

"They're waiting for someone called Dratshev to arrive in the morning," she whispered to Reynolds.

CHAPTER 36

KIEV, UKRAINE

"D o you think this miserable piece of shit whore's son understands English?" Reynolds said as a test. The man guarding them only looked toward him with no change in expression.

"I don't think so," Avramenko answered.

"Listen, Nicky. I think we're going to have to make an attempt to escape tonight. Once this Dratshev arrives there's no telling what might happen to us."

"What should we do?"

"The gun. You're going to have to get the gun hidden on your leg."

"Then what, Mark? My hands are still bound. There's nothing in the toilet to help us cut this tape binding our wrists."

"I know. It would be better with your hands free, but you can still do it. You have to. We have to assume they will kill us when they're done questioning us."

"Tell me what I must do."

"We'll give it another hour. Let this guy settle in. He's tired. Look at him yawn. Then you ask to go to the toilet. You retrieve your gun. Make sure the safety's off. Open the door. Stick the gun in his face. I mean in his face with the muzzle touching him.

You've got to scare the shit out of him. March him back in here. I'll take his gun. Then he takes the tape off our wrists."

"Yes. I see. I can do that."

The watcher yelled in Russian for them to shut up. They were not to talk.

"Nicky. Listen to me; you must be prepared to shot him if he doesn't cooperate. You shoot him immediately then pick up his gun and get the hell out of here if you can. Do you understand that?"

"I come back for you, Mark."

"No. The toilet is out in the warehouse area away from the offices. The others would be here once they heard the shot. Besides, one of them will be watching me. You wouldn't be able to do anything. Ok?"

"Yes."

Their watcher again yelled at them to stop talking.

After an hour, Reynolds could no longer hear voices from the nearby offices where the other men were. He hoped that at least two of them might be sleeping. Reynolds nodded to Avramenko. It was time.

The man yelled for one of his companions to come in and watch Reynolds while he escorted the woman to the toilet.

The toilet was located in a stand-alone structure twenty feet outside the rear door to the lunchroom. Once inside, Avramenko worked her bound hands down her panty hose and brought out the gun. She straightened her clothing.

There was no way to conceal the gun with her hands bound. She would have to go right for it. Success would be mostly a matter of luck. Their captors all held their guns in their hands at the ready. If the man reacted instinctively, she'd probably be shot. She might also shoot him, but she would most certainly lose to his larger caliber weapon.

She readied herself. Flushed the toilet. Remembered to switch off the gun's safety. Turned off the light. Opened the door.

The man was standing a few feet away having a cigarette. His gun was stuck in his waistband. In the dimly lit warehouse he didn't immediately see the gun in her hand. He was taken by surprise as she closed the distance between them quickly. As instructed, she stuck the gun right up against his left cheek.

She wasn't sure what to do next. She should get his weapon, but how? It would be risky to try to remove it from his waist with her hands bound together. She felt more in control with her gun in his face.

The man put his hands behind his head as ordered. Avramenko then moved behind him. She held him by the shirt collar with one hand while jamming the barrel of the gun into the back of his head.

In this fashion they made their way back to the door to the lunchroom. She ordered him to lower his hands, open the door, and then go in.

The man did as instructed.

As he entered, the man watching Reynolds looked at his colleague. "Where's the woman?" the man said since Avramenko was shielded by the other man.

Avramenko came from behind the man. "Don't move!" She was pointing the gun at the sitting man watching Reynolds. It was a precarious position. The man watching Reynolds had a gun in his hand, resting in his lap. The man that had been watching Avramenko still had a gun tucked into his waist. Avramenko had only her small .38.

Things happened quickly. The man watching Reynolds reacted, perhaps instinctively by raising his 9 mm weapon to counter the threat. Avramenko did not hesitate. She fired twice. Her target was only eight feet away. Both shots hit the man in the chest. His weapon discharged, but hit no one. The weapon fell from his hand as he dropped out of the chair clutching his chest.

The other man reached for his gun from his waist. Reynolds pushed violently on the cafeteria table catching the man hard on the hip as he was turning around toward Avramenko.

The blow caused him to turn back toward Reynolds. In that instant, Avramenko did not hesitate. She fired four times at a point blank range of only three feet. The one round that struck him in the head killed him.

Reynolds scurried across the floor to retrieve the two weapons. The wounded man was gasping for air. The two rounds had apparently hit his lungs. The other man looked dead.

Shouts came from outside the lunchroom. A translation wasn't necessary. The wounded man tried to say someone but it came out weakly. Reynolds struck him a hard blow to the head with one of the 9 mm automatics.

"Get the other gun, Nicky."

She dropped her .38 in favor of the heavier more lethal 9mm.

"Listen. We're going out the back door here into the warehouse. We need to try to find a way out."

Once outside the lunch room, Reynolds and Avramenko took a quick look around then sprinted across the open area in front of the toilets. At a run, they headed toward the rows of stacked goods on pallets.

As they reached the cover of the inventory goods, two shots were fired. The bullets missed. Reynolds and Avramenko ran down the aisle. At a cross aisle they turned, ran over several aisles, then did another left turn. Within a minute, they reached the other end of the warehouse. Logic suggested there must be at least a personnel door somewhere on that end of the building.

They found the door further down the wall. It was secured by a padlock.

"Shit! Get over there out of the way, Nicky. Keep watch. Shoot anyone you see."

The best bet was to shoot the hasp on the door lock. The lock itself was probably much harder steel. He stuck the barrel of the pistol against the hasp ring then turned his head away and fired.

It took a second shot before the padlock fell away. Reynolds opened the door. A gust of cold air struck him. Snow was falling. They couldn't go far in this weather without coats, especially in the middle of the night.

"Nicky, run outside and find some cover. If anyone comes out the door shoot at them."

"What will you do?"

"Going to try to ambush these other two guys. We can't get far without warm clothing. We've got no car, no passports, no money."

"What is *ambush*?"

"I'm going to catch them by surprise. I'm going to shoot them. We can then get our stuff and steal the car."

"You will be killed, Mark."

"Maybe, but I don't see another way. Now go!"

Reynolds pushed Avramenko out the metal door then closed it hard enough to create a loud noise. He then scurried behind a small forklift parked close to the wall. He was less than twenty feet from the door.

Within moments the two men ran toward the door. One opened the door cautiously then stepped out. Two shots rang out. Two holes punched through the sheet metal wall of the building to the right of the door. Avramenko had missed.

The man quickly ducked back in and closed the door. He and the other man were standing together. Reynolds rose from behind his concealment, steadied the 9mm automatic with both hands and fired twice at the smaller of the two men.

The man dropped to his knees. The larger man turned and fired a wildly unplaced shot. Reynolds fired five rounds at him.

More than one found its mark. He too went down, but there was no movement after he hit the floor.

Reynolds approached the other wounded man from behind. He could see the man still held his weapon in his right hand as he still remained kneeling on the floor.

"Drop the gun!"

The man did not drop his gun.

Reynolds quickly came up behind him and stuck his own gun in the back of the man's neck.

The man understood and dropped his weapon. His breathing was labored. Reynolds circled around to his front. The man held his left hand over his lower abdomen. Blood ran through his fingers. His eyes were wide in an expression of disbelief as he looked up at Reynolds.

Reynolds kicked the man's weapon a safe distance away. Then he opened the door a crack and yelled to Avramenko.

He listened for Avramenko's reply. He didn't want her to shoot him by mistake.

"Mark?"

"Yes. I'm all right. Get in here quickly." He opened the door to show himself.

Avramenko entered and Reynolds said, "Ask him who he's working for," pointing to the wounded man.

The man made no reply. Avramenko asked again. After no response, Reynolds stuck the gun to the side of his head. Avramenko asked again, but the man still said nothing.

"Search their pockets for the car keys, Nicky"

Avramenko hesitated at the task. "Nicky, now! Do it!"

She checked the dead man first, then the wounded man while Reynolds pressed the gun to his head. "No keys," Avramenko said.

"Fuck. Let's get back up front to the offices."

Reynolds gathered the two guns from the floor. The one man looked dead. The wounded man looked like he might be dead soon unless he got medical attention. Tough shit.

Returning back to the lunchroom, they found the man wounded in the chest sitting on the floor, propped up against the wall. His breathing was coming in short bursts. His lower body was soaked in blood. His face was ashen. He was going into shock.

This time Reynolds did the search for the Mercedes keys. Fortunately he found them on the dead man. He didn't relish checking the other wounded guy soaked in blood.

Reynolds and Avramenko retrieved their coats out of the pile of clothing scattered on the table. "Leave the rest, Nicky. We've got to get our passports then get the hell out of here. Be careful, the leader, the one called Stanislav, might still be here."

They found the office their captors had been using. It was littered with take-out food containers and beer bottles. The notebooks and their personal papers were not there.

"Sonofabitch. Let's get the hell out of here. Be careful," Reynolds said.

They exited the office. Reynolds checked the trunk to see if the computers might be there. They weren't.

He tossed the keys to Avramenko. "You drive. I'll open the door. No, wait a second. I'll be right back."

Reynolds went back inside to the lunchroom. He rifled the pockets again of the dead man, this time taking the man's wallet. There was a little cash, no credit cards. He then went to the wounded man. Sticking his gun to the man's head, he slipped his hand into the man's rear pocket. He pulled out the wallet. His hand was covered in blood.

He grabbed some of the scattered clothing and cleaned up as best he could. It proved worth the effort, yielding more cash and a credit card.

Reynolds ran back through the offices to the Mercedes. He opened the warehouse roll-up door and took a quick look around. It was the early hours of the morning, still dark. A couple of dim exterior lights illuminated the immediate area. No trucks or cars were about at this hour.

Avramenko drove out. Reynolds closed the door behind them.

"Why did you go back in there?"

"This." He held up the cash and credit card. "Not much, but it will help a bit."

Several blocks away, Avramenko said, "What are we to do now?"

"I don't know, Nicky. Do you know anyone in Kiev that would help us?"

"I don't think so. Mark, what are we to do? We have no papers, no money. We can't return to Russia. Those men were going to kill us. It's hopeless," Avramenko said. She was nearing the end of her emotional strength.

He was also near the end of his endurance. "Our only chance is to get to the American Consulate. That means here in Kiev or we must get out of Ukraine. No, Kiev's the best bet. I think trying to go anywhere else is an impossible journey. Besides, we must get rid of this car soon."

"Do you have any idea where we are?"

"No. I do not know Kiev," Avramenko said. Exhaustion and the prior rush of adrenaline were quickly overtaking her.

"Hang in there, Nicky. Drive us out of this industrial district. Go towards the left. There're more lights that way. Stop at the first hotel you see."

Kiev was a city of three million people. It was thirty minutes later before they found their way to a commercial area and a hotel. It didn't look like much. Reynolds sent Avramenko in to see about a room.

She returned running. "Yes. They have a room."

"Use this credit card. Tell them it's your husband's. Tell them he's parking the car. Which I am. But I'm going to leave it several blocks away. I'll be a little while getting back. Wait for me in the lobby."

Avramenko kissed him through the open car window. "Hurry. Please."

Reynolds drove down the street four blocks then turned right and went another three blocks. He found a parking space in front of a block of apartment buildings. Before leaving the Mercedes, he tried to retrieve the USB drives he had crammed down the rear seat. He could not get his hand very far into the crevice. After a couple of minutes he gave up. There was no way to find them short of removing the seats. That was not possible. There was too much risk of drawing unwanted attention during this early morning hour. Besides, copies were on their way back to New York.

It took Reynolds ten minutes to walk back to the hotel, Avramenko was waiting. She hugged him and took his arm as they mounted a flight of stairs. Their room was on the second floor. It was shoddy and worn, but at least appeared clean.

Avramenko sat on the bed. Tears streamed down her cheeks. She was actually shaking. Reynolds sat next to her and put his arm around her.

"God that was awful, Mark. I killed those men. I could see their faces as I shot them."

"You're just reacting. Natural under the circumstances. Don't shed tears for those assholes. They meant us harm. Probably were going to kill us. Torture us first if necessary to get us to give up our information."

"You're not troubled?" she asked.

"Not about shooting those guys. Martinelli Global and their stooges have tried to kill me before. It's very personal now."

Reynolds took the two 9 mm automatics and placed them on the nightstand. They were both exceedingly hungry but too exhausted to even think about how to get food at this hour. They both fell asleep with their clothes on.

CHAPTER 37

OZERSK, RUSSIAN FEDERATION

C olonel Bukerin was dining with a junior officer at a popular restaurant. As was typical, the restaurant was heavily frequented by military personnel working at the various nuclear facilities in this once closed city. Midway through their dinner a car parked in front of the restaurant exploded. The Colonel and his companion were among the twelve killed in the blast. The official position declared it the act of Chechen separatists.

In the city of Trekhgornyy, a young army major was found shot to death along with a woman in a hotel room. Police arrested the husband of the woman, another army officer, for the murder. Newspaper accounts attributed the murders to jealousy. The army officer maintained his innocence.

MOSCOW, RUSSIAN FEDERATION

General Oleg Ryndenko's and his mistress had just made love. She had been particularly attentive in response to his gift of an expensive watch. Afterwards she cooked dinner.

Ryndenko was in a relaxed mood. His mistress kept refilling his glass. It was a celebration, but he did not tell her why. Things had worked out the way Garnitsky planned. Ryndenko was suddenly wealthy beyond his imagination. He would resign his commission and take on this high paying job with Garnitsky. Life had turned very good.

After nearly a fifth of vodka, Ryndenko fell into a drunken stupor on the sofa. Once he started snoring loudly, his mistress went into the bathroom. She returned with a hypodermic needle.

When injecting medications, it is necessary to expel some fluid from the syringe to ensure no air is injected into the patient. An air bubble could cause an embolism, an obstruction to a blood vessel. The result could be a heart attack.

The woman injected Ryndenko with an entire syringe full of air.

Within minutes Ryndenko was in visible distress. The pain from his heart brought him to consciousness. He struggled for breath. His eyes widened in terror, not only from the pain of the heart attack taking place, but looking at his mistress. She was calmly standing across the room with her arms folded across her chest. She was smiling.

No matter how much she was paid to be with him, Ryndenko disgusted her. He would never humiliate her again.

KIEV, UKRAINE

Stanislav picked up Yuri Dratshev at the Kiev airport executive aircraft terminal. They drove immediately to the warehouse. Stanislav parked outside and entered the building. He called out several times for one of his men to come out of the office and open the roll-up door. Getting no response he uttered an expletive and opened it himself.

He got back into the idling Mercedes and drove into the building. He stopped abruptly and quickly exited the car ahead of Dratshev. He was intent on kicking someone's ass for their laxity.

Stanislav entered the office area. Finding no one there he sensed a problem and drew his handgun. As he entered the lunchroom he said, "дерьмо!"

Blood had pooled around each of the two men. Stanislav crouched down to the man propped against the wall. His face was drained of all color.

Stanislav shook the man's shoulder. There was a slight hint of life left as his eyelids fluttered. "What the hell happened. Where are Reynolds and Avramenko?"

The man's lips moved slightly but there was no sound. Stanislav opened the door into the warehouse area and looked around.

"What has happened here, Stanislav?" Dratshev asked as he walked into the lunchroom.

"I don't know, Yuri. It looks like my men were attacked by someone. There were four of them. Reynolds wasn't armed. He and the woman were tied up."

"Search the building. Quickly," Dratshev ordered.

Stanislav ran to the other end of the building. He came upon his other two men. One was still alive. He was in terrible agony with a wound to the lower abdomen. Stanislav crouched down. "What happened?"

The wounded man gritted his teeth. "Reynolds . . . had a gun . . . somehow hidden . . . got away."

"Reynolds did this? Shot all four of you?" Stanislav said. It sounded absurd, but he couldn't risk it repeated to Dratshev. He couldn't be responsible for another failure to capture Reynolds.

Stanislav stood up and looked back toward the other end of the warehouse making sure Dratshev had not followed him out of the offices. Turning back to the wounded man, he smashed the barrel of his gun to the side of the man's head. He delivered another blow to the man's head with the butt of his gun, hearing the skull crack.

Returning to the office where Dratshev waited, Stanislav said, "The other two are dead by the rear door. Shot. Must have been several attackers. My men were all experienced."

"Where were you during this time, Stanislav?"

"I left only two hours ago to pick you up."

Stanislav was lying. He had gone to a hotel to get a good meal and a short sleep in a real bed. He had been gone six hours. By Stanislav's expression, Dratshev suspected he was lying.

"Who would possibly know you were holding Reynolds and Avramenko here, Stanislav? Not only that, who would have the interest or capability to intervene?"

Stanislav swallowed. "I don't know. Perhaps the computer guy can tell us."

To Dratshev, Stanislav was just looking for a way to deflect his incompetence. He had become unreliable.

"Perhaps. Unless of course your two men taking him back to Moscow fuck that up too. For your sake, Stanislav, you should hope they don't. Now, what did you find on Reynolds and the woman?"

Stanislav fumbled through his pockets. He handed Dratshev the passports and wallets. "And I have their computers."

CHAPTER 38

SMOLENSK, RUSSIAN FEDERATION

Ilya Varvarinski was in a bad way after the car crossed the border into Russia. The two men had placed him in the trunk. It had been over two hours. His hands and feet were bound. His mouth was gagged with his own socks. Breathing was difficult in the trunk to the point of panic. He was shaking uncontrollably with the cold.

Once into Russia, they stopped off the main highway to let him relieve himself and drink some water. For the rest of the journey, he was placed in the back seat with one of the men. Placing him in the trunk was necessary to smuggle him across the border out of Ukraine.

"What's this about?" Varvarinski asked.

"Shut up."

"Who are you working for?"

The man sitting in the back seat with Varvarinski elbowed him hard in the chest. "I said shut up."

It was another three hour drive to the city of Smolensk.

The car made its way to a grimy industrial sector. It stopped in an alleyway next to a door. The stenciled name read Smolensk Logistics. The door was unlocked. Inside was a vast empty warehouse.

They cut the tape binding Varvarinski's ankles, then escorted him into the building. He was barefoot and forced to walk through the cold slush on the ground. His wrists were still bound.

The warehouse was unheated. The interior temperature was near freezing. Sunlight from the overcast day provided a weak illumination through the high windows near the roofline. Next to the wall were stacks of wooden pallets. Varvarinski was told to sit on the floor.

One man went back to the car and returned with a thermos of coffee. The two men lit cigarettes and shared the coffee, offering nothing to Varvarinski.

Two hours later a car drove up outside. The men dropped their cigarettes and took up positions with their handguns drawn. Feliks Garnitsky walked in followed by another man.

Garnitsky stood in front of Varvarinski. Varvarinski was shaking with a combination of the cold and fear.

"Ilya. Why?" Garnitsky asked.

"Why what?"

"Ilya. Do not insult me. We both know what you have done. You are this hacker that calls himself Rasputin. Only you didn't need to hack into our databases, you already had access."

"There is some mistake, Mr. Garnitsky. I am no hacker. I didn't steal anything."

"Yes you did, Ilya. You've been working with that American reporter, Reynolds. You were seen together at the railway station. Before that you were perhaps giving information to the Russian woman reporter, Avramenko. Do not continue to deny your guilt. But why, Ilya? After all I have done for you."

Varvarinski's anger took control over his fear. His normal bright and engaging countenance took on a hard edge. He stared directly at Garnitsky with an unmistakable expression of hatred. "Because you killed Leysa. You made her one of your whore's, then some sadistic bastard beat her to death."

"That's not true, Ilya. Leysa's death was a terrible tragedy. But it was just an unfortunate crime. The police investigation determined that someone broke into her apartment and strangled her. Why do you think otherwise?"

"She wasn't strangled. You don't have to be a doctor to see there was no strangulation. But you could see her face. She died because she was beaten to death! By someone associated with you. Someone you are protecting."

"Ilya, you are wrong. But I don't believe I can convince you of that. Whatever our differences are about the death of your sister is not the current problem. That problem is what you have done. What you have stolen from us. What you have done to harm us. That is why we are here in this dismal place."

Varvarinski maintained a glare of defiance. Inside he was shaking.

"Ilya, I want you to tell me what you've done. Don't deny it. We know you have stolen documents. I want you to tell me what documents. Who you have given them to. Then all of this unpleasantness will be over."

Varvarinski glared at Garnitsky. "Fuck you."

Garnitsky shook his head. "Ilya, that is not good. You know I must have this information. I wish to avoid the unpleasantness that will be inflicted if you do not tell us."

Varvarinski did not respond.

"Ilya, this man here is trained to extract information. He will succeed. He will use methods that are most painful. In the end you will tell me what I wish to know. Believe me, it is best if you just tell me now to avoid such torments."

Varvarinski bit his lip, but uttered no response.

"I'm sorry that it has come to this, Ilya. But I must have your information."

Garnitsky nodded to the man that had accompanied him.

"Strip him to the waist," the man ordered. "Tie him to those pallets. If he resists, shoot him in the foot."

The other two men slit the tape binding Varvarinski's wrists. They removed his coat and tore away his shirt. Once this was done, they pushed him down onto the stack of wooden pallets face-first. One man produced a roll of duct tape. The other forced Varvarinski to stretch out his left arm. His wrist was then secured to the pallet with duct tape. The maneuver was duplicated on his right wrist.

The man accompanying Garnitsky extracted a length of electrical cable from his pocket. He brought it down with full force across Varvarinski's back.

Varvarinski let out a loud scream. He had never experienced such pain. The cable cut into his back leaving a deep pattern of welts.

"Ilya. That is only a sample of the pain that will be inflicted. It will go on as long as necessary. You cannot endure. No one can endure. Tell me what I want to know."

Varvarinski shook his head.

The man proceeded to flog Varvarinski. After ten minutes, Varvarinski's back was a maze of bleeding wounds and deep bruising. The two men that had abducted him even turned their heads from the ugly sight.

Garnitsky bent close to Varvarinski's face. "Ilya, tell me. This is so unnecessary. I can make it stop if you just tell me."

Varvarinski's breathing was labored. "Yes. I will tell you. I have sent files to two people in New York. They were sent by Federal Express."

"Their names, Ilya. Their addresses."

"Rachel Stern. The other is Matthew Solomon. I can't remember their addresses."

"No, no, Ilya. You are very smart. You know the addresses. Now tell me."

Varvarinski did not answer. The man with the belt brought down another stroke across his back. Varvarinski hated himself for being so weak. But Garnitsky was right. No one could endure this. He gave up the addresses.

"How were they sent? And when?"

Varvarinski told him. Garnitsky nodded to the two men that had kidnapped Varvarinski. He and the man inflicting the torture left the building.

One of the men remaining withdrew his weapon. Placing the barrel inches from the back of Varvarinski's head, he pulled the trigger.

KIEV, UKRAINE

Reynolds woke as the sun rose. It was another overcast day. He sat up in the bed, cradling his face in his hands. Avramenko was still asleep. He hated to wake her but he was anxious to move forward.

"Nicky. It's time to get up." He touched her face gently.

Avramenko stirred and groaned, then came awake abruptly. "What? What's going on?" she said in Russian as she sat upright in bed.

"It's ok, Nicky," Reynolds said as he touched her shoulder. "It's time to go. We need to get to the U.S. Embassy as soon as we can."

Reynolds looked at the rubles he had in cash. "I have a little more than 300 rubles. Do you think that'll be enough for taxi fare?"

"I'll ask at the desk. Let me go to the toilet, then we'll leave."

The taxi fare in Ukrainian currency was equivalent to 250 Russian rubles. Reynolds gave the driver all the Russian currency he had.

The taxi deposited them at the gate to the U.S. Embassy. Like most U.S. legations throughout the world, this one was surrounded by a gated high wall.

Reynolds approached the Marine guard. He was asked for his papers. When Reynolds told him that his passport had been stolen, the Marine radioed the information to some superior. He was told to wait.

He and Avramenko looked around anxiously to see if they had been spotted. It was ten minutes later before the guard motioned to him. He grabbed Avramenko's hand and proceeded through the gate.

"Sir. I have authorization for you only. Not the lady. She must wait out here."

"No fucking way. She's with me. Listen to me, soldier. I need to see the Ambassador. Not some junior fucking secretary, the Ambassador. You tell whoever controls access here that it's a matter of national security. U.S. national security. And I'm not shitting you. I'm a newspaper reporter. The name is Mark Reynolds. New York Daily Press. Check it out. You want to make the front page in New York for being a dumb shit? Now go tell whoever you need to."

The Marine stiffened at Reynolds' outburst but turned without comment to make the call from his guard post.

Several minutes later a young woman in a business suit came to the gate station. "Mr. Reynolds? And this is?" looking at Avramenko.

"My name is Katerina Avramenko. I am Russian citizen. I work for a Russian newspaper."

"She's working with me," Reynolds said.

"Very well. Follow me," the woman said.

After signing in and receiving visitor badges, the woman escorted them to a small nondescript conference room. It was thirty minutes later before a man in his early thirties entered. He shook hands with Reynolds and Avramenko then sat down.

"We have done some checking. There is a Mark Reynolds formerly employed by the New York Daily Press. You're that person?"

"That's right."

"But you have no passport. How's that?"

"It's a long story. But suffice it to say it was stolen."

"Stolen? What were the circumstances?"

"Listen. They were stolen by some people bent on killing us. They're connected to the large multi-national, Martinelli Global. I've been writing some unflattering stuff about Martinelli Global."

"And you are also a journalist, Miss Avramenko? A Russian newspaper?"

"That is right."

"And how do you know Mr. Reynolds?"

"We work on same story. Story about Martinelli Global"

The man turned back to Reynolds. "Mr. Reynolds. There's another serious matter. You are aware that the Republic of Columbia has filed murder charges against you. Interpol has issued what is known as a Red Notice. That means any signatory country to the international treaty governing extradition is duty bound to arrest and deport that person."

"Shit. That's a bullshit charge. It wouldn't hold water in the U.S. It's Martinelli Global's people in Columbia. They've got heavy political clout. If you check I think you'll find the FBI got me out of Columbia after I was detained."

"Maybe they had the same problem with you as we do. You've placed us in an awkward situation, Mr. Reynolds. Legally you're on the equivalent of U.S. soil in the form of this embassy. As a U.S. national you are not subject to summary extradition from the U.S. But we are in a foreign country. However, let's leave that aside. You indicated you had information of national security interest. What is the nature of that information?"

"No offense, but you're not senior enough. I will only give this information to the Ambassador, or least the CIA Chief of Station."

"Listen, Mr. Reynolds, I can't pass you to someone higher up unless you tell me what this concerns."

Reynolds hesitated for a moment before saying, "It concerns nuclear weapons."

The man's eyes widened. He excused himself and left, closing the door behind him.

It was another thirty minutes later before the door opened and a middle aged man with glasses entered. He said his name was Johnson. He said he was the Commercial Attaché. Unfortunately, the Ambassador and his deputy were not in Kiev at the moment.

"Do I take it Mr. Johnson that you are the CIA Chief of Station?"

"Oh my no. I'm just a career foreign service employee. Trade relations mostly. Not connected with intelligence. Right now I'm the most senior official here. So we're both stuck with each other."

Reynolds still assumed he was CIA, perhaps not the head guy, but CIA nonetheless. At the mention of national security it would logically be handed to the local CIA contingent.

"Ok, Mr. Johnson. Here's what I have. First of all I've been working on a story about multi-national corporations' excesses and illegal practices. I'm using one corporation, Martinelli Global, to showcase the story. They've tried to stop me before. They've tried to kill me more than once."

"Tried to kill you in Ukraine?"

"Yes. That's why we are without passports. I have evidence against the senior executives about their illegal activities that I am about ready to publish. I can present the Justice Department with enough evidence to indict the top guys at Martinelli Global on a whole raft of major criminal charges. Implicates Russian businesses as well. But that's not the pressing issue. We've now uncovered something that is truly a matter of national security. It must get to the White House."

"The White House? Come now. If it wasn't for your reputation as a credible newspaper reporter and author, one might brand you a conspiracy crackpot. So what could be so earthshaking that the President needs to know about it?"

Reynolds glared at the man and his condescending manner. "Tell your superiors that we have strong evidence that Iran has obtained functional nuclear warheads. Tell them the origin of those warheads is Russia."

The color drained from the man's face. He looked at Reynolds and Avramenko trying to size up what they might be about.

"What kind of evidence?" Gone was the diplomatic officer veneer. He was CIA.

Reynolds told him about the cell phone recordings. Told him how they came about as a result of a disgruntled employee with access to their computer files. The guy was an accomplished hacker and found a way into his target's cell phone system.

The man he suspected as being CIA listened intently, asking several questions. "So where is all this evidence? Where are these telephone conversation recordings?"

"In the United States," Reynolds replied.

CHAPTER 39

MOSCOW, RUSSIAN FEDERATION

F eliks Garnitsky burst into Nikolai Krasin's office and closed the door behind him. Only yesterday he had told Krasin they had captured Reynolds and the Russian journalist who was helping him.

"I've some important news, Nikolai Mikhailovich. Some good, some bad. The bad news first. That idiot Stanislav somehow let Reynolds and Avramenko escape. Someone killed all four of his men. Yuri Dratshev is there now trying to sort it out."

"Stanislav's an incompetent. Why are you using him for something this important?" Krasin said. He was still seated at his desk.

"Because he was on the scene at the time. But I agree he's a problem. That will be taken care of."

"So who killed the four men? Is somebody with resources helping Reynolds?"

"That's a possibility we're looking into. Hard to see who that might be. But it would also seem unlikely that Reynolds and Avramenko could have overpowered four men with weapons."

"This is a major disappointment, Feliks. Glad I didn't tell Martinelli and Redek the news of Reynolds' capture. Bad enough now I've got to tell them we fucked up again. They're going to think we're just a bunch of dumb peasants. Am I to trust you to resolve this Reynolds problem, Feliks?" Krasin was now out of his chair pacing the office.

Garnitsky fumed inside. Only Krasin could talk to him like that, the arrogant prick. He knew nothing about how these things worked.

"But there's good news to counter that temporary problem. We have both Reynolds' and Avramenko's computers. They weren't caring any copies of files stolen from our computer system. They left behind their passports and credit cards also. It will be difficult for them to get far."

"And what are you doing to find them?"

"I know certain people in Kiev. They are spreading the word that there is much money to be made for information about this American. We have several members of the Ukrainian SBU that will provide information for money. Better than that, my sources at the FSB tell me they have assets within the SBU itself. They've already started a search. My senior contact at the FSB and I both agree that Reynolds would probably go to a U.S. embassy or consulate. The most obvious is Kiev. But we're looking at others. The only way they could have left Ukraine is if someone is assisting them."

The SBU was the Ukrainian Security Service. Garnitsky had personally called his principle senior contact, a one-star general in the Russian FSB. The General enjoyed a substantial salary on Garnitsky's payroll. He was highly placed enough that Garnitsky had access to almost any of the FSB's most classified information. Garnitsky could also run operations with FSB assets as if they were his own.

"When do you expect to find them?" Krasin asked.

"Within a matter of days. But I also have additional good news to report. The hacker was actually our own Ilya Varvarinski. He accessed our system and stole the evidence he was trying to give to Reynolds. He's an expert. Disguised himself as an outside hacker. He has been taken care of. We have his computers. The American experts Redek sent are trying to get into the files on the computer. Seems Varvarinski set up elaborate security on his own computers."

"And why did he steal from us?"

"Blamed us for the death of his sister."

Krasin glared at Garnitsky. "Don't you mean he blamed you, Feliks?"

Garnitsky did not respond to Krasin's comment.

"At least his removal is something positive I can convey to New York." Krasin said.

"There's something else we need to take care of however. Under questioning, Varvarinski said that before we picked him up he had sent copies of the computer files to the United States. Small envelopes containing USB storage devices. He said he sent them by Federal Express the day before yesterday. They may arrive in New York tomorrow."

"Jesus Christ, Feliks! You do not have further bad news do you? So what the hell are we to do about this?"

"Varvarinski gave us the names and addresses. He sent packages to two people in Manhattan. One's a lawyer named Matthew Solomon, the other's a woman named Rachel Stern. She works with Reynolds at the newspaper."

"So what can be done?"

"Give the information to Conrad Redek. Tell him he must hurry. Redek knows people who can handle this. Best approach is to intercept these deliveries. If delivery cannot be stopped, then they need to forcibly recover these storage devices. And they need to do so quickly, before anyone copies them to a computer. Dratshev has looked at some of the documents on Reynolds' computer. It would be very damaging in the United States. It would damage us here in Russian as well."

"That's even worse news, Feliks. I'm calling Redek right now. What a fucking disaster."

It took a few minutes for Conrad Redek to be located. It was early morning in New York. Krasin went through the whole string of events with Redek. The conversation lasted twenty minutes.

"I'll tell Steven. He'll be very upset of course. The key here, Nikolai, is to resolve this matter about Reynolds. When you call me next time, I hope it's to tell me that Reynolds is dead. I'll take care of these file devices on their way to New York."

"We will find Reynolds. But, Conrad, Feliks has told me the electronic files Varvarinski stole are very bad for all of us. You must get them at any cost. If that means killing this woman and lawyer, don't hesitate."

"I understand, Nikolai."

Krasin disconnect the call. He turned to Garnitsky, "When you find Reynolds and this woman, they're to be killed. Quickly and quietly. Their bodies are not to be found. They're too dangerous to all of us."

MANHATTAN, NEW YORK

It was three o'clock in the afternoon on the Upper West Side. The FedEx delivery van parked in front of Rachel Stern's apartment building. The driver went to the row of buzzers and rang Stern's apartment. No answer. He simply left the FedEx envelope propped against the wall next to the mail boxes. Once he left, a man in a windbreaker picked up the envelope.

At about the same time in Downtown Manhattan, another FedEx truck parked in the delivery zone of an office building. The driver had a number of deliveries for this professional building. A man in a smart gray business suit stood outside the door marked *Law Offices of Cohen, Miller & Solomon*. As the FedEx driver approached from down the hall, the man opened the office door then immediately closed it. He intended to make it look as if he had just left the office.

"Do you have a package for Matthew Solomon?" the gray suit said to the FedEx delivery man as he approached.

"Right here."

"Excellent. I've been waiting for this for days. A settlement check. A big goddamn check!" the man said and signed for the package. He reached into pocket and gave the FedEx guy a twenty as a tip. "You have a good day."

Conrad Redek brought Steven Martinelli up to speed with the events in Russia.

"So you're saying that even though Reynolds is still on the loose, that none of these incriminating electronic files exist any longer?"

"That's right. They have Reynolds computer, and for that matter the Russian journalist's computer too. We intercepted the files sent to New York. And the source of the leak has been eliminated."

"Conrad. I want this Reynolds matter concluded. We've let it go on for too long. It must be done quickly. That was the whole point to deal with him while he was in Russia. But Nikolai has bungled this whole opportunity."

"I am confident it will get repaired. Reynolds is out of options. He has no passport or credit cards. If he's arrested outside of the U.S. he gets deported to Columbia. And he doesn't have any more materials then he had before he left for Russia."

"What if he has made it to a U.S. Embassy?" Martinelli asked.

"Can't see that will be a problem. He's got no evidence. The Justice Department didn't act on his earlier information. I'm told there was some violence in Ukraine that Reynolds could be linked to. Then of course there is this murder warrant from Columbia."

"Regardless, this matter must be concluded as soon as possible, Conrad. They're truly cowboys over there in Russia. Letting this computer systems guy get his hands on incriminating files suggests sloppy security. Should the files even have existed? I wonder where else we might be exposed? I trust you're reviewing our own security measures, Conrad?"

"Absolutely. The same guys who found the obscure trail left by this Varvarinski are going to do a full audit of our computer security here in New York," Redek said.

"That's good, however we need to go further. Are there electronic files that could prove incriminating? Do we even know?"

"The short answer is we probably don't know. We have always been very careful to avoid any obvious audit trails for anything knowingly illegal. But besides that, it's impossible to ensure that we do not have documents that when put together with other documents might prove incriminating. We employ too many people to control everything."

"How about e-mails? They seem to be sources of a lot of problems. Every time a member of Congress is caught screwing around it seems it's leaked through an e-mail."

"I have a plan. Durbin's chief computer guy will do it personally. It's a little painful. A lot of our people are going to be pissed off," Redek said.

"What are you suggesting?"

"Destroy our entire e-mail archives. Ostensibly it will be a cyber-attack, a computer virus. Which it actually will be. But one that we create ourselves then leave behind as evidence of the reason for the lost files. We even have insurance for such an event."

CHAPTER 40

KIEV, UKRAINE

R eynolds and Avramenko were forced to sit in the embassy conference room for another two hours. Someone brought them sandwiches and coffee.

The man calling himself Johnson eventually returned. Accompanying him was a younger man with a military style haircut. "This is FBI Special Agent Franks. He's our FBI liaison officer here at the embassy."

"Mr. Reynolds, Miss Avramenko," the agent said and shook hands. He and Johnson took seats on the opposite side of the conference table.

"We have checked on both you and Miss Avramenko," Agent Franks said. "You are who you claim to be. Now, Mr. Johnson has told me your story. I must say it's quite a story. Tell it to me again."

For the next two hours, Reynolds went over the story starting with his investigations of Martinelli Global going all the back to the Nigerian chemical plant disaster. The agent interrupted repeatedly to ask questions. He had a legal pad but made only occasional notes.

Reynolds omitted the details about escaping their abductors by killing four men. No telling what complications that would present with the Ukrainian authorities if they were informed of the deaths. He explained their escape as a result of the kidnappers' carelessness.

After Reynolds concluded his narrative the agent said, "That's a helluva story, Mr. Reynolds. Sounds more like a novel if I'm to believe all of these narrow escapes. And this stuff about stolen nuclear weapons. Frankly that's just plain bizarre. My superiors would have my head if I gave that any credibility."

"You calling me a liar?"

"I don't know. You've given us no evidence. For that matter, there's nothing to substantiate your charges against Martinelli Global. For all I know it's just your paranoia. Or maybe you're just obsessed with this corporation."

"There were photographs. There was no mistaking what they showed," Reynolds said not disguising his anger.

The agent shrugged then continued, "Your account of what went on in Columbia differs with the Columbian government."

"Christ. Martinelli Global has them in their pocket."

"Well they apparently made enough of a case to get a Red Notice issued by Interpol. Interpol isn't a bunch of idiots."

"Listen. The U.S. Ambassador in Bogotá didn't buy the Columbians' bullshit. Because of him I got out of that corrupt shithole. I was escorted back to the United States by the FBI no less. Check it out."

"I did. That part's correct. But the information you provided proved inconclusive. The investigation was abandoned. The Bureau's report suggests you may have even fabricated the information to get out of Columbia."

"The FBI didn't want to investigate. Somebody applied political pressure to squelch the investigation."

"More speculation? I suppose it was these people from Martinelli Global again?"

Reynolds held his anger in check. "We can fence forever over this, Agent Franks. Believe me, evidence exists. It's enough to destroy Martinelli Global."

"So you say. And its in New York. But you won't tell us where. How do we know this isn't just another one of your flights of fantasy? Just like when you promised evidence in exchange for getting you out of Columbia."

"Fuck you. I'm tired of listening to this. You're nothing but fucking bureaucrats."

"Fine. You're free to leave. You came to us. Consular Services will get you a replacement passport within a couple of days."

Reynolds knew they must leave Ukraine as soon as possible. He had to turn this around. Attacking Agent Franks was counterproductive.

"You know we can't leave. We've no money. No place to go. The people that held us captive would undoubtedly be looking for us. I'm telling you evidence exists in New York. "

"But you won't tell us where. Why is that?"

"If I tell you where, then you'll retrieve it. There's a lot of data there. The stuff's in Russian. It's not organized. That's what Miss Avramenko and I were doing. God knows how long you'll take before you decide to send us home. That makes me uncomfortable."

"Home? Miss Avramenko is Russian. You expect her to go with you to the United States? I can't get her a new passport."

"She'll be invaluable in helping to sort out the files. We made a lot of progress before we were kidnapped and our computers stolen. You can get her a visa."

"So how is it that this data is in New York?"

"Copies of everything were sent there independently as a safeguard. Documents. Real evidence. This stuff's too valuable to lose."

"Sounds like you're trying to blackmail the U.S. Government," Agent Franks said trying to make up his mind how to handle this.

Reynolds did not rise to the provocation.

Johnson, the suspected CIA guy said, "Let's go over how you got these telephone intercepts of this Feliks Garnitsky." Johnson had checked on the name. Garnitsky was suspected as being involved in large scale smuggling in Russia. He was ex-KGB and to Reynolds credibility, Garnitsky was associated with the well connected billionaire, Nikolai Krasin. Krasin's enterprises were financially linked with Martinelli Global. That much was corroborated. If what Reynolds was alleging about nuclear weapon thefts proved credible, this would be a major professional coup.

"Like I told you. It was a disgruntled employee. He had personal reasons to get revenge on Garnitsky. He's the source of a lot of the other incriminating evidence against Martinelli Global. Taken from their own files."

"But to get audio recordings of telephone calls on this guy?"

"Why not? I'm no computer expert, but he is. Apparently an accomplished hacker. If hackers can access highly secured databases of the Government and financial institutions, why not a cell phone system? Especially a Russian system."

"And Garnitsky was talking to one of his subordinates?"

"Apparently. The subordinate seemed to be supervising the theft close to the scene."

"Seems kind of loose to talk over a cell phone."

"What choice did he have? E-mail is insecure. My own problems prove that. They also leave a trail. Not likely the cell phone calls would be monitored. If they were, it would be some government eavesdropping computer program looking for key words. Isn't that what the NSA does? I think he avoided such words. Our hacker friend put it together only by the association of circumstances, and of course the photos. Besides that, he was targeting Garnitsky."

"You're correct about this getting us nowhere," FBI Agent Franks said. "I'll need to discuss this with Washington. Mr. Johnson will need to discuss this with the Ambassador. In the meantime, you'll be put up in some makeshift accommodations here at the embassy."

"One more suggestion," Reynolds said. "Call a deputy U.S. Attorney. His name is Albert Thorne. He's in the Manhattan office. I had a conversation with him after returning from Columbia. I think he can vouch for me." Reynolds said.

He hoped Thorne might take an interest. He hoped Thorne would remember that suspicious pressure had halted investigation into Reynolds previous accusations against Martinelli Global.

Reynolds and Avramenko were escorted by a Marine to a storage room in the basement. Two cots had been prepared. Each was piled with a set of sheets, a blanket, and a pillow.

Reynolds kissed Avramenko. "It'll workout, Nicky."

"I do not believe they will allow me to go to the United States with you."

"They will. I won't leave you here."

Avramenko was an emotional wreck. Reynolds was not much better.

FBI Agent Franks and the man known as Johnson discussed the problem of Reynolds and Avramenko. Actually they argued. Franks didn't like journalists in general. He sure as hell didn't like negotiating with one. Yet as Johnson pointed out, Reynolds was a recognized investigative reporter of some standing. Author of two books. One on Russian nuclear weapons stockpiles. For that matter, Katerina Avramenko was a well regarded journalist, critical of the Russian Government.

Obviously this intelligence would be passed on in detail to their superiors. Critical to their careers however were their personal interpretations and recommendations. For that reason, Agent Franks gave a non-committal recommendation as to the voracity of Reynolds information. He supported Reynolds suggestion to talk to the U.S. District Attorney Thorne. Reluctantly he recommended that both Reynolds and

Avramenko be returned to the United States if Thorne agreed. Make it the Attorney General's problem.

Johnson was a bit more positive with his spin as he reported to Langley, Virginia. The CIA was used to more imperfect intelligence. Reynolds was basically credible. Avramenko supported everything he said. The background made sense. If he passed the intelligence on with a too much cover-your-ass assessment and Reynolds' story panned out, he'd look like a clerk. If he over played it and it turned out to be a dry hole, he'd be labeled gullible. But Johnson had been at this for over twenty years. He knew how to frame his reports in the appropriate CIA language that kept the options open.

In the morning, a woman staffer knocked on their door. She handed Reynolds a stack of clothing assembled for both of them. She told them they could use a shower down the hall. Some basic toiletries were provided. Breakfast was arranged when they were finished. They were expected at a meeting at 8:30 that morning.

The sleep, a shower, and a hearty breakfast of eggs and ham in the embassy kitchen restored Reynolds and Avramenko. A Marine escorted them to a large conference room. Franks and Johnson were already seated.

"Have a seat," Franks said. "In a moment we're going to have U.S. Deputy District Attorney Thorne on the phone."

In fact it was not only Albert Thorne but another U.S. attorney named Ellsberg. Ellsberg had been the attorney that was ordered off pursuing Reynolds earlier information after returning from Columbia. He was a specialist at investigating complex financial crimes.

FBI Agent Franks had filed his report, as had Johnson with the CIA. With the mention of a theft of nuclear materials the information moved quickly up the chains of command. Contrary to normal practice, both the FBI and CIA were coordinated on this at least for the moment. Thorne had been contacted. He vouched for Reynolds credentials. He readily agreed to talk to Reynolds and suggested to his superiors that he be joined by Ellsberg. These particular criminal areas were Ellsberg's expertise.

Ellsberg had also told Thorne something else a couple of weeks after being ordered not to pursue Reynolds previous information. Ellsberg looked at Reynolds materials in some detail. Contrary to orders, he did some preliminary work on his own. The information should clearly have been pursued. He was certain Martinelli Global had exercised pressure. Pressure at a very senior level. It had upset him ever since. When Thorne contacted him, he leaped at the chance. He told his boss that Thorne had requested his consultation on a matter of some evidence that was in the area of Ellsberg's expertise.

A telephone connection with Washington was established. Deputy U.S. Attorney Albert Thorne introduced himself, followed by the others in Kiev.

"Mr. Reynolds, I have with me a colleague, Deputy U.S. Attorney Phillip Ellsberg. He is familiar with previous evidence you presented us regarding Martinelli Global. It seems you lead a colorful life, Mr. Reynolds. A dangerous one as well if we're to believe these latest reports. It would certainly improve the situation if you would allow us to retrieve this new documentation you say you have."

Reynolds was encouraged by this telephone call. It was 1:30am in the morning in New York. The people on the other end must see this as important.

"I understand that. But you must understand my position. I'm stuck out here swinging in the wind. It's a matter of trust. You should see this as vital. If you do, you'd want me back on secure ground in the United States. Short of that, you're just jerking me around. I've been there before. You guys ignored information I gave you before."

"Let me ask you this, Mr. Reynolds," Ellsberg said. "Your allegations about the theft of nuclear weapons is being processed by U.S. intelligence. Do you have reason to believe this theft involves others at Martinelli Global?"

"I don't know. All we have is the information on the telephone recordings of Feliks Garnitsky."

"But Garnitsky is connected with Martinelli Global?"

Avramenko answered. "Of course he's connected. He's a senior executive working for Nikolai Krasin. Krasin's enterprises are largely owned by Martinelli Global. Garnitsky's also a major criminal."

"I assume that was Miss Avramenko," Ellsberg said. "And how did you become involved with Mr. Reynolds investigations."

"In much of my reporting on Russian criminals I have come across Feliks Garnitsky. I began receiving incriminating information about Garnitsky by e-mail from someone calling himself Rasputin. Later on, Rasputin said there was an American reporter who was investigating this big multi-national corporation called Martinelli Global. I learned that the Russian financier, Nikolai Krasin was heavily connected with Martinelli Global. Garnitsky was connected with Krasin. Then Rasputin said the American was coming to Russia. Of course I was interested in working with the American."

"And you have seen these files that Mr. Reynolds claims are now in the United States?"

"Yes. We have worked together to organize these files."

"And these audio recordings of Garnitsky? The digital photographs?"

"Yes. Those as well."

"You realize, Miss Avramenko, that if you are allowed entry into the United States, it is solely based upon your help in this matter," Ellsberg said.

"Yes."

"Mr. Reynolds, we have the reports of your interviews there in Kiev. Tell me in summary terms what it is you have on Martinelli Global."

Reynolds took a moment to organize his thoughts. "I had enough evidence on Martinelli Global before even going to Russia. The Justice Department did nothing with it. Don't know whether that's incompetence, the lack of will, or political pressure. But the documents I can give you from Martinelli Global's Russian connections are more incriminating. They cover a range of new things.

"Connections to Russian subsidiaries through specific offshore shell corporations. Documentation of briberies, Foreign Corrupt Practices Act, I believe. Money laundering. Smuggling. SEC violations for not identifying foreign investments, for falsifying financial reports. Tax violations. Wire fraud of course. And whatever laws must be violated for secret investment in a foreign military weapons programs. This documentation nails them."

The discussion went on for another half hour. Ellsberg concluded with, "I hope to get back to you with a decision about your situation within the next twenty-four hours. Do we need to coordinate with anyone at State, Mr. Johnson?"

Johnson, acting in his cover role as a State Department officer answered, "No. I'll take care of advising the Ambassador and Washington."

CHAPTER 41

Moscow, Russian Federation

F eliks Garnitsky sat in his office waiting. Waiting for news from all quarters. He was sipping a coffee and smoking. It was late afternoon. He had just received the most important news. Krasin had just called after hearing from Conrad Redek. The USB devices with the incriminating files had been intercepted prior to their delivery. Now if he were only to hear that Reynolds had been located.

Garnitsky needed to see exactly what files Varvarinski had found. Dratshev still had Reynolds' and Avramenko's computers in Kiev. Once Varvarinsky had been implicated, his computers had been confiscated and given to the American computer experts to attempt to decode the files. His own experts had not been successful.

His telephone rang. "Yes?"

Raisa, the head of the information systems department said, "Sir, the American experts asked me to call you. Whatever they've been working on, they would like you to come down."

Raisa sounded shaky. She was still traumatized from a few days earlier after being questioned for hours. The men doing the questioning were frightening enough with just their appearances. They had hammered at her about theft of company files. Now the Americans wanted to see Garnitsky. Was she to be accused of something?"

Down meant the computer department in the basement. Garnitsky met Raisa who escorted him to the locked room where the two Americans had been working on Varvarinski's computers. She knocked. The older American opened the door and ushered her and Garnitsky inside. The man told her to translate to Garnitsky that they had found Varvarinski's encryption key and were able to open his files. Even first-rate hackers make mistakes.

"Raisa. I must apologize for having those security people question you," Garnitsky said. "You see there were some highly confidential files illegally accessed. I was told it had to be either you or Varvarinski. It was Varvarinski. He won't be returning to work here. These are his computers. I need to review what he stole. You can help me navigate the files."

The two Americans left the room.

Garnitsky sat down at the table alongside Raisa. In front of her was Varvarinski's notebook computer. Raisa began clicking on folders and certain files commenting to Garnitsky when he asked more specific questions.

This went on for over half an hour when Raisa came to a folder containing audio files. "This is unusual," she said.

"What?" Garnitsky said.

"This folder. It's full of audio files. Recordings."

Raisa did not want to open any of these files. She didn't want to know what they contained. These files were not from Moscow Capital Partners databases. "If these are confidential, perhaps I should leave now that you know how to navigate."

"Perhaps that is best, Raisa. I believe I can manage."

Raisa couldn't leave fast enough. Garnitsky scared her.

Garnitsky opened the first file. After a few words of the audio recording he abruptly leaned in toward the computer. It was his own voice he heard. It took him a minute to place what the call was about. Once he recognized it was a conversation with Dratshev he was visibly shaken as he listened. He let the recording conclude before opening the next file. He repeated this through the list of files, not necessarily listening to each entire recording. He didn't have to. Then he came to the digital photographs.

Garnitsky just sat there for several minutes. What did this mean? Where else do these recordings exist? On the USB devices and Reynolds' and Avramenko's computers. And Varvarinski's two computers.

The first thing Garnitsky did was delete the audio files then delete them from the recycle folder. He had heard that even such deleted files could sometimes be recovered. For the moment, his deletions would suffice.

He opened the door. "Raisa. Have the two Americans join us."

Garnitsky explained that he wanted the hard drive removed from Varvarinski's desktop computer. The younger American produced a screw driver. Within a couple of minutes he removed the hard drive and then handed it to Garnitsky.

"Raisa, thank them for their excellent work. I will be sure to compliment their work to Conrad Redek in New York."

Garnitsky left with Varvarinsky's notebook computer and the hard drive removed from his other computer.

Back in his office, he called Krasin. "Nikolai. The file devices Conrad intercepted in New York; what has he done with them?"

"I told him to destroy them. We already had the other computers with the files. These USB devices were only copies. Too dangerous to keep. My guess is Conrad tried to look at the files but they were probably almost all in Russian. He couldn't very likely go get a translator. So I think he probably destroyed them. Why?"

"Because I took a look at some of the files. We could have been ruined, Nikolai. Dratshev has Reynolds' and the woman's computers. I'm calling him now to destroy them. I will now have the only copy. They're on Varvarinski's computer. It's locked in my safe. Only you and I should review them."

KIEV, UKRAINE

Garnitsky called Dratshev. "Yuri. Listen to me. I need you to destroy Reynolds' and Avramenko's computers. We have identified the stolen files on Varvarinski's computers. The data on these computers is too dangerous. Do you know how to do that?"

"Of course. I'll remove the hard drives then physically destroy them."

"Immediately, Yuri. Do it right now."

"Yes, Sir. Have we heard anything on Reynolds yet?"

"No. Do you have any of our people with you in case Reynolds is located in the Ukraine?"

"Only Stanislav."

"That fucking idiot is worse than useless. There can be no more failures in removing Reynolds and the woman."

These audio recordings of his cell phone conversations with Dratshev made killing Reynolds and Avramenko an imperative. Even without the recordings they might convince someone to look more closely. Krasin had already sanctioned their killing so Garnitsky didn't have to act independently.

"Yuri. I think the best possibility is that Reynolds is at the United States Embassy there in Kiev. We need to get some people in place. I know someone there in Ukraine that might be able to help us. I'll call him. His name is Tischenko. He's a bigtime arms smuggler in Odessa. We've done business together. Old school. I did some favors for him in the past. He should be able to arrange for some people to help you. I will have him call you directly."

"And if Reynolds is at the Embassy, what do you want me to do?"

"Get surveillance in place. Make a plan. They must leave sometime. Probably for the airport. You need to intercept them. They must be killed at any cost, Yuri."

"They might be escorted by people from the Embassy. Could get ugly with other casualties."

"Can't be helped. Reynolds and the woman cannot be allowed to leave Kiev. Do what you have to."

Garnitsky didn't have to wait long. He was having breakfast at his favorite morning restaurant when his cell phone rang.

"We've located Reynolds," the FSB general said. "As we suspected, he's at the U.S. Embassy in Kiev."

"That is excellent work, General. Were you able to gather any further information?"

"No. Only that Reynolds and the reporter Avramenkova have been there two days. Our source within the embassy is not highly placed."

"Would your source be able to give us a warning when Reynolds is about to leave?"

"I don't know. That would depend on the communications capability with the control officer. I will inquire."

"Such information would be of considerable value, General."

The General understood that meant a healthy fee if he could get the information.

Garnitsky immediately called Dratshev.

Dratshev told Garnitsky that his friend Tischenko had sent four men from Odessa. They had arrived in Kiev only a few hours earlier. The men came armed with AK-47 assault rifles. They looked capable. They also brought a large quantity of Semtex plastic explosive as requested by Dratshev.

"Do you have a plan on how to do this, Yuri?" Garnitsky asked.

"Yes. Explosives I think will be the surest way. The firepower will be an alternative or backup. But it would be helpful if we knew when Reynolds might be leaving the Embassy. It's going to be difficult to identify if Reynolds is in a particular vehicle."

"I'll see what I can do. In the meantime you must simply be ready to execute your plan on a moments notice."

In the parking structure of Dratshev's hotel, the four men assembled the Semtex explosive with detonators in the trunk of the Mercedes they drove from Odessa. Once the rigging of the car as a bomb was completed, they drove to the U.S. Embassy on Yuriy Kotsiubynsky Street.

Stanislav was already on lone surveillance at the Embassy. He was sitting in his car located across the street from the Embassy.

Dratshev got into Stanislav's car and explained the plan. It called for Dratshev and two men in one car to watch the Embassy. Another car with the other two Odessa men would alternate surveillance. Stanislav would drive the heavier Mercedes the Odessa men brought. He understood the plan to be that he was to crash the Mercedes into the car carrying Reynolds as it left the Embassy.

If the embassy car came up the street as expected, Stanislav would simply have to pull out in front of it to cause the accident. The two other vehicles following would drive up and box in the car with Reynolds. The four gunmen would then exit their vehicles and assault the car with heavy automatic weapons fire killing Reynolds and everyone else.

If the car left the Embassy going in the opposite direction, Stanislav would turn around quickly and fall in behind. At an opportune time, he would pull along the embassy car and force it off the street.

Dratshev escorted Stanislav back to the Mercedes. He tossed Stanislav's car keys to the two Odessa men as they passed him to get into Stanislav's smaller sedan. After a few words of encouragement to Stanislav, Dratshev returned to the other car. As instructed, Stanislav took the Mercedes down the street a block from the Embassy. It was a guess, but Dratshev determined by the map that it was the direction they would most likely take if going to the airport. Dratshev's car took up the surveillance position.

At some point they would have to take turns to get food and use a toilet. That would mean he would be short two men and a car if Reynolds were to leave at that time. Dratshev wished he had more manpower and more time to develop a better plan. The idiot Stanislav would get no relief. He could piss in his pants for all Dratshev cared.

Those thoughts proved academic when his cell phone rang after only two hours into the surveillance. It was Garnitsky. "The FSB has a source inside the Embassy. I just received word that Reynolds is expected to be leaving within the hour. It will be a large, black American car. Appears to be just one car. Probably two or three people besides Reynolds and the woman."

Dratshev called the other two cars using two cell phones. He left the connection open to both and put them on mute. He then turned to the man in the rear seat. The man handed Dratshev a control box slightly larger than a cell phone, with a twelve-inch antennae. He moved a toggle switch marked *activate system*.

"The green light indicates the system is activated. You press the arming switch to arm the detonator. The red light will display. You then move this toggle switch to detonate," the man explained.

"How close does the car need to be from the target?"

"Perhaps five meters or less to ensure everyone is killed. Best if it's right next to the target. Then it's a sure thing," the man said.

"How far away should we be?"

"I'd like to be well over a hundred meters away. The controller signal will work at even a much greater distance."

Dratshev nodded his understanding.

"This man in the other car. Why is he willing to be a suicide bomber?" the man in the rear asked.

Dratshev turned around to look at him. "Because he doesn't know. He thinks he's to stop the car by crashing into it. Then you guys will come up and kill everybody with automatic weapons."

Close to an hour later, the Embassy gates opened. A black Lincoln with tinted windows pulled out and headed in the anticipated direction.

"Stanislav. The car is heading toward you. Get ready," Dratshev said into his cell phone. He moved the arming toggle switch. The red light on the controller came on.

Stanislav started the Mercedes. In the rearview mirror he could see the American car approaching. He was anxious to get this done. Once Reynolds and the woman were killed, his earlier failures might be overlooked.

As the Lincoln approached, Stanislav pulled the Mercedes hard to the left into the street. He was a second late. The Lincoln accelerated and swerved hard to the left to avoid the collision. The reaction to accelerate was counter to the instinctive response to hit the brakes. But the embassy driver was State Department security, trained in defensive driving techniques.

The Mercedes caught the Lincoln a hard blow in the right rear spinning the Lincoln around 180 degrees and skidding just past the Mercedes.

Dratshev moved the detonation switch.

The explosion tore away the entire rear half of the Mercedes. The shock wave rocked Dratshev's vehicle. "Get closer!" Dratshev shouted to the driver. The gutted, burning Mercedes blocked the view of the embassy car that had skidded around then came to a stop beyond the Mercedes.

"Go around to the left!" Dratshev ordered.

The driver inched around the burning Mercedes. Two other parked cars were overturned by the blast. One was on fire. The targeted Lincoln sat in the middle of the street pointing back in the direction it had come from. It was upright about twenty meters away from the Mercedes.

As the Lincoln spun after the collision, the front took the blast. The engine hood was gone. One front wheel had collapsed. The engine had been pushed back through the firewall much like from a front-end collision. The front windshield was destroyed.

Dratshev's car pulled close to the Lincoln. The second car pulled up behind. "Finish it," Dratshev ordered into his cell phone to the other car.

The gunman from Dratshev's car and two from the other car exited with their assault rifles. No people were visible in the Lincoln. Presumably they were slumped down in their seats, killed by the blast. As the gunmen approached the Lincoln they were distracted by screeching brakes from the other side of the burning Mercedes.

Dratshev and his driver exited their vehicle. The driver fired a short burst from his AK-47 at two U.S. Marines that were running toward them on foot around the destroyed Mercedes. The Marines stopped and pulled back for cover.

The other three men turned back to the Lincoln and fired several bursts of fire into its passenger side. The men ran to the side of the Lincoln. Inside was a scene of carnage.

Dratshev waved for them to return. More security was arriving to support the two embassy Marines. Sirens could be heard in the distance.

The two assailant cars sped away down the street at high speed.

CHAPTER 42

KIEV, UKRAINE

E mbassy security, backed by additional Marines secured the scene of the car bombing. Kiev city police arrived within minutes. A senior commander of the Ukrainian national police arrived shortly after.

CIA agent Johnson arrived just ahead of the police and emergency medical personnel. He looked inside the shattered car. The driver and front passenger were a mass of gore. Their faces were not recognizable. The blast had driven the shattered windshield into their heads and upper bodies. The passenger was FBI Special Agent Franks.

Reynolds and the woman were slumped in the rear seat. They were unconscious. Blood streamed from multiple head wounds on both. They looked dead to Johnson.

The embassy medical officer arrived right behind Johnson. He looked at the passengers in the front seat. No hope there. Pushing Johnson aside, he opened the rear passenger side door. It was punctured with a line of bullet entry holes.

Katerina Avramenko was leaning against Mark Reynolds. Her sweater was soaked in blood. Besides the head lacerations, there appeared to be a bullet wound to the side of her head. The doctor felt her neck for a pulse.

"She's dead," he said, as much to himself as to Johnson. Reaching over Avramenko, he felt Reynolds neck. "Shit, this guy's still alive!"

The doctor backed out of the car as the first ambulance arrived. He moved quickly around to the other side of the Lincoln. With Johnson's help he eased the door open, cradling Reynolds from falling out. With the help of the emergency medical staff, Reynolds was placed on a gurney.

"We'll be going to the Kiev City Emergency Hospital. I'm going with the ambulance," the doctor told Johnson. "Get me someone over there right away that speaks Ukrainian. I need to know what kind of treatment and medication they're using. Ukrainian medical care sucks. This is not a place where you want to go to the hospital."

The embassy doctor called Johnson from the hospital three hours later. "Ok, here's the deal on Reynolds. All the blood you saw is mostly superficial lacerations, glass from the windshield probably. Both eardrums are ruptured. Severe concussion. He's still unconscious. Broken ribs and punctured left lung. Broken wrist. Dislocated shoulder. He just got out of surgery to repair the lung penetrations and remove fragments of two shattered ribs. The surgeon did a good job. I assisted."

"So he'll make it?"

"Yes. Unless there's some brain trauma we don't know about. The MRI unit here is not operating so we can't do a scan. We'll have a better fix on his status in another twenty-four hours."

"And the others?"

"The two men in the front were probably killed instantly from the blast. Both had fractured vertebrae at the neck. The massive tissue damage to the face and head came from the windshield. The woman might have survived the blast like Reynolds, but she was struck twice by bullets; one ruptured the liver, the other struck her head above her ear. Either shot would have caused death."

The Kiev Embassy was a frantic madhouse of activity consuming everyone from the Ambassador down. The secure telephone transmission lines were in constant use. State Department, Justice, and the CIA all had an interest.

The number-two FBI agent stationed at the Embassy became nominally in charge of what was essentially a criminal situation involving assaults on U.S. nationals. He was young and inexperienced. He couldn't wait until a very senior agent arrived from London to take over.

The FBI agent's immediate responsibility was to ensure Reynolds safety at the hospital. He welcomed Johnson's experienced hand in recommending how to allocate his limited personnel. With Johnson's assistance, the Ambassador placed three embassy security staff at his disposal, along with four Marines.

Johnson was also making his reports to Langley. With what was most likely an attempt on Reynolds' life, Reynolds' story about missing nuclear warheads had ratcheted up several notches. Johnson's communications moved quickly to the Deputy Director levels at both Operations and Analysis.

Through his own chain of command, Deputy U.S. Attorney Ellsberg made it clear to the FBI that he wanted Reynolds back in the United States as soon as medically permitted. His new boss agreed with him. His old boss had left the Justice Department. There were rumors of investigative decisions being influenced by political interests.

Ellsberg resurrected Reynolds' earlier allegations. Coupled with the attempt on Reynolds' life and his claim of new incriminating documentation, the request to open an investigation got a green light – directly from the head of the Criminal Division.

It was two days after the bombing before Reynolds regained consciousness. He was in terrible pain once he awoke. He couldn't hear anything. Yelling questions about what happened to Avramenko's didn't work. Trying to read the lips of the medical staff yielded nothing. They probably weren't even speaking English. The heavy dosage of pain medication soon put him to sleep.

When he awoke hours later, Johnson was seated in a chair across the room. There was another younger man there as well.

"I can't hear. What happened to Katerina Avramenko?" Reynolds asked, not knowing if his words were intelligible.

Johnson moved closer to the bed. He bent down towards Reynolds' face. "I'm sorry. She was killed," he said loudly.

Reynolds shook his head conveying he did not understand.

Johnson took a notebook from his pocket and wrote the phase, "She died in the bombing." He tore off the notebook sheet then turned it toward Reynolds to read.

Reynolds just stared at the words. After a moment he turned his head to the side and closed his eyes. Tears ran down his face. He let the intravenous drip of pain medication take him back into sleep.

It was a week later before the embassy medical officer felt Reynolds was up to traveling. He was still in bad shape. His face and head were a mass of healing wounds. The effects of the surgery were still painful. His torso was tightly wrapped in bandages for support. His arm was in a sling. The right wrist was in a cast. The pain medication kept him perpetually drowsy. He still could not hear. The loss of Nicky was altogether the most painful. He had been in a deep depression since he was told of her death. It was easy to tune everyone out when you couldn't hear.

MOSCOW, RUSSIAN FEDERATION

Feliks Garnitsky entered Nikolai Krasin's office. Once again he had bad news to report.

"Dratshev failed to kill Reynolds."

"What do you mean he failed?"

"Reynolds survived."

"Survived what?"

"Yuri attempted to detonate a car bomb to kill Reynolds as he left the United States Embassy in Kiev. It was too rushed. Not enough time to create a proper plan."

Krasin glared at Garnitsky. "Sonofabitch! You're making excuses, Feliks. I don't like that. All of your people have continually fucked up this affair with Reynolds. What am I to think? What am I to do about this?"

Garnitsky did not rise to the provocation of Krasin's rhetorical question.

"What happened?"

"A car bomb was detonated as the car carrying Reynolds left the embassy. We've learned that everyone in the car was killed except Reynolds."

"Who was killed?"

"The Russian reporter, Avramenko and two others from the United States Embassy."

"So now we've stirred up a hornet's nest by killing U.S. diplomatic staff. What are the Ukrainians going to say about the attack? Can it be blamed on Muslim extremists?"

Garnitsky was well aware of the added failure of Dratshev's plan.

"Probably not. The car used to carry the explosives was rented in Odessa. Dratshev used some people from there, a criminal group we've had dealings with. He needed some manpower quickly. He used Stanislav to drive the Mercedes.

Stanislav died in the blast. Any remains are not going to point to Muslims."

"And Reynolds?"

"In a Kiev hospital. Injured, but he'll survive. Heavily guarded of course."

Krasin was silent for a few moments. "You're not to pursue anything further against Reynolds. Without any documented evidence he cannot do much. I'll have to tell Martinelli. But I want to tell him that any connection to us has been eliminated. Do you understand my meaning, Feliks Alekseev?"

Garnitsky understood. Dratshev must be eliminated. It solved his own problem as well. Dratshev was the last link to the warheads theft. The harder part was killing the four Odessa men. It would cost a lot of money to compensate their boss in Odessa to keep the peace. He would contract with the Lebedyenko syndicate to do the dirty work. That would also cost a lot of money.

Two days later, Yuri Dratshev was abducted at gunpoint as he exited a restaurant. He was taken to a scrap yard and shot in the head. The body was fed into a large compactor used for compressing automobiles to dense metal cubes.

One week after the Kiev bombing, the Ukrainian press reported an incident of organized crime rivalry erupting into violence. Four men had been gunned down in separate attacks in Odessa. All of the victims had alleged associations with a known criminal organization. The media reported that police suspected the murders were perpetrated by a rival criminal faction.

MANHATTAN, NEW YORK

Steven Martinelli walked into Conrad Redek's office. He threw down a copy of that morning's newspaper. "Seen the front page?"

"Redek looked at the newspaper. Yes, what do you mean?"

"I just got off the phone with Nikolai. They located Reynolds then that idiot Garnitsky tried to kill him. A car bomb no less. That bombing at the U.S. Embassy in Kiev was his doing. Reynolds survived. They killed the Russian reporter, but they also killed an FBI agent and a State Department security guy."

"Christ."

"Nikolai says he is removing any link that could be traced back to them?"

"Does that include Feliks Garnitsky?"

"No. I asked that too. Krasin waffled. I think he might be afraid of Garnitsky. At any rate, that means that Reynolds will be talking."

"But there's no evidence to back up his allegations, Steven."

"I know that. But with this attempt on his life, the Government will listen. Especially with the murder of an FBI agent and a State Department employee.

"That means we need to start taking precautions. I want you personally to supervise an audit of all of our databases, files, whatever, for anything that the Government could use against us."

"We've always been scrupulously careful, Steven."

"Conrad, just do it. I want nothing taken for granted. You already warned me about e-mails. Too late to consider destroying them through your bogus cyber-sabotage idea. It would be too coincidental. Especially look at everything involving our Russian holdings. I can't trust Krasin's organization. They're a bunch of cowboys."

CHAPTER 43

MANHATTAN, NEW YORK

Reynolds disembarked at New York's JFK International at 3:00pm. Two FBI agents sent from London accompanied him on the eleven-hour non-stop flight from Kiev. The FBI agents turned him over to two waiting U.S. Marshals outside Customs. The marshals were to accompany him to his apartment, then bring him to the Federal Building in downtown Manhattan the following day.

Reynolds rode in silence from the airport. Little else he could do. Still unable to hear, those around him tended to gesture or just guide him. Back at the apartment, one marshal stayed with him. The other went out to get food.

Reynolds got a bottle of scotch from the kitchen cabinet. He offered the marshal a drink but the man declined with a wave of the hand. Reynolds went to his office area. He thought about calling Rachel, but realized that wouldn't work. He still couldn't hear. The doctor said the damaged ear drums should heal within two months. His hearing should return gradually.

Two hours and three drinks later he fell asleep in the chair.

The next morning was a struggle. He hurt badly. Showering was awkward with the cast and bandages. Most of all he couldn't stop thinking about Nicky Avramenko. It was another death caused by Martinelli Global. Because of him. Because of his obsession. Because of his carelessness. She was the third person to die for his cause.

"Care for breakfast, Mr. Reynolds?" the other marshal asked holding up an egg to convey his meaning. "I can fix some eggs?"

"No thanks. I'll just take some coffee," he said as best he could.

Reynolds and the marshals arrived at the Federal Building on One Saint Andrew's Plaza in Lower Manhattan. At 9:00 a.m. promptly, he was escorted to a conference room in the offices of the U.S. District Attorney for the Southern District of New York.

Reynolds turned his head as the door opened and several people walked in and took seats. A man leaned over and handed him a note. "I am Deputy U.S. District Attorney, Phillip Ellsberg. All of us extend our condolences to the loss of your colleague Katerina Avramenko. We realize that you are still unable to hear. I will therefore type my questions for you to see on the screen. I will try to phrase my questions to look for as short an answer as possible. Realizing that speaking might be awkward without the ability to hear, you can type a response if you prefer on the notebook computer in front of you.

"The meeting is informal but will be transcribed. Lastly, we will try to be brief. I prepared a summary based upon your previous allegations and the new developments you spoke of while you were in Kiev. That summary has been distributed to everyone here. Now let me introduce everyone."

Ellsberg started with the woman at the head of the conference table. The names and titles displayed on the digital projection. "In charge is U.S. District Attorney for the Southern District of New York, Eileen Maguire."

The others included two FBI agents, a Central Intelligence Agency representative, a representative from the Defense Intelligence Agency, and a stenographer.

"Let's begin," Ellsberg said. "We want to focus on these new allegations that you claim are supported by evidentiary proof,

Mr. Reynolds. You claim those materials are in the U.S. Where exactly?"

Reynolds slowly typed Rachel Stern's name and his attorney Matthew Solomon.

"And their relationship to you?"

"Miss Stern is a colleague from the Daily Press. She's a researcher. Mr. Solomon is my attorney," Reynolds typed.

"And you will accompany us to secure these documents?"

"Yes."

"You were very short on specifics when we spoke on the telephone when you were still in the Ukraine. For the benefit of everyone here, I would like you to reaffirm the scope of your allegations"

Reynolds nodded in the affirmative.

"You allege that Martinelli Global has violated SEC disclosure laws related to foreign investments?"

"Yes."

"That Martinelli Global executives have been complicit in bribing foreign officials through their subsidiaries?"

"Yes."

"That Martinelli Global engages in money laundering on a staggering scale. And that some of those funds come from drug trafficking?"

"Yes."

"That Martinelli Global uses offshore foreign corporations to conceal illegal investments and transactions? And that you have documentation to identifying many of these foreign holdings?"

"Yes."

"That Martinelli Global executives in the United States have knowledge of criminal acts, even homicides, committed on their behalf or on behalf of their subsidiaries?"

"Yes."

"You also allege that Martinelli Global has a financial interest in enterprises that engage in controlled technology without U.S. Government authorization. And perhaps more importantly, actually engages in commerce directly with a foreign military without U.S. authorization."

"Yes."

"And I believe the most jarring allegation is that Martinelli Global personnel may be complicit in the possible theft of Russian nuclear weapons?"

Everyone sat a little forward to hear what Reynolds said on that question.

Reynolds waved off the question. He typed in, "Someone connected with Martinelli Global's Russian holdings. Senior guy working for the billionaire financial mogul, Nikolai Krasin. Krasin's a partner with Martinelli Global. I don't know how deep this involvement goes with Martinelli Global's Russian subsidiaries."

"What kind of idiot would leave a document trail of such a theft?" the CIA man asked shaking his head with an incredulous expression. Ellsberg typed the question.

Reynolds typed, "Not documents. Cell phone calls. Recorded as digital files. And cell phone digital photographs."

"How did you tap into these calls?" the CIA man asked.

Reynolds typed, "I didn't. A hacker did. A pissed off employee. Same person that got into their databases. It's the source of all this Russian subsidiary stuff that incriminates Martinelli Global."

"And this hacker. Are you going to tell us who that is?" the CIA man asked. Ellsberg continued to type the questions.

Reynolds shook his head no.

"Thought as much. Typical reporter. Supposed to believe what they say but they wouldn't divulge the source so it can be corroborated," the CIA commented.

Reynolds typed, "Listen to the audio recordings. Even the CIA should be able to draw an accurate conclusion."

"Mr. Reynolds, the fact that these materials were stolen could prove problematic to a prosecution," the U.S. District Attorney said.

Reynolds typed, "I'm no lawyer, but doesn't the fact they were stolen from outside the U.S., and by what amounts to a whistleblower allow their use?"

Eileen Maguire smiled. "We're studying that. Even if there are problems as to admissibility as evidence it could still be valuable. If the materials are all you say, then it should point us toward targeted avenues of investigation. Since someone tried to kill you, I have high expectations. Which brings us to how you're going to provide us with those materials? And I mean immediately, Mr. Reynolds."

Reynolds typed. "Easy. Take me to the New York Daily Press offices. Rachel Stern will be at work there. The materials are electronic files stored on a couple of USB drives."

Maguire nodded to the two FBI agents. "That should not take long then. Please bring the materials directly back here. I'd like to see how good this stuff is."

Reynolds typed. "Most of it's in Russian. You'll need someone to translate."

"I'll get someone, Mr. Reynolds. Now get me that evidence."

The two FBI agents drove Reynolds the short distance to the offices of the New York Daily Press. Even with mid-day Manhattan traffic it took only fifteen minutes.

As they ascended in the elevator to the tenth floor, Reynolds felt guilty about seeing Rachel for the first time since his return in this impersonal way. He hoped she'd understand why he didn't see her yesterday when he returned to New York. Why he didn't even call. After all he couldn't hear. But this way in the office she wouldn't even be able to kiss him. He felt like a shit. It was more about not being forthright with Rachel. The sense that he betrayed her with Katerina.

The receptionist was startled when she looked up. "Oh my God! Mr. Reynolds? What happened?"

The FBI agent answered for him, "Mr. Reynolds was in a bad accident." The agent showed his badge. "We'd like to see Rachel Stern. Is she here?"

The flustered woman said, "Yes. Yes she is. I'll call her." The girl dialed a number. "Rachel. My God, you've got to come to reception right away. Mark Reynolds is here. And he's with the FBI."

The receptionist said. "She'll be right here." She then took off her headset and left the reception area.

The receptionist returned within moments followed by John Fredericks the managing editor.

"Jesus Christ, Mark. What the hell happened?"

The senior agent again answered for Reynolds. "A bad accident. I'm afraid that Mr. Reynolds suffered perforated eardrums and is temporarily unable to hear."

"Hi, John," Reynolds said, not knowing how it came out.

Fredericks started to extend his hand but realized Reynolds right wrist was in a cast. He touched him gently on the left shoulder instead.

Rachel Stern entered the reception area.

"Oh no, Mark!" she rushed to him and embraced him carefully. "What happened?"

The agent showed her his badge.

"The FBI? Are you in trouble, Mark?"

Reynolds' expression conveyed he couldn't hear.

The FBI agent explained again. "Mr. Reynolds is temporarily deaf. We realize you may have a lot of personal questions having not seen him for a number of weeks. However, we have something urgent and of utmost importance we must discuss with you. Is there somewhere we can talk privately?"

Rachel led them to a small conference room. John Fredericks attempted to follow, but the FBI agent said, "I'm afraid this is confidential, Sir."

"What? I'm the fucking managing editor here. You can't come in here and start questioning my staff without a warrant!"

Reynolds interceded. As best he could say, not sure the words were coming out intelligibly, "John, it's all right. We need to talk to Rachel. About something that's important to me. I'll explain later. Please."

Fredericks backed away glaring at the agents.

Reynolds closed the door behind him.

The lead agent said, "Miss Stern, someone sent a package to you from the Ukraine over a week ago. Two USB devices. They contain evidence related to a criminal investigation. Where are they?"

Her expression showed she did not understand. "What do you mean? I never received any package from Ukraine. What's on these USB's, Mark?"

"What?" Reynolds asked looking at the agents.

The agents proceeded to question Stern. Reynolds couldn't follow what was going on. Finally the lead agent scribbled on his note pad, "She says she never received a package."

"Rachel. Please. I want you to give them the USB's. I'm in trouble if you don't give them to them."

"Miss Stern, we would like to search your apartment if you will let us."

"Hell no! Why should I?"

"If you don't, I can have a search warrant issued within a matter of minutes. This is a national security matter. We'd rather have your cooperation."

Stern looked at Reynolds. He nodded yes to indicate he wanted her to cooperate with whatever the agents were asking.

It took an hour to search Stern's apartment. While the agents were about the search, Stern *talked* with Reynolds. He was starting to understand a little by reading lips. Stern quickly picked up on exaggerating her forming of words to assist him.

From the difficult verbal exchange assisted by scribbled notes, Stern understood the brief outline of Reynolds story since he left for Moscow. About the kidnapping. His escape and the killings. Meeting Rasputin. The nuclear weapons. The car bombing. Avramenko's death. A duplicate set of the files sent to his attorney.

After completing their search, the FBI agents thanked Stern and left with Reynolds. He promised Stern he'd return that evening. If the FBI let him go that is.

The agents said nothing on the short trip to Matthew Solomon's law offices. There was a repeat scene with a stunned Solomon upon seeing Reynolds looking the way he did. Then, no, he had not received a package from Ukraine.

Back at the Justice Department offices, U.S. DA Maguire asked sharply, "Well, Mr. Reynolds, what would you suggest? If it wasn't for the fact that someone tried to kill you, I'd say you made this up. I'm still not all that sure. Maybe exaggerated is the more accurate term. At any rate you've made us look pretty stupid."

Maguire gave Assistant DA Ellsberg a withering look.

"Rasputin sent them. Unless someone got to him first. It was important to him personally as well," Reynolds typed into the computer.

"But you won't tell us his name?"

Back to typing his responses, Reynolds said, "Can't. I'd be putting his life in jeopardy."

"We need to check if any deliveries were addressed to Stern and Solomon," Ellsberg said to the senior FBI agent. "If there were delivery records then we would have to conclude they were intercepted. If they were shipped but not delivered, where are they?"

"I know what's happened!" Reynolds suddenly typed. A terrible expression came over his face. "They must have found Rasputin. Maybe before, maybe after he sent the USB's to New York. They picked up Avramneko and me shortly after we separated from Rasputin. The USB's may never have been sent. Either way Rasputin would now be dead."

"It's easy enough to check if there were ever any shipments addressed to Stern and Solomon," Ellsberg said turning to the FBI agents.

The senior FBI agent sighed. "We'll check it out. I'd bet we find there were never any shipments."

"There is nothing more to be done now," District Attorney Maguire said. "If there were in fact deliveries posted to Stern and Solomon that would at least validate that part of your story. If not, then you're either very unlucky or just a liar, Mr. Reynolds. If it's the later you're going to find yourself in some very deep shit."

Reynolds was driven to his apartment by a marshal. The marshal did not stay. Apparently he did not warrant protection any longer.

He poured a Scotch and sat in the dark looking out the window. Without the files he still had enough for a book, but it would not be the same. Now that he knew much more, but couldn't write about it. And the nuclear weapons in Iran? What would that mean? Especially if no one in the U.S. Government believed him.

So many lives lost helping him. Was any of it worth the price? Was he obsessed with this story beyond good judgment? What had Katerina become to him? Had he fallen in love? Did it matter now?

After a second drink he decided to he should honor his promise to see Stern. He poured his drink into a plastic cup to go. If he couldn't flag a taxi, he'd take the subway.

Reynolds rang Stern's buzzer. She was waiting with the door open when he arrived on the elevator.

Reynolds was still asleep in Stern's bed at 10:00 a.m. the next morning. He had been exhausted and slept twelve hours straight.

"Mark, wake up. It's somebody named Ellsberg. He wants to talk to you. Oh shit. I guess you can't hear."

Reynolds took the telephone. "I can't hear you, Mr. Ellsberg. Talk to Miss Stern."

Stern took the phone back and listened for a few moments. "Hang on, let me tell him. He says the FBI has traced Federal Express shipments addressed both to me and Matthew Solomon. They were sent from Kiev eleven days ago. The one to me was recorded as *left by mailbox*. The package for Solomon was signed for by Solomon. They've visited Solomon. It wasn't his signature."

Stern thanked Ellsberg and hung up.

"Sonofabitch. That's it then. They intercepted them. All Rasputin's files have been destroyed. The last possibly was Rasputin's own files - the originals. Now they're gone for sure too."

"How do you know that?"

"Because he's dead. They got to him. There's no way they would have known Rasputin had sent anything, much less to whom, unless he told them. Forced him. Shit. I'm still calling him Rasputin. His real name was Ilya Varvarinski. A brave guy. And another person that died helping me."

With Stern's prodding, Reynolds contacted his literary agent Francis Kline. He had Stern arrange lunch.

"Oh my God, Mark. You look awful. And you can't hear?"

He took out a note pad and wrote, 'Thanks Francis. Nice social skills you have.'

He was getting fairly proficient at reading lips, but talking was awkward with no audible feedback. Mostly by writing on a pad he now carried, he recounted events since he left for Russia. He omitted about the nuclear weapons theft. Not sure she would believe that.

"Holy shit. That's one hell of story, Mark. I'm sorry about those two people that were helping you. How much can you back up?"

"Some, not all. Some I can relate but I just can't claim that it was Martinelli Global's doing. At any rate, you said what I had before going to Russia was pretty powerful stuff. Have you floated the book proposal around yet?"

"Oh yes. Three publishers expressed interest. Been back and forth with all of them answering questions. I'm expecting to hear something in the next couple of weeks. I think it looks good. Tell you what. I'll give all of them a call this afternoon. See where it stands."

That next morning, Kline came to see him at his apartment.

"Mark. I'm not sure what's going on but there's a problem."

He gave her a notepad.

"Problem? About what?" Reynolds scribbled back on the notepad.

"Your book proposal. All three editors told me they were passing on it."

"I thought you said they had expressed interest?"

"More than interest. Real enthusiasm. I was actually expecting three offers."

"So what's happened?"

"I'm not sure. One editor said she was overruled. They had too many business related projects going. Needed to balance this year's publications with other stuff. Ok, whatever. The next editor was really pissed off. His boss simply told him to decline. No explanation. According to him, when he pressed the point his boss told him it came from higher up. Just drop it he was told."

"And the other publisher?"

"The other guy said he changed his mind. With the way he expressed his earlier interest that doesn't ring true. He was the most enthusiastic."

"It's obvious, Francis. Martinelli Global put pressure on them."

Kline's tone suggested skepticism. "I think you give them too much credit. You really think they have that kind of influence? These are major publishing houses."

"I don't know anymore. How do you explain these publishers abrupt change of heart?"

Reynolds did little for the next two few weeks. He was too distracted to write. The whole idea of his book held no interest. It would not be what it could have been. Even if he wrote it, how would he get it published?

He e-mailed U.S. Attorney Ellsberg, "Is any progress being made on the Martinelli Global investigation?"

Ellsberg responded, "Not really, Mr. Reynolds. Actually I'm not working on it anymore. Maguire has two other attorneys assigned to the investigation. The consensus seems to be that there isn't enough to take to a grand jury. Even if that does develop, the charges may be comparatively bland. SEC violations. Maybe tax issues in transfer pricing irregularities."

"What about Foreign Corrupt Practices Act violations? Bribing foreign officials.?"

"The evidence you gave us probably is not going to prove strong enough. But there's still an open investigation. We'll try to keep you informed of any progress."

"What about the nuclear weapons?"

"We shouldn't discuss those kinds of things in e-mail. That's the CIA's and other intelligence agencies turf. I don't know what's happening there. From your testimony, I'm afraid they're skeptical. At any rate, you should not discuss this with anyone. People will paint you as a crackpot."

"Do you believe me?"

"I believe you about hearing telephone recordings. If I were to hear them I don't know if I'd draw the same conclusions. How are you mending from your injuries?"

"Getting better." Psychologically he wasn't mending.

CHAPTER 44

MANHATTAN, NEW YORK

"Steven, it's Farley," the ranking member of the Senate Judiciary Committee said. With Farley Haberstom's distinctive southern accent it was hardly necessary to announce who he was to Steven Martinelli.

"Good of you to call, Farley," Martinelli responded. He was alone in his office taking the call.

"I did a little checking with my contacts over at Justice. They're looking into these allegations made by this reporter Reynolds. There's little documented evidence apparently. They've got some old stuff Reynolds gave them a while ago. My source tells me they have passed on some of his allegations to the SEC. Any problems in that area, Steven?"

"Don't believe so, Farley. But in today's complex international business, it's easy to make accounting errors. We employ some top notch attorneys to make sure we don't violate any laws."

"My source says their interest is around offshore corporations."

"Well that would only be natural. Every major corporation uses offshore foreign subsidiary corporations for tax reasons. Legally allowed under U.S. law. Most large corporations have hundreds of foreign business entities. But you know all that,

Farley. This is just an obsessed reporter trying to make headlines. He doesn't even have a job at the moment. The Daily Press fired him."

"Well it's still unwelcome attention to your company. Wouldn't want this to become something like an Enron frenzy."

"Different thing altogether, Farley. Enron was using tax haven corporations to create all sorts of false financial numbers. All designed to hide real financial problems while pushing share prices up. Their whole business model was a house of cards. Martinelli Global has traditional businesses. We've been around for a hundred years."

"Good to hear there's nothing to this, Steven."

"On a personal note, Farley. Are you and Florence free to come up to New York on Saturday the twenty-first? We're having a dinner party. Some people you'll find interesting." Martinelli told him who else was expected.

"We would like to have you two stay with us for the weekend if you can manage it. I can send the Gulfstream down to pick you up."

"Sounds good, Steven. I'll tell Florence to get a new dress."

Reynolds' hearing was gradually returning. The other injuries were healing. Unfortunately his emotional condition had only worsened.

He was a hunter. This time the beast won - gored him badly and left him for dead. He was left emotionally crippled. This Martinelli Global quest had cost far too much. It may have been an obsession. Lives were lost. Nothing ultimately was achieved. Martinelli Global had only been slightly wounded. In the end they won. It was just a cost of doing business for them.

Reynolds reflected on his circumstances. How could this have gone so badly? There was no platform from which to present his material about Martinelli Global. No job, no book, perhaps no prospects. He had never felt so discouraged in his life.

He felt badly for Rachel Stern. He cared for her, genuinely liked being with her. But he didn't think he was in love with her. Had he ever been in love? With Denise? With Nicky? He didn't know. Was it all more sex than love?

For the three weeks he had been back in New York, he had seen Rachel only a few times. He deflected her attempts at affection claiming his injuries, especially his ribs. They had not made love. There was a growing distance between them. He reluctantly agreed to dinner at her apartment that evening.

From the moment he entered, he wondered if it was a mistake. She was dressed in shear white silk dress with a plunging neckline. Makeup was perfect. She had every intention to seduce him. She kissed him passionately at the door.

Dinner was lobster and asparagus. Well prepared. An expensive Burgundy. Everything perfect except the conversation was forced. Stern had to talk loudly for Reynolds to understand. She was cautious about her questions of the events in Russia. For Reynolds' part, he was unusually quiet.

After dinner Stern could not resist any longer. She came around the table and sat on Reynolds' lap. Holding his head with both hands she said, "Mark, please make love to me. Right now. Please?"

Guilt is not a good aphrodisiac. Stern did her best to sexually arouse him. Reynolds did make love to her but it was forced. Both lay in bed for some time. Stern cried softly. Reynolds stared at the ceiling.

At midnight he left. It was a tearful departure, for him as well. He walked a number of blocks before hailing a taxi to return to his own apartment.

The next morning he felt worse than ever. He avoided the temptation to get drunk in favor of starting to look for a new job. The first order of business would be to construct a list of all the people he knew in the business. From the list he would send out e-mails. He was good at networking.

Reynolds had been at the computer for a couple of hours. He took a break to make some coffee. When he returned, there was a new e-mail. He spilled his coffee when he noticed the sender's name. It was Rasputin.

The message read, "Mark Reynolds, if you are receiving this e-mail, I am probably dead. How is that you say? Because it would not be sent if I were able to control this automatic e-mail. And because I am very good with computer technology. Perhaps the best? I must now brag and tell you how this was done. I placed these files on an internet service provider's server. Then I created program to send this to your e-mail address after 30 days if I did not log in to reset date. To get around their security firewalls was elegant piece of work. I am not modest. Nowhere in cyberspace is safe! Ha, ha! I must be sure that you have evidence. Hope this is unnecessary. Hope you have already used this evidence to destroy these people. This was my life insurance. You are my beneficiary. You shall receive many more e-mails with attached files spread over two days. I have compressed files but must be sure that each e-mail is not too large and your mail box is not overwhelmed. Goodbye Mark Reynolds. We fucked the bad guys very good! Rasputin"

Reynolds sat stunned for several moments. Then he clicked on the attachments. They were all in Russian. These were the files that were lost. Sonofabitch! You're right my friend. This *will* fuck the bad guys!

He sat at his computer the entire afternoon. As Rasputin promised, there were periodic e-mail receipts, each with a measured amount of attachments to control the size of each e-mail. Reynolds moved them out of his e-mail in-box as they came in then stored them on the hard drive. As this went along, he made backups on several USB drives. The evidence was not going to be lost again. There would be numerous backup copies.

Over the hours, Reynolds periodically fixed something to eat. He did not leave his computer throughout the night, dosing only for short periods in the chair. He did not answer his phone. This continued into the following day and that night. The last e-mails carried the audio files of Garnitsky's cell phone conversations with his subordinate.

Reynolds was exhausted at the end of the two days, but wired with excitement. He needed some sleep. A couple of Scotches to celebrate helped to knock him out.

The world looked very different the following morning. He was back in the game. What to do next? He could take the files as they were to the U.S. District Attorney, or he could first try to reconstruct the work he and Avramenko had begun.

The Justice Department could wait. When he was ready, he would deliver a work product they couldn't ignore. One he would shove up the Government's ass.

The first task was to translate the files which were mostly in Russian. He didn't have Avramenko. He wasn't about to try to find a translator. These files couldn't be exposed to just anyone. He had used the various on-line translation websites before. They gave you the essential meaning but the syntax was terrible. He wondered if there wasn't something more sophisticated out there. Something to translate large amounts of text with better grammatical structure.

He found some pricy software on the Internet that touted it was useable for corporate and government applications. It took some searching to locate the software in a computer store near Columbia University on Manhattan's Upper West Side. He took a taxi there immediately.

It took well into the following night to convert all the Rasputin files into English. The translation software worked remarkably well. The English syntax was surprisingly good.

The next morning he began the task of trying to organize the files. Some were familiar from his work with Avramenko. It soon became apparent that her understanding of names, places, and how things worked in Russia had been invaluable. He could read these files but putting them into a meaningful context was going to be a long process. He could use help. Should he call Rachel? Would she want to help? Would he be giving her false expectations? Might he eventually fall in love with her?

To himself he said of course he should call her. She was always part of this Martinelli Global project. It was unfair not to let her participate. She was a professional. All true, but rationalizations? Maybe he was just a selfish sonofabitch after all. Anything for the story? Anything for Mark Reynolds? At least he wouldn't be risking Stern's life.

He called her at the Newspaper. His hearing had returned enough to use the telephone. After apologizing for not answering her calls for the last two days he asked, "Rachel. Can you come over tonight? I've got my hands on the missing files. The ones that Rasputin sent from Russia. It's the mother load. But I need your help, Rachel. It's a helluva research project. Names and places will head us down all sorts of paths. Just organizing the stuff alone is a large task. I'm not sure I have a right to ask it of you."

"Of course. I'll be there at six, Mark." Rachel Stern was equally tenacious. She too wanted to topple Martinelli Global. And she still wanted Mark Reynolds.

They worked well into the night. They broke for a brief dinner break of omelets with a good bottle of wine. It was like old times. Reynolds did not regret his decision. Stern was exceedingly good at her work. She set up various electronic file folders after questioning Reynolds to understand what these Russian affiliates of Martinelli Global might be doing. She filed various documents in more than one folder. She setup a cross reference index to link various documents to key names or key words.

Like Reynolds, she was enthusiastic when she worked. Watching her he felt less guilty and where that might lead emotionally.

Exhausted at two in the morning, they fell into bed. Reynolds was energized to once again be deep into the project. He reflected on how close he had come to utter despair. Watching Rachel's excitement and the application of her skills confirmed he had been right to involve her. It was her project too.

He was in a perfectly pliable mood. When Stern took off her clothes there was no faking his arousal. He focused his attention on giving her pleasure as they made love. Afterwards he felt good about being with her. For the first time he didn't feel guilty about emotionally deceiving her with their physical intimacy. Why not see how things developed?

They worked for two weeks nonstop. Most week days Stern was at the Newspaper doing her regular job, but she found a way to get a couple of days off. At work, she often cheated by doing research on subjects suggested by some of Varvarinski's files.

Reynolds had prepared a summary with references to specific documents. Stern's research of businesses and people often clarified what a file meant.

It was a Sunday afternoon. Stern had just completed reading the summary.

"This is powerful stuff, Mark. Should be plenty of evidence for the Justice Department to get indictments. Are you ready to take it to them?"

"I think so. I'm going to call Ellsberg tomorrow."

"I thought Ellsberg was not working on the case?"

"He's not. But I owe him one for believing me and getting me out of Kiev. This should be a real feather in his cap."

"What's-her-name, the U.S. District Attorney, she's not going to like the snub."

"Does it look like I give a shit? She never believed me after I couldn't produce the evidence."

"And the book?"

"I'm starting on it tomorrow. My guess is that once the Justice Department investigations become public, Martinelli Global won't be able to pressure any publishing house to suppress the book. That and the newspaper stories will make for powerful marketing. Francis will love to take a bite out of several editors' asses for turning her down before."

"Are you going to give this stuff to the media?"

"Absolutely. At least selectively. I'll give the Government some time before I go public with some of the stuff. No need to give Martinelli Global warning to start covering their tracks."

Reynolds was quiet for a moment. He had debated about telling Rachel of the audio files of Garnitsky's cell phone conversations. "Rachel, there's something else I want to tell you about."

Stern was apprehensive about what Reynolds wanted to say. She prayed it was not something that would destroy their developing relationship. No declaration that he had been in love with Katerina Avramenko. Even if she was dead, Stern didn't want to hear that.

"What's that, Mark?"

"There's another set of files here," he said and held up a USB drive. "They're audio files. This is what compelled Ilya Varvarinski, aka Rasputin to meet with us face to face in Kiev. It's what may have cost him his life. It's why Garnitsky went to such lengths to have us killed."

"What's on them?"

"Conversations. A couple of digital photographs. Cell phone conversations between Garnitsky and one of his henchmen. I listened to them. Listened to someone translate them that is. They're in Russian of course. If you hear all of them in sequence, you have to draw the obvious conclusion. Someone stole Russian nuclear warheads. Now Iran has them."

"Oh my God! Are you sure?"

"Varvarinski and Nicky drew the same conclusion as I did. When you piece together Martinelli Global's Russian partner's investment in the Russian nuclear industry you can see how there was access to the weapons."

"Are you saying that a Martinelli Global subsidiary may be responsible for arming Iran with nuclear weapons?"

"Maybe. I don't know. Could be a rogue operation. After all, this Feliks Garnitsky has a criminal past. He's also ex-KGB. Might know how to pull off something like this. Hard to see why Martinelli Global as an organization would be directly involved."

"Even so, if some of their people were involved it'll be a blockbuster revelation. Are you going to release that information too?"

"I don't know. That's bigger than just my story or my book."

"You know the Government will try to suppress you from going public on that."

"Of course. I'll give them the benefit of the doubt. I'll at least give them time to investigate."

The following morning, Reynolds called Assistant U.S. District Attorney Phillip Ellsberg. "I have come into possession of the documents I told you about previously. The materials that never arrived in New York."

"You have them! How?" Ellsberg said.

"I'll explain when I see you. I'd like to come to your office at two o'clock if that works for you."

"How about right now? In fact I'll send a car for you."

"No need. I have another commitment this morning. I'll see you at two," Reynolds said and hung up.

His other commitment was a stop at his attorney's office, followed by an excellent lunch. He gave Matthew Solomon two sets of USB drives with the Rasputin files. One set was to be held in Solomon's office, the second set to be placed in a safety deposit box under the law firm's name.

"That's a little paranoid isn't it, Mark?" Solomon said.

"I'll tell you soon what's on these tapes. You'll agree with my precautions. The material is going to the Justice Department. They might want to suppress some of the stuff. It'll bring down Martinelli Global. That's for certain. But there's other even more explosive material in those files. It was enough to almost get me killed. It did get others close to me killed. So humor me, Matt. Now, can I treat you to lunch? I'll tell you about what happened in Ukraine. It's one hell of a story."

Arriving at the federal building in downtown Manhattan, Reynolds was escorted to the same conference room as before. The same people were there as before along with two new U.S. attorneys, presumably working on the Martinelli Global investigation.

U.S. District Attorney Eileen Maguire chaired the meeting. "Well, Mr. Reynolds, I trust this will be more productive than our previous meeting."

Reynolds extracted three small USB drives from his sport coat pocket. He slid them across the conference table to Maguire. They stopped when they bumped against her legal pad.

She glared at Reynolds. "And these contain what, Mr. Reynolds?" she asked in a sarcastic tone.

"One is the raw data given to me by the person calling himself Rasputin, the computer hacker. The pissed off Martinelli Global Russian subsidiary employee. Most of it's in Russian. The second drive has the same files translated in English. It also represents additional work I did so far to organize and collate with other information I had."

"You mean you've had this data without turning it over as you originally promised?" Maguire said angrily.

"That's right."

"So you simply lied the last time you were here?"

"No I didn't. I came into possession of the documents again only two weeks ago. It was sent if you will from beyond the grave. An automatic e-mail transmission by Rasputin. He set up the data to transmit via e-mail to me if he did not reset the program on whatever server he hid it on. Because it was sent, I have to believe he is now dead. His e-mail in there explains it."

"And this third USB, what does it contain?"

"That's the audio recordings of cell phone conversations between a ranking person within Martinelli Global's affiliated Russian company and a subordinate. It's the stuff I conclude points to a theft of Russian nuclear warheads. Not nuclear material, the whole fucking operational part of advanced nuclear bombs. It's in Russian. Listen to it through a translator. Look at the photographs. See for yourselves if you draw the same conclusion."

Ellsberg said, "What are you going to do with this information, Mr. Reynolds?"

"Publish it of course."

"Mr. Reynolds, it would be more helpful to our investigation if you didn't go public with this information right away," Maguire said. "As for the stuff about nuclear weapons thefts, this might fall within prohibitions under national security statutes. I would warn you . . ."

"You know you could just ask. But no, the first instinct for a petty bureaucrat is to exercise power. So let me tell you what I'm going to do. And what I want.

"First, on all the potential criminal stuff, I'll give you sixty days before I release anything to the media. Gives you time to begin investigations without alerting Martinelli Global. That's of course if there are no leaks. Any reports in the media about

Martinelli Global being investigated, I will do as I see fit. First Amendment preemption. You can't do anything about it according to my lawyer. I'm not open to discussion on that. I've done all the work. People have been killed getting this information. At the least, the Justice Department has done nothing but sit on their hands. At the worse, it was illegally pressured to suppress an investigation.

"As to other stuff about Iran having operational nuclear warheads, well I want a deal there. I've no love for the Islamic fundamentalist Iranian government. I'm anxious that the United States find some way to counter this new threat. I'll hold off publishing anything about that. We'll have to see. At the least, I will warn you if I change my intentions. To persuade me to cooperate, I want this Interpol Red Notice rescinded. I'm not about to have that hanging over my head."

"Mr. Reynolds, I've been briefed about your troubles while you were in Columbia," Maguire said. "You must realize that we cannot dictate to Interpol. They're an independent body. We also cannot dictate to the Columbian government."

"Bullshit. The U.S. must carry a lot of clout with Interpol. Look at the evidence. It's fabricated nonsense from a corrupt banana republic. If you look deeper, you'll see Martinelli Global's hand in this. But you know, I don't give a shit how you do it. That's my price for conditional silence on the nuclear thing."

"I warn you, Mr. Reynolds, taking that position may get you into a lot of trouble," Maguire said, holding her anger in check.

"I think I'm done here," Reynolds said and rose from his chair. "I appreciate the Government's expression of thanks."

"Mr. Reynolds, you do have our thanks," Phillip Ellsberg said. "You've been investigating Martinelli Global for some time. Can we count on your assistance as we examine this body of material you've just given us?"

Ellsberg was a cooler head. Maybe Maguire was the only jerk in the room. But he did provoke her. "Sure. Whatever I can do."

"Mr. Reynolds, we don't know yet what these cell phone recordings might mean," The CIA man said. "If you are correct, I don't need to tell you what extraordinary international implications it has. I can't stress too strongly that you must not talk about this to anyone. True or not, public speculation alone would change the dynamics. Can we count on that?"

"Listen I understand all too well the implications of this. Remember my source probably gave up his life because of it. The criminal stuff is a story. I recognize this is something more."

CHAPTER 45

MANHATTAN, NEW YORK

O ver the next several weeks Reynolds spent considerable time at the Federal Building in Lower Manhattan. Deputy U.S. Attorney Ellsberg had been reassigned to head up the investigation into Martinelli Global. Once U.S. Attorney Eileen Maguire examined Reynolds' newly presented evidence she understood this had the potential for a major case.

Ellsberg and his associates were impressed not only with the evidence, but Reynolds' own work with the material. His broadened research gave them a jump start to develop various paths of inquiry. Reynolds' had even provided a rough organizational chart of Martinelli Global's holdings.

In a meeting with Phillip Ellsberg and his boss Eileen Maguire, Maguire opened with, "Mr. Reynolds, I owe you an apology. My previous skepticism was misplaced. I've been following the progress of Mr. Ellsberg's team closely. Seems your allegations of Martinelli Global's criminal actions are largely correct. Some might be difficult to prove but there's enough to go to the next step."

"Which is what?"

"I'm ready to take this to the Attorney General. If he buys off on it, and I am confident he will, then we're ready to seek warrants to seize documents from Martinelli Global."

"Then what?"

"When we exercise the warrants it will become known to the media that Martinelli Global is being investigated. About a week ago we also turned certain evidence over to the Securities and Exchange Commission. My point being that there will be a lot more people aware that an investigation has been instituted. It won't be a secret any longer."

"That's too be expected," Reynolds agreed. "And you want to know what my intentions are relative to going public?"

"Precisely," Maguire said. "It would be helpful if Martinelli Global did not know where they might be exposed. Less ability for them to hide or destroy evidence."

"Tell you what. I will hold off on going public until you pursue seizing documents. At that point, it will be all over the media," Reynolds said. "Apart from that I have no reason to go public in the form of giving either the print or broadcast media any specifics. I don't work for a newspaper currently. I'm also not motivated to selling them information.

"My focus is on writing a book. There's no profit in my releasing all the personally detailed information piecemeal to the Press. So other than pursuing book proposal discussions with publishers, I wouldn't be impeding the investigation."

"We appreciate that, Mr. Reynolds," Maguire said.

"I would also add that the Justice Department extends our thanks for the invaluable assistance in interpreting this body of evidence. The structuring of their use of offshore corporations has opened up all sorts of avenues for investigation. And of course our thanks again for laying this on our doorstep," Ellsberg said.

"You're welcome. I hope it drives a stake in the heart of Martinelli Global. I hope it's also career-enhancing to you as well."

Even Maguire smiled.

"One other thing. What's going on with pursuing the Russian nuclear weapons?"

Ellsberg looked at his boss.

Maguire said, "The truth is I don't know, Mr. Reynolds. That's gone way up over my head. Might even be outside the Justice Department's purview unless it proves to be a Martinelli Global corporate deal rather than just some of their employees. The intelligence agencies have not confided in us. As far as this Feliks Garnitsky, the FBI is pursuing an investigation over his possible involvement in the attack on you. An FBI agent and a State Department employee were killed making it a Justice Department investigation. I take it that no one from the CIA has been in touch with you?"

"Nope. They haven't. Guess I wouldn't expect them to. I have nothing else to offer other than the recordings of Garnitsky's telephone calls. But it does bring me to my demand about getting this Interpol Red Notice rescinded."

"I realize the importance of getting that suppressed, Mr. Reynolds. On my request, the FBI liaison to Interpol has delved into the details of Columbia's evidence. The evidence is thin; witness accounts, police statements. It wouldn't get an indictment in the U.S. I'm surprised that it went this far, but I'm not that familiar with Interpol's evidentiary threshold."

"So what are you saying?" Reynolds asked.

"First, I strongly suggest you keep your suspicions about a nuclear theft in Russia to yourself. This must have reached the White House at least at a briefing level. You don't want to get cross-wise with that kind of power.

"Take my advice and hold off. What I'm going to do is brief the Attorney General and recommend that the U.S. Government somehow get this Red Notice rescinded. The AG's connected to the White House, the State Department follows White House orders, we have clout and pressure points with the Columbians, and all the realpolitik mechanics that goes on down there. We at least owe you that."

Reynolds wasn't going to let go of this. Martinelli Global could fall and this stupid Columbian bullshit murder charge could haunt him forever. But Maguire was being straight with him.

"I appreciate your efforts, Ms. Maguire. I'll do as you suggest for now, but make it known to the powers up high that I'm adamant on this. Whatever happens, I'm ultimately putting the transcripts of Garnitsky's calls in my book. I'm not yet convinced it wasn't a Martinelli Global deal. At the least, the players are connected to Martinelli Global. It will certainly be included in my book. But that's a ways off before it goes into print. After all, I need to write about the demise of Martinelli Global as the last chapter."

"Harvey. Good to her from you. Doing well I trust?" Steven Martinelli said to the caller. The caller was one of the five Securities and Exchange Commissioners. Politically well connected and a direct beneficiary of Martinelli's largess.

"Steven, I've got some disturbing news. The Justice Department has started a criminal investigation against Martinelli Global."

"And how do you know this, Harvey?"

"They've shared evidence with SEC investigators of potential violations by Martinelli Global."

"Evidence of what?"

"I don't have access to the details, but I understand they claim you guys falsified financial reporting. Potentially issues of Sarbanes-Oxley violations. What's going on, Steven?"

"I don't know, Harvey. First I've heard of any such thing. I'm not going to get excited until I hear more. International business has become so complex there's lots of opportunities for mistakes. But mistakes do not equate to intent. Probably just some young Turks at the Justice Department wanting to make their mark. I'll have my legal people look into it."

"You don't sound concerned, Steven. That makes me feel better."

"Just part of business nowadays. But all the same, I appreciate your advance warning, Harvey. Anything I can do for you?"

Martinelli hung up. He was stunned by the news. He called Conrad Redek and Paul Belden to his office immediately. After explaining the situation to his two senior lieutenants, Martinelli asked, "Recommendations?"

Belden responded. "First, any discussions where I'm involved are attorney-client privileged. We should be cautious to adhere to that. Secondly, we should hire some outside legal horsepower right away. It's always better to get legal help early before things become a crisis."

"Who?" Martinelli asked.

"For this sort of thing, the firm of Frenzel & Levi I think."

"Ok, do it."

"What else?"

"Do an audit of our sensitive areas. Let's see where we are most vulnerable."

"Sensitive? You mean illegal don't you," Redek said. "And what do you mean an audit?"

"We need to know what documentation exists that could support criminal charges. Preplan how to counter its effects."

"Shouldn't we just purge them as we identify them?" Redek asked.

"No, no. We've got to be careful. Somebody on staff would have to be involved. That means potential witnesses. Obstruction of justice at the least. Prejudicial to our defensive position for sure.

"Let's back up, gentlemen. What do we think the Government might have?" Martinelli said.

"I think it's just the old allegations made by that reporter Reynolds. We know that all copies of the information stolen from Moscow Capital's databases were recovered," Redek said.

"What stolen information are you talking about, Conrad?" Belden asked.

"Never mind, Paul. As corporate counsel, you don't want to know," Martinelli said. "So what's your assessment, Paul?"

Belden was not happy about being excluded from whatever Martinelli and Redek were referring to. He moved on. "We're into a lot of stuff that violates U.S. statutes. We know that and we have done an elegant job of architecting mechanisms to shield ourselves. But having said that, the level of organizational complexity is so great it's both an asset as well as a liability."

"Explain," Martinelli said.

"As an asset, the interconnection of subsidiaries and foreign corporations, and the myriad layers of transactions makes any investigation enormously complex. It's so complex it would be difficult to make a case understandable to a jury. Enron was such an example."

"Christ, Paul, the top guys at Enron *were* convicted!" Martinelli said.

"That's because they screwed a lot of people; stockholders, lenders, employees. And in the end, they did a sloppy job with using the offshore corporations." Belden said. "Our situation is different."

"And the liability associated with this complexity?"

"The inherent audit trails that are created as a necessary part of doing business. The level of documentation is commensurate with the level of complexity. Electronic, paper, people. No way around it. That's always the area of risk. Couldn't destroy all of it even if we wanted to."

Five days later, a team of twenty FBI agents and U.S. marshals descended on Martinelli Global's headquarters in

Manhattan. They were armed with broad federal search warrants. The core of the team was comprised of white-collar crime specialists supported by several of the FBI's best computer experts.

New York Daily Press – Financial Section:

Federal agents served warrants to seize documents from the Manhattan headquarters of Martinelli Global on Monday. Martinelli Global is a large multi-national corporation with business activities in a range of markets. The Justice Department's interest in Martinelli Global came as a surprise to the financial community. A spokesperson for the U.S. District Attorney's office for the Southern District of Manhattan acknowledged the exercising of warrants but declined to explain the nature of the investigation. A spokesperson for Martinelli Global said they had no knowledge of the Justice Department's investigation. None of Martinelli Global's senior management could be reached for comment.

"Goddamnit, Steven, what the fuck's going on?" Senator Farley Haberstrom yelled. "Christ, you told me just last weekend there was nothing to worry about."

"Farley, calm yourself," Steven Martinelli said.

"Calm myself? Listen, Steven, I think you've got more to worry about. My source at Justice says there's some new evidence they have. Apparently very damaging stuff against Martinelli Global. Went all the way up to the Attorney General."

Martinelli felt like he had been hit in the stomach. "Where did this evidence come from?"

"That same pain in the ass reporter my source says. The one you said was no longer a threat. Tell me how bad this is, Steven."

"I told you before, Farley, there's nothing of substance in all this. It's the complexity of doing business internationally. Martinelli Global is aggressive in using every inch of the law. We push the envelope. There's a risk in that. But I assure you, this is not serious. All major corporations sooner or later suffer a conflict with interpretation of regulations."

"Bullshit, Steven. This is not about regulatory compliance. This is about serious criminal violations. My source says they're using terms like tax evasion, conspiracy, money-laundering, Sarbanes-Oxley violations, and god knows what else. The source says in all probability they'll soon be sending this to a grand jury to seek criminal indictments."

"Farley, I appreciate the intelligence. But trust me, we'll handle this."

"You do that, Steven. I've got a tough reelection coming up in two years. I wouldn't want our past associations becoming a political liability around my neck."

It was the middle of the afternoon when the buzzer sounded in Reynolds' apartment.

"Yes?"

"Mr. Reynolds. My name is Lane. I'm Central Intelligence. May I come up and talk to you?" the voice said over the intercom.

Reynolds checked the man's ID through the security lens in the door before allowing him to enter. He offered the guy a seat.

"I'll get right to why I'm here, Mr. Reynolds. What is your intention about publishing this story about Russian nuclear weapons being stolen?"

"It's going in my book. It's not yet mentioned in my proposal being floated to publishers. The book's about Martinelli Global. In part, this theft involves Martinelli Global. I'm printing transcripts of the conversations. I'll let the public draw their own conclusions."

"I'm directed to ask you in the interest of national security to consider not making those conversations public."

"Who's asking?"

"It comes from the White House."

"If I publish, am I violating any U.S. law?"

"Possibly. But we'd prefer it didn't come to that. I'm to tell you that Interpol has rescinded the arrest warrant against you. Columbia has also withdrawn charges against you.

Reynolds nodded. That was a relief. "That's very good. Can you tell me what's being done to investigate if this theft happened?"

"I'm afraid I can't comment. Personally I don't even know. All of that is highly classified."

"So you expect me to remain silent on this indefinitely? Or will the Government let me know when it's ok?"

"I'm simply instructed to ask for your cooperation."

"Tell your bosses that I am going to eventually publish this stuff. Tell them at the White House if a President can make claims of WMD's based on half-assed intelligence, I can certainly publish my claims based on solid evidence. This needs to be public. And if you could stop me legally you wouldn't ask for my cooperation, you'd simply threaten me."

"Very well, Mr. Reynolds. I'll convey your answer. You know of course the Government will renounce your conclusions as ridiculous. May not help the success of your book."

"That'll be my problem."

The CIA agent turned as he was about to leave. "This meeting never occurred, Mr. Reynolds."

The initial coverage of the Justice Department investigation against Martinelli Global moved quickly from the financial section to the front page. As with any such situation involving so many people, details began to leak from all directions. The story quickly became the next broadcast media spectacle. It involved important people. Better still, it had the prospect of staying front center for a long time.

CNN News:

> Unnamed sources within the Justice Department claim that Martinelli Global is facing serious criminal charges. Those same sources say that grand jury indictments are expected to be handed down within a matter of weeks against Martinelli Global senior management.

> Martinelli Global is an international giant with revenues over one hundred billion dollars annually. Martinelli Global has diversified businesses, heavily focused in natural resources, agricultural products, and logistics. Martinelli Global has been particularly successful operating in third world countries, and has large subsidiary holdings in Russia and other former Soviet-era republics. Martinelli Global traces its origins back a hundred years. The current CEO, Steven Martinelli, is the great-grandson of the founder.

> Martinelli Global is not a household name. As a major corporation, Martinelli Global is unusual, not only with their business model, but their avoidance of publicity. Like other major corporations, Martinelli Global does engage heavily in political contributions both in the U.S. as well as foreign countries where they do business, but otherwise maintains a low profile.

> On news of their legal difficulties, Martinelli Global stock fell fifteen percent in the last two days of trading on the New York Stock Exchange. Martinelli Global has been largely silent in their public rebuttal of allegations of corporate wrongdoing. Steven Martinelli and his senior executives have made no public comments, leaving all communications to their lawyers from the legal firm of Frenzel & Levi.

Accusations of alleged wrongdoing by Martinelli Global foreign subsidiaries were first reported months ago in a series of articles in the New York Daily Press. It is not known if Martinelli Global's current legal troubles are directly connected with those earlier allegations.

New York Daily Press – New York:
Speculation continues to rise over the extent of Martinelli Global's legal troubles. Attempts to obtain statements from Martinelli Global executives continue to be unsuccessful. Several members of Martinelli Global's Board of Directors have issued statements claiming they have no knowledge of any wrongdoing on the part of the Company. In a seeming expression of confidence, Martinelli Global CEO, Steven Martinelli is reported to be on holiday in Italy.

Fox News:
We are switching to breaking news for live coverage of a press conference from the Federal Building in Manhattan, New York. It is believed that the Justice Department will be making an announcement about the ongoing investigation targeting the multi-national corporation, Martinelli Global.
"I am U.S. District Attorney for the Southern District of New York, Eileen Maguire. I have called this press conference to announce progress of the Justice Department's investigation into Martinelli Global Incorporated. A federal grand jury has just handed down a list of indictments, the extent of which goes well beyond the level and types of corporate wrongdoing seen in other high profile corporate prosecutions of the last decade. In times of economic turmoil the United States has recently experienced, uncovering a pervasive level of

criminal conduct by a major U.S. corporation can only further diminish public confidence.

"Martinelli Global and several of its officers have been indicted on a range of criminal charges. You can find the details of the charges in the handout you will receive at the end of my remarks. The indictments have been handed down on multiple counts of criminal violations. These include violations of the Foreign Corrupt Practices Act, the International Anti-Bribery and Fair Competition Act, wire fraud, money laundering, tax evasion, Securities and Exchange violations, and conspiracy. Martinelli Global has engineered its success using organizationally sanctioned criminal methods. In their broad range of international operations they have sought to partner with corrupt government officials in countries having poor regulatory mechanisms. They have even partnered with international criminal organizations.

"Indictments have also been handed down by the same grand jury for the auditing firm of Kellogg-Tyler. Kellogg-Tyler has audited Martinelli Global for over ten years. The indictments are for violations under Title Two of the Sarbanes-Oxley Act, and for conspiracy.

"I'll now take questions."

The details of the indictments revealed that Steven Martinelli, Conrad Redek, Paul Belden, and three other Martinelli Global senior executives had been personally indicted.

"Mark. Have you heard," Stern said. Reynolds was working at his computer in his apartment when she called.

"Heard what?"

"Turn the TV on. All the news channels are covering it. Martinelli Global's been indicted. All sorts of criminal charges. You beat them, Mark."

Reynolds switched on the TV. He watched what was the beginning of the death watch of Martinelli Global Incorporated.

After talking to Stern, his phone didn't stop ringing. The first was his former editor at the Daily Press. John Fredericks was alternately congratulatory then apologetic for events of the past. In the end there was the offer to return to his old job.

The last to call before he unplugged the telephone was his literary agent. "I think this means we're back in business, Mark. I can't wait to float your proposal again. I'll make those bastards choke on what I'll be asking. I'm expecting well into seven figures."

CNN News:

   On continued bad news over legal troubles, trading was suspended on Martinelli Global stock at the New York Stock Exchange today. After the share price had fallen another forty percent by mid-afternoon, trading was suspended. A spokesperson for the NYSE indicated that it was unlikely trading in Martinelli Global stock would resume tomorrow.

CHAPTER 46

MOSCOW, RUSSIAN FEDERATION

"Mr. Secretary, I will repeat my previous assertions that no nuclear weapons are missing from our inventories. The Ministry of Defense has thoroughly investigated these sites operated by the Rusatomic corporation," the Russian Foreign Minister said to the U.S. Secretary of State. They were meeting at his office in the Kremlin.

"Our own intelligence people have offered other possible scenarios to account for these telephone call intercepts."

"What other scenarios for example?" the U.S. Secretary asked.

"Smuggling. Some sort of high value goods."

The U.S. Secretary did not respond. The photos transmitted over the cell phones clearly pointed to warheads. The Russians were simply choosing to deny. Maybe the theft was brilliant. Maybe Russian official were involved. Maybe the Russians can't even confirm they have nuclear warheads missing.

"With all due respect, Mr. Minister, I am told these intercepted telephone calls make a compelling case. The digital photos confirm that."

"Our experts do not agree."

"Have you at least found this Feliks Garnitsky yet?"

The Minister sat back in his chair in a defensive posture. "Unfortunately no. But it's just a matter of time. We have his boss, Nikolai Krasin under arrest. Not for this bizarre idea that nuclear weapons were stolen, but for violating various Russian laws. It seems his business associations with this company Martinelli Global have gotten him into considerable trouble. With information provided by your Department of Justice, it appears that Russian laws were violated. At any rate, Krasin claims no knowledge of anything about stolen nuclear weapons."

"That's comforting." The Secretary of State made no attempt to hide his sarcasm.

Nikolai Krasin was detained in the notorious Lubyanka prison in Moscow. It was now operated by the Russian FSB. During Soviet times it was a feared place of torture and execution during the Stalinist purges. It still provoked fear.

Around midnight, two burly guards entered his cell. Krasin was sleeping soundly, the effects of drugs placed in his food earlier. The Lubyanka was old. Exposed pipes still crossed the cell ceilings.

The two men lifted Krasin off the bed and placed him on the floor. They removed the sheet from the bed and then ripped it in half. Rolling it up made for a crude rope. One man stood on the bed and tied the makeshift rope to the pipe near the ceiling. The other end was tied in a slip knot.

One man hoisted the still unconscious Nikolai Krasin over his shoulder while the other man still standing on the bed placed Krasin's head in the noose. The other man released Krasin. The noose tightened as it took the weight. The bed was pushed aside leaving Krasin's feet dangling a foot above the floor.

Krasin regained consciousness. His eyes bulged in terror as his hands clawed at the fabric about his neck.

The men waited for several minutes after Krasin's body went limp. Their orders were clear about making no mistakes. It would officially be ruled suicide.

Other Russian government officials had also been arrested in the wake of the information provided from the United States. The Russian President was selective about which were arrested. It was an opportunity to purge certain people, while others became indebted for their reprieve.

The exception was Feliks Garnitsky. The President wanted his head even more than Nikolai Krasin's. But Garnitsky had vanished.

MANHATTAN, NEW YORK

U.S. District Attorney Eileen Maguire had been negotiating with Conrad Redek and his attorney for half an hour.

"Your offer of fifteen years is ridiculous. The charges against Mr. Redek do not support anything like that."

"Those may not be all the charges leveled against your client," Maguire said. You see there are some troubling irregularities at the Russian corporation known as Rusatomic. Rusatomic is effectively a subsidiary of Martinelli Global, through a veil of offshore corporations of course. But we can still prove Martinelli Global was heavily invested."

"My client's already charged along those lines. What's different about this particular Russian corporation."

"Rusatomic was involved with Russian military nuclear weapons. Much of what is known is classified. However I can tell you that fissionable material is missing. Information suggests it may be in the hands of terrorists."

The attorney did not respond. Maguire continued. "There is ample evidence to tie ownership in Rusatomic to Martinelli Global. As Chief Operating Officer, that makes your client

Martinelli Global. Even if we can't prove charges of providing material support to terrorists, there's a whole raft of charges under chapter 113B of the U.S. Code that will add years if convicted. I suggest your client accept our offer."

New York Daily Press - Front Page:

A spokesperson for the Justice Department officially acknowledged that Martinelli Global Chief Operating Officer, Conrad Redek, and General Counsel, Paul Belden have entered into plea agreements with the Government. These plea agreements put to rest rumors that had circulated for days about an impeding deal with two of the central figures in the Martinelli Global scandal. The spokesperson indicated that each had agreed to unspecified prison sentences in exchange for full cooperation and disclosure in pursuing the Government's case.

The spokesperson added that the agreement would facilitate other prosecutions within the ranks of Martinelli Global's former management, and would further an understanding of the Byzantine structure of Martinelli Global's international business dealings.

The agreements will add to the legal pressures on Steven Martinelli, the former Martinelli Global Chief Executive Officer. Martinelli is currently residing in Italy. The U.S. Government has been pursuing his extradition back to the United States within the Italian courts since his indictment on multiple criminal counts. A source at the Justice Department who wished not to be identified suggested that Martinelli had considerable influence in Italy which was adding difficulties in pursuing the legal process there to seek his extradition.

CNN News:

Martinelli Global announced the filing for bankruptcy protection under Chapter 11. In recent days, the move had been rumored to be inevitable in the wake of the unfolding scandal surrounding the Company. In making the announcement, former Martinelli Global Board of Director and newly appointed interim CEO, Ralph Dillard said that the recent criminal indictments and other negative publicity had heavily damaged Martinelli Global's ability to sustain revenues. Dillard indicated revenues had fallen 50% in recent weeks. Attempts to reduce costs are not expected to stem the decline into insolvency. Many on Wall Street believe a Chapter 11 filing is merely a stopgap measure that will soon move to a full liquidation. None of those questioned thought that Martinelli Global would be purchased as an ongoing business entity, leaving only the prospect of a liquidation of its assets.

The NYSE de-listed Martinelli Global a week ago. Trading had been halted two weeks earlier and never resumed after continued revelations of corporate wrongdoing.

In the growing Martinelli Global scandal, Manhattan Commercial Bank disclosed they were writing down losses due to Martinelli Global loans of $6.5 billion dollars. Manhattan Commercial was closely allied with Martinelli Global. The Bank's total exposure is over $9 billion. Experts say that the losses may also make Manhattan Commercial a fatality.

The surprise announcement so early in the Chapter 11 court supervised process further adds weight to the speculation that Martinelli Global is headed for liquidation. Martinelli Global had total secured debt of $18.5 billion, suggesting that Manhattan Commercial's move may soon be followed by other secured creditors. Some of these creditors are foreign banks. Martinelli Global assets are expected to cover only a small fraction of its debt. Unsecured creditors are not expected to see any payments on their outstanding receivables.

Reminiscent of Enron's demise, the human tragedy of Martinelli Global will be staggering. All of the 15,000 employees will not only lose their jobs, but much of their investments. Most employees purchased Martinelli Global stock at discounted prices for their personal investment. Many will also see their 401K accounts severely damaged if they were invested in Martinelli Global.

The collapse of a giant multi-national such as Martinelli Global has delivered a dampening effect to securities markets throughout the world. With Martinelli Global's extensive investments worldwide, the fate of many Martinelli Global foreign subsidiary companies is certain. While Martinelli Global was known for its risk taking ventures often in difficult political climates, their success and longevity made them a secure company within the investment community. Governments throughout the world are expected to rethink their regulatory controls to guard against future corporate excesses of the Martinelli Global type. Some in Congress are calling for increased limitations on the use of tax haven foreign subsidiaries.

Associated Press Release – Rome, Italy:

The Italian Ministry of Justice announced today that they have issued an arrest warrant for Steven Martinelli. Martinelli is the former CEO of U.S. based Martinelli Global which collapsed under a torrent of criminal charges. Martinelli had been fighting extradition within the Italian legal system for many weeks. The U.S. State Department was reportedly exerting pressure at the highest levels of the Italian Government for the extradition of Martinelli. Martinelli's exact whereabouts in Italy has been a secret during this time, with his attorneys arguing his case in the Italian courts.

SPELLO, UMBRIA, ITALY

Steven Martinelli was living in a rented villa outside of the Umbrian hilltop city of Spello. The surrounding areas were devoted to vineyards and olive groves. It was the ancestral home of his family. There were many distantly related Martinellis living in the area. In a moment of nostalgia, Steven Martinelli had loaned money to a distant relative to improve the old olive oil business once owned by his great-grandfather.

That association now proved useful. The owner of the olive business, a second cousin named Guidotti, rented the villa in his name. A man and wife lived in the guest cottage on the estate. The woman cooked meals and did the laundry for the man she knew as Signore Bartolo.

The night was devoid of any light with both the clouds and a heavy fog when three men approached the large stone house on foot. The old lock on a rear door to the kitchen proved easy to open. The men were dressed in black with rubber soled shoes. The stone floors even on the second level betrayed no squeaks.

Steven Martinelli was asleep with his body turned on its side. The only light came from the pencil-thin beam of a small flashlight. At a nod from one of the intruders, the two others rolled Martinelli on his side and held him down. The third put a plastic bag over his head.

Within ten minutes after murdering Steven Martinelli, the men had packed his clothes and toiletries and carried his body down the driveway to their van. Before dawn Martinelli's body was buried in a prepared area of a construction site. The site was scheduled to have concrete foundations poured the following day. Steven Martinelli would simply vanish in the style of Jimmy Hoffa.

ROME, ITALY

Boris Stepanov Lebedyenko, the Russian Mafiya boss operating in Italy, met Feliks Garnitsky at the Hotel Locarno.

"What brings you to Rome my old friend?" Lebedyenko said as he joined Garnitsky in the garden patio next to the hotel. It was a gloriously sunny afternoon. Garnitsky had the bartender make them drinks.

"Some difficulties back home, Boris. I decided to leave for health reasons."

"Serious health matters?"

"Very. That's why I came to you. I want to disappear. I also want to buy protection. So I thought of my old friend, Boris."

"Does this have to do with the work we did for you in Odessa?"

It gave Garnitsky an out rather than fabricating something else to account for his predicament. "Unfortunately, yes."

The vodka martinis arrived. Garnitsky leaned forward. "I can pay an awful lot of money for this help, Boris."

"And who is it that you have offended? I don't want to inherit your enemies, Feliks Alekseev."

"The Government. You've heard about this fall of the American company Martinelli Global and my former associate, Nikolai Krasin. The businesses were connected. Krasin was arrested in Russia. Committed suicide the Government said. That of course didn't happen. He was killed so he wouldn't have a chance to implicate others in the Government. I intend to avoid that same fate."

"And how much would you pay for my help?"

"Two million Euros, Boris. Plus expenses."

Lebedyenko was startled by the amount. "You must have really pissed off some important people."

"Can you help me, Boris?"

Lebedyenko looked at Garnitsky for a moment before answering. "Yes. We have a deal. Where do you wish to go?"

"Here in Italy somewhere. A larger city where I will not be noticed. A new identity. Resident status in Italy."

"What documents are you traveling under?"

"The same false Polish passport I have used before. I speak a little Polish. I'd like a new identity of course. Better to continue to obscure the trail. Ukrainian I think. Explains speaking Russian without being Russian. Can that be arranged, Boris?"

"Of course, I have a very good source. Expensive, but he uses real stolen blank passports. I'll have to see about Ukrainian. But it can be done.

"Now about location. Do you know of Catania?"

"Only that it's in Sicily."

"Large enough city so you will not stand out. Good restaurants. Airport. More importantly, I have a business associate there. Young guy. Italian Mafia. Took over from his old man. Understands modern methods, but still respects the old ways. Powerful. Has at least the local police on his payroll. Smart guy. I'll discuss your situation with him. You'll need to pay him too."

"I would expect to. When can you set this up?"

"I'll need at least a day. I'll send two of my people to pick you up here at noon the day after tomorrow. Italian guys. Angelo and Tommaso. They'll take you to the airport. It's a short flight to Catania. They'll have your ticket and your Catania hotel information. If my friend agrees to help, they'll have information on how he will contact you."

"I appreciate this, Boris. You're a dependable friend."

"Thank you, Feliks Alekseev."

Lebedyenko took the napkin from the table and a pen from his pocket. He wrote out a long series of numbers on the napkin and handed it to Garnitsky. "Swiss numbered account. I trust you can make the deposit tomorrow?"

Garnitsky nodded. He knew that the money would have to be transferred before he would get to Catania. This was ultimately about business. Lebedyenko got up and embraced Garnitsky and kissed him on each cheek.

As promised Lebedyenko's two Italians showed up at the Hotel Locarno at the appointed time. They were polite but said little in the drive to Rome's Aeroporto Leonardo da Vinci.

As they left the city, the driver called Angelo did not take the sign marked to the airport via the Autostrada. Garnitsky started to look around with some anxiety. They spoke only Italian and English. Garnitsky only spoke Russian and bits of Polish and English. The guy in the back seat next to him tried to explain in poor English and hand gestures there was an accident on the Autostrada. They were taking the route to Ostia south of the airport.

Garnitsky relaxed after getting the general idea of what the Italians meant. That was until they passed the sign indicating route 296 north to the airport. When he turned his head there was a silenced 9mm automatic pointed at him.

Angelo parked the car in the parking lot next to the marina. Garnitsky was escorted aboard a thirty-five foot sport fishing boat with its engine running. The boat left the slip immediately as the three men boarded.

Once out into the Mediterranean, Boris Lebedyenko emerged from below deck. "Hello, Feliks Alekseev. I must say I am not glad to see you. This is most unpleasant what I must do.

You did indeed piss off very powerful people in Russia. Unfortunately they're more powerful than you. You also lied to me, Feliks. It was not about killing those people in Odessa. It was something much worse."

"Then you're to kill me, Boris?"

"Yes. But sadly I have more unpleasantness, old comrade. My orders are that it should be a bad death."

Lebedyenko nodded to Tommaso holding his gun on Garnitsky. The man shot Garnitsky in each thigh. Garnitsky writhed in agony but said nothing. He was to die and there would be no reprieve.

Tommaso and Angelo then brought out a chain and secured it to Garnitsky's legs. The chain was attached to a hundred-pound anchor. The anchor was hung over the side of the boat. The two men then lifted Garnitsky so his body would ease over the railing. He slipped into the sea without saying anything, only terror in his eyes.

MANHATTAN, NEW YORK

Mark Reynolds' book, *Shell Game,* came out with a major marketing effort. The publisher was motivated to recoup Reynolds' $2.5 million advance. It made the top of the best seller list the first week. It was still number one six weeks later and into a second major printing. The speculation about Russian nuclear weapons possibly in the hands of Iran was a bombshell.

The book reviews were overwhelmingly favorable:

"Makes complex international business understand-able."

"A story of truly scary white-collar criminals."

"If half of what Mark Reynolds did is true, he should be recruited by the FBI."

"A thinking man's Indiana Jones tale of adventure with a new breed of bad guys."

One review particularly captured the book's popularity: "For what amounts to a business exposé, *Shell Game* reads like a thriller. Reynolds explains the complexities of a large corporation gone bad, while giving the reader a hell of a ride."

Reviews critical of *Shell Game* were centered on criticizing Reynolds' assertions about a theft of Russian nuclear warheads as just speculation, without foundation, farfetched, the photos unconvincing. Various experts weighed in on both sides of the debate in competing rounds of talking-heads on television news shows.

The whole range of U.S. Government agencies and the White House collectively declared Reynolds' speculation about missing Russian nuclear weapons as being totally unfounded. Reynolds was accused of adding it to the book for promotional publicity. The U.S. Government declared that Russia had firm control over their nuclear weapons inventories, and that those inventories are regularly monitored by U.S. inspectors under treaty agreements. No irregularities have been uncovered. The White House Press Secretary said the President regarded these speculations as only further complicating efforts in dealing with the belligerent regime in power in Iran.

The Kremlin declared there were no missing nuclear warheads. They criticized the allegations as a media stunt to promote the book.

The State of Israel officially declared the evidence presented in the book was inconclusive and unsubstantiated.

Broadcast media news formats and talk shows couldn't get enough of the debate. Mark Reynolds' appearances were in high demand. He was often frustrated with the focus on the nuclear weapons overwhelming the real thrust of the book. *Shell Game* was an exposé of a major international corporation going criminal. The nuclear weapons theft speculation was only a horrific byproduct of their corrupt culture.

Shell Game concluded with the verbatim transcripts of the Garnitsky-Dratshev calls, along with the digital photographs. Reynolds annotated the conversations with explanations of Garnitsky's and Dratshev business affiliations with Martinelli Global, and their connection to Russian nuclear weapons inventories. A map of the Caspian Sea region was included to provide geographic perspective. The evidence was brief but clearly compelling.

Reynolds ended *Shell Game* with:

These are my conclusions. I hope they are incorrect. But I felt the evidence must be made public. Both the United States and Russia deny that nuclear warheads are missing. Was Martinelli Global complicit through their Russian subsidiaries, or was this the work of a group of rogue individuals? Can we be sure Russian nuclear warheads are not missing? If they were, would the Russians admit to it? Would the United States government admit to it? How will Israel react? Does Iran now have a nuclear weapons capability? If they do, how will they leverage that power?

I believe we shall soon find out.

www.ingramcontent.com/pod-product-compliance
Lightning Source LLC
Chambersburg PA
CBHW030749030726
47497CB00001B/197